Andie [...] around the age of four, and is still doing it today—only now the sparkly fairies have made way for spirited heroines and sexy heroes. Thankfully she now has some real friends, as well as a husband and three children—plus a grumpy but lovable cat. Andie lives in Bristol, and when not actually writing might well be plotting her next passionate romance story.

Clare Connelly was raised in small-town Australia among a family of avid readers. She spent much of her childhood up a tree, Mills & Boon book in hand. Clare is married to her own real-life hero and they live in a bungalow near the sea with their two children. She is frequently found staring into space—a surefire sign that she is in the world of her characters. She has a penchant for French food and ice-cold champagne, and Mills & Boon novels continue to be her favourite ever books. Writing for Modern Romance is a long-held dream. Clare can be contacted via clareconnelly.com or at her Facebook page.

VIERI'S CONVENIENT VOWS

ANDIE BROCK

HER WEDDING NIGHT SURRENDER

CLARE CONNELLY

MILLS & BOON

First Published in Great Britain 2018
by Mills & Boon, an imprint of HarperCollins*Publishers*
1 London Bridge Street, London, SE1 9GF

Vieri's Convenient Vows © 2018 by Andie Brock

Her Wedding Night Surrender © 2018 by Clare Connelly

ISBN: 978-0-263-93528-8

MIX
Paper from
responsible sources
FSC™ C007454

This book is produced from independently certified FSC™ paper
to ensure responsible forest management.
For more information visit www.harpercollins.co.uk/green.

Printed and bound in Spain
by CPI, Barcelona

VIERI'S CONVENIENT VOWS

ANDIE BROCK

For my sisters, Linda, Jo and Diana.

Love you loads. xxx

CHAPTER ONE

HARPER MCDONALD GAZED at the mass of bodies writhing on the dance floor. With green and blue laser lights playing over their jerky movements they somehow produced a mesmerising whole, like a choppy sea. A DJ was performing on the elevated stage, the pulsing music so invasive that Harper could feel it reverberating through her body, defying her to stand still. She had never witnessed anything so hedonistic, so tribal. Even the air felt different, heavy with the scent of luxury and indulgence and wealth.

As another impossibly glamorous couple swept past her, Harper pulled in a breath, trying to ignore the way her stomach was knotting inside her. She felt so out of place she might as well have had a pair of antlers on her head. But she wasn't here to blend in or to dance or to schmooze with the beautiful people. She was here for one reason only. To find her sister.

Descending the stairs, she tentatively started to skirt the edge of the dance floor, looking for someone who might be able to help her. Somebody here had to have some information, had to know what had happened to Leah. But she had only gone a few steps when she was physically halted. With a shriek of terror she found herself airborne, both arms grabbed in a vice-like grip, the hold so powerful that her feet were lifted clean off the ground.

'Get off me! Put me down!' Frantically turning her head, she saw a pair of giant, suited men, their wide, impassive faces eerily shadowed by the coloured lights, giving nothing away. With a surge of adrenaline she tried to twist inside their grasp but this only made their brutish hands tighten further. Panic washed over her.

'I insist that you put me down.' She tried again, raising her voice over the incessant throb of noise, kicking her legs beneath her. 'You're hurting me.'

'Then stop squirmin'.'

Offering no more than this one piece of advice, the pair of man beasts continued to move forward, Harper trapped between them like the filling of a sandwich. The crowd of revellers parted to let them through with surprisingly little interest in her plight. No one seemed remotely interested in helping her.

'Stop this!' She battled to halt the hysteria that was rising in her throat. She didn't have a clue who these thugs were, only that she was being forcibly escorted against her will. And not even towards the entrance where the idea of being evicted into the chill of the night suddenly seemed all too inviting. No, she was being propelled in the opposite direction, further into the mysterious depths of this dark and dangerous place. A series of terrifying images flashed through her mind—abduction, murder, rape. And then the worst dread of all—was this what had happened to Leah?

Well, there was no way she would let herself be taken. She would fight with everything she had to save herself and her sister. 'I'm warning you.' She kicked her legs wildly beneath her once more. 'If you don't put me down right now I will scream so loud I will burst your eardrums.'

'I wouldn't advise that,' a low voice growled in her ear. 'If I were you I'd keep nice an' quiet. When you've done what you've done you've gotta expect consequences. Makin' a fuss ain't gonna help nothing.'

Done? What had she done? Surely they weren't talking about her fooling the security at the door?

Gaining entrance to this exclusive, members' only nightclub had proved to be surprisingly easy. Sidling up to the bouncer, she had been prepared for trouble, deciding she would have to throw herself on his mercy and explain why she was here. But no explanation had been necessary. The guy had moved aside and waved her straight in, uttering, 'Nice of you to join us again,' in a deep, mocking voice. Because of course he had thought she was her sister. He had thought she was Leah.

The last Harper had heard from her twin had been over a month ago, a drunken phone call in the wee small hours, Leah never having had any respect for the time difference between Scotland and New York. Harper's sleep-fuddled brain had struggled to understand what Leah was telling her—something about having met a man who was going to make her rich, how the family would never have to worry about money again.

And then nothing. As time had gone on the creeping concern that something was wrong had quickly escalated into a full-blown panic that a dreadful fate must have befallen her sister. Enough to see Harper maxing out her credit card to fly to New York and make her way to this alien venue, deep in the heart of Manhattan. Spectrum nightclub, where Leah had been working as a hostess since she'd left their home in Scotland six months ago. The last place she had been seen before she had disappeared and the only place Harper could think of to start looking for her.

Now, as she was physically propelled forward by these fearsome man beasts towards God knew what end, Harper couldn't help but panic that in coming to try and save her sister, she was about to suffer the same unknown fate.

At the back of the club, she found herself being bundled through a concealed door behind the stage and into a dark passageway. It was so narrow that the trio had to go in single file, her minders finally letting go of her arms but positioning themselves in front of and behind her, so close that she could feel the heat coming off them, smell the sweat. They ascended a dimly lit flight of stairs until they reached a door at the top and they moved beside her again. One of them rapped his knuckles against the matte black paint.

'Enter.'

Harper was shoved into a small, square office, lit by a single florescent strip light. A dark-haired man sat at a desk facing the door, his head bent, his fingers rapidly tapping at the keys of a computer. Behind him, a long rectangle of glass, a two-way mirror, gave an uninterrupted view of the undulating mass below.

'Thanks, guys.' Still he didn't look up. Harper noticed the way the light shone blue-black on the thick waves of his hair. 'You may go.'

With subservient grunts the pair shuffled out, closing the door behind them.

Harper desperately tried to steady her heart rate, to think clearly. Her eyes flitted around the room to see if there was any means of escape. It was almost totally silent in here, she realised. The pulsating beat that had been with her ever since she had entered the nightclub had gone, replaced by the roaring of blood in her ears and the gentle tap of the laptop keyboard.

She stared at the man before her. Even though he was seated and steadfastly ignoring her, she could sense the power of him. But there was something else, something worse, an enmity that was radiating from him like a palpable force. Suddenly being left alone with this silent, formidable figure was worse than being manhandled by those gorillas. She was almost tempted to run after them, ask them to take her with them.

'So.' Still he refused to look at her. 'The wanderer returns.'

'No!' With a rush of breath, Harper hurried to put him right. 'You don't understand…'

'Spare me the excuses.' Finally closing his laptop, the dark figure rose gracefully to his feet and Harper realised with a gulp how tall he was, how handsome, how effortlessly cool. 'I'm really not interested.' Still refusing to look her in the eye, he strolled casually to the door behind her. She heard him turn a key in the lock before slipping the key into his trouser pocket as he returned to his desk.

'W…what are you doing?'

'What does it look like I'm doing?' He stood by his seat. 'I'm making sure you don't escape. Again.'

'No.' Harper tried again. 'You're making a mistake. I'm not—'

'Sit down.' He barked the order, gesturing to the chair opposite his. 'There is no point in making this any harder than it already is.'

Harper edged forward and did as she was told. She felt as if she had fallen into some sort of rabbit hole. That none of this was real.

Seating himself, her captor folded his arms across his chest, his eyes finally meeting hers for the first time. And only then did his icy composure slip.

Che diavolo? What the hell? Vieri Romano ground down on his jaw. *It was the wrong damned woman!* A surge of frustration went through him as he clenched his fists. The person before him looked like Leah McDonald and she sounded like Leah McDonald, with that soft, lilting Scottish accent. But now that he was glaring at her beneath the harsh overhead light he knew with irritating certainty that she was *not* Leah McDonald.

Hell. He raked a hand through his hair as he continued to stare at this imposter. They were certainly very alike, obviously twins, but the subtle differences were now clear to see. This young woman's eyes were wider apart, the lips fuller, the nose a tad longer. Her hair was different too, falling in careless auburn waves compared to Leah's more styled tresses. But even without these differences, Vieri would have known this wasn't Leah, simply by her manner.

The woman before him was all serious determination. There was no sign of Leah's flirty confidence—something that Vieri suspected Leah would be trying to use right now to get herself out of trouble, had he managed to get the correct sister in front of him. Leah was well aware of her assets and knew how to use them, whereas her sister appeared uncomfortable beneath his scrutiny, wrapping her arms around herself to cover up her slender but shapely figure. And if Leah's eyes would have been batting seductively by now, her sister's glared at him, full of fire. She reminded Vieri of a cornered animal, one that was most definitely not going to give up without a fight.

But then neither did he. Vieri ran a hand over his jaw, rapidly assessing this new situation. Maybe they were in it together, this pair of Celtic beauties. He wouldn't put it past them. Perhaps this one had been sent as backup. They might just be dumb enough to think they could get away with it. Although dumb was not a word he would use to describe the woman sitting across from him now. There was something about her that suggested a sharp intelligence. If nothing else, it was possible she might be able to lead him to her double-crossing sister. One thing was for sure, she wouldn't be leaving here until she had been thoroughly interrogated.

'Name?' He barked the question at her.

'Harper.' She shifted in her seat. 'Harper McDonald.'

When he didn't immediately reply she tipped her chin in a show of defiance. 'And you are?'

Vieri's brows snapped together. He wasn't accustomed to being asked who he was. Least of all in one of his own establishments.

'Vieri Romano.' He kept his tone steady. 'Owner of Spectrum nightclub.'

'Oh.' He watched her full pink lips purse closed as re-alisation dawned. 'Then I should like to formally com-plain about the way I have been treated here. You have absolutely no right to—'

'Where is your sister, Ms McDonald?' Raising his voice, Vieri cut short her futile protests. He had no time to listen to her pathetic accusations.

She bit down on her lip, nipping the soft flesh with her front teeth, the action engaging Vieri more than it should. 'I don't know.' He could hear the panic in her voice. 'That's why I'm here, to try and find her. I haven't heard from her in over a month.'

Pulling his eyes away from her seductive mouth, Vieri let out a derisive grunt. 'Well, that makes two of us.'

'So she's not here?' The panic escalated. 'She quit her job?'

'She has walked out, if that's what you mean. Along with my bar manager, Max Rodriguez.'

'Walked out?'

'*Si*. Disappeared without a trace.'

'Oh, God.' Harper reached forward to grip the edge of the desk with hands that visibly shook. 'Where has she gone?'

Vieri shrugged his lack of knowledge, watching her reaction closely.

'You have no idea what might have happened to her?'

'Not yet.' He picked up some papers on his desk, tidying them into a pile. 'But I intend to find out. And when I do, her troubles will be just beginning.'

'Wh…what do you mean by that?' Harper's remarkable green-brown eyes widened.

'I mean that I don't take kindly to my employees disappearing off the face of the earth. Especially with thirty thousand dollars of my money.'

'Thirty thousand dollars?' Her hands flew to her mouth. 'You mean Leah and this Max guy have stolen money from you?'

'Your sister and I had a business arrangement, or so I thought. I made the mistake of paying her the first instalment up front. She has absconded with the money.'

'No! Oh, I'm so sorry!'

She looked suitably shocked, enough to convince Vieri that she knew nothing about it, but he noted with interest that she didn't challenge the facts.

'She will be too, believe me.'

He leant back in his chair. Much as he blamed Leah for her devious deceit, most of his fury was directed at himself. How could he have been so stupid as to fall for her sob story and give her the payment in advance? All that garbage about needing the money straight away to send back home to her family, for her father who was struggling to keep his job. It smarted like a smack in the face. Not the thirty thousand dollars—he didn't give a damn about that. If she had had the guts to ask him outright for the money he might well have given it to her. But the fact was that he, Vieri Romano, billionaire businessman, international tycoon, a man both revered and feared in the corporate world, had been taken for a fool. By a woman. Something he had sworn would never happen again.

But Leah McDonald had caught him at a low point, when his defences had been down. And what had seemed like a good idea at the time, the ideal solution in fact, had now spectacularly backfired.

He had been drinking in the club one evening, uncharacteristically feeling the need to drown his sorrows after the news he had received earlier that day. Leah had been his waitress. She had been attentive but discreet, just the way he liked his staff to be. On another night he might have made a mental note to congratulate the management on their staff training. But tonight, to his surprise, he found he just wanted to talk. And so he had, sharing a quiet booth and a bottle of Scotch, appropriately enough, with this bright-eyed Scottish woman. With her soothing encouragement he had told her about his godfather, the man who meant more to Vieri than anyone else in the world. The only person who meant anything to him. How he had received an email from the man that morning, confirming Vieri's worst fears. His godfather was dying. It was just a matter of time.

Had he left it there no harm would have been done. He would have gone home to continue his drinking and Leah would have pocketed a handsome tip, just another night and another guy offloading his troubles. Even if this time the guy was the boss. But something about her gentle voice had drawn him in, made him go further, and he had found himself telling her about the last time he had seen his godfather, the heart-to-heart they had had. How Alfonso had revealed to him what he had suspected at the time and now knew for sure, his dying wish. To see Vieri settled. With a wife. A family. The one thing Vieri had never had. Nor ever would have.

And Leah's response had been remarkably practical. If that was his godfather's last wish then it had to be accomplished. It was Vieri's duty. She had been quite adamant about it. If there were no genuine contenders for the role of fiancée, then he would have to find somebody, pay someone if necessary. Anything to make his godfather happy.

And to Vieri's surprise he found himself wondering if maybe this young woman was right. Maybe that was the solution. He had always made his godfather proud, he didn't doubt that, but this was different. This was about happiness. Something that for all his wealth and success Vieri had never fully understood. But he did know that if there was any way of fulfilling his godfather's dying wish, he would give it a go. Even if it meant a bit of subterfuge.

And so, by the time he had savoured the last of the peaty whisky at the bottom of his glass, the deal had been struck. Leah needed money and he needed a fake fiancée. In return for a down payment of thirty thousand dollars, Leah would pretend to be engaged to him for a couple of months, or for as long as it took. At the time, his alcohol-soaked brain had thought it the ideal solution. A way of making his godfather happy that didn't involve messy emotions. The potentially insoluble problem had suddenly shaped into something that he could control, something he understood better than anything else—a business deal.

But that was then. No sooner had Vieri paid the money into Leah's account than she had absconded. But, crucially, not before he had announced to his delighted godfather that he had taken his advice. That his wish had been granted and Vieri would be introducing him to his fiancée in the very near future.

Now he was left with a problem. When security had alerted him that Leah was back he had made the short journey from his offices in Midtown Manhattan, determined to have it out with her, to make her honour the deal. But the defiant young woman perched on the seat before him wasn't Leah McDonald and he was no closer to solving the infuriating situation.

Or was he? Harper McDonald said she had no idea where Leah was and he believed her. But maybe she could help him in another way.

Vieri coldly assessed the twin sister in front of him, his eyes narrowing as he waited for common sense to veto the crazy idea that had popped into his mind. Because it was crazy, wasn't it?

'So what do you intend to do?' Harper's anxious voice cut through his thoughts. 'About Leah, I mean. Have you involved the police?'

'Not yet. I prefer to deal with these things in my own way. For the time being at least.' He drummed his fingers meaningfully on the desk.

It had the desired effect. He saw her swallow hard, her imagination no doubt running away with her. Well, he wasn't going to try and stop it. For the time being it would suit his purposes to let her fear him. The fact that he abhorred physical violence and had striven to eradicate any organised crime from his establishments was of no consequence.

'Look, I can help you find her.' Like a fish on a hook, Harper squirmed about, trying to come up with something that would appease him. 'And I'll pay the money back myself if I have to. All of it.'

'And how exactly will you do that?' Vieri regarded her coolly. 'From what Leah tells me, your family are destitute.'

He saw the flush creep up her neck. 'She had no right to say such a thing!'

'So it's not true? Paying back thirty thousand dollars won't be a problem?'

'Well, of course it will a problem, the same as it would be for any normal family. But that doesn't mean I won't do it.'

'Really?'

'Yes, really.' She pushed her hair away from her heated face. 'I could work here, for example, for free, I mean.'

'I think one McDonald sister working in this establishment was more than enough, thank you.' Sarcasm scored his words.

'Well, some other job, then. I'm practical and capable and a fast learner. I'll do anything. I just need a bit of time and the chance to try and find Leah myself.'

'Anything, you say?'

'Yes.' Sheer determination was written all over her pretty face.

'In that case maybe there is something you could help me with.' He deliberately held her gaze. 'You could honour the commitment made by your sister.'

'Yes, of course.' She blinked, thick lashes sweeping low over those wide hazel eyes. 'What is it?'

A beat of silence hung in the air.

'To become my fiancée.'

CHAPTER TWO

'YOUR FIANCÉE?'

The word sounded just as ridiculous when choked from Harper's closing throat as it had done uttered from Vieri's now purposefully drawn lips.

'*Si*, that is correct.'

'You want me to marry you?'

'No.' He gave a harsh laugh. 'I can assure you it won't come to that.'

'What, then? I don't understand.'

'Your sister and I made a deal. In return for a generous payment she agreed to play the part of my fiancée for a limited period of time. It's really not that complicated.'

Not to him maybe, or her loony sister. But Harper was certainly struggling with the concept. 'But why? And what does limited mean?'

'In answer to your first question, in order to please my godfather. And as for the second, it will just be for a matter of weeks, months at the most.' He paused and took a breath. 'My godfather is dying.'

'Oh.' Harper could see the pain in Vieri's eyes. 'I'm so sorry.'

Vieri shrugged. 'His last wish is for me to settle down, take a wife, start a family. I would like to be able to fulfil that wish, in part at least.'

'But how? I mean, if it's just a lie…surely that wouldn't be right?'

'I prefer to think of it as a small deception.'

Harper frowned. It still sounded like a lie to her. 'And Leah agreed to this?' She didn't know why she was bothering to ask. It was just the sort of madcap idea that her sister would leap at.

'Actually, it was her idea.'

That figured.

'So what exactly is the deal? What did Leah sign up for?' She swallowed hard, bracing herself for the answer, a kick of dread in her stomach. Thirty thousand dollars was a huge sum of money. And had she heard him say that was the first instalment? But she knew Leah—she could have agreed to just about anything for such riches. An *anything* that Harper herself might now have to honour. It was a terrifying thought.

'Flying to Sicily, meeting my godfather, acting like the doting fiancée.'

Harper nervously chewed her fingernail, waiting for more information.

'It may entail several visits, maybe some lengthier stays. I would like to spend as much time with him as possible.'

'I see.' A tight silence fell between them as Harper tried to get to grips with this. 'Go on.'

'That's it. The arrangement between Leah and myself was left deliberately fluid.'

Deliberately fluid? What the hell did that mean? Faced with this formidably handsome man, Harper found her thoughts flying in some very surprising directions. Reining herself in, she stared at him primly. 'Obviously before I agree to anything I need to know what else would be expected of me.'

Vieri made a low noise in his throat. 'If you mean will

you have to share my bed, then the answer is no.' His dark, mocking gaze slashed across her hot cheeks. 'I am not in the habit of paying women to sleep with me.'

'No, of course not.' Harper hurriedly tried to erase the erotic image of being in Vieri's bed. 'Anyway, I know my sister would never have agreed to such a thing.' That had to be true. Didn't it? 'And neither would I, to be clear.'

Argh. Why didn't she stop digging and shut up?

'I'm very pleased to hear it.' His deep blue gaze slid over her. 'So, do we have a deal? Are you prepared to take on your sister's debt?'

'I don't know.' Still Harper hesitated. 'If I did, what would happen about Leah?'

'I would have no further interest in her.'

If Harper had thought his bald statement would be a comfort, she was wrong. Suddenly the idea that Vieri Romano had lost all interest in her sister worried her almost as much as the thought of him hounding her. She didn't know how to start tracking Leah down, whereas Vieri knew people; he would have contacts, resources at his disposal.

'But what about this Rodriguez guy? You must want to speak to him?' A sudden spark of hope mixed with fear lit inside her. 'He might be the one responsible for stealing your money. He might have kidnapped Leah.'

'Unlikely. From the little I saw of your sister she didn't look like kidnap material.'

'And what exactly does *kidnap material* look like?' Harper indignantly challenged the idea that no one would want to kidnap Leah, and, by association, her too.

'Heiresses, high-profile celebrities, children of the filthy rich.'

Clearly the McDonald sisters were none of those things.

'Well, there's the thirty thousand dollars. Rodriguez

might have somehow lured Leah away to try and get his hands on that.'

'Possible, though unlikely. Rodriguez has been working as a bar manager here for some time, having access to large sums of money every night of the week. There's never been any suggestion that he's stolen from us before. My guess is that, if anything, your sister has lured him away. Though I've no idea why.'

Neither did Harper. But right now she didn't have the capacity to try and work it out.

'But you are right.' Ruthlessly, Vieri continued. 'If a member of my staff walks out with no warning, regardless of the circumstances, I make it my business to investigate. I will find Rodriguez. And if your sister is still with him, then I will see that she is returned to her family.'

'Without involving the police?'

'I see no reason to contact the police.'

'Or violence. I would hate to think anyone would get hurt.'

Rising to his feet, Vieri walked around the desk until he was standing in front of her, towering over her, all formidable dark presence.

'I think perhaps I need to make a few things clear, Ms McDonald.' He locked eyes with hers, the dark intensity of his words matched by the stark angles of his handsome face. 'I will deal with this incident as I see fit. I make the decisions. I make the rules. You should consider yourself extremely fortunate that you have this opportunity to prevent Leah from a possible prison sentence.'

Fortunate? That was not a word Harper would use to describe herself right now. Her head was spinning with the shock and sheer enormity of what was being asked of her. But what choice did she have?

'So what do you say?' Vieri fixed her with a punishing

stare. 'Are you prepared to go along with my plan to save your sister's skin?'

Harper looked away, balling her hands into fists. Right now she would like to flay Leah herself, string her up and set about her, make her see what a completely stupid, totally irresponsible person she was. But Leah was her sister, her twin, almost a part of her. Of course she would save her—she would do anything to keep her safe, to protect her. It was what she had been doing the whole of their lives. Because Harper was the older twin, the sensible one, the *healthy* one. The one that shouldered the responsibility, took charge, tried to make everything right. Which in this case meant temporarily shackling herself to this shockingly attractive but coldly calculating man.

'Yes.' Her voice came out as little more than a whisper but as she raised her eyes to meet Vieri's she saw the look of satisfaction reflected in his midnight stare. Her fate had been sealed.

Harper peered through the window as the island of Sicily came into view, its iconic position off the toe of Italy's boot clearly visible from the air. As Vieri's private jet started to descend she craned her neck for a better look, taking in the rivers and the mountains, the clumps of towns and cities and, the most amazing of all, Mount Etna, shrouded in snow but puffing out a stream of smoke in welcome.

She had only ever been abroad once before, a bargain break holiday to the Costa del Sol in Spain when she was nineteen. Which might have been fun if she hadn't ended up trailing around after Leah trying to keep her out of trouble.

And nothing had changed. Here she was again, still trying to sort one of her sister's messes. But this time it was serious, really serious. Leah had stolen a large sum of money and Harper didn't doubt that if Vieri decided to press charges she could well go to prison.

Which was why she'd had no choice but to put her own life on hold and climb into Vieri's private jet to be flown back across the world to take part in this hateful little charade. She could kill Leah. She really could.

And it had all happened ridiculously fast—less than twenty-four hours had passed since she had first set foot in Spectrum nightclub. Once she had agreed to go along with the plan Vieri had leapt into action, insisting on sending a car to pick up Harper's suitcase from the hostel she had checked into earlier, refusing to even let her go with it. No doubt he was worried that if he let her out of his sight she would abscond—just like her sister. So now here she was, thousands of miles away, about to embark on a crazy deception.

It had been a long flight, starting in the small hours of the morning, and even though Harper had been shown to a sumptuous bedroom she had found sleep impossible, eventually venturing into the lounge area, where Vieri had been immersed in work, the light from the screen of his laptop suffusing his handsome face with an eerie glow. He had shown no interest in conversing with her so instead she had scrolled through the movies on the widescreen television, in the hope of finding something to take her mind off things. Which was impossible. How was she supposed to divert herself from the mad reality of what she was doing? Pitching up with a man who was almost a total stranger and pretending to be his fiancée.

But it was happening. As the plane landed she looked across at her 'fiancé', watching as he closed his laptop, unbuckled his seat belt and drew himself up to his full height. He shrugged on a dark cashmere coat, then ushered her down the steps of the plane and across the tarmac to the waiting car.

'Castello di Trevente,' Vieri instructed the driver once they were both seated inside, before settling back against the soft leather.

'Where are we going?' Harper addressed his strong profile.

'Castello di Trevente,' Vieri repeated. 'It's where my godfather lives.'

'He lives in a castle?' Harper's Sicilian was non-existent but even she could understand that.

'Yes, it's been in the Calleroni family for generations.' Vieri turned to look at her. 'Far too big and cold and draughty for him, of course, but Alfonso would never agree to move to anywhere more sensible.'

'I see.' Harper tucked her unruly hair behind her ears. 'But aren't we going to the hotel first, to freshen up, I mean?'

'I don't want to leave it too late. My godfather gets very tired and it's already six p.m. here.' Removing his heavy gold watch, he deftly adjusted the time before refastening it and raising his eyes to coldly assess her. In the dim light of the car his eyes flicked mercilessly over her body and Harper flinched beneath his scrutiny, tugging at the collar of her waxed jacket. Without saying a word he had managed to convey her obvious shortcomings, the world of difference between them. He oozed dark sophistication, whereas she felt as craggy and unkempt as the wild moorlands she came from.

But she refused to be intimidated by him. He might have all the wealth and power, and thanks to Leah's stupid deal it seemed he as good as owned Harper for the foreseeable future. But she still had her self-respect. And she would hang onto that for dear life.

Sitting up a little straighter, she sneaked a look at her companion. He was facing ahead again now, the collar of his coat turned up, but she could still see the dark shadow of stubble along his jaw, the loose curls of his dark hair that softened his austere profile. His hands rested in his lap, beautiful hands with long, strong fingers that invited their touch, making Harper wonder what they would feel like against her skin.

Which was ridiculous and totally uncalled for. With a jolt she put the brakes on her imagination. She and Vieri Romano had entered into a business deal, nothing more. And wondering what it would feel like to be caressed by his hands was most definitely not part of that deal. She needed to focus on the practicalities. That was what she was good at.

'So, what's the plan, then?' She broke the silence and Vieri turned to look at her, his dark brows raised. 'How am I supposed to act in front of your godfather?'

'Like my fiancée,' he replied coolly. 'I thought we had established that.'

'But shouldn't we have some sort of story mapped out?' Ever the pragmatist, she pressed on. 'How we met, how long we have known each other, that sort of thing?'

'You can leave the talking to me.'

Harper bristled. The idea that she was just going to be paraded in front of this man like some sort of inanimate object didn't sit well with her feminist principles. But then who was she kidding? None of this sat well with any of her principles. Even so, a thought occurred to her.

'Perhaps your godfather doesn't speak English?' That would explain Vieri's high-handed manner.

'Aflonso speaks perfect English.'

So that was that theory crushed. And it would make her job harder, even though Vieri didn't seem to recognise it.

'Then obviously I need to be able to converse with him.' She tried to assert some authority. 'And to do that I need to know more about him. And we need to know more about each other.' She tailed off, her authority already slipping away. Talking about herself was not a subject she was comfortable with.

'Very well.' Vieri immediately pounced on her reluctance, his full attention suddenly on her. 'Tell me your life story, Ms Harper McDonald.'

Harper swallowed hard. Her life story was not something she was fond of recounting. Everyone in her home town of Glenruie knew it anyway—those poor wee girls, left motherless by a tragic accident that took their mother then drove their father to drink. Left struggling to make ends meet, to keep a roof over their heads. But where strangers were concerned, Harper was careful to keep her tale of woe to herself. Except now this particular stranger was silently, unnervingly waiting for answers. She decided she would stick firmly to the facts.

'Umm, well, I am twenty-five years old and I've lived all my life in a small town called Glenruie on the west coast of Scotland with my father and my sister.' She paused. 'My father is a gamekeeper for the Craigmore estate. He manages the birds and the fishing for Craigmore Lodge, which is still owned by the Laird but now run as a hotel. Leah and I work there sometimes, housekeeping, waitressing, that sort of thing.'

'And your mother?'

'She died.' Harper pursed her lips, then forced herself to continue. 'A long time ago now. An accident with a shotgun.'

'I'm sorry.' Vieri lowered his voice.

'That's okay.' But of course it wasn't. In truth the accident had all but decimated their lives.

'And I gather there are problems with your father.'

Harper silently cursed her sister again. 'Umm, he hasn't been well lately so things have been a bit tough.'

'Leah said he's a drinker.' She really would kill Leah. 'Is it true that if he loses his job you lose your home?'

'Well, in theory that could happen. But I'm sure it won't come to that. Anyway…' she folded her arms over her chest '…that's enough about me.' She attempted a small laugh that died in the purring quiet of the car. 'What should I know about you?'

Vieri laid his arm on the armrest between them, his fingers curling over the end. He turned to the front. 'Thirty-two. Sicilian by birth but I've been living in New York for fourteen years. CEO of Romano Holdings. I started in the hotel and leisure industry, but now control over a hundred companies, and that number is growing all the time.'

Harper frowned. This wasn't the sort of information she wanted. She wasn't looking to invest or compiling a list of the world's most successful businesses, though she had no doubt that if she did Romano Holdings would be up there at the top. She was supposed to be engaged to him, for heaven's sake; she was supposed to know him *personally*.

'What about your family?' She focussed on his proud profile. 'Parents, brothers and sisters?'

'No, none.' His voice was bleak, his hand tightening on the armrest.

'What, no living relatives at all?' His obvious reticence only made her want to push further.

'No.' A muscle now twitched in his cheek. 'I was raised in a children's home.'

'Oh.' The word seemed ridiculously inadequate. 'Did your parents die, then?'

'I've no idea. But if not they might as well have done. I was left on the steps of a church when I was a few hours old.'

'Oh, how sad.' The image of the tiny abandoned bundle lodged in her mind and refused to be shifted.

'Not really. I've done pretty well for myself.'

'Well, yes, of course, but—'

'And from what I've seen of other people's families, maybe I was better off without one.'

Was that a swipe at her? Harper scowled to herself.

'But actually I was very lucky. Alfonso Calleroni was a trustee of the children's home. He looked out for me, became my godfather. Without him I may well have strayed down the wrong path.'

'You owe him a lot?'

'Everything.' Harper could hear the emotion in his voice. 'Which is why I want to do this one last thing for him. His happiness means a great deal to me.'

Harper hesitated. A thought had occurred to her that wouldn't be pushed away. 'Do you not think…' she started cautiously, all too aware that Vieri was not the sort of man who liked to be challenged '…that your godfather is thinking about *your* happiness when he says he wants to see you married? Not his own.'

Swinging round to face her again, Vieri positively shimmered with hostility. 'In the unlikely event that I should ever want your opinion, Harper McDonald, I will ask for it.' His voice was a low hiss. 'Until then I will thank you to keep your thoughts to yourself and do the job your sister has been paid to do. Is that understood?'

'Perfectly.' Harper straightened her back and turned to look out of the window. From now on she would keep her mouth shut. Even if she was the only one who could see this whole charade was stupid.

The rest of the short journey was travelled in silence until the car slowed before turning off the main road and up a long driveway. Only when it drew to a halt did Vieri turn to look at her again.

'Before we go in, you will be needing this.' Slipping his hand into his trouser pocket, he brought out a ring box and passed it to her. The velvet box was still warm from where it had nestled against his thigh. 'If it doesn't fit we can get it resized.'

Harper cautiously opened the box, realising she was holding her breath as she did so. Which was stupid. What did it matter what the ring looked like, or indeed if it was as fake as their engagement? Nevertheless as she removed it from the box, felt the weight of the green stone, saw its mocking sparkle in the dim light of the car, she had no doubt that this was the real thing. When she slid it onto her finger it fitted perfectly. Which only made her feel more uncomfortable. As did Vieri's dark gaze, which drifted from her hand to her face, making her stomach do an inexplicable swoop.

'You are ready?'

Harper nodded, stuffing the offending hand into her coat pocket to keep it from view as the driver came around to open her car door for her. 'Yes.' Somehow the right word came out, even though every part of her body was screaming no.

'*Bene*. Then let's do this.'

CHAPTER THREE

'COME A LITTLE closer so that I can see you better, *mia cara.*'

Harper did as she was told, edging towards the reclining chair where Alfonso Calleroni was propped up by a pile of cushions, a blanket draped over his bony knees.

'Ah, that's better. Sit here beside me. Vieri, don't just stand there. Pull up a chair for your young lady.'

Vieri dutifully produced a chair and placed it beside his godfather. Harper awkwardly settled herself down. If this whole situation weren't bad enough, Vieri was making it worse by standing right behind her, his hands on the back of the chair, his unnerving presence all around her.

'So, Harper, you say. Have I got that right?'

'Yes.' Harper suspected from her very brief acquaintance with Alfonso Calleroni that he probably got most things right. Despite his age and frailty and the poor state of his health she could tell he was still a very astute man. Which meant he wasn't going to be easy to fool. Only now did she realise that she had been hoping Vieri's godfather's faculties would be somewhat impaired. Which was an awful thing to hope for. Ashamed of herself, she tried to make up for her nastiness by giving him a bright smile. 'That's right.'

'And is that a Scottish name? Am I correctly attributing that wonderful accent of yours?'

'Yes.' He was as sharp as a pin. 'But the name came from my mother's favourite book, *To Kill a Mockingbird*. She called me and my twin sister Harper and Leah. As a loose sort of tribute.'

'So there are two of you? How wonderful.'

'Yes.' Although it felt slightly less wonderful from where she was sitting.

'And you met in New York, Vieri was telling me? A long way from home.'

'Harper's sister, Leah, was working in one of my clubs. Harper came to visit her,' Vieri smoothly interjected.

'And the two of you fell in love.' One gnarled, arthritic hand reached out to take hold of Harper's, holding it in his shaky grasp so that he could inspect the traitorous ring. 'How wonderful.' He raised his rheumy eyes to Harper's face. 'And your parents? I trust Vieri has done the right thing and spoken to your father to ask for your hand in marriage.'

Harper swallowed.

'Not yet, Alfonso.' Vieri cut in again. 'This has all happened rather fast. We wanted you to be the first to know.'

'Of course you did.' Alfonso's eyes travelled to Vieri's face, lingering there for several seconds. 'After all, I won't be around much longer. It would have been such a shame for me to die without knowing you had chosen a wife for yourself, wouldn't it now?'

'Let's not talk about dying, *padrino*.'

'Ah, but I am afraid we must, *mio figlio*. There are things that need to be discussed now that my time on this earth is short.' Raising Harper's hand, he brought it to his lips and gave the back of it a dry kiss. 'But I am tired now so I think they must wait for another day. Thank you so much for coming to see me, my dear.' He shifted in his seat, his face suddenly contorting with pain so that his nurse, who had been hovering in the background, rushed forward to help him. 'You have chosen well, Vieri. She is a lovely girl.'

As he pressed a button on his chair it slowly started to lever him upright until he was able to lean forward and grasp the walking frame that had been positioned in front of him by his nurse. 'Now, if you will excuse me.'

'Of course.' Vieri bent to give his godfather a kiss on the cheek. 'We will see you tomorrow.'

'Tomorrow, yes.' Alfonso gave him a weak smile. 'Let us see what tomorrow will bring.'

The next day's visit involved a longer stay, as did the day after that. Alfonso obviously delighted in his godson's company, the affection between them clear to see. But the affection between Vieri and Harper was another matter. Far from treating her like the love of his life, Vieri merely paraded her like some sort of trophy, to be perched on a chair and then ignored. With Alfonso's sharp intelligence missing nothing, Harper was becoming more and more convinced that they weren't putting on a good enough act.

On the third day, after returning to Vieri's stunning penthouse apartment in the luxury hotel he owned in Palermo, she decided she couldn't keep quiet any longer. Shrugging off her coat, she confronted Vieri.

'I'm worried that Alfonso knows we are not a real couple.'

'Why do you say that?' Vieri had made straight for the bar. 'I thought he seemed very cheerful today. He had more colour in his cheeks, less of that grey pallor.' Uncorking a bottle of wine, he poured Harper a glass and handed it to her.

'Yes, that's true.'

She watched as Vieri dropped ice cubes into his glass, pouring in a generous measure of whisky. With his shirt-sleeves rolled up, his hair casually messed, he was the epitome of the billionaire playboy at ease. He was strikingly tall, his physique a perfect combination of long limbs and honed muscle beneath taut olive skin, his movements both graceful and dangerous, like a tiger on the prowl. Yes, he was far more handsome than was good for him. Or her for that matter. Despite her best intentions to remain aloof, he seemed to have the bizarre capacity to heat her skin from within whenever he looked at her, to set her body tingling with anticipation at the mere sound of his faint, but deeply sexy Sicilian accent.

Taking a healthy sip of her wine, she turned away. She knew she had to be on her guard. She knew she really, really shouldn't be starting to look forward to this brief, early evening time they spent together. It wasn't as if Vieri had ever given her the slightest encouragement, shown any interest in her at all.

In the few days since arriving in Sicily they had fallen into a routine of sorts. Vieri would work all morning while Harper was left to amuse herself. She had taken to wandering into Palermo, exploring the narrow, cobbled side streets and the exotic markets or ordering a cup of bitter dark coffee and sitting outside to watch the bustling crowds go by. The city was full of such colour and vibrancy, she was already starting to love it. Their afternoons would be spent visiting Alfonso and then in the evening Vieri would disappear into his office and she wouldn't see him again. Despite being able to choose from the hotel's extensive menu, prepared by one of Sicily's top chefs, Harper had little appetite. Eating alone on the sofa, she would spend her time making calls to her father or searching social media sites on the Internet in the hope of finding some information about Leah. But there was nothing. Which only made her worry deepen still further.

Now she moved to sit on one of the cream leather sofas. 'I did think Alfonso was looking better today, but that doesn't alter the fact that he knows our engagement is a sham. You underestimate how sharp he is.'

'I can assure you I never underestimate anything about my godfather.' Vieri seated himself on the sofa opposite her, the ice clinking in the glass. He sounded vaguely ir-ritated, as if she was a slightly annoying appendage that had to be tolerated in order to solve a problem. Which she supposed she was. But the more he treated her like that, the more Harper found she couldn't hold her tongue. She was forthright by nature, and if something needed to be said, she couldn't help but say it. Even if every broodingly dark muscle of Vieri's finely honed body was silently tell-ing her to shut up.

'Then you must have noticed the way he looks at us, the way he takes everything in. He is not fooled by our pretence for a minute, Vieri. If you think he believes us, the only one being fooled is you.'

A muscle twitched ominously in Vieri's cheek, silently conveying just how close she had come to overstepping the mark.

'Well.' With an exhalation of breath he leant back into the sofa, crossing one long leg over the other, his relaxed posture not fooling Harper for a minute. 'As you seem to be so much more perceptive than me perhaps you would like to suggest what we do about it.'

'Fine, I will.' Refusing to be cowed, Harper placed her glass down on the table beside her. It was already half fin-ished. She was drinking far too quickly. 'First off we need to look as if we like each other—that would be a good start. Make eye contact, for example.'

'I wasn't aware we didn't do that.'

'Really? You spend more time looking at Alfonso's nurse than you do me.'

Vieri gave a wry laugh. 'Not jealous are we, Harper?'

'Hardly.' Her reply was too fast, too vehement. 'Why would I be?'

'Why indeed?' Dark brows quirked upwards. 'So, lack of eye contact, duly noted. What else am I doing wrong? I'm sure you are bursting to tell me.'

Harper frowned as she scanned his supremely confident pose. Yes, there were several things that she would be only too happy to point out to him, but many more she would keep to herself. Like the frantic beat of her blood when she was faced with that midnight-blue stare of his. And the fact that, far from lessening on a longer acquaintance, the impact of his powerful persona and stunning good looks seemed to be having an even more potent effect on her nervous system.

He altered his position, uncrossing his legs and running a hand over his jaw. For all his arrogant ease, Harper could see that he was waiting to hear what she had to say, even if he did intend to totally disregard it. Because beneath that languid exterior, Vieri Romano was as stubborn and unyielding as an iron girder. Well, fine, she was stubborn too. Something her father liked to hurl at her, along with a lot more colourful adjectives, when he couldn't get her to procure another bottle of whisky for him from the bar at the Lodge, or give him the money so that he could stumble down to the pub for himself.

'Well, your body language is all wrong,' she began purposefully. Vieri had asked for his shortcomings so she would give them to him. It was too good an opportunity to miss. 'And you are far too evasive when Alfonso asks you questions about us. And you jump in all the time, when he is trying to talk to me.'

'Is that so? Clearly I am no good at this.' Vieri took another sip of whisky and set the glass down beside him. 'So, shifty-eyed, stilted posture, evasive and interfering. Is there anything else you would like to add?'

'No.' Harper pursed her lips to suppress a rogue smile. 'I think that's enough to be going on with.'

'*Bene*, then we had better do something about it.'

Harper's smile knotted inside her. Something about the glint in his eye told her she wasn't going to like what was coming next. Ditto, his use of the word *we*.

'What do you mean?'

'I suggest we try some role play.' Somehow he managed to make the idea burn with seductive intent.

Harper's anxiety spiked. 'Role play?'

'Yes.' His eyes travelled lazily over her increasingly tense frame. 'A little role play will help us be more comfortable in one another's presence.'

Being in Vieri's presence made Harper feel many things but *comfortable* wasn't one of them. And she strongly suspected that the sort of role play he was talking about would do nothing to help with that.

'I'm not sure that's such a good idea.' She turned her head away, flustered, desperately trying to escape from the trap that was of her own making.

'No?' Rising to his feet, Vieri moved to stand in front of her. 'Well, it has to be worth a try. Come on, up you get.'

Holding out his hands towards her, he gave them an impatient shake.

Harper swallowed, her mind struggling to come up with something to veto this crazy idea, the excitement tingling through her disobedient body already making this impossible.

Slowly she reached out towards him, preparing herself for the inevitable jolt of awareness that shot through her whenever their hands touched. And yep, there it was again, like a fizz of electricity running through her.

Pulled to her feet, she found herself standing mere inches from Vieri's towering form, trapped by his height and power and sheer magnetic pull. And when Vieri lightly took hold of her shoulders, drawing her towards him, her heart, which was already beating double time, threatened to leap out of her chest altogether, to make a bid for freedom to prevent any further assaults on its ability to function.

But worse was to come. With a shudder of pleasure, Harper felt his hands skim over her shoulders and down her back, where they settled possessively on either side of her waist, spanning the waistband of her jeans. She tried to move beneath his possessive grip but that only brought her into closer contact with him and as their bodies joined she became acutely aware of his honed shape; the muscles that rippled beneath his broad shoulders, the granite-hard chest pressed against her breasts, the long limbs, one leg slowly edging between her own, sending a thrill of awareness through her as she sensed his growing arousal. Harper let out a gasp.

'Hmm.' Vieri moved his hands to her back and, lowering his head, whispered in her ear. 'Interesting.' Sweeping aside her hair, he very gently pressed his lips below her earlobe, before lightly travelling down the sweep of her neck. *Oh, dear Lord.* Eyes tightly closed, Harper involuntarily angled her head to allow him more access.

'It seems we have found a connection.' He raised his head and Harper opened her eyes to meet his. 'Perhaps this won't be as hard as we thought.'

Or a whole lot harder. Fighting to catch her breath, she moved inside his hold, intent on finding some control. But Vieri hadn't finished with her yet.

'Maybe we should try a kiss.' He looked at her as if she were some sort of experiment. 'In the interest of authenticity, I mean.'

'I really don't think that will be necess—'

But before she could even gasp out the words his mouth was on hers, with the lightest of touches, just resting there as if to see what might happen next. Harper's breath stalled. No way could this be construed as a passionate kiss, not yet, but that didn't stop it from feeling intimate, sexual, heavy with promise. With a thrilling certainty she knew just where this kiss could go, what it could lead to. And as Vieri increased the pressure she found herself responding, feeling the thrum of excitement explode inside her head as her lips parted and his tongue found hers, sliding against it, around it, softly persuasive, hot, wet and druggingly sensual, tasting and teasing in a way that made her whole body shake with longing. Pulling away, she just caught the briefest hint of surprise in his eyes before he lowered his head again to continue his relentless assault. She had no sense of how long it was before, light-headed from lack of air and the sheer, potent sexuality of the kiss, she finally managed to push herself away from him and drag in a gulp of air.

She tried to hide the tremble of her body. Never had she imagined a kiss could be anything like that, so intensely hot and wild and powerful, leaving her knees shaking and her ears ringing. It wasn't as if she had never been kissed before. She had dated a couple of the local lads back home in Glenruie and it had been pleasant enough. Though not sufficiently pleasant for her to want to take the relationships much further. But she most certainly had never been kissed like *that* before. Thoroughly, utterly and completely possessed by a man who knew exactly what he was doing.

But it was just role play. Harper smoothed down her blouse, touching her lips with shaking fingers to check they were still there, that they hadn't somehow melted or fused with the heat. What they had just done wasn't real—whatever else, she had to remember that. Except now, of course, he had totally ruined her for any other man's touch. Thanks for that, Mr Romano.

Bracing herself, she raised her eyes to meet his. And there it was, that assurance, the deeply held complacency of a man who knew exactly the effect he had had on her. It was almost as if he had branded her as his own. Well, they would see about that.

'That's quite enough of that.' She deliberately moved away from him.

'Really?' A wicked smile played around his lips. 'I was just starting to enjoy myself. I believe you were too.'

'Whether or not either of us enjoyed it is entirely of no consequence.' Harper pulled at the neck of her blouse. Why was it so damned hot in here?

'Oh, I don't know. I found it of considerable consequence.' Mocking dark brows raised fractionally. 'You may have noticed.'

Harper flushed violently. Why was it that Vieri was crowing over his physical attraction to her, whereas she felt she had to frantically try and cover it up? Because Vieri had been in control, that was why. Because he was used to seducing women, no doubt bedding a different woman every night, revelling in the power he had over them, using them to satisfy his casual sexual urges and then discarding them without a second thought. It was written all over his smugly arrogant face.

Well, there was no way she was going to fall for his

smooth, well-practised seduction routine, no matter how good it might have felt.

'We were supposed to be learning how to be easy around one another in front of Alfonso to try and make our engagement believable. Not getting involved with...' she hesitated, hating the breathless catch in her voice, the way her cheeks still burned '...that sort of thing.'

'That sort of thing?' He was deliberately mocking her, loving every moment of her discomfort.

'Yes.' Her voice went up a notch. 'You know perfectly well what I'm talking about.'

He certainly did. Vieri let his eyes travel slowly over her flushed face, lingering on the swollen pout of her mouth. His very physical reaction to her had taken him by surprise, as clearly it had her, the passionate nature of the kiss catching him unawares. He had thought himself firmly in control, never doubted it for a second but somehow, lost in the heat of Harper's mouth, that control had slipped dangerously. In fact, if Harper hadn't called time on their little role-playing exercise he wasn't sure he would have had the willpower to do so himself. And then where would they be? In bed, that was where, at least if he'd had any say in the matter.

The image of Harper splayed across his bed had lodged in his mind and refused to be shifted. Her copper-coloured hair spread across the pillows, that shapely figure of hers waiting to be divested of its clothes, the no doubt sensible underwear he'd find and the pleasure he would take in slowly removing it. There was something incredibly sexy about Harper McDonald, something he couldn't quite put his finger on, though his traitorous body would have him putting his finger pretty much everywhere. And that would be just the start.

He gazed at her now, at the way those remarkable tawny

eyes glittered with a mixture of arousal and defiance. She really had no idea how attractive she was and that made a welcome change from the sort of women he usually found himself surrounded with who, frankly, suffered from the opposite problem. But it was more than that. There was an earthiness to her, a sensuality that was entirely unwitting, just a part of who she was. Perhaps it was her Scottish heritage. Somehow she conjured up purple heather and damp bracken and soft green moss and how it would feel to lay her down on such a bed and make love to her.

Enough! Moving a couple of steps away, he adjusted the fit of his trousers. Taking Harper to bed was not part of the plan. He just needed to remember that.

'Well—' he adopted a businesslike approach '—if you are sure we are done here, I will go and get on with some work.'

Turning to leave, he had reached the doorway when he remembered something. 'Oh, by the way.' He looked back to where Harper was still rooted to the spot. 'I meant to say, there is a charity gala here in Palermo on Saturday. Alfonso is a patron. He would like us to go.'

'Oh, right.' She didn't even try to hide the despondency in her voice and for some reason that riled him. He wasn't used to his dates being anything less than wildly enthusiastic when they were chosen to accompany him to glittering social events.

'You will need an appropriate outfit.' He raked his eyes dismissively over her casual jeans-and-top ensemble. 'In fact, you should choose several outfits. There may be a number of social engagements we need to attend while we are here.'

'I see.'

'My driver will be at your disposal. And obviously you will charge everything to my account.' Still she refused to look remotely grateful. Weren't women supposed to like shopping? 'I trust that won't be a problem?'

'No problem at all.' She tipped her chin haughtily. 'It's your money.'

'Indeed it is. And you are, to all intents and purposes, my fiancée.' Mounting irritation scored his voice. 'So please make sure you choose appropriately.'

'Yes, sir.' She tossed her hair dramatically over her shoulder. 'Heaven forbid that I should embarrass you in any way.'

Vieri ground down on his jaw. Embarrassment was not one of the emotions this infuriating young woman stirred up in him. But right now he had no intention of examining the ones that she did.

'*Bene*, that's settled, then.' He turned and strode from the room. Suddenly the need to put some space between them seemed vitally important.

CHAPTER FOUR

HARPER HAD TO admit that there was a certain heady excitement about going into these exclusive designer boutiques and knowing she could buy anything she wanted. At the mention of Vieri Romano's name, the snooty shop assistants were falling over themselves to help her, parading a dazzling array of garments before her. In the end she bought a cocktail dress, a pair of tailored trousers and a fitted jacket, all of which, she decided sourly, would be considered sufficiently appropriate.

But still no ball gown. As she breathed in the expensively scented air of yet another boutique, Harper determined that she would not leave this one without the requisite purchase. She was quite sure that there were any number of beautiful dresses here that would be more than suitable. The fact that she didn't feel right in any of them was because of the circumstances, not the gowns.

Finally she made her choice, a dark green lightweight velvet creation with a demure neckline and a full-length skirt. It was considerably less daring than some of the outfits, which was why she picked it. She didn't want to feel sexy around Vieri. Not when just the memory of that clinch, that kiss, was enough to set her knees wobbling again.

She was arranging to have it delivered to the hotel when she was interrupted by a tall, striking-looking middle-aged woman who she had noticed idly flicking through a rail of clothes and who had now silently come to stand beside her.

'Excuse me.'

Harper turned and gave her a friendly smile. It wasn't returned.

'Did I hear you say that you are a guest of Vieri Romano?' The woman spoke perfect English.

'Yes.' Harper wasn't sure what business it was of hers but she politely replied.

'How very interesting.' Perfectly made-up eyes swept over her from top to toe, taking in every little detail until Harper felt she was staring at her very bones. 'And that outfit you are buying.' She pointed a manicured finger at the dress being held by the sales assistant. 'It is for the Winter Ball?'

'Yes, that's right.'

'Then how fortunate for you that we bumped into each other. A dress like that will never do. Vieri will hate it.'

Harper frowned. She didn't like being spoken to like this by a woman she didn't know from Adam. In fact, instinctively she didn't like this woman at all, but, positioned firmly beside her as she was, she was impossible to ignore. Sensing Harper's reluctance, the woman gave her a forced smile.

'How rude you must think me, my dear.' She extended a hand weighed down with jewelled rings. 'Allow me to introduce myself. My name is Donatella Sorrentino. I am an old friend of Vieri's.'

'Harper McDonald.' Harper took her hand but found herself pulled into an awkward embrace, the soft fur of the woman's mink coat crushed against her chest as several heavily perfumed air kisses were wafted on either side of her. Pulling away, Donatella studied her with highly critical eyes.

'So tell me, Harper McDonald, how do you come to be accompanying Vieri to the ball?'

Harper moved a step away. 'Alfonso, Vieri's godfather, is a patron of the charity that hosts the ball.'

'You hardly need to tell me that, my dear.' Donatella's eyes glittered coldly. 'I suspect I know rather more about Sicilian society than you do. And quite apart from that, Alfonso Calleroni is my uncle.'

'Oh.' Harper was suitably chastened. 'I'm sorry, I didn't know.'

'Why would you? How is the old man, by the way?' She only just managed to stifle a bored yawn. 'I have been meaning to pay him a visit.'

'He is very frail.' Harper chose her words carefully. She wasn't going to be the one to tell this woman her uncle was dying, even if she suspected she wouldn't give a damn. 'But I think having Vieri here is cheering him up.'

'I'm sure. And you? Where do you fit into this cosy little scenario?'

Harper hesitated. Apart from Alfonso, no one else knew about their engagement and she only ever wore the tell-tale ring when they were visiting him. To tell a woman like this, who looked as if *malicious gossip* could be her middle names, might be a dangerous thing. But on the other hand, what did it matter? People were bound to find out sooner or later and frankly the temptation to try and shock that supercilious face out of its Botoxed grimace was too great to resist. She took in a breath.

'I am Vieri's fiancée.'

The look of total astonishment on Donatella's face was so great that Harper wasn't sure she had actually taken the information in. She decided to clarify, just for good measure. 'We are engaged to be married.'

'Mio Dio!' The words rasped from her throat before Do-

natella had time to stop them. But she quickly recovered herself. 'How simply wonderful. Come, let me embrace you.' She tugged Harper against her again, speaking over her shoulder. 'Why, that means we are almost family.'

Harper suppressed a shudder. If she had thought her own family was bad enough, this woman was on another level altogether.

Pulling away, Donatella held her at arm's length, gripping her shoulders that bit too hard with bony hands that felt more like claws. 'To think that Vieri is finally to marry. You must tell me simply everything, my dear, where you met, how you came to fall in love, although Vieri of course has always been totally irresistible and you…you are such a pretty young thing. When is the wedding to be? This is all so romantic!' She was babbling now, the words coming out in a rabid torrent. 'We must have lunch.' Fishing in her bag, she produced a diary, hurriedly flicking through the pages. 'Now, let me see—'

'That's very kind of you,' Harper interrupted, 'but I can't give you a date right now. I'm not really sure what my plans are.'

This brought Donatella's head back up. '*Your* plans?' Immediately she pounced on Harper's mistake. 'I'm sure Vieri will have everything mapped out for you both. He has always been so frightfully organised. When did you say the wedding was?'

'I didn't,' Harper replied firmly. 'We haven't fixed a date yet.'

'So this is all quite sudden?' Cold blue eyes drilled into her. 'You haven't known Vieri very long?'

'Not long, no.'

'I thought as much. You would never be considering buying that ghastly dress if you knew Vieri like I do. Look…' she glanced at her watch '… I can give you fifteen minutes. At least let me choose a suitable dress for you.' She moved over to the rails, snapping her fingers at the sales assistants, who rushed to her side to take hold of the garments she was rapidly selecting in a frantic rustle of taffeta and silk.

'Now run along and try these on and I will wait here to give you my final verdict.' She decorously draped herself on a velvet chaise longue, all eagle-eyed determination.

'We can't have you letting our Vieri down, now, can we?'

Sitting at the pavement café, Vieri took a sip of his espresso and opened his newspaper. His morning had gone well, a successful business meeting seeing him acquire a large plot of land ripe for development to add to his portfolio here in Sicily. And right now, even though he had vowed never to live here again, he couldn't deny that being back in Palermo felt good, felt like coming home.

A flash of auburn-coloured hair across the road caught his eye and suddenly there was Harper, striding along in the sunshine, her shoulder bag bouncing against her side. She seemed completely oblivious to the admiring glances of the men around her but Vieri wasn't. He found his grip tightening on the handle of his cup.

In truth, seeing her here wasn't entirely coincidental. At breakfast that morning she had told him she was going to visit the antiquities museum, which happened to be just around the corner. He had offered her a lift into town with him, which of course she had declined. It seemed she preferred to walk.

Now he watched as she bent down to stroke the head of a mangy-looking dog belonging to a beggar sheltering in a doorway. Vieri closed his newspaper, observing them intently. He saw Harper take her purse from her bag, pull out some notes, then turn the purse to shake out the coins

before offering the whole lot to the man, who was getting
to his feet, his hands cupped before him eagerly. Vieri
stood up, his protective instinct on high alert. The beggar
was pulling Harper towards him, either in some sort of
embrace, or he was about to go through her pockets—or
worse. Whichever, it was enough to see Vieri leap through
two lanes of traffic with horns blaring, to land by her side.

'That's enough.' Speaking in Sicilian he pulled the man
away by his shoulder, the beggar looking at him with a
mixture of annoyance and surprise. 'Get your hands off
her.'

'Vieri!' Harper rounded on him in outrage. 'What do
you think you're doing?'

'I could ask the same of you.' Moving his hand to the
small of her back, he propelled her forward along the pavement, tucking her arm through his to secure her to his
side. 'I just saw you giving him the entire contents of
your purse.'

'So what if I did.' She tripped angrily along beside him.
'It wasn't your money, if that's what you're worried about.'

'I don't give a damn about the money.' He navigated
them between the pedestrians. 'But I do worry about you
getting yourself into dangerous situations.'

'Well, don't. I can take care of myself. And besides,
there was nothing dangerous about that. The poor man
was hungry, that's all, and so was the dog.'

'That's as may be. But that doesn't mean he's not a violent criminal.'

'Oh, for God's sake!' Jerking to a halt, Harper pulled
her arm from under his and held it across her chest. 'I don't
know how you live like that, thinking the worst of everyone. I feel sorry for you, I really do.'

'Save your pity for the beggars, *cara*.' He met her heated
stare full on. 'And besides, I don't think the worst of ev-

eryone. When it came to your sister it seems I didn't think badly enough.'

He watched, not without some satisfaction, as the famous pout put in another appearance. She really had the most luscious lips, pink and full and perfectly formed. It was all he could do to stop himself from raising his fingers to touch them or, better still, bending his head to feel them against his own. The fact was, he hadn't been the same since that kiss they had shared. Even though a couple of days had passed, the memory of it still burned in his head—in his groin.

At the time he had pretended he was doing it to test Harper, to see how she would react. With arousal already stirring in his body he had wanted confirmation that she was feeling it too—at least that was what he'd told himself. But the fact was, the sight of those swollen lips had been impossible to resist, especially when coupled with her heavy-lidded eyes and that sensuous take-me-to-bed body.

That, at least, he had managed to force himself to resist. So far anyway. Harper's bedroom was at the opposite end of the hotel apartment from his and he had expressly forbidden himself from going anywhere near it. Just the thought of the delights that lay in wait for him on the other side of that door was enough to see him heading for the shower and swinging the dial round to cold.

If anyone had told him that he would be obsessing over this relatively ordinary young Scottish woman he would have told them they were mad. She was not his type, she wasn't glamorous or sophisticated or worldly. But she was warm and clever and kind. Despite the telling-off he had given her, the compassion she had shown that beggar, the way she had let him pull her into his arms, even though he must have smelled decidedly rank, had touched Vieri. It was typical of her, always thinking of others. Couple that with a natural prettiness and an innate sexiness and you had a special kind of person. Had he just called her *ordinary*? Who was he trying to kid?

But she was also as stubborn as a mule. Linking his arm through hers once more, he started them walking again. His car was parked only a few streets away. He wasn't even going to tell her that he'd just decided he was taking her out for lunch. She'd only start kicking up a fuss.

'So.' He turned them down a side street. 'Did you enjoy the antiquities museum?'

'Yes, I did.' He felt her relief at the change of subject. 'There are some amazing works of art in there. It's hard to believe that some of them date back thousands of years.'

'Sicily has a very rich history.'

'But some things never change.' Following her gaze, he saw she had spotted another beggar on the other side of the street. He groaned inwardly, preparing himself for another lecture. And sure enough it soon came. 'Doesn't it bother you?' She shot him an upward glance. 'Living a life of such wealth and privilege, when there is still so much poverty all around?'

Vieri drew in an exasperated breath. 'For your information, I have earned the life that I lead through hard work and determination.' He had no idea why he felt the need to defend himself, why he should give a toss what this opinionated young woman thought of him. He only knew that he did. 'And quite apart from that, me living like a pauper is not going to help these guys.' He gestured across the road. 'But by continuing to invest in this country I am providing employment and security for families who in turn pay taxes that go towards helping those less fortunate. Plus I am actively involved with a number of charities. Throwing down a handful of coins is not the long-term solution.'

'Well, no, I suppose not,' she conceded quietly. 'But

sometimes a short-term solution is better than nothing.'
Their eyes clashed before Harper dragged her gaze away.
'Oh…' She looked around her, suddenly realising they had
stopped. 'Is this your car?'

'It is.' Opening the door, Vieri gestured to her to get inside. 'If you would like to get in, I know a nice restaurant
not far along the coast. I thought I could buy you lunch
before we go and see Alfonso this afternoon. That is, if
your socialist principles will allow it, of course.'

Harper hesitated, biting down on her lip. Unless Vieri
was very much mistaken she was trying to hide the hint
of a smile. Finally she slipped into the passenger seat and
turned to face him as he got in beside her, tucking her hair
behind her ears. And there it was, the distinct and heart-
warming twinkle of mirth dancing in those autumn-coloured eyes.

'Lunch would be lovely.' She even reached out to touch
his arm, albeit very briefly. 'Thank you.'

Through the arched windows of the overheated sitting
room, Vieri watched Harper and his godfather in the garden. Bundled up in a thick coat and with a rug across
his knees, Alfonso was seated in his wheelchair, Harper
slowly pushing him along the neat paths that meandered
between flower beds that had more bare earth than flowers at this time of year.

Alfonso had been quite determined that he wanted to
go out and get some fresh air, and that it should be Harper,
and Harper alone, who was to accompany him. His nurse,
Maria, had been told to take some time for herself and
Vieri, somewhat unwillingly, left to his own devices.

They had stopped now, Harper coming round to Alfonso's side, squatting down so that she was level with him.
Alfonso was pointing to a bird perched on a holly bush, a

goldfinch if Vieri wasn't mistaken, though he was no expert on ornithology. He was more interested in the way Harper's hand rested on Alfonso's knee, the way Alfonso's own hand went to protectively cover it. The bird flew off and Harper tucked in the scarf around Alfonso's neck and they smiled at each other before she stood up and went back to pushing the wheelchair.

Vieri frowned. His godfather clearly adored Harper. And she him, if the tender way she fussed over him was anything to go by. Vieri had noticed the way Maria had started to defer to her, obviously happy that Alfonso was in safe hands when Harper was around.

Turning away, he sat himself down on the ancient sofa, drumming his fingers on the cracked leather of the arm as he waited for them to return. It was good that they got on so well, that Alfonso so obviously approved of his choice of 'fiancée'. But at the same time, it left him with more than a slight sense of unease. Somehow this close friendship they were forming troubled him because of course it was all built on a lie. Somehow it would have been easier if they had remained more emotionally distant from one another, then Vieri wouldn't have ended up feeling such a fraud. He was starting to realise that he hadn't thought this thing through at all.

His lunch with Harper had been surprisingly relaxed. Choosing the fresh catch of the day, Harper had ploughed her way through a large platter of seafood with surprising speed, enthusiastically mopping up the juices with hunks of bread. It had been a real delight to see her enjoying her food, although Vieri had been careful to avert his eyes to the twinkling expanse of the Mediterranean Sea when she had finally come up for air, dabbing her mouth with the napkin and declaring it was the nicest meal she had ever had. Even so, he felt a foolish swell of pride that he had finally managed to do something that had made her happy.

A buzz from his phone alerted him to a new email message from Bernie, his head of security. Vieri clicked it open. Rodriguez had been found and was back in New York. But Leah McDonald was no longer with him. Bernie was awaiting further instructions. Vieri narrowed his eyes for a moment, then tapped out his reply.

Leave Rodriguez to me. Find Leah McDonald asap.

He heard a door opening and the sound of Harper and his godfather returning. Harper was laughing at something Alfonso had said and when they appeared in the sitting room she was still smiling, her cheeks flushed from the cold, her hair a mass of untamed curls. She looked… gorgeous. Dragging his gaze away, he was suddenly conscious of Alfonso's eyes on him, a knowing smile playing about his lips.

'Let me help you into your chair, *padrino*.' For some unknown reason he felt flustered, as if he had been exposed. 'I do hope you haven't caught a chill.'

'Stop fussing, my boy, I am fine. With your fiancée, I have been in the very best hands.' He smiled at Harper before easing himself into his chair. 'But I think I will go for a lie-down in a minute. Harper, perhaps you would be so good as to find Maria for me.'

'Of course.'

As she left the room, Alfonso signalled to Vieri to close the door behind her.

'Come here, my son. Quickly. I want to talk to you before Harper returns.'

Vieri pulled up a wooden chair and seated himself opposite his godfather.

'What is it, *padrino*?'

'I may be old,' he started, fixing his godson with a watery stare, 'but I like to think I am still pretty astute.'

'Indeed you are.' Vieri didn't doubt that for a second.

'And it is fairly obvious to me that you have rushed ahead with this engagement because you want to make your old godfather happy.'

Vieri inhaled sharply. Was this it? Had they been rumbled? Had Harper been right all along? With Alfonso's penetrating gaze firmly trained on his face, Vieri decided that if necessary he would come clean, admit that this was all a sham. He wasn't prepared to dig the hole of this lie any deeper.

'And I want you to know that you have succeeded.' His lined face lit up. 'Harper is a wonderful girl. I am delighted that you have fallen in love with someone so perfect for you.' He raised his eyebrows.

'Well…yes, thank you,' Vieri mumbled quietly.

'In fact I would go as far as to say you are very lucky to have found her. Young women like Harper are few and far between. Don't lose her, Vieri.'

'I'll try not to.'

But his attempt to be light-hearted was met with a sudden seriousness as Alfonso reached to take hold of his hand.

'I mean it.' His eyes glittered. 'You have to trust me on this one. As someone who probably knows you better than you know yourself, I'm telling you, if you let Harper slip through your fingers you will regret it.'

'Alfonso—'

'No, hear me out, *figlio*. As you know, I never married, never had a family, not because I didn't want to but because of the terrible vendetta between my family and the Sorrentinos. The vendetta that took the life of my dear brother.'

Alfonso's voice faltered but with a look of grim determination he carried on. 'Now I am the very last Calleroni so when I die the name will die with me and the generations of murder can finally cease.'

'I know this, *padrino*.' Vieri's voice was soft. 'I have always known.'

'And you also know that this is the reason that I could never adopt you as my son, much as I wanted to, because I would never burden you with the Calleroni name.'

'I do, *padrino*. But to be your godson has been more than honour enough.'

'And it has been my pleasure. To see the success you have made of your life has been my greatest achievement. Especially...' He paused and reached for a glass of water by his side to moisten his throat. 'Especially as there were times, in the early days, when I thought I had lost you.'

'Never, *padrino*. I would never have turned my back on you.'

But they both knew the time that Alfonso referred to. That black period in Vieri's youth when the course of his life could so easily have changed for ever. Or more likely ended—with a bullet through his head.

Vieri had been just eighteen, little more than a kid, when Donatella Sorrentino had deliberately sought out her uncle's handsome young protégé. At the time she had appeared to Vieri to be the height of sophistication: wealthy, extremely attractive and impossibly glamorous. He had known she was dangerous, but in Vieri's naive eyes that had only made her all the more alluring.

Some years before, Donatella Calleroni, as she had been then, had done the unthinkable and crossed the divide, forsaking her own family to marry into the Sorrentino dynasty. The fallout between the two warring clans had been predictably catastrophic. In the name of honour but blinded by revenge, her father, Eduardo Calleroni, had retaliated in the only way he knew how—with violence, ending up with him splattered across the tarmac in a hail of bullets. His brother's death had broken Alfonso's heart but if Donatella had felt any guilt, any remorse, she never had shown it.

But even knowing all this, to Vieri's intense shame, he had still fallen under her spell.

In hindsight he could see how he had been groomed. Donatella had taken such an interest in him, buying him clothes, taking him to the theatre, the opera, for meals out in expensive restaurants. By keeping her entertained Vieri was doing her husband a favour, she had insisted, because Frank never did anything but work.

In actual fact Frank Sorrentino had known full well what was going on, to start with at least. One of Sicily's most notorious gangsters, he had thought it wise to keep tabs on the clever Romano boy who was a son in all but name to Alfonso Calleroni. Donatella had been dispatched to keep a close eye on him. Something she had done all too well.

Before long the idea of them going to bed together had shifted from an erotic fantasy to an inevitability. And Vieri, still a virgin, had wanted it, badly. The thought of Donatella being his first, maybe even his only, had filled his head, consumed his young body, sent his teenage hormones into overdrive. So he had readily agreed to Donatella's terms that nobody could ever, *ever* discover their illicit relationship. Despite knowing the possible consequences, they had embarked on a passionate affair.

And then, as suddenly as it had begun, it was over. Donatella was bored, she told him. He was becoming too possessive, anyway he was far too young for her. It was only ever meant to have been a brief fling. From being a constant presence in his life she abruptly severed all contact.

And Vieri had accepted her decision, respected her wishes. Despite being shocked, bruised, broken-hearted even, for he had genuinely believed himself to be in love with her, he had backed right off, walked away. Done as he was told.

It was only several months later that he had discovered the full, horrifying truth. And such had been his all-consuming rage, his thirst for revenge, that he knew he would have been capable of almost anything. With fire raging in his blood and his contacts in the world of organised crime, the situation could so easily have ended in disaster, destruction, death.

But then Alfonso had stepped in. Without ever discussing anything a position in New York had rapidly been found for him, together with a considerable amount of money to enable him to make a new life for himself. Which of course he had done, becoming a billionaire businessman in under ten years. He had his godfather to thank for his success. But more than that, he had him to thank for his life.

Now he squeezed Alfonso's hand. 'You know you mean the world to me, *padrino*.'

'I do indeed, *mio figlio*. Which is why you are going to accept this one piece of advice.' His voice quavered. 'Build a family for yourself, Vieri, a wife and children. Don't live an empty life like mine.'

'You have not led an empty life, Alfonso! How can you even say that?'

'It has been empty in here.' He punched at his bony chest with a frail fist. 'Inside, where it matters. I had to deliberately end my family line but you, you have the chance to start one. Don't you see, Vieri, by being an orphan, by having no background, you have a blank canvas? You are free from the shackles that restrained me. Make the most of that opportunity.'

'What are you saying?'

'I'm saying it is time to alter the course of your life. Don't put it off any longer. Take this opportunity to marry your lovely fiancée and settle down.'

'Alfonso, I—'

'Set a date, Vieri.'

'I'm sorry?'

'For the wedding, set a date. And don't make it too far away. If I am to stand any chance of seeing you two walk down the aisle it will need to be within the next month.'

CHAPTER FIVE

HARPER SURVEYED HERSELF in the full-length mirror. She had to admit that awful Sorrentino woman had chosen the most beautiful dress, even though she would never have picked it for herself. Not in a thousand years.

Made of shimmering satin, it had a slim-fitting bodice, ingeniously styled so that the two straps only went over one shoulder leaving a tantalising sliver of cleavage in between and a wide expanse of bare back behind. Slightly ruched around the hips and bottom, it hugged her tightly, giving her a sexy shape she hadn't even known she had, before it fell in soft folds to the floor. But it was the colour that was the most shocking of all. Red. Bright red. Harper was quite sure that someone of her colouring should never wear red and yet here she was wearing it, and looking pretty darned hot—even if she did say so herself.

She turned, twisting to get a better view of the back, so intent on her own reflection that she failed to notice Vieri standing in the doorway of her dressing room.

'*Molto bella.*' His deep, sultry voice spun her around and she reached out a hand to steady herself against the dresser. As he slowly advanced towards her, her grip tightened against the polished wood. 'You have made a good choice.'

'Thank you.' His unexpected compliment went to her

head like a glass of champagne. She was just about to blurt out that she hadn't actually chosen it herself but remembered Donatella's strict instructions that she wasn't to mention her input, or indeed that she had met her at all. Harper had wondered if it was because she had no intention of going to visit Alfonso, that maybe this was just a flying visit. Harper gathered she now lived in Milan. 'You look pretty smart yourself.'

Smart was a massive understatement. He looked completely, heart-stoppingly, drop-dead gorgeous. Wearing a tuxedo and a white dress shirt with a black bow tie, he was the epitome of suave, elegant handsomeness, as if he had been created solely for the purpose of showing how it should be done. Long limbs were effortlessly encased in the fine fabric, giving him an easy, cat-like grace. He was clean shaven, Harper noticed, his usual designer stubble missing, and his hair was still wet from the shower, pushed back from his forehead so that the thick dark curls were temporarily tamed. He smelled divine too, his subtle aftershave invading her senses now that he was so close. Too close. Way too close.

'Are you wearing your hair down?' Harper's breath stuttered to a halt as he reached forward to move her hair to one side, exposing the sweep of her neck. 'I think the dress would suit an upstyle, don't you, maybe with some suitable earrings to set it off?'

'Maybe.' Harper pursed her lips. 'But I don't happen to have any suitable earrings.' What did he think, that she had a selection of diamond jewellery that she could dip into for any occasion?

'I wish I'd thought of that before.' Vieri's intense dark blue gaze seared into her. 'I would have bought you some.'

'Well, it doesn't matter.' With a small shake of her head, Harper dislodged his hand so that she could start to breathe again. By taking her caustic comment and turning it around with his offer to buy her jewellery he had disarmed her. More than that, something about the intensity of his stare was doing alarming things to her insides. She wasn't used to being the focus of such close attention, to have someone looking at her, really looking at her, almost as if they cared. She quickly brushed the silly notion away. 'I'll put my hair up anyway.'

Briskly sweeping past him, she fled for the sanctuary of her bedroom where her make-up bag held a few grips and an assortment of hair bands. 'Do you want to wait for me down in the lobby?'

'That's okay. I'm fine here.'

Harper's heart plummeted. He might be *fine* there, decorously lounging about in her dressing room, but she felt anything but fine, as a quick glimpse in the mirror brutally revealed.

She looked different somehow, as if some sort of banned substance had entered her bloodstream, changing her features. It took her a second to work out what the peculiar look was, and when she did she wished she hadn't. Because it was arousal. Her cheeks were lightly flushed and her hazel eyes had darkened to a sultry amber glow as the devastating effect of his lethal attraction continued to pump in her veins.

This evening was going to be awful. However was she going to be able to stand beside Vieri, trying to be the elegant and sophisticated fiancée, when the merest touch of his breath on her neck did *this* to her?

Staring at the emerald ring on her finger, she fought the temptation to pull the wretched thing off and hurl it across the room. What good would that do? She had signed up to this deal—she had to see it through.

Picking up her hairbrush, she started to tug it forcefully

through her curls, giving herself a stern talking-to with each vicious stroke. Then, capturing the thick swathe of hair, she twisted it into a knot on the top of her head and, with a mouth full of hair grips, set about securing the stray tendrils as best she could. Then, setting her features in what she hoped was a suitably bland expression, she went back through to the dressing room.

Vieri, who had been sprawled in a chair, one long leg casually draped over the arm, rose to meet her. His blue eyes raked all over her but he made no comment as she brushed past him to retrieve the shoe box from the dresser, self-consciously lifting out the silver shoes and quickly slipping them onto her feet as if there were nothing remotely unusual about her wearing a pair of sparkly stilettos with a price tag that had made her eyes water, in much the same way as she suspected the shoes themselves would by the end of the night. Throwing a cashmere wrap around her shoulders, she then picked up the silver clutch bag and, drawing in a breath, turned to face Vieri again.

He came towards her, his right arm crooked as he waited for her to slide her arm through it. Nestled so closely beside him, Harper felt her pulse set off at a gallop.

'*Sei pronto*, you are ready?'

Harper nodded, although she felt anything but. She gathered the wrap closer to her in a vain attempt to ward off his nearness.

'Then let's go.'

As they moved towards the doorway Harper felt the wobble in her step. And it wasn't just the four-inch heels.

The Winter Ball was a magnificently glittering affair held in a stunning, floodlit medieval castle not far from Palermo. The guests were escorted across the moat and through the echoing anterooms to a ballroom that had been transformed into a winter wonderland. Giant icicles twirled above their heads, snowflakes danced across the walls, and enormous ice sculptures of fantastical beasts adorned the walls. It was certainly breathtaking, if a little dazzling. As Harper gazed about in awe she realised that most of the women were dressed in appropriately winter colours; ice blue was very popular, as were silver and white. Even the staff were dressed from head to toe in snowy white. And there she was in flaming scarlet.

'Why didn't you tell me?' she snapped in Vieri's ear as she reluctantly relinquished her wrap, the idea that she might be able to keep it on for the entire evening quickly taken out of her hands by the helpful cloakroom attendant.

'Tell you what?'

'That everyone would be dressed in…in cold colours.'

'I didn't know they would.' Vieri surveyed the room dismissively.

Harper followed his even gaze, feeling like a hedge-row poppy about to infiltrate a room full of lilies. But it was too late now. With his arm snaking around her waist, Vieri was confidently escorting her into the room, all eyes turning to look at them. Or so it seemed to Harper. She felt their curious stares, their blatant scrutiny of this boldly dressed stranger who had the audacity to be on the arm of Sicily's most eligible bachelor. As they advanced further into the room the crowd parted, almost reverentially, to let them through until a middle-aged man came forward to shake Vieri's hand, demanding to know who this beautiful young woman was. When Vieri casually introduced her as his fiancée there was an audible intake of breath before a group of people closed around them, congratulations flying as the women edged forward to get a better look at her, eyeing the ring on her finger with burning curiosity, while the men were slapping Vieri on the back.

Harper quickly downed half a glass of champagne. She was about as far out of her comfort zone as it was possible to go. Unlike her sister, she had never aspired to live the high life, the affairs of the rich and famous holding no interest for her. While Leah would be poring over celebrity magazines, she would be more likely to be found running her finger down the column of barely legible figures in their father's accounts ledger, trying to make sure that everything balanced before it was handed over to the estate accountant. Her biggest dread was that the Laird would be forced to sack her father, that they would lose their livelihood, their home. Gordon Gillespie, Laird of Craigmore, was a good man but fundamentally the Craigmore estate was a business, and if Angus McDonald was seen as a liability, Harper knew he would have to go. Which was why she worried herself sick fighting the losing battle to keep him sober, covering his tracks, essentially doing as much of his job as she could for him.

But tonight she had another job to do. Tonight she had to play the part of the adoring fiancée. Although how she was supposed to do that when Vieri was virtually ignoring her, she had no idea. Despite the fact that he had stressed in the car the importance of them giving a convincing performance because the gossip from the night would be sure to find its way back to Alfonso, now they were actually here he seemed to have forgotten all about her. As the great and the good of Sicilian high society swarmed around them, not to mention royalty and A-list celebrities from all over Europe, she watched him being borne away on a tide of adoring females, scarcely giving her a glance as he disappeared into the crowd. Well, maybe it was a much-needed reality check. When Vieri had looked at her in her dressing room, just for that moment, he had made her feel beautiful. He had made her feel *special*. Now, as she watched the smooth way he charmed the women around him, she realised it had simply been an act. A minor charm offensive. And like a fool she had fallen for it.

Draining the last of the champagne, she swapped the empty glass for a full one from a passing waiter. She wished she could shrink into the background, pretend she wasn't here, but, given her choice of attire, that wouldn't be easy. A shriek of laughter turned her head in time to see a beautiful blonde with icicle earrings grasp Vieri's arm then lean forward to giggle something into his ear. Harper turned back, squashing down the pang of hurt, refusing to let herself feel anything.

'Signorina?' A rather dashing young man wearing some sort of military uniform stepped forward. 'Would you do me the great honour of having the next dance?'

Pasting on a smile and accepting his hand, Harper allowed herself to be led to the dance floor, grateful that at least someone was paying her some attention. She would allow him the honour, and anyone else who might want to dance with her. They would be no substitute for Vieri, of course, but right now her bruised confidence would take anything that was on offer.

From his table at the side of the ballroom, Vieri's narrow-eyed gaze flitted across the crowded dance floor. She wasn't difficult to spot, the flash of that scarlet dress as Harper was twirled around by yet another partner, male guests of all ages queuing up for the chance to take her hand, slide their arm around her waist, hold her just that little bit too close.

Well, it was time to put a stop to it. Vieri pushed his drink away and rose to his feet. He thought he had made himself clear. He thought he had explained that her role as his 'fiancée' was to spend the evening by his side, look decorous and say little. Instead of that she had disappeared the first chance she'd had, already on the dance floor when he had looked up to see where she was within minutes of their arrival.

Irritation spiked through him, along with some other emotion that felt suspiciously like jealousy. He ground his jaw. If she was dancing with anyone it should be him.

Was she doing this deliberately? Trying to prove some sort of point? Vieri had never concerned himself with the inner workings of a woman's mind and he certainly had no time for playing silly games, as the few women who had tried that on with him had soon found out to their cost. But he would never have thought that of Harper. She was too open, altogether too straightforward. It was one of the things he liked about her. But tonight she had overstepped the mark. If she wasn't playing games it was time he reminded her of her duty. To him.

Weaving his way through the dancers, he zoned in on his target, briefly pausing behind the swaying figure of Harper's partner, Hans Langenberg, the Crown Prince of a small European principality, before tapping him briskly on the shoulder.

'Excuse me.'

'Vieri Romano.' Hans turned to face him. 'I hope you haven't come to spoil my fun.'

'If you mean claiming my fiancée for a dance, then yes, I have.'

'Fiancée, eh, Romano?' The Crown Prince looked at him with renewed respect. 'So it's true. You are finally committing after all this time?'

Vieri gave a brisk nod. 'I said so, didn't I?'

'Well, hats off to you, old chap. You have made an excellent choice.'

Vieri scowled. Why did everyone persist in telling him

what an excellent choice he had made when in point of fact he hadn't made the choice at all?

'Though I can't pretend I'm not disappointed,' Hans continued. 'I was hoping I might be in with a chance myself.'

'Well, I can assure you, you are not.' With a surge of possessiveness Vieri stepped in between the two of them, slipping his arm around Harper's waist. A tingle of awareness shot through him as his fingers touched the bare skin of her lower back. Swiftly followed by the hot rush of annoyance when he thought of the other men who had had their hands there tonight.

'I am here, you know, I can speak for myself,' Harper finally piped up. But her voice held none of the usual edge Vieri had expected to hear. Instead there was a hint of triumph, a light in her eyes that told him he had been sussed—that he had given himself away. Something she decided to put to the test by leaning into him so that the sexy warmth of her body worked its way through the fabric of his suit, setting off a chain reaction that he battled to contain.

'I don't doubt it for one moment, Miss McDonald.' Hans reached for Harper's hand, kissing the back of it before letting go and giving her a formal bow. 'Can I just say it has been a pleasure? And should you, you know, ever change your mind…'

There was a low growl and it took Vieri a second to realise it had come from him. Pulling Harper closer to him, he fixed Hans with a menacing stare. 'Back off, Langenberg.'

'Sorry, old chap.' Hans frowned. 'Didn't mean to tread on your toes.'

'It didn't stop you treading on mine.' Both men turned to look at Harper, who was stifling a giggle.

Vieri glared at her. She was drunk; she had to be. 'You, young lady, need some fresh air.' Loosening his arm, he took hold of Harper's hand. 'We are leaving.'

He started to weave his way out of the ballroom, keeping Harper's hand in a firm grip as he negotiated a path through the noisy throng of people, ignoring all attempts to stop them from leaving. They made their way down a corridor, Harper's shoes clicking on the flagstoned floor as she hurried to keep up with him, until they reached an ancient oak-panelled door, and, sliding the heavy iron bolt across, Vieri ushered them out into a secluded courtyard. It was quiet and dark out here, the music from the ballroom reduced to little more than a dull thud. High castle walls on all four sides protected them from the breeze but the air was still cold and Vieri felt Harper shiver beside him.

'Here.' Shrugging off his jacket, he draped it over her shoulders. 'So…' He held her at arm's length. 'How much have you had to drink?'

'I don't know.' She tipped her chin. 'I wasn't counting. How much have you had?'

'For your information I am stone-cold sober.'

'Really?' Her nose wrinkled. 'How boring.' Shrugging off his jacket, she tried to give it back to him. 'I don't need this. I am used to properly cold winters. Where I come from this would be considered positively balmy.'

'Well, from where I come from it isn't and I'm not letting you get hypothermia.' He positioned the jacket over her shoulders again.

'What is it with you, bossing me around all the time?' Without waiting for an answer, Harper took a few steps away and twirled herself around, holding the lapels of the jacket across her chest. 'But thank you for bringing me here. I have actually had a lovely evening.'

He'd noticed. Vieri ground down on his jaw. But if she was baiting him, he refused to bite. 'It's Alfonso you should be thanking. It was his idea.'

'Then I will, the next time we visit. He is such a lovely man. And so generous. Everyone here thinks the world of him.'

'Yes.' Vieri's voice sounded gruff in the dim light. 'I know.'

'It is so sad to think that he is dying.' She turned mournful wide eyes in his direction.

'Everyone has to die eventually.'

'I guess.' Vieri watched as she moved to the centre of the courtyard, throwing back her head and looking up into the sky. 'When my mother died, Leah and I were told that she had become a star in the sky. We didn't really believe it, even then.' She paused, staring intently upwards. 'But on a starlit night like tonight I still find myself wondering which one she might be. Silly, I know.'

'That's not silly.' Vieri quietly closed the gap between them, coming to stand next to her. 'It's a way of remembering her.' There was a beat of silence. 'How old were you, when she died?'

'Twelve.' Harper turned to look at him.

'And it was an accident with a shotgun, you say?'

'Yes.' Her voice was very small.

'What happened?' Suddenly Vieri found he wanted to know the details. To try and understand the event that had so obviously shaped this young woman's life.

'My father was away one night, helping out on a neighbouring estate.' Vieri could see the effort it took for Harper to talk about this, even now, years after the event. 'My mother heard a disturbance, someone trying to poach the birds, so she took the shotgun to try and scare them off. It was dark, she wasn't used to handling a gun, she tripped…'

'I'm sorry.' Vieri held her gaze. 'That must have been very hard for you all.'

'Yep.' Harper touched the slender column of her throat. 'Pretty tough. She died trying to protect a few birds that were going to end up getting shot anyway. Ironic when you think about it. And Dad never forgave himself. He was convinced it was his fault.'

And she had been left to pick up the pieces. She didn't say as much, but as Vieri studied Harper's proud silhouette in the dim light it was plain to see—the care and compassion, the *responsibility*, that sat so heavily on her slender shoulders. It was clear that she would do anything for her family, even if, as he strongly suspected, they didn't appreciate her. He wondered if her father and sister had any idea how lucky they were to have her, to have a family at all, in fact. But if they were guilty of taking her for granted, where did that leave him? He was using her entirely for his own gain. It was an uncomfortable thought.

'Anyway...' she gave him a forced smile '...that's enough talk about sad things for one night. What I'd really like to do is dance.' She looked at him boldly. 'With you, I mean.'

Vieri shook his head. 'We're not going back in there.'

'Who said anything about going inside?' Removing his jacket, she held it at arm's length. 'We can dance here, under the stars.' The jacket was dropped theatrically to the ground.

'Harper...'

'Come on, it will be fun.'

Suddenly she was advancing towards him, holding out her arms invitingly. Too invitingly. The scarlet dress glowed in the dim light, the sheer fabric of the bodice pulling tight around the swell of her breasts as she closed the gap between them, positioning herself in front of him like a defiant temptress. It was a lethal combination and suddenly Vieri understood why red meant danger. A danger that increased tenfold as she slid her arms around his neck.

He managed to resist for all of two seconds. But then suddenly his arms were around her waist, and he was drawing her into his body, her bare flesh tantalisingly cold beneath his hot hands. They began to sway, Harper's softly sensual body leaning into his as their feet moved beneath them to the barely audible strains of music coming from inside.

Vieri closed his eyes, just for a moment. This felt good. *Too good.* He was already guilty of using Harper; he could not let himself take advantage of her any further. But as his hands strayed lightly over the ruched fabric of that firm little behind it was so hard to hold back. His body was already defying him, reacting wildly to the feel of her luscious body against his, the scent of her hair, the small but erotic movement as she swayed in his arms. As the tightening in his groin intensified, with supreme effort Vieri forced himself to stop.

'That's enough.' His words were harsher than he had intended, and he saw Harper's eyes widen as he roughly moved to hold her at arm's length. He meant to apologise but before he had the chance Harper had launched into an attack.

'Okay, fine, I get the message.' Smoothing down the fabric over her hips, she turned to glare at him. 'Heaven forbid that we should actually start to enjoy ourselves.'

'I think you have enjoyed yourself quite enough for one evening.'

'And you haven't, I suppose? Apart from when you took the time to glare at me, of course.'

'I'm surprised you noticed. You seemed to be far too busy throwing yourself at every available man.'

'Perhaps if you had paid me a bit more attention I wouldn't have needed to *throw myself* at anyone.' She drew in a sharp breath that pushed her breasts seductively upwards. 'You were the one who said we needed to put on a convincing performance and yet within minutes of arriving you were swanning off with your gaggle of female admirers.'

'I was merely engaging in the normal rules of social etiquette.'

'Well perhaps you should have spent more time *engaging* with the person you are actually *engaged* to.'

'I would have done, if I could have got a look in.'

'You didn't even try, Vieri.'

They glared at each other, childish hostility shimmering between them.

'So that's what all that unbecoming behaviour was about.' Keeping his tone low, Vieri gestured towards the party inside. 'You were trying to make me jealous.'

'Ha!' Harper gave a contemptuous laugh. 'I'm sorry to disappoint you and your mountainous ego but my *unbecoming* behaviour was simply me having a good time. Enjoying the company of some civilised men.'

'Civilised be damned.' Vieri's voice boomed around the courtyard. 'I saw the way Hans looked at you and there was nothing civilised about that.'

'Excuse me, you're the one who just accused me of trying to make you jealous.' Harper leapt on his words. 'But it's clear that you don't need any help in that department. You are more than capable of turning all green-eyed monster without any help from me.'

'Nonsense.'

'And while we are on the subject, what was all that chest beating in front of Hans? All that, *"Back off, Langenberg."*' She mimicked Vieri's voice, piling on a heavy Sicilian accent to perfectly capture his ill humour.

Vieri felt the blood fire through his veins. 'That's enough.' Harper was in danger of seriously overstepping the line. 'I'm taking you home.'

'And supposing I don't want to go. Supposing I want to stay and have some more fun.'

'Trust me, Harper, you don't get the choice. The fun is over.' Striding over to pick up his jacket from the ground, Vieri pointedly gave it a shake before looping his finger through the label and tossing it over his shoulder. 'We are leaving. Now!'

CHAPTER SIX

'HERE, DRINK THIS.' Vieri slid the cup of espresso coffee across the table towards her.

'For the last time, I am *not* drunk.' Harper angrily folded her arms across her chest, glaring at Vieri, who was seated on the sofa opposite her.

It was true. Maybe she had had one too many glasses of champagne at the ball—why else would she have been stupid enough to ask Vieri to dance with her? But the way he had rebuffed her, his surly silence in the car on the way back to the apartment and now his patronising refusal to believe anything she said had sobered her up nicely, thank you very much.

She probably should have gone straight to her room. That had been her intention as she had simmered beside him in the warm, purring darkness of the car. Even when they were back at the apartment, Vieri noisily making coffee, she had intended to show her defiance by sweeping past him and marching to her room, firmly closing the door behind her. But halfway there she had realised that that was actually more cowardly than agreeing to sit down and have a cup of coffee with him. That fleeing to her bedroom would send out the message that she was upset by what had happened between them. Which of course she was.

Asking him to dance had been a stupid idea; she should

never have done it. But his display of possessiveness in front of Hans, and then the way he had asked about her family, the surprising tenderness in his expression, had emboldened her, made her drop her guard. Only for him to throw her foolishness back in her face by rebuffing her, shoving her away as if she was nothing, no one.

She lifted her cup to her lips, sullenly eyeing her adversary over the rim. He had pulled loose the bow tie so that it lay flat against the crisp white of his shirt, which had the top buttons undone, the sleeves rolled up to reveal dark-skinned forearms. He looked as stunningly drop-dead gorgeous as ever but there was something about him, a sharpness that stiffened his posture, tempering his usual languid style.

Perhaps he was afraid she was going to leap on him. Forget her place once again and demand that he take her to bed, make love to her. That thought did very disturbing things to her insides and she hastily swallowed a mouthful of hot coffee to try and drown them. Vieri Romano need have no fear of that. She had learned her lesson. From now on she intended to show him just how much she didn't care.

She watched as he refilled his cup. 'Well, in that case there are a couple of things I would like to discuss with you.'

'Go on.' With studied indifference, Harper arranged the scarlet folds of her dress.

'First, I thought you would like to know that your sister has turned up.'

'Leah?' Leaping to her feet, all pretence of coolness gone, Harper flew to his side, perching herself down on the sofa next to him. 'Oh, thank God.' She searched his face for information. 'Is she okay?'

'As far as I know.'

'Oh, thank God.' She repeated the words on a long exhalation of breath. 'Where is she? How did you find her?'

'She was tracked down to a casino in Atlantic City. She has been collected from those premises.'

'Collected from those premises?' Immediately alarm surged through her. It was always the same with Leah; she evoked this hugely protective instinct in Harper, as if she had been put on this earth solely to save her twin sister. Which in a way she had.

A sickly child, Leah had been diagnosed with kidney failure shortly after their mother's death, compounding the family's distress. They were told she would need a kidney transplant and Harper was found to be the perfect match but legally they still had to wait four long years until the girls were old enough before the transplant could go ahead. But finally it had happened and Harper was able to give her sister the precious gift of a healthy life. But it did mean that she still worried obsessively over Leah, probably far more than she should.

'So what does that mean?' She cross-examined Vieri. 'You had your security guys go and pick her up?'

'Correct.'

Harper remembered the two brutes who had grabbed her in Spectrum nightclub, the way they had manhandled her when they had thought she was Leah. And they had been obeying Vieri's orders. Were they the same goons who had been sent to 'collect' Leah?

'Well, I hope they didn't hurt her. I'm telling you now, Vieri, if one of your bully-boy thugs has harmed so much as a hair on my sister's head...'

Vieri let out a low scoff. 'Forgive me if I don't appear too terrified.'

'I mean it. If any harm has come to Leah you will have me to answer to.' His sarcasm only served to fire her temper more. 'You can forget about this whole charade with your godfather. I will go right round there and tell him everything.'

'Really?' Vieri leant back into the sofa. 'And will this *everything* include how your precious sister wilfully cheated me out of thirty thousand dollars?'

Harper paused, searching for a firmer footing. 'If necessary, yes. Alfonso will understand. He is a good man. Maybe he deserves to know the truth.'

'And maybe you should think very carefully before you continue this conversation. I am not going to be held to ransom over this, Harper. You knew the score when you agreed to take on your sister's debt. Either you continue with our arrangement or you pack your bags and get the hell out of here. The choice is yours.' Dark blue eyes flashed at her. 'But rest assured, if that happens, the debt will still have to be paid.'

Harper glared at him, the blood pounding in her ears, fear and anger and frustration coursing through her body.

'Is that a threat?'

'Take it any way you want.'

'And what do you think Alfonso would make of that? The fact that you are prepared to hound two young women for a sum of money that is nothing more than a pittance to you.'

'You leave my godfather out of this.' Danger tinged Vieri's voice.

'Maybe he needs to know just what a bully and a thug you really are.'

'*Chiedo scusa*, I beg your pardon?' With a flash of anger, Vieri leant in, so close that she could feel his hot breath on her cheeks. 'What did you just call me?'

Harper swallowed hard. Perhaps she had gone too far. But stubborn pride refused to let her back down. She was too worried about Leah, and about what might happen to her if she did try and pull out of this hateful deception. She was trapped and, worse than that, trapped by a man who did the most terrible things to her. Who right now, despite everything, was firing her senses, making her body throb with need.

But if she was trapped she would fight, no matter how useless it might be, like a fox caught in one of her father's snares. Because the alternative was to give in, surrender to this man, and she would never do that.

'You heard,' she obstinately fired back.

'Indeed I did.' His voice was terrifyingly soft.

Grimly Harper hung onto her defiance. 'You don't intimidate me, Vieri.'

'No?' His gaze deliberately burned into hers, the small space between them humming with threat. 'You call me a bully and a thug and yet you are not intimidated by me. Doesn't that make you rather stupid?'

'Oh, you would love that, wouldn't you?' Still she pushed. 'For me to be scared of you.'

'On the contrary.' Reaching forward, he brushed his fingers along her jawline, before curling his hand possessively under her chin. 'What I would love would be for you to honour the clearly laid-out terms of our agreement and start behaving like my fiancée.'

'But…' His finger pressed against her lip to silence her.

'What I would really *love* would be for you to start showing me some respect.'

Harper swallowed against her closing throat. The heat of his fingers was setting her face alight, hammering her heart wildly in her chest. In theory she only had to turn her head to release his grip but somehow she couldn't do it. His punishing gaze was holding her captive and it was as much as she could do to drag in a ragged breath.

'I will start showing you some respect when I think you have earned it.' Somehow she managed to choke out some words.

'Is that right?' With a cold laugh Vieri moved his body fractionally closer. 'So tell me, just for argument's sake, what exactly *do* I have to do to earn your respect? Obviously letting you step in for your thief of a sister hasn't done the trick, despite the fact that I could so easily have gone to the police and got her into serious trouble. And then there's the time and effort I have put into finding her, not to mention giving her money and putting her on a plane back to Scotland. Clearly that is not enough.'

'I'm sorry?' Harper croaked. 'What did you just say?'

'I said that Leah is on her way back to Scotland. For your information that is what my "bully-boy thugs" have been doing. On my instructions and at my expense they have been putting your precious sister on a plane back to her homeland.' He twisted the hand that still held her chin to look at the watch on his wrist. 'She should be landing in Glasgow in a couple of hours.'

'Oh.'

'Yes, oh.'

There was a heavy pause, the air between them thickening as suddenly the swirling hostility began to morph into something much more slick and dark and dangerous. Harper could only watch, her breath caught in her throat, as Vieri let go of her chin and slid his hand around the nape of her neck, drawing her closer to him until their lips were only fractionally apart. And then they were touching.

Harper closed her eyes against the white-hot bolt of sensation that stormed through her, flooding her core. Immediately the kiss took on a life of its own, hot and damp and deeply sensual, leaving Harper no power to resist. Her lips willingly parted to allow Vieri's sweet assault, her own body responding with blind need as she pressed herself against him to feel more of his silken mouth and the raw, sexual promise beneath.

Slowly Vieri's fingers stroked upwards from the base of her neck and Harper shuddered with pleasure. Threading his fingers through her hair now, he dislodged the hair-pins until her hair cascaded over her shoulders in a tumble of soft curls. Then, pulling away from her mouth, he stared at her. Harper blinked back, her heart thundering like fury. She would defy anyone to be immune to those eyes. She had no defences against their drugging power.

Gathering up a thick swathe of her hair, he twisted it so that he could hold it in his grip, tugging so that it pulled lightly against her scalp, in a blatant display of seduction and control. And then his mouth was on hers again, glori-ously hot and wonderfully soft, yet firm too, like a wicked promise covered in satin.

Harper moved her arms around his neck, her fingers threading through his hair, pushing up through the thick dark waves, her nails digging into his scalp, almost to the point of pain. And Vieri responded in kind, possessively tightening his hold on her hair so that the kiss deepened, their bodies closing together. Pinpricks of pain tingled across her scalp, heightening the wild sensation of plea-sure as Vieri's free arm snaked round her waist, then up over her bare back, the flat of his palm pressing firmly between her shoulder blades.

Their mouths parted for a second, just long enough for Harper to take a gasp of breath and then he was claiming her again, pushing her back against the sofa and leaning forward to cover her body with his own.

'You drive me crazy, d'you know that?' Vieri's low voice growled hot in her ear. 'You and this damned dress have been taunting me all evening.'

'We have?'

'Yes, you have.' His growl deepened. 'Don't pretend you didn't know. Ever since I walked into your room and saw you standing there admiring yourself I have been thinking of ways to get you out of it.'

Propping himself up on one arm, he stared down at her face before lowering his head so that his hair brushed tantalisingly across the bare skin of her chest. Harper closed her eyes as the damp heat of his mouth started to trace the swell of her breasts, his lips dragging against the skin and leaving a rash of goosebumps in their wake.

'Well…' she sighed over his head '…that was never my intention.'

'No?' Vieri murmured against her. 'Well, you could have fooled me.' Raising his head, he moved his hand to the strap of her dress, sliding it slowly, seductively over her shoulder. Harper arched against his touch, her heart hammering wildly against her ribcage. 'You had every man at that ball lusting after you, Ms McDonald, as I'm sure you well know. I suspect you knew exactly what you were doing when you chose this dress.'

'Ah, but that's just it.' Her words stuttered in her throat as Vieri continued his assault, lathing his tongue into the valley between her breasts. 'I didn't choose it.'

'No?' Moving his hand to cup one swollen breast, Vieri squeezed it gently in his palm. 'Then who did? I feel I should thank them.' He altered his position so that he settled his groin against hers, the shockingly hard evidence of his arousal shooting arrows of lust through Harper.

'It was someone I met by chance in the boutique.' She croaked the words.

'Oh, yes?'

'Yes. She knows you, as a matter of fact. She said you wouldn't like the dress I had originally chosen.'

'Interesting. Who is this mystery woman with impeccable taste?'

'Umm, I can't tell you. I've just remembered I'm not supposed to say.'

'Then I can see I am going to have to think of a way to prise the information out of you. Now, let me see…' He paused, his eyes flitting darkly over her heated face, over the swell of her breasts that rose and fell with each ragged breath. 'Where shall I start?'

His fingers slid under the bodice of her dress, releasing her breasts. For a moment he just stared at her, his eyes full of hunger, and Harper's nipples, already almost unbearably hard, tightened still further. Then his hands reached to cup her breasts and he held their swollen weight with such care, such obvious appreciation, it was all she could do to stop herself from whimpering with pleasure.

He lowered his head until his mouth was only a fraction away from one breast, his hot, silky breath caressing her skin until slowly, very slowly, he took the puckered nipple in his mouth. Now Harper did moan, a blissful, guttural sound, coming from somewhere deep in the back of her throat. And as Vieri started to rasp his tongue over her aching peak, stopping only to suck again, to repeat his deliriously wonderful assault, Harper's hands flew to the back of his head, holding him tightly against her, desperate for this torturous pleasure never to stop.

But eventually he moved, his head coming back up, a half-smile twisting his mouth. 'Am I any nearer to breaking your code of silence? If not I am more than happy to continue.'

Please, yes. Harper screamed the words inside her head. He was teasing her, she knew that; he didn't give a damn about who had picked out her dress. They were playing a game here but she had no idea what the rules were. Only that Vieri had made them up, that everything was on his terms. It felt forbidden, dangerous, and as if it was only going to end one way. Badly. But it also felt wildly exciting, exhilarating, like nothing she had ever experienced before. And deep down, somewhere inside that sex-befuddled brain of hers, she knew she would never have the strength to make it stop. She had no alternative but to play along.

'I'll give you a clue.' She arched her back, jutting her chest forward, inviting him to take her once more. 'She is almost related to you.'

Vieri frowned, then dipped his head again. 'Well, that is going to be difficult.' His hand cupped her other breast, his tongue delicately tracing the outline of her nipple. 'Seeing as I have no living relatives. Not that I'm aware of anyway.' Slowly his mouth closed around her nipple and Harper let herself surrender to the pleasure.

'Think of your godfather, then.'

'Alfonso?' He abandoned her breast long enough to say the name, returning to muffle the next sentence against it. 'What does he have to do with it?'

'Because it was his niece, Donatella!'

'Donatella?'

His reaction to her name was extreme—brutal. As if venom had somehow entered his bloodstream, his body went suddenly rigid, his head jerking back to expose the strong column of his neck.

'Y…yes.' Stuttering with surprise, Harper could only stare up at him in astonishment.

'You are telling me that Donatella Sorrentino chose this dress for you?'

'Yes. Why, does it matter?'

His reply was a violent oath in a foreign tongue. Releasing her shoulders, he leapt to his feet, for a second glaring down at her dishevelled body with undisguised hatred burning in his eyes. Then turning, he moved as if he was desperate to get away from her.

Harper stared at the broad expanse of his back in total shock. She could see the bunched muscles of his biceps flexing as he folded his arms in front of him, his shoulder blades jutted rigidly beneath the fine fabric of his shirt.

She pulled her eyes away, looking down at herself with distress, horror even. Her breasts were fully exposed, still tingling from where Vieri's mouth had been, her nipples hard and throbbing. Snatching up the strap of the dress, she pulled it back over her shoulder, struggling to tuck herself back into the tight bodice. And only just in time.

Vieri swung back round to look at her again, resentment scoring his face, as if he had somehow hoped she had disappeared while his back was turned.

'You need to go to bed.' It was an order, a cruel dismissal, his blue-black eyes still alight with fury.

Harper certainly wasn't going to challenge him. She couldn't get away fast enough. Leaping off the sofa, she snatched up the skirt of her dress and swept past him, heading for her rooms as fast as she could, marching through her dressing room and into her bedroom and slamming the door behind her. Only then did she let herself breathe, leaning back against the door, slowly sliding down until she was crouched on the floor in a puddle of red satin. Only then did she let herself surrender to the misery and injustice of it all, to the painful burn of tears that blocked her throat.

CHAPTER SEVEN

'NEED ANY COMPANY?'

Vieri tightened his grip around the tumbler of whisky in his hand. He growled his negative reply, leaving the heavily perfumed female hovering beside him no room for doubt. The only company he wanted right now was the alcohol in his glass and the hope that enough of it would numb his murderous thoughts.

He had chosen this dingy bar, in a far from salubrious area of Palermo, because he didn't want to talk to anyone, didn't want to see anyone. Signalling to the barman to refill his glass, he took another deep slug of whisky, returning the glass to the sticky bar top with a thud. He'd drink this and then he'd go. Being here was doing nothing to improve his state of mind and he could already feel the beginnings of an alcohol-induced headache starting to thrum at his temples.

Donatella Sorrentino. He repeated her name in his head, feeling his muscles tighten, his skin crawl. The idea that she was here, somewhere in Palermo, at the same time as him filled him with a bitter loathing that refused to abate. He imagined that he could feel her evil presence all around him, even though he knew she would never frequent a place like this. But like a rat in a sewer she was there, unseen, a dark, malevolent presence.

Presumably she was back in Palermo because she had heard about Alfonso and was circling the water like a predatory shark. Well, she was going to be sorely disappointed. She might be Alfonso's niece, his only living relative, but, as his godfather's executor, Vieri knew for a fact that she wasn't going to get a cent of his inheritance. The entire estate was to be divided between the many charities he supported. Alfonso had disowned his niece long ago, on the night his brother had been gunned down in the street—the night Donatella hadn't so much as shed a tear for her father.

It disgusted Vieri to think that he could ever have been taken in by that woman. That he could have gone to bed with her, made love to her, planned a future with her. Blind to her faults, he had still been pining for her even after she had so unceremoniously dumped him. But discovering her final act of treachery had changed all that. And his misplaced devotion had turned into a heavy, poisonous weight that had sat inside him ever since.

He had only found out the truth by accident. Months after he and Donatella had gone their separate ways, Vieri had been dating a local girl when she had let slip that her sister was a nurse in a private clinic and that Donatella Sorrentino had been in for a termination. With a tidal wave of fury Vieri had known, right at that very moment, that the child had been his. Dates had been demanded, his poor unsuspecting girlfriend left with no choice but to extract the details from her sister. And they fitted perfectly. The child was his. Without even mentioning it to him, Donatella Sorrentino had had an abortion, terminated his child. A child that would have been the only family he had ever had.

Thanks to Alfonso, he had never had the chance to exact his revenge. Instead of tracking down Donatella with a view to God knew what, he had been put on a flight to

New York, forced to concentrate on making a new life for himself. And now, of course, he was very grateful for that. He hadn't laid eyes on Donatella since the day she had told him their affair was over. But the thought of her here, in Palermo, filled him with a towering rage. And the idea that she had chosen Harper's dress, come anywhere near her, in fact, exploded white lights behind his eyes.

Swirling the last of the liquor around in his glass, Vieri swallowed it in one gulp. It wasn't helping. It couldn't erase the thought of that evil woman tainting his Harper. *His Harper?* Where had that come from? Since when had he started to think of Harper McDonald as *his*? He drummed his fingers on the bar top. But there was no denying that Harper filled his thoughts more and more, that something about her, *everything about her*, made her impossible to ignore. Not just in a sexual way, although that was a powerful force, but in a more deep-rooted emotional way that was totally unfamiliar to him. A way that he didn't want to examine.

Vieri put his head in his hands. This evening had been a disaster. His plan had been to let Harper enjoy the ball, then take her back to the apartment, soften her up by telling her that Leah was safe and well and then hit her with the fact that their 'arrangement' had been changed. That they were, in fact, going to have to get married. Vieri suspected that Harper wouldn't take the news well, as indeed he hadn't, but there was no alternative. They were in too deep. This was going to have to happen and somehow they had to deal with it.

But the plan had started to unravel very early on, triggered by seeing those predatory men's hands all over Harper on the dance floor. And taking her out to the courtyard hadn't helped, his control slipping dangerously when faced with the fierce temptation of her seductively sexy body. He had just about managed to keep a hold of himself and get her back to the apartment when they had started to argue, any ideas he had had of coaxing her into compliance replaced by bitter recriminations, macho chest-beating and veiled threats. It was not the way he had intended it to go. Especially when, on hearing himself telling her she could pack her bags and leave, the strangest sensation had crept over him. A sort of hollow emptiness, a panic almost, at the thought of losing her. It had come out of nowhere, that acute sense of loss, of abandonment. And the worst of it was, he knew it had nothing whatever to do with their 'arrangement' and everything to do with the way he was starting to feel about her. The way she had got to him.

Something that had been all too evident when he had given in to the thundering in his head and started to kiss her. One minute he had been incensed by the totally unjustified way she'd been laying into him and the next that fiery defiance was turning him on like a tap on full pressure. Somehow her incredible sexiness had got to him, hotwired his libido into life until all he'd been able to think about was taking her in his arms and making love to her. Making her sweet body his.

And then she had mentioned Donatella. Vieri recalled her stunned expression when he had pushed her away, the hurt and pain that had been drawn across her face before she had collected herself, finally sweeping past him to the sanctuary of her room.

A couple of whisky-soaked hours had passed since then, but the memory still made Vieri grind down hard on his jaw. She hadn't deserved that, the cruelly dismissive way he had treated her. He shouldn't have taken out his seething anger for Donatella on her.

But maybe it was for the best. Throwing a handful of notes onto the bar, he rose unsteadily from the stool. For

Harper's sake they needed to keep their relationship professional, businesslike. Anything else, no matter how tempting, would just complicate matters, muddy the waters. He needed to protect her, against himself, because he couldn't bear for her to get hurt. And that was what would happen if she tried to get close to him. Because he was emotionally sterile, he had nothing to give her. Donatella had seen to that.

It occurred to him that in a funny sort of way she had done him a favour by turning up, interfering in Harper's choice of dress. If she hadn't, the evening might well have ended in a very different way; it had certainly been heading rapidly down that path. He could have been in bed with Harper now, making love to her, maybe even for the second or third time. Because Vieri already knew that once with Harper would never be enough. Yes, it was just as well they had parted when they did.

Pushing open the door of the bar, he stumbled out, the cold air hitting his face, sobering him up. Shoving his hands into the pockets of his trousers he set off in search of a taxi to take him home. The fact was, Harper McDonald was too good for him. He gave a gruff laugh into the night air. And that was something he had never imagined saying about any woman, ever.

'Harper? Is that you?' Harper had never, *ever* been so glad to hear her sister's sleep-muffled voice.

'Yes, Leah, it's me.'

Awake for most of the night, Harper had been waiting for the hours to slowly drag by before she could finally call home. She had held her breath as the phone rang, willing her sister to answer it, terrified that she wasn't there, that somehow she had gone missing again.

'What time is it?' Leah whispered groggily.

'It's nearly seven a.m. in Sicily.'

'Sicily?' This cut through the fog of sleep.

'Yes, that's where I am, Leah. In Sicily.'

'What on earth are you doing there?'

'What *on earth* do you think I'm doing here?' Somewhere in amongst the massive relief that Leah was safe, Harper felt a surge of anger. 'I'm clearing up your mess, of course.' She gripped her phone tightly to her ear. 'How could you do it, Leah? How could you disappear with thirty thousand dollars of Vieri Romano's money?'

'Oh.' Harper could perfectly picture her sister's guilty face. 'You know about that?'

'Of course I know about that. That's why I'm here, repaying your debt.'

'But how? I mean, I don't understand.'

'When you disappeared without a trace, thanks for that by the way, I had to go looking for you. I went to Spectrum...'

'You flew to New York?'

'No, I swam. Of course I bloody flew to New York.' Harper took in a breath. 'I was manhandled by Vieri's henchmen because they thought I was you, then delivered to the great man himself, only to be told, once he'd established who I was, that you had scarpered with his money.'

'Oh, God, Harper. I'm so sorry.'

'So you should be. But frankly sorry isn't going to cut it. So come on, then, I'm waiting. Why the hell did you do it?'

There was a pause on the other end of the phone.

'It's a bit of a long story.'

'I thought it might be.'

'I met this guy, Max Rodriguez.' Leah started tentatively. 'He was a bar manager at Spectrum but he was also a professional gambler. He said if I gave him the thirty thousand he could double it, maybe even triple it, in just one night.'

'And you believed him?'

'He was really convincing, Harper.'

'And it didn't occur to you to wonder why, if he was such a whizz at the gaming tables, he still needed to work in the bar of a nightclub?'

'Not really.'

'Honestly, Leah!'

'It's all very well for you to scoff now, with the benefit of hindsight. But at the time it seemed like an excellent plan. I thought I could repay Vieri, then send the rest of the money back home, take some of the pressure off you and Dad.'

'How very kind.' Harper kept the sarcasm in her voice but she could feel her anger starting to melt. This was typical of Leah, to get involved in a stupid, crazy scheme that brought nothing but trouble for those all around her, especially herself, but only because she was trying to help. Generous to a fault, and she had plenty of those, Leah did all the wrong things for the right reasons. 'So what went wrong with this brilliant plan?'

'Max lost the money.' She sounded genuinely crestfallen. 'Every last cent. I'd gone with him, to this casino in Atlantic City. Obviously I wasn't going to let him just take my money without me being there to make sure he didn't just run off with it.'

'Obviously.'

'But after he'd lost the money he did a disappearing act. I ended up having to stay on at the casino, working in the kitchens to cover the drinks bill he'd run up, pay for the suite of rooms he'd booked, all using my money.'

'Technically I think it was Vieri's money.'

'Well, yes.'

'But you're okay?' Harper's anxiety spiked. 'I mean, they didn't treat you badly?'

'No. The staff at the casino were decent enough, given the circumstances. But owing Mr Romano thirty thousand dollars was bad enough in itself.'

'Oh, Leah. Why didn't you ring me?'

'Because I was ashamed, I guess. Because I'd messed up yet again. I think I was hoping I would somehow get the money to repay him and no one need ever know anything about it.'

'And how, exactly, were you going to do that?'

'I don't know. Rob a bank, marry a rich man, sell my body to the highest bidder?'

'Leah!'

'I had no idea, Harper, beyond going into hiding and getting as many jobs as I could and saving like hell so that I could at least start to pay some of the money back. I was being trained to work in the casino, on the tables, when Vieri's goons burst in and bundled me into a limo. I had no idea where we were going. Turned out to be the nearest airport.'

'But whatever were you thinking?' Harper moved the phone to her other ear. 'Even if by some miracle you hadn't lost all the money, what about the original deal you had made with Vieri?'

'I was going to pay him back his money and then pull out. I knew I'd have to look for a job somewhere else, but I figured it would be worth it.'

'Didn't you care about letting him down?'

'Oh, come on, Harper. You don't feel sorry for men like Vieri Romano! It was a stupid idea anyway.'

'Yeah, a stupid idea that I now have to see through.'

'So is that what you're doing in Sicily?' Leah breathed into the phone. 'Honouring my agreement?'

'Yes, Leah. That's exactly what I'm doing.'

'*You* are pretending to be engaged to Vieri Romano?' She had the nerve to laugh.

'I said so, didn't I?' Harper bristled with annoyance. 'I'm glad you find it so hilarious.'

'No, not hilarious.' Leah steadied herself. 'I'm just surprised, that's all.'

'What, surprised that I'm having to pick up the pieces of your shattered life yet again?'

There was silence from the other end of the phone.

'I'm sorry, Lea.' Instantly Harper regretted her sharp tongue. 'I didn't mean it like that.'

'Yes, you did.' Leah let out a deep sigh. 'And you're right. We both know that I owe you everything. And all I want is to try and make it up to you.'

'How many times? You don't need to make anything up to me. Especially if it means coming up with harebrained schemes like becoming engaged to billionaire Sicilian businessmen.'

She was relieved to hear her sister laugh.

'Okay, point taken. But at least I can sort this mess out myself. If you can book me a flight to Sicily—I'd do it myself except I have literally no money—then we can swap places and you can come home.'

'No, Leah.'

'But why not? It's the obvious solution.'

'Because it's way too late for that. I've been introduced to people, got to know his godfather. And besides, Vieri would never agree to it. Your name is mud as far as he is concerned.'

'But we look so alike. He probably wouldn't even notice the difference.'

'Trust me, he would notice.'

Harper bit down on her lip. She had answered too quickly, given herself away.

'So, you and Vieri…' Leah probed quietly. 'Have you got close?'

'No.'

'Oh, my God, you have, haven't you? You have fallen for him!'

'No! Of course I haven't!'

'Oh, Harps, be careful. I mean, I know he's a complete hunk with enough sex appeal to decimate a small planet, but even so, a man like Vieri Romano… He breaks hearts for a living.'

'I have not fallen for Vieri Romano! He's an arrogant, overbearing egotist. Why ever would I fall for a man like that?'

'I don't know. You tell me.' Her voice was laced with amusement.

'Look, Leah, I'm not going to discuss this any further. We need to make plans for the next few weeks.'

'I suspect you've already done that.'

'I'm being serious, Leah. I'm not sure when I'm going to get back to Glenruie, but in the meantime you are in charge. How is Dad? Have you seen him?'

'Not yet. It was late when I got in last night. The kitchen looked in a bit of a state.'

'I can imagine. You are going to have to be tough with him, you know.'

'I know.'

'And I'm down to do quite a few shifts at the Lodge. I was going to ring and cancel them but now you're back you can do them for me. They're all written on the calendar.'

'Okay, fine.' She sighed heavily. 'Why does it feel as if I've drawn the short straw?'

'Don't even go there, Leah!' Harper gave a brisk laugh. 'Look, I'm going to have to go now. So glad you are safe, sis.'

'Thanks. And sorry…you know…'

'Forget it.'

'Love you, sis.'

'You too.'

Ending the call, Harper moved over to the window. Dawn was just beginning to break over the city, the rising sun defining the jagged black mountains in the distance, picking out the orange brickwork of the chaotic conglomeration of houses below.

It was so beautiful here, and yet Harper had never felt more isolated, more alone. The torture of what had happened between her and Vieri the evening before had robbed her of a night's sleep and still coursed shamefully through her veins. The way she had responded to his touch, been so near to giving herself to him, exposing her feelings, now scored her cheeks with humiliation. One minute she had been melting beneath the seductive power of his mouth and the next he had cruelly dismissed her, brutally reminding her of who was in charge. He pulled her strings and she danced. He cut them and she fell.

Turning away from the window, she went back and sat on the edge of the bed, bunching the bedcover between her fingers. It had been the mention of that Donatella woman that had thrown him into a rage—clearly something had gone on between the two of them. Was it possible they had been lovers? Were they *still* lovers? The thought cut through her like a blade. Sucking in a breath, she made herself focus on the reality of her situation. Whoever Vieri saw, whatever he did, was none of her business. Their engagement was only for a few, short weeks. She just had to wrap up her emotions and get through this. Although the fact that their arrangement would only end because of Alfonso's death was something Harper had yet to come to terms with.

But when the inevitable happened she would go back to

Scotland and get on with her life and put this whole, crazy episode behind her. It would be as if Vieri had never existed. And somehow, her poor virgin heart would have to find a way to heal itself.

Pulling back the feather-light duvet, she slipped underneath and curled herself into a tight ball. And finally sleep came.

CHAPTER EIGHT

A SERIES OF loud raps on her bedroom door saw Harper burrowing out of the duvet, blinking against the light.

'Harper!' There was no mistaking the deeply sonorous voice.

'Yes,' she croaked back, fumbling for her phone to see what the time was. Ten-thirty? How could that be? But before she had the chance to order her thoughts Vieri was striding into her bedroom, full of his usual command.

'You need to get up.'

Harper pushed herself up against the pillows, brushing the hair out of her eyes with a shaky hand. By the look on Vieri's face, something was wrong.

'What's the matter? What's happened?'

'I have received a message from Alfonso's nurse.' Vieri's voice was tight. 'We need to get over there right away.'

'Oh, no!' Harper felt her heart lurch. 'Alfonso…he hasn't…?' She pulled back the covers, scrambling to get out of bed.

'No, no. It's Maria. Some sort of family emergency, apparently. She has had to leave.'

'Oh, thank goodness.' Harper gave a huge sigh of relief. 'Not that I don't feel sorry for Maria, of course.' She stopped, suddenly aware of Vieri's cool blue eyes raking over her. She was wearing a pair of old fleecy tartan pyjamas, perfect for keeping out the winter chill back home, but, judging by Vieri's expression, not the sort of female night attire he was familiar with.

She gazed at him, desperately trying to ignore the stutter of her heart. Wearing faded, low-slung jeans and a grey sweatshirt, he was more casually dressed than usual, but no less devastatingly attractive. The dark shadow that shaded his jawline gave him a feral, untamed look, and his ruffled hair, that didn't appear to have been brushed any time recently, only made him seem all the more dangerously tempting. Harper bit down on her lip. Maybe this unkempt look meant he had had a bad night too. After the way he had treated her, she couldn't help but hope so.

'So, what's the plan?' She tried to sound normal, running a hand over her own sleep-tangled hair and tucking it behind her ears. But all the time she was acutely conscious of Vieri's unwavering stare. 'Can you hire a temporary nurse?'

'Already done. But Alfonso is being difficult. It seems that he wants you there.'

'Oh.' Harper nodded. 'Well, I'll get dressed and we can head straight over there.'

'I mean he wants you to move in with him.' Vieri hesitated. 'Until Maria gets back.'

'I see.' Harper bit back her surprise. 'Well, that's okay. I can do that.' Already her affection for Alfonso was such that she would do anything for him.

'Obviously I will accompany you.'

Obviously. Harper felt her stomach twist with nervous apprehension. All brisk businesslike command, there was no trace of the Vieri of last night. Of the seductive lover who had so easily smashed through her fragile defences, or the angry stranger that had followed. It occurred to her that she had no idea at all what went on in this man's head.

'Maria doesn't know how long she will have to be away,' Vieri continued. 'Do you have any commitments, at home, I mean?'

This took Harper aback. It was the first time Vieri had even mentioned the life she had had to put on hold for him.

'Actually I spoke to Leah this morning.' She fiddled with the hem of her pyjama top. 'She's safely back in Glenruie and she has agreed to do my shifts at Craigmore Lodge for me. And look after Dad.'

Vieri gave a brief nod.

'She explained to me what had happened, about the money, Vieri. How that man gambled it all away and then disappeared.' Harper took a tentative step towards him. 'Leah didn't deliberately set out to steal from you, you know. She intended to pay you back.' For some reason she felt she had to try and clear her sister's name.

'It makes no difference to me either way.' Vieri looked profoundly unconvinced, his profile set hard in silhouette against the window. 'As far as I am concerned the matter is closed. Once our arrangement has been concluded, of course.'

'Of course.' Harper chewed the inside of her lip. What was the point of even trying to get through to this man? She sighed heavily.

'We will leave in twenty minutes.'

'Fine.'

She watched as his broad-shouldered frame turned and left the room. Heading for the bathroom, she stripped off her pyjamas and stepped under the shower, hoping that the thundering water would drown out her sense of foreboding.

It seemed that no matter how hard she tried to protect herself, the web she was caught in was tightening all the time. Somehow, Vieri's control over her life was becoming more and more inescapable.

* * *

'*Benvenuto*, welcome.' Alfonso stretched out a skinny arm towards Harper, taking her hand and patting it with his own. 'Thank you so much for coming to save me in my hour of need.'

'It's nothing, Alfonso.' Harper leant in to kiss his papery cheek. 'It will be a pleasure to stay here and look after you until Maria returns.'

'You are very kind but I know what an imposition it must be for you. And for Vieri.' He shot Vieri a look. 'But I hope you will forgive the selfishness of a very old man.'

'There is nothing to forgive, Alfonso.' Vieri gave his godfather a hug, the reality of how frail Alfonso had become gripping his heart.

'Harper, my dear.' Alfonso turned to where Harper still stood beside his chair. 'Perhaps you would like to go and check your room? My housekeeper has made it ready for you but I want to make sure everything is just as you want it before she leaves for the day.'

'I'm sure it will be perfect.'

'Even so.' He touched her hand again. 'It would put my mind at rest.'

'Very well, I'll go and unpack.'

Both men watched as she left the room.

'Come and sit down, my son.' Alfonso patted the chair beside him, speaking in his native Sicilian. 'You are making me anxious, standing there with that forbidding look on your face. I hope this situation...' he waved his hand around expressively '...isn't inconveniencing you too much.'

'Not at all, *padrino*.' Vieri seated himself in a high-backed chair.

'Then what? You look troubled.'

Vieri took in a breath. 'Did you know that Donatella is

back in Palermo?' He could feel a vein pulsing in his neck at the very mention of her name.

'Ah, yes, I did hear as much.'

'And that doesn't worry you?'

'Not in the least. She knows better than to show her face here.'

'But she will still try and make trouble,' Vieri replied. 'You can bet on that.'

'Donatella Sorrentino will only make trouble if we let her, Vieri. And I have no intention of doing any such thing.'

Vieri bit down hard on his jaw. Alfonso was right. Hadn't he already let her do just that by reacting so violently when he'd found out she had chosen Harper's dress? He had played right into her vicious hands.

Taking a breath, he strode over to the window, gazing out at the calm vista.

'Let it go, Vieri.' Alfonso's soft voice spoke behind him. 'That woman may have blighted your past, but don't let her blight your future.'

Vieri turned and the two men locked eyes, the air thick with words that weren't spoken. So wise, so caring—it worried Vieri considerably that Alfonso's view of his future was built on a construct of lies and deceit. It worried him, too, that his rosy picture would never happen. But it was too late for regrets. He had started this stupid charade, he had no choice but to see it through.

Harper sat down heavily on the bed. *Her* side of the bed. The housekeeper had left after Harper had insisted that the room was perfect, that there was nothing more she needed. But even though the room was perfect, the reality of the situation was far from it. Because it was evident that Harper wasn't going to be the sole occupant of this bedroom. She would be sharing it with Vieri.

She looked around in dismay. At the two sets of towels on the bed, the two white dressing gowns on the back of the door. Sharing Vieri's enormous hotel penthouse apartment had been bad enough. How on earth was she going to cope with sharing a bedroom—a bed? No, it couldn't happen! Somehow the sleeping arrangements would have to be changed.

Two pairs of eyes turned in her direction as she walked back into the salon. Alfonso gestured to her to come forward. 'I hope everything was to your satisfaction?'

'Yes, *our* room is lovely.' She ground out the words, flashing Vieri a pointed stare.

'*Bene, bene.* I thought you would like it. That bed is very special, you know. It's known as a marriage bed, hundreds of years old, I believe. Superstition has it that the couple that lie in that bed will soon be granted the blessing of a child.' His dark eyes twinkled. 'Although I suspect they may need to do more than just lie in it.'

'Alfonso!' Vieri rested his hand on his godfather's shoulder.

'Forgive me. But in my situation you can't blame me for trying to speed things up a bit. I'm not old-fashioned enough to think you have to wait to be married these days to share a bed.'

Harper sat down on the sofa, tightly crossing her legs. How awkward was this?

'Speaking of which, have you set a date yet?'

'A date?' She frowned at Alfonso, her mind still whirring with the sleeping arrangements.

'Yes.' Alfonso sat forward in his chair. 'I asked Vieri if you would be so kind as to make the wedding soon. So that I might be able to attend.'

'The w-wedding?' She shot a horrified glance at Vieri,

who steadfastly refused to meet her eyes. Instead he addressed his godfather.

'We haven't had the chance to discuss it yet, *padrino*.'

'No? Well, there's no time like the present.' Clearly Alfonso wasn't going to be deterred. 'Why don't we sort it out now? Harper, pass me my diary, will you? It's in the top drawer of my desk.'

As if in a trance, Harper did as she was told, crossing the room to retrieve Alfonso's diary and placing it in his outstretched hand.

'*Grazie*, thank you, my dear. Now let me see.' His shaky hands started to turn over the pages. 'Ah, now how about this week?' He turned the diary around, holding open the pages. Vieri and Harper peered at it. Harper's heart stopped. It was a mere two weeks away. 'Shall we say the twenty-third?'

'The twenty-third?' To Harper's horror, Vieri appeared to be considering it, worse, drawing her in. 'I think that might be possible. What do you say, Harper?'

There was a lot she wanted to say. *An awful lot.* But trapped between Alfonso's hopeful gaze and Vieri's shuttered calm she didn't know where to begin.

'I think that may be a little soon.' Her voice was tight with suppressed tension. 'Weddings take some time to organise, I believe.'

'Sadly time is not something I have a lot of.' Alfonso smiled weakly at her. 'As you know.'

Harper bit down hard on her lip. How was she supposed to counter that?

'What sort of wedding do you have in mind?' Alfonso continued unabashed. 'Do you envisage a lavish affair?'

'No!' Harper swallowed. Five minutes ago she hadn't had any sort of wedding in mind. 'Not at all.'

'Well, I don't think a small, intimate gathering will be

difficult to organise. And finding a venue certainly won't be a problem. Vieri owns several luxury hotels in Sicily alone. In fact, I have a better idea.' He pushed himself upright. 'Why don't you get married here? In the *castello* chapel. You would be doing me the greatest honour.'

'That is very kind of you, Alfonso. But all the arrangements, the disruption, will it not be too much for you?' Harper fired a surreptitious glare at Vieri. Why was he not putting a stop to this nonsense right now?

'Not at all. It will give me something to look forward to. So, is that settled, then? Saturday the twenty-third.'

Harper found herself nodding weakly.

'Eccellente.' Alfonso gave them both a beaming smile. 'Now, if you will call that new nurse of mine, I think it's time I took a nap.'

'And just when, *exactly*, were you going to tell me about this wedding?'

Shaking with outrage, Harper turned on Vieri as they stepped outside into the cool air.

'Keep your voice down.' Linking his arm through hers, Vieri moved them away from the *castello*. 'Getting hysterical is not going to help anyone.'

'I think I have every right to be hysterical!' Balling her hands into fists, Harper dug them further into her coat pockets. The shock of what she had just agreed to was still ringing in her ears, and having Vieri locked beside her, his towering, powerful body controlling her steps as they moved through the gardens, was doing nothing to calm her down. 'How could you have told Alfonso we would be getting married without even *asking* me first?'

'I intended to explain the situation.' Vieri stared straight ahead, his proud profile showing nothing in the way of remorse as he moved them along the gravel pathway in the direction of the formal gardens. 'But Alfonso got in there first.'

Explain the situation! Was that all he thought he had to do? Harper could hardly believe the man's arrogance. She wanted to scream and shout, to beat her fists against his conceited, iron-hard chest, but she knew she had to concentrate on the practicalities. She fought to hold her voice steady. 'This is *not* what I signed up for, Vieri. This is *not* part of the deal!'

'I appreciate that.' He walked them under the archway of the brick wall and into the formal gardens. 'I realise that the terms of our agreement will need to be renegotiated.'

'Renegotiated?' Harper brought them to a sudden stop. 'Do you really think that's all there is to it?' Her eyes flashed with fire. 'Do you really think I will agree to marry you, just like that, without you even having the courtesy to ask me?'

'Unless I am mistaken, it would seem you have already agreed.' Vieri met her blazing temper with cold, calculating eyes.

With the blood boiling in her veins, Harper didn't trust herself to speak. Because he was right, of course. She had already consented to this wedding. Acknowledging her silence with a single quirk of his dark brow, Vieri pulled her closer to him, tucking her arm against the warmth of his body as he moved them on again, between the towering box topiary. Reaching a stone bench, he released her and waited for her to sit down before seating himself beside her.

'Look, Harper, this wedding was not my idea but we can make it work.' His voice was low, confident. 'I know how fond you are of Alfonso. I know you would do anything to make his final weeks happy.' She could feel him scanning her grim profile, sense how sure he was of himself. Of her. Because, of course, she would do anything for Alfonso. Including marrying this darkly dangerous man.

'Financially I will make it worth your while,' he continued smoothly. 'You will be fully recompensed for your inconvenience.'

'I don't want your money!' Leaping to her feet, Harper rounded on him. 'And having to marry you is not an *inconvenience*. It's a total nightmare!'

She turned away, biting down on her lip to try and stop it from trembling. That had come out all wrong, had revealed far too much. Somehow her thin veil of protection had slipped, revealing her dangerously turbulent feelings beneath.

'Not necessarily.' Behind her she heard Vieri get to his feet, his voice infuriatingly calm.

'No?' She spun around. 'How can you say that? This whole thing has got completely out of hand. Quite apart from the marriage, you do realise that Alfonso expects us to share a bedroom while we are staying at the *castello*?'

'I gathered as much.' Vieri's intense stare found hers, the memory of last night after the ball, of what had so nearly happened between them, shining in their deep blue depths.

'So what exactly do you intend to do about that?' Harper hurriedly tried to suppress the fresh flutter of panic in her chest.

Vieri's mouth twitched before he finally spoke. 'I will sort it out. If that's what you want.'

'Of course it's what I want!'

'Fine.' He raised his hand dismissively, as if the matter was of no consequence, as if she was somehow being unreasonable. 'There are more than enough rooms in this *castello* for us both to have our own personal space. Alfonso need never know about our sleeping arrangements.'

'Well, see that it happens.' She threw back her head, then had to steady herself, suddenly feeling dizzy with the madness of it all.

'Are you okay?' Vieri immediately noticed the pallor of her face. 'It's cold out here. Perhaps we should go back inside.'

'No.' She dug in her heels. 'I'm going nowhere.'

'Then let me at least warm you up.' Suddenly he had gathered her in his arms, pulling her against the strong, muscled heat of his body.

For a second Harper let herself be held, her eyes closed in blissful surrender until the yearning for what could never be saw her struggle to release herself.

'Actually I would like to be left on my own.' She moved a step away and sat down heavily on the stone bench. 'I need to think things through.'

'As you wish.' But he sat down beside her again. What part of *alone* did he not understand? Several highly charged seconds of silence rolled by.

'Harper?' He rested his hand on her thigh, the heat of his palm branding her skin through the fabric of her dress.

'What?' She deliberately moved to dislodge his hand.

'I do understand that this is a big thing I am asking of you.' He closed the gap between them until his thigh was pressed against hers. She could feel the warmth radiating off him, see his soft breath in the air. 'But it doesn't have to be such an ordeal. Alfonso knows that we are only getting married so quickly for his benefit, so he will understand if it's a very private affair.'

'But we will still be married in the eyes of the law.'

'Yes, this is true. But when Alfonso…when the time comes, the marriage can be annulled.'

He had thought this all through, hadn't he? And for

some reason, that only made his calculated deceit, both to his godfather and to her, seem even worse.

'However, if you decide that you can't go through with it, then I will respect that decision. I will go in there and tell Alfonso the truth, this afternoon, as soon as he awakes from his nap. You will be free to go. You need never see him again.'

Harper felt her heart plummet. The thought of not even saying goodbye to Alfonso was unthinkable. But then so was the idea of confessing that they had lied to him, that the whole engagement was a sham. He would be so disappointed. No, more than that, he would be devastated. Harper knew she could never do that to him.

She dragged in a breath of cold air to steady herself.

'Okay, I will do it.' She forced herself to meet Vieri's midnight stare. 'For Alfonso's sake, because I can't bear to think of him upset, I will agree to marry you.'

'Thank you.' Taking hold of her hand, Vieri squeezed her cold fingers in his firm, warm grasp. 'I do appreciate it.' He rose to his feet, dropping her hand but still holding her eyes. 'I will see to the arrangements right away.'

He turned, his job obviously done, and began to stride purposefully back towards the *castello*.

Harper watched his retreating figure, so tall and imposing. So unmistakeably Vieri. This impossible, arrogant, gloriously perfect specimen of manhood who had turned her life upside down. Who drove her completely crazy in every possible way. And from whom, no matter how short their so-called marriage might be, whatever might happen in the future, she feared she would never fully recover.

CHAPTER NINE

THE NEXT TWO weeks passed in a dizzying daze. Preparations for the wedding were rapidly organised, Vieri taking charge, the way he always did. And even though he did consult her, asking her opinion over some of the details, the flowers for the chapel, the food for the wedding breakfast, Harper didn't have the heart to get involved. So in the end she left it all to him.

A small guest list was drawn up, mostly comprising a few of Alfonso's trusted colleagues associated with his charities and a handful of old friends. 'There are so few of us left,' he had mournfully stated as he had turned the pages of his address book. 'That's what comes of being so ancient.'

Vieri had only invited one guest, a Sicilian friend called Jaco Valentino, someone he had known since childhood, apparently. Even that had been Alfonso's doing, casually mentioning that it would be nice to see Jaco again and why didn't Vieri see if he was free that day. Vieri had been left with no option but to agree.

Harper, herself, had no intention of inviting anybody, despite Alfonso's obvious surprise and concern that her father wouldn't be attending. She had explained, as best she could, that it would be too difficult for Angus to get away at such short notice. This, at least, was partly true.

His job as gamekeeper on the Craigmore estate did make it very difficult for him to take any time off. The fact that he had absolutely no idea that his daughter was actually getting married, she kept to herself.

And now the day of their wedding had arrived. Gazing out of the window at the sparkling sunshine, Harper tried to swallow down the nerves inside her. These were not the normal jitters a bride might feel on her big day, those of anticipation and excitement. No, Harper's nerves were of the more sinister kind, sitting like a leaden weight in her stomach.

Never had she imagined her wedding day would be like this—that she would be facing it so completely alone, without even Leah by her side. Vieri had offered to pay her flight, insisting that her being here wouldn't be a problem for him, that whatever had gone on between them was all in the past. But Harper had declined. She had no intention of even telling Leah that she was marrying Vieri. What was the point? It wasn't real. In a few months the marriage would be annulled and it would be as if it had never happened. And besides, if she told Leah it would be all round Glenruie before you could say capercaillie. Leah couldn't keep a secret to save her life.

Taking her dress from the wardrobe, Harper unzipped it from its garment bag and laid it over her arm. It was made of fine cream silk, with a loose cowl neck and a low back. This was the first time she had actually held it in her hands, and she was taken aback by just how lovely it was.

She had bought it online, having no intention of going to any of the bridal boutiques in Palermo and running into another of Vieri's admirers. Instead she had chosen it from the vast array of wedding dresses available, rapidly scrolling through them, refusing to spend too much time deliberating over the seductive creations because what did it matter what she looked like anyway? It wasn't as if she had a lover waiting for her at the altar, desperate to see his beautiful bride. Vieri would probably barely even notice what she was wearing.

Taking off her robe, she slipped the dress over her head. It slithered down over her body, pooling in a perfect circle at her feet. It was almost laughable the way it was such a perfect fit, as if it had been made for her. The slippery silk encased her slender body, showcasing her bare arms, her décolletage, the gentle swell of her hips, her long legs. Allowing herself only the briefest of glances in the mirror, she sat herself down at the dressing table and set about taming her curls into some sort of order, sweeping them up into a loose chignon. She would do this, she would put on some make-up, then she would make her way to the chapel and she would marry Vieri Romano. What she wouldn't do was think. Because thinking about what she was doing had the capacity to break her heart.

'This is all very sudden, *mio amico*.'

Vieri glanced across at his oldest friend. He and Jaco had been raised together in the children's home but, unlike him, Jaco had been adopted at the age of eleven and whisked away to a shiny new life. At the time they had pretty much lost touch, but years later, when Jaco was living in New York, they had renewed their acquaintance. By then they were both highly successful businessmen and both enjoying the playboy lifestyle. Standing well over six feet tall but having lost none of his boyish charm, Jaco had rivalled Vieri for the affections of the city's most beautiful women, or so he liked to keep telling him. But there was no doubting that the two of them had been a formidable force when they had hit the town together.

'Well, you know how it is, Jac.' Deliberately vague, Vieri shifted his weight from one leg to the other, checking his watch again.

The two men were standing beside the altar of the chapel, waiting for the bride to appear. The small congregation was chattering amongst themselves, the priest bending down to talk to Alfonso, who had had his wheelchair positioned right at the front so that he would miss nothing.

'I'm not sure I do.' Jaco gave his friend a sideways glance. 'I thought we had both agreed that the whole marriage thing wasn't for us.'

'Well, yes.' Vieri tugged at the sleeve of his shirt. 'But things change, don't they?'

'And would this sudden change be anything to do with your godfather?' Jaco narrowed his eyes. 'I understand he doesn't have a lot longer on this earth.'

'I want to make him happy, Jac. It's the least I can do.'

'Even so, getting married... Isn't that a bit extreme?'

Vieri shrugged and Jaco followed his gaze in the direction of Alfonso, who looked up and gave them a beaming smile.

'There's your answer.' Vieri returned his eyes to the front. 'That look has got to be worth a bit of self-sacrifice.'

'If you say so, old friend.' Jaco patted Vieri on the shoulder. 'If you say so.'

With a low rumble and a couple of hollow squeaks, the organ music started up and the congregation fell silent. Moving into position in front of the altar, Vieri stood tall and straight, pushing back his shoulders, gazing up at the arched stained-glass window. As the slightly wheezy strains of Vivaldi's Primavera filled the intimate but echoing space he found himself saying a silent prayer, asking for guidance, or absolution, or at least some sort of indication that he really was doing the right thing. For suddenly this wedding felt terrifyingly real.

A sharp dig in the ribs from his friend interrupted his thoughts. 'Self-sacrifice, eh?' With a low laugh, Jaco, who had been looking over his shoulder, returned to face the front. 'I'm not sure that's what I'd call it. She's a stunner Vieri.'

But Vieri had no time to reply. With a swish of silk Harper had come to stand beside him and finally he turned to look at her, only for the breath to be sucked from his lungs. Because she looked exquisite. The simple dress sheathed her gentle curves and slithered to the floor. She carried a small bouquet of white gardenia, with a single bloom tucked into her hair behind one ear, and as he stared at her a shaft of coloured light flickered over her face and down her body, giving her an ethereal, almost other-worldly appearance.

Vieri forced himself to drag in some air. He had never expected this, to have such a visceral reaction to his bride, so strong that it threatened to undo him completely. He told himself that it had to be guilt, for what he was making her do, what he was putting her through. But the way his mind was already slipping the silky garment down her body, his fingers itching to explore the exposed skin beneath, had nothing to do with guilt. Neither did the inexplicable surge of emotion that had suddenly consumed him, coming out of nowhere, so strong that it burned behind his eyes, held his muscles taut. It was a wave of tenderness, of posses-siveness. The feeling, no, the certainty that Harper would be his and his alone. From this day forth.

They held each other's gaze and for a split second Vieri saw all the torment and confusion he was experiencing re-flected in Harper's remarkable hazel eyes. *And the desire.*

Yes, she felt it too, no matter how much she might try and deny it. That, at least, gave salve to his masculine pride.

The priest gave a small cough, opening the heavy bible in his hands, preparing to start the ceremony. But he had barely uttered more than a few words from the opening address before the door at the rear of the chapel squeaked open, then closed again, followed by footsteps hastening down the aisle that defied all but the most stoic not to turn and see who this latecomer might be.

'Sorry, sorry.' There was no mistaking that accent or who it belonged to as the apologies continued and the guests shuffled along to make room for her at the end of a pew.

'Leah!' Harper had turned to look at her sister, whispering her name in astonishment before frantically mouthing, What are you doing here?

Seated now, Leah gave her an apologetic grin, followed by a little wave, which turned into a dismissive gesture to get on with it.

Harper turned back to the front. 'Your doing, I take it?' she whispered under her breath, her eyes fixed straight ahead, but there was a smile in her voice.

Vieri shrugged in admission. It was true he had ignored Harper's instructions not to invite her sister, going behind her back and sending Leah the money for her flight here. He wasn't even sure why he'd done it, except that he had strongly felt that it was time Harper's family supported her, instead of it always being the other way round. It was time they realised just how lucky they were to have her.

When Leah hadn't shown this morning he had written her off, assumed she had just taken the money, ripped him off again. But it seemed he had been wrong.

'There are *two* of them?' To his right he heard Jaco utter

his astonishment but Vieri wasn't going to start explaining now. He would, however, put his friend right about that young woman the first chance he got. If ever anyone had trouble written through them like a stick of rock, she did.

As Harper took her seat at the head of the table she hardly recognised the ancient dining room that had been transformed for the wedding breakfast. The draughty, echoing room had had a serious makeover: colourful antique rugs covered the cold flagstone floor, red velvet chairs replaced the uncomfortable carved wooden ones, and the table had been beautifully laid with a white damask tablecloth set with silver gilt cutlery and sparkling crystal. Arrangements of winter flowers, interspersed with cream candles in gilt candlesticks, ran the length of the table. In fact there were candles everywhere, positioned on the polished wood furniture at the sides of the room and in the heavy iron candelabra above their heads. A roaring fire blazed in the enormous grate.

'The wedding planners have done a good job.' Vieri eased himself into the seat beside her. 'I'll have to remember to use them again.'

'For your next wedding, do you mean?' Avoiding his eyes, Harper smiled sweetly at the assembled guests as she shook out her napkin and placed it on her lap.

'I actually meant commercially—my hotels host a lot of weddings.' Vieri gave her a dark stare. 'I have no intention of marrying again.'

'Oh, my mistake.' Accepting a glass of wine from the waiter, Harper let her shoulders drop from where they had been hovering up around her ears. They were married now, deed was done, there was no point in being all prickly with Vieri. That would solve nothing. She might just as well relax and enjoy the meal as best she could.

She cast her eyes down the long table. Leah was sitting about halfway down, next to Vieri's friend, Jaco. Harper had to admit it was lovely to have her here, and secretly she was touched that Vieri had gone to the trouble of arranging it. She couldn't hear what they were saying but under Jaco's instruction Leah was swilling the wine around in her glass, then holding it to her nose to inhale the bouquet. Jaco was laughing.

At the far end of the table, Alfonso was holding court with a couple of elderly friends. Feeling Harper's eyes on him, he looked up and smiled, raising his glass.

'Look at him.' Vieri leant in closer and immediately Harper's senses leapt about in response. 'I can't remember the last time I saw him so happy.' Raising his own glass in return, he waited for Harper to do the same. 'We did the right thing, you know.'

Harper nodded. For the first time this whole crazy venture made sense. For the first time she could see why they had done it. To give pleasure to a kind and generous man who deserved happiness at the very end of his life. For the first time it felt as if they had done something good.

'Yes, we did, didn't we?' She turned and smiled at Vieri, clinking her glass against his, and as their eyes met Harper felt her stomach somersault inside her.

'I'm glad you agree.' Holding her gaze, Vieri studied her face intently before covering her hand with his own. 'You have a lovely smile, by the way. You should use it more often.'

Harper quickly looked away, battling against the crippling effect of the unexpected compliment. Gripping the stem of her glass, she took a sip of the velvety wine. If her smile was lovely, his was deadly, used for the sole purpose of killing his prey.

She had been fighting his devastating attraction all day,

since the moment she had come to stand beside him in the chapel. Dressed in an immaculate grey suit, with matching waistcoat, and a blue silk tie that mirrored his ultramarine eyes, Vieri was the embodiment of sheer masculine perfection. His dark hair was pushed back from his forehead, curling behind his ears. When he was clean-shaven, his thick sideburns appeared more obvious, as did his square jaw and that oh-so-sensuous pink mouth. A mouth that brought back the memory of how it had felt against her own. That begged to be felt there again.

Setting down her glass, Harper took a shaky breath. Today, more than any day, she needed to be careful. She had to be on her guard, protect herself from the deadly onslaught of Vieri's charm. And step one was to try and steady the traitorous thump of her heart right now.

In true Sicilian style, the meal went on for hours. Course after course of delicious food was served, accompanied by freely flowing wine that ensured all the guests had a good time. Day soon turned to night, and as the more elderly guests started to leave Alfonso eventually announced that he was going to retire. Calling Vieri and Harper over, he embraced them warmly as they bent to kiss his cheek, taking hold of Harper's hand as she straightened up and patting it affectionately.

'Thank you so much, both of you. This has been wonderful.' He smiled up at them but as the smile faded a seriousness crept into his eyes. 'I hope you know how much it means to me.'

'We do, *padrino*.' Vieri squeezed his shoulder. 'And we are very glad that you have enjoyed the day.'

'I don't just mean the day.' A hint of impatience crept in as Alfonso gripped Harper's hand with surprising force. 'I'm talking about the two of you being officially married.' He paused and Harper could see just how tired he was. 'I must admit, I had my doubts. You might even call them suspicions.' His bushy eyebrows lowered over eyes that flicked between Harper and Vieri. 'In fact I did wonder at first if the two of you had cooked this up between you. A well-intentioned but misguided plan to fool an old man.' Harper froze, her gaze locked on Alfonso's hand so that she wouldn't have to meet Vieri's eye.

'But then I saw the two of you together and my mind was put at rest. Because I could see it in your eyes, feel it here, in my heart.' He banged his chest with his fist. 'I could see that you loved each other. And that was all that mattered. Which was why I hurried things along a bit.' He gave a low chuckle.

'You mean it wasn't because you are dying!' With a leap of hope, Harper blurted out the words.

'Oh, bless you, my dear. I'm dying all right.' Alfonso kissed her hand. 'But now, I can die in peace, safe in the knowledge that my godson has finally found the happiness he deserves.'

Harper forced down the lump in her throat, fighting the tears that pricked the backs of her eyes.

'Anyway, enough of my old-man ramblings. I hope that you young people will continue to celebrate long into the night. Oh, I nearly forgot.' Reaching into his inside jacket pocket, he withdrew an envelope and passed it to Vieri. 'A wedding present. Open it later.'

'Thank you, *padrino*.' Vieri put the envelope into his pocket. 'You are very kind.'

'And you are very dear to me, both of you, I want you to know that. Come, one last embrace.' Holding out his arms, he pulled them down into a long hug before kissing them in turn on the cheek. 'Now it is time to say goodbye.' His voice wavered. *'Addio, miei cari!'*

He signalled to Maria, who had returned to the *castello*

just in time for the wedding. Taking hold of the handles of his wheelchair, she waited for Alfonso to release the brake before slowly wheeling him out of the room. As Harper and Vieri watched him go, he raised a shaky hand of farewell above his head.

CHAPTER TEN

'WELL, GOODNIGHT, YOU TWO.'

Always the last to leave a party, Leah finally got to her feet and moved unsteadily around the debris-strewn table. She kissed Harper, and then, rather more awkwardly, Vieri.

'Thank you so much for inviting me, Vieri, and for paying for my flight and everything so I could be here. That was very generous of you. Especially after what I did... letting you down like that.'

'Forget it.' Vieri waved his hand in a dismissive gesture but Harper noticed there was no rancour in his voice. He looked and sounded positively mellow.

'And can I just say...?' She paused, a smile spreading across her face. 'You two make a lovely couple.'

'Leah!' Harper shot her sister a warning glare.

This was typical of Leah, stirring things up. They had had very little time to talk but during a hushed conversation in the privacy of the bathroom Harper had made sure that her sister knew the score, that this was a marriage in name only. Except, of course, Leah refused to believe it.

'I can't help it if that's what I think.' Leah refused to be silenced. 'And I'm not the only one. Everyone has been saying so all day.'

Had they? Even though Harper knew that that was just what people said at weddings, she couldn't help but feel a little surge of pleasure. Because somehow, despite everything, even though it shouldn't have, today had been lovely. It had felt right.

She put it down to the fact that she and Vieri had achieved their aim—they had made Alfonso happy. In fact, he had appeared positively delighted, a beaming smile across his face for most of the day. Which in turn had made Vieri relax. Harper had seen a new side to him as he had chatted to the guests, laughed with Jaco, clearly enjoying himself. Even now, at this late hour, he appeared to be in no hurry to end the day; instead he cradled a glass of brandy in his hand, absently swilling the liquid around as he watched the sisterly exchange going on. If Harper wasn't mistaken, there was the tug of a smile pulling at the corners of his mouth.

'Go to bed, Leah.' Sitting up straighter, Harper shooed Leah away. 'I'll see you in the morning.'

'I'm going, I'm going.' Blowing them both a kiss, Leah tottered off, her feet bare, her strappy shoes held over her shoulder by one finger. 'Have a good night, you two.'

Alone at last, a dangerous silence settled over the room. Harper cleared her throat.

'Well, I guess I had better be thinking about going to bed too.'

'Yes, it's been a long day.'

'A successful one though.' She looked across at Vieri for confirmation but immediately found herself caught in the midnight blue of his eyes. Pulling her gaze away, she only made it as far as the long length of his body lounging back in his chair. With one leg crossed over the other, he appeared completely at ease and even more dangerously handsome than ever. The jacket had gone, the fitted waistcoat emphasising his broad shoulders, his narrow waist. He had loosened his tie and pushed up the sleeves of his shirt to reveal tanned forearms, covered in a liberal dusting of dark hair. He looked casual, relaxed, but most of all deeply, heart-wrenchingly sexy. Harper felt her chest tighten.

'No regrets, then?' Lightly asked, his question nevertheless demanded an answer.

'No. I'm glad that we were able to do this for Alfonso.'

'Good.' He took a sip of brandy. 'That makes me feel less guilty.'

'Guilty?' Harper laughed. 'I can't imagine you ever feeling guilty about anything.'

'Then that shows how little you know me.' Suddenly serious, Vieri leant forward in his chair.

Harper blinked. 'That's true.' She really did know very little about this enigmatic man who was now, remarkably, *ridiculously*, her husband.

'Then perhaps we should do something about it.'

'Like what?' Her words came out as a gasp.

Vieri shrugged his elegant shoulders. 'I would be lying if I didn't admit that a few things were coming to mind.'

Their gazes clashed, the *few things* he was referring to all too clear in the swirling depths of his eyes. Harper felt the frantic beat of her heart in her throat.

'You are a very special person, Harper.' The sincerity of his gaze held her captive. 'I really mean that.'

'Well, thank you.' Harper gave an embarrassed laugh but it was silenced by a fingertip pressed against her lips.

'And I would very much like to make love to you.'

Shock ricocheted through her, swiftly followed by a clench of lust, deep in her groin. It was the way he had just *said* it, as if it were so easily possible, as if it could just happen. Which of course it could. Harper swallowed hard. But it *shouldn't*, should it?

Fighting to find some logic, some reason in this swirl of madness, Harper stood up, gazing at the vaulted ceiling as if the answer had to be hiding there somewhere. 'But this was never part of our agreement.' Her voice sounded husky, as if it belonged to someone else.

'Hang the agreement.' Suddenly up on his feet, Vieri came and stood before her, cupping her chin in his hand. His cool façade had slipped, revealing the dark passion beneath. 'Right now I want you, Harper. You have no idea how much.' His breath feathered across her heated face, his words sending spasms of yearning right through her. 'And I believe you want me too.'

'Yes.' Harper stared into his eyes, suddenly unable to hide the truth any longer.

A smile curved Vieri's sensuous mouth. '*Bene*. So what do you say? Will you let me take you to bed tonight?'

Oh, God. Harper had never wanted anything more in her life. But she couldn't just say yes. Could she?

'I… I don't know, Vieri.' Still she tried to rationalise her thoughts that now only drummed with one, sensuous beat.

Reaching forward, Vieri picked up a stray tendril of hair and, after a moment's hesitation, tucked it behind her ear. 'One night together, Harper, that's all I'm asking, all I'm offering. One night of pleasure.'

It was so tempting. He was so, so tempting.

'I think we deserve that.'

Did they? Harper had no idea what they deserved. But as Vieri's face came towards her she felt her eyelids flutter closed and when his lips touched hers she knew she was powerless to resist. The kiss deepened immediately, the tidal wave of sensation kicking in again until the pleasure was so strong she couldn't feel her feet any more, didn't know which way up she was. With his lips moulded against her own, firm and tight, yet silky and persuasive, their hot possession left no room for doubt or thought of any kind, and she could do nothing but let herself be pulled into the swirling abyss, dragged under by the current, left gasping for air. It was suffocating. It was drowning. And it was impossible to fight.

She wanted him! And even though a quiet voice told her to be careful, warned her of the consequences, a much louder one was screaming at her to do this. To let go, to live for the moment. That if she didn't, she would regret it. The sort of regret that would stay with her for the rest of her life.

Breaking away from the kiss, she felt for his hand, tipping her head to look up at him, still needing that final confirmation. And there it was. With his pupils dilated until his eyes were almost black, Harper had her proof. She could see that he was hanging onto the very last threads of his control and that was all she needed to know. He wanted her every bit as much as she wanted him. And that was the most empowering feeling ever.

'Let's go.' With a confidence that surprised her, she tugged on his hand, leading him out of the dining room. But by the time they had reached the echoing hallway, Vieri was beside her, one arm around her waist, hurrying them both up the long flight of stairs as if the very devil were on their heels. They flew down the corridor together until they reached their bedroom door.

Or at least the bedroom that they supposedly shared. In fact, as far as Harper knew, Vieri had never so much as set foot in there. True to his word, from day one he had found himself another room in the *castello*, Harper didn't know where. She had told herself she didn't care. So she alone had used this bedroom, slept in the ornate 'marriage' bed, dressed in front of the fancy gilt mirror. And even though she had told herself it was a relief, that the last thing she had wanted was the awkwardness of sharing a room with Vieri and all the mixed emotions that would have stirred up, in truth it had only made her feel more alone.

But tonight all that was going to change. Opening the

door, Vieri pulled her in behind him but the sight that met Harper's eyes stopped her in her tracks. The bedroom had been filled with candles, burning low now that several hours had passed. In the flickering light, Harper could see a trail of rose petals leading to the bed, the four posts of which had been decorated with winter foliage and long-stemmed red roses, twisting up and around and over the canopy, giving it a wonderful, Sleeping-Beauty-like quality.

'It seems the wedding planners have been busy.' She gave a light laugh, intended to show that she knew this ridiculously romantic setting had no real heart behind it, had nothing to do with Vieri.

'So it would seem.' He looked around him, puzzled.

'I think we can probably guess whose idea this was.' She raised her eyebrows, giving Vieri a neutral smile.

'Alfonso!' They spoke his name together.

With a low laugh Vieri took hold of her hand and navigated them along the path of petals towards the bed. 'He is completely shameless. He will stop at nothing to bring us together.'

'I know.' They sat down together on the bed, Harper's heart banging loud enough to wake the entire *castello* as she looked at their hands clasped together in Vieri's lap, thought of where they might soon travel. 'And it seems he has succeeded.'

'Yes.' The air between them thickened, vibrating with desire. With his fingers stroking against her palm, Harper felt her eyelids close, her whole body tingle with erotic awareness.

'You want this?' His breath whispered softly against her face.

'I want this, Vieri.'

She had never wanted anything so much in her entire life. It was an all-consuming yearning that obliterated all doubt, took all reason and turned it into so much dust. The need for him to be hers, to possess her, as no man ever had, was so strong, so overwhelming, that it didn't matter that she knew they had no future together. Tomorrow didn't matter. *Hell*, an hour's time didn't matter. All that mattered was that Vieri took her in his arms and made love to her right now.

Opening her eyes, she gazed at the chiselled features of his handsome face, registering the slash of heat beneath the olive skin, the determined set of his jaw showing his restraint, the way he was holding back. But most of all she saw the swirling depths of desire in his eyes; she saw how much he wanted her. And that was all she needed.

Her hands flew to his chest, rapidly unbuttoning his waistcoat and pushing it over his shoulders before pulling his tie undone. She moved to start on the buttons of his shirt but Vieri took over, sweeping her effortlessly from the bed and setting her onto the floor where his hot gaze swept over her, scorching her flesh from head to toe. Kicking off her shoes, Harper stood on tiptoe to reach for him, linking her arms behind his head, suddenly aware of the difference in their heights, how very tall he was. But feeling for her hands, Vieri released their grasp and took her arms above her head, so that her breasts tugged upwards. Their eyes met.

'Stay like that.' It was a hoarse demand, a whisper of promise.

Bending down, he took hold of the hem of her dress, bunching the slippery fabric in his hands and starting to lift it up, revealing her ankles, then her calves. As he rose to standing he took the dress with him until it had slithered past her bottom and her waist and, with a final flourish, like a triumphant matador, he pulled it up and over her head.

'Molto bella.' Tossing the dress to one side, Vieri took a moment to look at her, his eyes travelling hungrily over the white silk stockings, the matching panties, and then to

her breasts, naked and heavy with need. But Harper felt
no shyness as his gaze raked over her, no embarrassment
or awkwardness. Instead his intense gaze empowered her,
made her feel beautiful, as if she could do anything. She
tingled with a glorious heat that spread to every cell in her
body, finding its way to her core where it burned hot and
bright and insistent.

Only when his eyes alighted on the scar that arced down
one side of her belly did she falter, her arm instinctively
moving to cover it. But Vieri lifted her hand, running his
finger tenderly along the fine ridge of the scar tissue.

'What's this?'

'A kidney transplant. Years ago, when I was sixteen.' She
spoke quickly, hoping that would be explanation enough.

'You needed a kidney transplant?'

'No, not me, Leah. I was the donor.'

'*Cristo*, Harper.' Vieri moved his hands to her shoulders, bringing her closer to him. 'Has your entire life been
dedicated to saving others?'

'Pretty much.' Harper pulled back to look into his eyes.

'And now?'

'Not now. Trust me, Vieri, this…' She moved provoca-
tively against him. 'This is just for me.'

'For us.'

'Yes,' she corrected herself. 'For us.'

With a slow, sinful smile, Vieri reached to release the
pins in her hair and Harper shook her head so that the loose
curls tumbled over her shoulders, over her naked breasts.

'You look…' he swallowed hard '…incredible.'

His words brought a heady surge of power, stripping
away any last inhibitions, making her bold, making her
sure. Never had anyone looked at her like that before, made
her feel like this before.

Her hands moved back to his shirt again, fumbling with

the buttons until she was able to push the fabric apart, expose Vieri's broad, muscled chest to her greedy eyes, her
itching fingers. She placed the flat of her palms against
the wall of his chest, revelling in the feel of his hot, hard
skin, the brush of tight, coarse hair. His muscles flexed
beneath her touch, his obvious strength and power thrilling her senses, tightening her core still further. She closed
her eyes, letting herself feel the beat of his heart, picking
up the rhythm with her own pulse that pumped the blood
rapidly through her veins.

Vieri moved to shrug off his shirt, then dealt with the
buttons of his fly, pulling off his trousers, along with his
shoes and socks. Down to black boxers now, straining
against the power of his arousal, he stood gazing at her for
a couple of long seconds, silent apart from the telling rasp
of his breath. Then, dispensing with his last item of clothing, he waited, watching her watching him. Harper's eyes
widened. With his naked body illuminated by the candlelight he looked like the embodiment of perfection in masculine form. So virile, so potent, so totally magnificent.

He reached for her again, sweeping aside the curtain of
her hair and leaning forward to breathe against her neck,
then plant a trail of hot, heavy kisses from below her earlobe to the base of her throat.

Trembling with anticipation, Harper felt his hands slide
down her arms, over her waist, to the top of her thighs
above her stockings where his fingers sensuously traced
the bare flesh, circling inwards towards her very centre.
Harper gasped, his velvet touch stealing her breath, clenching every muscle in her body, turning her inside out.

Her small step closed the space between them, trapping
his hands where she wanted to feel them so very badly,
at the very heart of her, the heat of her, her most sensitive
core. But Vieri took his hands away, pressing them firmly

against her buttocks, clenching hard to pull her against him so that the gloriously, shocking swell of his arousal pressed against her tummy. Harper drew in a sharp breath of shock.

'For you, Harper,' he moaned softly before covering her mouth with his own, kissing her tenderly, but with such possession, such need, that there was no doubting his intent. 'Just wait one second.'

Pulling away, he crossed over to where his trousers had been discarded on the floor and, slipping his hand into the pocket, he brought out a foil wrapper. Ripping it open with his teeth, he turned to face her again, sliding the condom over his magnificent form with practised ease.

Then he was hers again, spanning her hips with his hands and lifting her effortlessly off her feet. Harper threaded her arms around his neck, Vieri's soft Sicilian curse sounding like the most erotic word in the world as he moved them backwards onto the bed where he laid her down, his body held over her by locked elbows on either side of her head.

He kissed her again, his hand moving between them to trace the flimsy silk of her panties, before removing them to brush against her tight curls as his fingers found their way to her centre that throbbed, hot and wet and desperate with need. Harper squirmed into his touch, silently urging him on until one finger unerringly found just the right spot and he started a torturous, teasing, circular movement. With a wild gasp, she grasped at his shoulders to anchor him down, to give her more. He expertly increased the pressure until Harper felt herself start to shake, a tremor spreading through her body, taking her over completely. With a sigh she gave herself over to it, closing her eyes and drifting with it, shuddering more dramatically with each wave that rippled through her, dimly aware, but not caring in the least, that her small mews were growing louder with each blissful, clenching contraction.

Eventually she stilled as Vieri's hand withdrew. She opened her eyes.

'Sie bellissima!'

His lips closed over her mouth again as he repositioned himself until he was exactly where he wanted to be and with a deep, shuddering thrust, accompanied by a groan of pleasure, he was inside her.

She gasped out loud, the sharp twinge of pain holding her rigid, clawing her nails into his back.

'Harper?' Immediately he stopped, pushing himself up on forearms ridged with corded veins as he stared down into her face.

'It's nothing.' Harper made herself breathe and the pain was gone, replaced by the most glorious sensation of fullness, of being joined, as she felt her tightness expand to hold him. She put her arms around his neck to pull him back down. 'Really.'

'Harper, if you want me to stop...'

'No!' That was the very last thing she wanted. She raised her head to find his lips, digging her hands into his hair. And after a moment of hesitation he was kissing her back, lowering his body, sliding further into her with slick, juddering sureness that felt more right than anything she had ever felt before.

He started to move, slowly at first, but increasing the speed with the rasp of his breath, his thrusts becoming deeper, faster, until Harper felt the dark waves of ecstasy start to roll again and, with a glorious sense of abandonment, she gave herself over to this most incredible of sensations. She heard Vieri groan, utter something low and primal in his native tongue as with one, last punishing thrust he shuddered his own release, deep inside her, before falling down to be wrapped in her arms.

CHAPTER ELEVEN

VIERI STIRRED, OPENING his eyes to see a shaft of moonlight illuminating the bed. He looked down to where Harper was asleep in his arms, her face buried in his chest so that all he could see was the tangle of auburn curls. His heart swelled. She looked completely adorable.

A strange feeling of pride came over him, a sense of peace. Closing his eyes again, he listened to her soft, even breathing, inhaling her unique scent, so different from his own, mixed in with the smell of flowers and candle wax in the room.

He had never expected to find himself here. At the start of yesterday he had been thinking about nothing other than getting the wedding ceremony over with, getting the day over with. He had been totally convinced that this was to be a union in name only, and a very temporary one at that. But as the day had worn on, something had shifted inside him.

Spending time with Harper, watching her talking to the guests, to Alfonso, always with that quiet charm, that easy grace, had made him realise just how exceptional she was. He had found his eyes following her around the room, seeking her out, an unfamiliar sense of pleasure stealing over him when she returned to his side. Jaco had soon picked up on the vibe, ribbing his old friend about *getting a room*, steadfastly refusing to accept Vieri's account that this marriage was simply a means to an end. In fact it had been Jaco who had slipped the condom into his pocket, giving him a hug and muttering 'just in case' in his ear before retiring to bed.

And, of course, Jaco was right. What Vieri felt for Harper went way beyond an appreciation of her social skills, or her ability to make his godfather happy. The idea that that was all it was was laughable. The simmering attraction between them had been there right from the start but slowly it had become more than that. It had become something bigger, more whole, affecting him on a deeper level altogether. He had refused to face up to it. Until tonight.

Tonight he could ignore his feelings no longer. Tonight he had been able to think of nothing else but taking her in his arms and making love to her. The attraction between them, both physical and mental, had become an all-consuming need that he had been powerless to resist. Suddenly he'd found himself asking why not? They were consenting adults. They were actually married, for God's sake. What was to stop them enjoying one night together? And once that idea had taken hold, nothing was going to budge it.

And the reality had been better than even his overheated imagination could have come up with. Sex with Harper had been amazing. *Special.* Maybe too special. Vieri realised that for the first time ever the sexual act had actually meant something, gone far beyond simple physical pleasure and taken him somewhere he had never been before, deep into unknown realms of emotions that he hadn't even known existed. It felt dangerously like losing control, but for this one night he was going to allow himself to live solely in the moment, enjoy the here and now. He wasn't going to think, he wasn't going to analyse what had hap-

pened between them, or indeed the fact that Harper had
clearly been a virgin. Not now. Not with her nuzzled like
this in his arms. He felt himself drifting off into a con-
tented sleep but when Harper moved softly against him,
his arousal, which had already half woken from its slumber, defiantly made itself known.

'Vieri.' His name, uttered sleepily from her open lips,
only served to stoke the fire, and when she reached for
him, pressing her full breasts up against him, winding
her legs around his, there was only one possible outcome.
One hot and sensual, deeply sexual and infinitely satisfy-
ing conclusion.

Harper awoke with a start. The room was very still. A
watery, early morning daylight was filtering through the
gaps in the old wooden shutters. Pulling the covers under
her chin, she stared at the foliage twisted around the posts
of the bed, the roses that had lost their just-picked bloom.

She was alone. She knew that much without turning to
look or spreading out a limb to check. She could sense the
space where Vieri had been, feel it with a twitch of pain,
like a hole in a tooth.

He had gone. Screwing her eyes shut, she forced herself to get a grip, to ignore the clenching of her heart, the
acute sense of loss, abandonment.

She had known the deal when she had agreed to go to
bed with Vieri. *One night of pleasure.* That was what they
had signed up for. And clearly that night was over.

She turned on her side, staring at the indentation on
the pillow where Vieri's head had been. Despite the sense
of emptiness inside her, she didn't regret what they had
done—she could never regret it. Because making love
with Vieri had been the most wonderful experience of
her life. She had felt it; it had happened. She was irrevo-

cably changed. And even though the bed beside her was empty now, nothing could take that away.

Pulling back the covers, she caught sight of the crumpled pair of white stockings, remembering how Vieri had peeled them from her legs, some time in the middle of the night. How they had made love again, with such passion, such tenderness…but without a condom. She recalled Vieri cursing with frustration, searching his pockets again, coming back to bed empty-handed. But the power of their passion had been too strong and neither of them had had the willpower to stop. Instead Vieri had insisted that he would be very careful. She just hoped he was right.

Picking up the stockings, she rolled them into a ball and tossed them onto a chair before heading for the bathroom and a long, hot shower.

She sensed something had happened the moment she stepped out into the corridor. At first all seemed eerily quiet, but as she strained her ears she could hear low male voices and as she started to descend the sweeping staircase the two men in the hall looked up at her. Friends of Alfonso's, they had stayed overnight. Harper started to smile at them but her smile froze as she got closer and caught the sombre expressions on their faces.

'My dear.' One of them reached out and touched her arm. 'I am so sorry.'

Panic clawed at her heart. 'W…what?'

'You…you haven't heard?' The two men exchanged a glance.

'No, tell me, please. What has happened?'

Just then the door to the study opened and Vieri appeared, his face ashen grey.

'Vieri!' Harper rushed towards him but he seemed to look straight through her.

A man in a dark suit followed him out and together they walked to the front door, speaking in soft but rapid Sicilian. Harper watched in frantic silence as they shook hands, the man pulling Vieri into a hug, patting him on the back, before turning to leave.

'Vieri! Please, tell me what has happened!' She ran to him again, putting her hands on his chest to bar his way, to prevent him from walking straight past her.

Vieri stopped, looking at her for the first time, and Harper felt her heart contract with pain. His handsome face was taut with grief, his eyes the colour of dull stone. He dragged in a breath, as if having to speak to her was costing him too much, more than he was prepared to give. But eventually he found the coldly terse words.

'It's Alfonso, Harper.' He averted his gaze, as if he couldn't bear to look at her. 'He's dead.'

'No!' Harper choked on the word, tears immediately brimming in her eyes. 'But how…when?'

'Some time last night.'

'Oh, Vieri.' Harper stared back at him, tears starting to roll down her cheeks. He took several steps away from her, then stood tall and straight, as imposing as ever, but with every plane of his body rigid with tension. As if, were she to touch him, he might snap. 'I'm so sorry.'

He angled his head, giving an almost imperceptible shrug, as if to say her platitudes were of no interest to him. As if she were of no interest to him. This man, who only a few hours ago had looked at her as if she was the centre of his world, taking her to unknown heights of ecstasy, *stealing her heart*, was now regarding her with something bordering on disgust.

But he was grieving. Taking a shuddering breath, Harper wiped the tears from her cheeks with the back of her hand. He looked so devastated, so lost, that she thought her heart might break for him.

Her feet took her towards him again, the overwhelming need to comfort him blocking out all other emotions. Throwing her arms around his waist, she tried to hug him to her, but it was like hugging a block of stone. And when she crushed her head against his chest, her tears dampening the front of his shirt, it seemed as if his heart beating against her ear had slowed to a cold, hard thud.

He made an impatient noise over the top of her head. 'I need to get on. There are a lot of things I have to see to.'

'Yes, of course.' Harper sniffed noisily, pulling herself away. She cleared her throat, tucking her hair behind her ears. 'Can you just tell me…was anyone with him when he died?'

'Maria was with him.' His voice was dry, detached. 'She said it was very peaceful.'

'Well, that's something to be thankful for.' Harper sniffed again. She waited for some sort of reply but his silence made it all too clear that she was being dismissed. 'Okay, I'll…um…let you get on, then.' She started to move away. 'But if there's anything I can do to help, anything at all, you will say, won't you?'

'Actually there is.' The force of his reply turned her hopefully back to face him.

'Yes?'

'Get rid of the guests.' His mouth flattened into a hard line. 'All of them. Right away.'

Harper hesitated, but only for a second. 'Yes, of course.' She hated the thought of having to tell people that Alfonso had died but if it saved Vieri the painful chore then she would do it.

'And that includes your sister.' He fixed her with a cold stare, devoid of all emotion.

'Very well.' With a sombre nod, Harper moved away. She would do as she was told. Now was definitely not the time to question his orders.

'Entra.' Vieri briskly replied to the tap on the office door. Pinching the bridge of his nose, he tried to stem the headache that was building behind his eyes. He had been dealing with all the paperwork involved with Alfonso's death for a couple of hours now, and, even though he was grateful to have something to keep his mind occupied, he knew he needed a break. He sat back in his chair waiting to see who the visitor was, inexplicably finding himself hoping it was Harper. He had been unnecessarily brusque with her—she was probably owed an apology.

But it wasn't Harper. And as the door opened the sight of who it actually was saw Vieri leap to his feet.

'You!' Anger surged through him, hot and fierce. 'What the hell are you doing here?'

'Well, that's not much of a welcome, I must say.' Advancing into the room, Donatella moved around the desk to stand beside him. 'You seem to have forgotten your manners, Vieri.'

She was wearing a fur coat and had some sort of small dog tucked under her arm, who stared at Vieri with bulging eyes.

'I have forgotten nothing, trust me. And you are not welcome here.'

'Now, don't be like that.' She tried to offer her cheek to be kissed but Vieri jerked his head away, stepping to the side. The thought of kissing this woman made him want to be sick.

'I mean it, Donatella.' Her name tasted like poison on his tongue. 'I want you to leave.'

Totally ignoring him, Donatella moved to seat herself

in the chair opposite the desk, settling the dog on her lap. 'Surely you will allow me to pay my respects.'

'*Respects?*' Vieri spat the word back at her, his body rigid with tension. 'I think it's a little late for that. I don't recall you showing Alfonso any respect when he was alive.'

'As I recall, *he* disowned *me*.' She stroked the dog's fur with a hand heavy with jewelled rings. 'And me his only living relative.'

'And you know full well why. You made your lethal choice when you married into the Sorrentino family.'

'Ah, yes, of course. I am the evil witch responsible for the extermination of the Calleroni family.'

'For the murder of your father, Alfonso's only brother, yes.'

'Look at you, Vieri, so high and mighty, so morally upright.' A sneer curled her lip. 'And yet I seem to recall a time when even knowing who I was, *what* I was, didn't stop you from coming to my bed.'

Vieri ground down hard on his jaw, not trusting himself to speak.

'You were crazy for me once, Vieri. You can't deny that.'

'I was crazy, all right, crazy to ever have anything to do with you.'

'Ah, I see the years have twisted the truth, *il mio amore*, made you bitter. But I'm sure you must remember the good times. I know I do.'

'What I remember—' Vieri sucked in a breath '—is that you made the decision to terminate our unborn child!'

Shock flickered across Donatella's face, fighting to move the chemically frozen muscles. 'So you know about that?'

A murderous silence filled the air. 'I do.'

'Then you should be grateful.' Swiftly recovering her composure, Donatella lifted her chin.

'Grateful?' The word roared between them.

'Yes, grateful that I swiftly dealt with the situation. Surely you didn't think you and I would ever be playing happy families?'

'Maybe not.' Fury slowed his words to a low drawl. 'But that doesn't mean I couldn't have raised the child myself. Had I ever been consulted, that is.'

'Trust me.' She gave a harsh laugh. 'No amount of *consultation* would have persuaded me to keep that baby.'

Rage flowed thickly through Vieri's veins like molten lava. He towered over her, his fists clenching and unclenching as he fought to find some control. 'Leave! Now!'

'Very well, I will go.' Rising to her feet, Donatella tucked the dog under her arm and started towards the door, but then stopped, turning to look at him again. 'Oh, how rude of me. I haven't congratulated you on your marriage.' She met his searing glare. 'Such a charming young girl, that little wife of yours. Did she tell you we had met?'

Pure hatred whitened the skin around Vieri's mouth.

'Yes, of course she did. I'm sure you two don't have any secrets.' She gave him a sly smile. 'No doubt she will be only too happy to bless you with any number of little brats if that's what you want. I wish you a long and fertile life together.'

Vieri's low growl gave him away and Donatella's gaze sharpened.

'Or have I got that wrong? Perhaps there is another reason for this hasty marriage?' She raised a painted talon to her lip, pretending to think. The dog squirmed in her grasp. 'Could it be something to do with your godfather's imminent demise, I wonder? Something in the terms of his will that meant if you weren't married, his money, this *castello*, would have come to me?'

'Ha!' Vieri laughed in her face. How typical of Donatella to assume that she was the reason for his rushed marriage. 'Trust me, that was never going to happen.'

'That's just it, I don't trust you, Vieri.' She stared at him with calculating eyes. 'I have watched your meteoric rise to fame, seen the way you have acquired exposed businesses, taken over failing companies. That takes ruthlessness, determination, grit. Qualities I like to think, in some small way, you may have learnt from me.' She studied her fingernails.

'Or to put it another way, I believe that over the years you have become every bit as manipulative and underhanded as me. I believe you will stop at nothing to get what you want, especially if that means depriving me of any inheritance. I just hope that poor unsuspecting young woman you have taken as your bride knows what she's let herself in for. For her sake, I hope she knows the man you really are.'

'Get out!' Vieri roared with a violence that made the dog growl, bare its teeth. Marching past her, he flung open the door, standing sentry as she came towards him.

'Don't worry, I'm going. *Ciao, mio caro.*' She reached up to touch his cheek but Vieri ducked away from her hand. 'Until we meet again.'

Ushering her out into the hallway, Vieri turned and strode back into the office, slamming the door behind him.

One thing was for sure: if he had any say in it, they would never, *ever*, meet again.

Harper heard the slam of the door before she turned the stairs and saw Donatella Sorrentino standing outside the office. She stopped, her hand gripping the banister, a cold fear creeping up her spine. There was something about this woman and her relationship with Vieri that felt bad, dangerous. Harper had never forgotten the way Vieri had reacted when she had told him about Donatella choosing her dress. It had been extreme, violent even. And now this, the door slamming, the high colour of Donatella's cheeks as she headed for the front door, proof positive that emotions between her and Vieri were running high. Harper didn't know what those emotions were but she did know that they were deeply felt and still very much alive. Which logically only led her to the conclusion she had already suspected. At some point in time, Vieri and Donatella had been lovers. And they possibly still were.

Pushing that hideously painful thought to the back of her mind, she watched as Donatella reached the front door, desperate for the woman to be gone. But at the last minute Donatella turned, fixing Harper with an icy stare, and for a moment their eyes locked.

'Good luck.' Donatella broke the heavy silence with a caw of sarcasm. 'You are going to need it.' Then with a cruel laugh she turned and swept through the front door.

Harper sucked in a breath. She refused to be intimidated by her, refused to even think about who this woman was, what part she played in Vieri's life. Not today, not on the day of Alfonso's death.

Moving to stand outside the office, she was trying to pull her composure into place when the door flew open and she was suddenly confronted with Vieri's towering figure. And judging by the murderous look in his eye, a towering mood to match.

Harper's heart lurched with love and compassion and a myriad other emotions that she couldn't begin to process right now.

'Hi.' She sounded ridiculously chirpy. 'I was just coming to tell you that I've done as you asked. All the visitors have left or are leaving. They asked me to pass on their condolences, and Jaco said to tell you he will be in touch later today.'

'Fine, whatever.' With a shrug, Vieri looked over her shoulder, scanning the empty hallway.

'If you are looking for Donatella, she has just left.' Harper fought to keep the bitterness, any sign that she cared, out of her voice.

'But you are still here.' The dark blue eyes swung back in her direction, coldly focussing on her face.

'Well, yes, of course.'

'There's no of course about it. I want you to leave too.'

'Me?' Harper stared at him in astonishment.

'Yes, you.' He squared his shoulders, determination setting in. 'I want you to go. I don't want anybody here.'

'But I'm not "anybody", Vieri.' Harper gasped. 'I'm your...' She hesitated, the word *wife* refusing to come. Despite what had happened last night she was not his wife, not in the true sense of the word. And she never would be. 'I loved Alfonso, you know I did.'

'You barely knew him.'

'Not like you, no, but that doesn't mean I'm not deeply saddened by his death, that I'm not grieving too.'

'Well, you can go and grieve somewhere else.'

'Vieri!' Horror stiffened her spine. That he could be so hurtful, so cruel, cut her to the quick. But he was in shock. Dragging in a stuttering breath, she forced herself to calm down. 'Look, you're upset. I'm sure you don't mean that.'

'I can assure you, I do.'

She stared back at him, the glimpse of his vulnerability beneath his granite façade the only thing keeping her strong. 'Let's not discuss this now. We can talk things over later.'

'There is nothing to talk about, Harper.'

'Don't do this, Vieri. Don't push me away. I want to be here for you, to be able to support you.'

'The way you *support* everybody else, I suppose?'

Harper flinched at the bite of his words. 'What do you mean by that?'

'I mean that I don't need your support, Harper. More than that, I don't want it. You don't need to fix me, the way you seem to have to fix everyone else in your life.'

'That's not fair, Vieri.'

'No? Well, that's the way it looks to me. It strikes me that you are so busy solving everyone else's problems that you have never stopped to take a long hard look at your own. Not content with saving your sister's life, it seems you have to carry on running it for her. And the same with your father, trying to control everything he does.' He paused, his eyes glittering like flint. 'Perhaps if you spent a bit less time meddling in other people's lives and a bit more concentrating on your own you wouldn't still be a virgin at the age of twenty-five.'

Harper gasped, her eyes widening in horror. It took a second or two for his vicious words to permeate, for it to sink in that he had really said them. But when it did her knees started to tremble beneath her and she had to reach for the wall to support herself. The blood drained from her face, taking her breath along with it, so that she had to fight to remain upright. She swallowed, made herself breathe, then swallowed again.

She could feel his eyes on her but she would not look at him. There were a thousand things she wanted to say but none of them would come. And none of them mattered, anyway. All the words in the world wouldn't have made any difference. With his short, brutal analysis Vieri had made it quite clear what he thought of her. He had shown just what a sad, pathetic creature he considered her to be. And maybe he was right. Maybe she had spent all her life looking out for other people because she had no life of her own. Maybe to still be a virgin at the age of twenty-five was pathetic. Pitiful. And if that wasn't, finally giving her virginity away to a man such as Vieri Romano certainly was.

But worse than that, far far worse, was the fact that her virginity wasn't the only thing she had given him. She had given him her heart. And for that she would never forgive herself.

Moving away, she headed blindly for the stairs, tightly gripping hold of the banister to help in her ascent, all too aware of Vieri's cold, cruel eyes trained on her every step. She forced her shoulders back and straightened her spine, determined at least to hang onto her last modicum of pride while she still had it. Because right now, it felt as if that was all she had left.

CHAPTER TWELVE

VIERI WATCHED AS Harper climbed the stairs, her chin up, her head held high. But he could see just how much effort it was costing her, just how much his spiteful words had hurt her. He cursed violently under his breath, only just stopping himself from screaming out loud. Why the hell had he done that? Taunting her about her virginity, of all things. Why had he taken out his fury and hatred for Donatella on Harper? It was unforgivable.

But deep down he knew why. *Guilt*.

Much as he hated to admit it, Donatella had been right when she had called him manipulative and underhand. That was the man he had become. Hadn't he demonstrated both of those qualities in the way he had treated Harper, using her purely for his own gain? *His own pleasure*. She had been right too, when she'd said he had learnt from her, but not in the way she'd meant. His poisoned relationship with Donatella had taught him never to trust anyone, never to get close to anyone. Never to give his heart away again. Something he had to guard against now, in a way he never had before.

He jammed his hands deep into his pockets, pacing to and fro across the echoing hallway.

Discovering that Harper had been a virgin had shocked him to the core. He had taken something from her that she would never get back. Something that he most certainly didn't deserve. Now the shame of his action refused to go away. So when Harper had looked at him with those wide hazel eyes, piercing his protective armour, his guilt had made him lash out.

But maybe she had brought it upon herself. Vieri allowed his twisted logic to kick in. Maybe it was her fault for insisting on searching for the goodness in him, looking for something that wasn't there. Didn't she realise there was no goodness to be had? For all his wealth and success, all his urbane charm and effortless good looks, he was nothing more than a fraud. An empty vessel, a hollow shell. The baby his parents hadn't wanted, the boy no one had adopted, the misguided young lover who had been rejected, the father he was never allowed to be. He certainly didn't deserve her kindness and compassion. Much less her virginity. *Or her love.* If he allowed her to get close to him now he would only end up dragging her down, ruining her life, and he would never let that happen. He had to set her free.

Turning to go back into the office, he blinked against the tortured image of her face as he had delivered his spiteful words—the shock, hurt and pain, that awful pain that had stolen the light from her eyes.

He had to be strong. Alfonso was dead; there was no longer any reason for them to be together. It was better to be cruel now and have a clean break than prolong this agony any longer.

His phone buzzed in his pocket and he viciously swiped to accept the call from the funeral directors. *'Si, pronto.'* Kicking the office door shut with his foot, he spoke in rapid Sicilian, instructing them to come and collect Alfonso's body as soon as possible. No, he did not want them to leave his godfather at the *castello* for a period of mourning. He had no intention of prolonging this particular agony either. As painful as it was, he would say his goodbyes now, and that would be an end to it.

Standing outside Alfonso's bedroom door, Vieri steeled himself for what was on the other side. Slowly turning the handle, he let himself in. The large, panelled room was dimly lit and a chilly breeze stirred the air. The shutters were closed against the bright daylight outside but one window was open behind them so that, in accordance with Sicilian tradition, the deceased soul could fly off to heaven.

As his eyes adjusted, Vieri could make out the motionless shape in the bed. Alfonso, his dear *padrino*, really was dead. The harsh reality slammed into him again. He silently stepped forward and only then did he realise that there was someone else in the room. Harper. Sitting quietly by the bedside, her head bowed, her hand clasping one of Alfonso's that lay stiffly outside the covers. But the second she saw Vieri she was on her feet.

'Oh, it's you,' she whispered hoarsely. 'I'll go.'

'You don't have to.' His voice sounded gruff, unsteady.

'Yes, yes, I must.' She refused to look at him. 'You will want to pay your respects in private.'

He moved to stand beside her, inexorably drawn to her the way he always was. The masochist in him made him want to see her face and he reached to take hold of her chin, lifting it so that she had no alternative but to meet his stare. But what he saw shrivelled his very soul. Her eyes were red from crying, long eyelashes clumped together, the tears still damp on her cheeks. She looked so unutterably sad he simply couldn't bear it.

'What I said earlier, Harper.' All his resolve had vanished at the sight of her misery and he slipped an arm around her shoulder to pull her against him. 'I'm sorry.'

'Not here, Vieri.' She put a shaky hand to his chest, lightly pushing him away. Vieri could feel the heat from her palm warming his heart. 'This is not the time or the place.'

'No.' Letting his arm drop, Vieri glanced down at his godfather. 'Of course not.'

For a moment she held his gaze, her eyes dark, unfathomable. Then, blinking, she turned away, bending to plant a soft kiss on Alfonso's forehead.

'I'm going now, Vieri.' Straightening up, she tossed her hair over her shoulders, tucking it behind her ears, suddenly in control. But Vieri saw the pale column of her throat work with the effort of swallowing. 'I have never seen the point of long goodbyes.'

'No. I understand.' He moved to let her pass. 'The undertakers will be here soon anyway.'

Giving him one last heart-rending look, Harper brushed past him and left the room.

Vieri took the seat where she had been and picked up the hand that she had been holding. Old and gnarled, it felt cold to his touch. He raised it to his lips, letting his breath warm it, just for a minute, before replacing it carefully down on the coverlet. He gazed at his godfather's face, so familiar, so much loved, and yet somehow already different. As if he was no longer there. As if his soul had already left his body.

He would miss him so much, this man who had always been there for him, guided his path in life, steered him in the right direction, stopped him from making the worst mistake of his life. They had never discussed the whole Donatella debacle. Not once. Because that wasn't Alfonso's way. He knew how stubborn Vieri was, how proud. Instead he had cleverly manipulated him away from trouble, given him the means to start a whole new life.

With a flash of long-overdue insight, Vieri realised that Alfonso had been manipulating him right up to the end. His marriage to Harper. He raised his eyes heavenward. Was it possible that the wise old goat had been right about that too? Certainly everything about last night had felt right, more than right. Amidst the shock and grief of Alfonso's passing it didn't seem appropriate to let his mind go there but if he did…then he knew that his body still thrummed with the high of it, yearned for more. He knew that no other sexual experience had come close, that making love to Harper had been on another level completely. It had touched him. It had *meant* something.

I have never seen the point of long goodbyes. Suddenly Harper's words came back to him and he knew, with a bone-chilling certainty, that she hadn't just been talking about saying goodbye to Alfonso. She had been saying goodbye to him.

He jumped to his feet, his heart racing in his chest, his first instinct to run and find her, to stop her, to beg her forgiveness. *To ask her to stay.* But dredging up a depth of willpower he scarcely knew he possessed, he forced himself to stop. He would not go after her. For her sake he *had* to let her go.

There was a light knock on the door and Agnese, Alfonso's housekeeper, appeared in the doorway. 'Signore Romano, I thought you should know that the funeral directors are here.'

'*Si, grazie.*' With a heart laden with sadness, Vieri bent over his godfather to place one last kiss on his cheek. Then, straightening up, he took a deep breath and nodded. 'Tell them I will be right there.'

The sun shone brightly on a thin scattering of snow that coated the rugged landscape as Harper neared her home on the Craigmore estate. Ahead of her Mount Craigmore, one of the Scottish Munros so beloved by serious climbers, stood tall and proud, its jagged white peak stark against the blue sky.

It felt strange to be back, even though she'd only been away for a few weeks. Everything looked the same, but felt different, as if there had been some imperceptible change. With a twist of sadness Harper realised that she was the one who had changed. Irrevocably and for ever.

Leaving Sicily, leaving Vieri, had all but torn her apart. But she had done it, somehow made the arrangements, taking the first flight she could from Palermo, and spending half the night at Amsterdam airport waiting for a connection rather than spending another moment on Sicilian soil.

And despite the fact that she felt as if she had been passed through a grater, mercilessly shredded, a quick glance down revealed that she was still in one piece. Still breathing. Nobody died of a broken heart. She would get over this, be strong, carry on. Because that was who she was, what she did.

The first test of her strength had been telling Leah, who had been sleeping soundly through the drama going on around her at Castello di Trevente. Harper had already woken her to tell her the news of Alfonso's death and the fact that Vieri wanted her to leave. But Leah was still in bed when Harper returned with the knowledge that she too would be going.

'Hurry up, Leah.' She pulled impatiently at the bedclothes. 'I've already told you, we have to leave.'

'We?' Pushing herself up onto one arm, Leah had stared incredulously at her sister. 'Surely you're not leaving too?'

'Yes. I told you, Vieri wants everyone to go.'

'But not you, surely?' She frowned deeply. 'I mean, you and Vieri, yesterday, you seemed so close.'

'It was an act, Leah. You of all people should know that.' In the effort to cover up her pain and hurt she knew she sounded harsh, cold. But it was either that or break down and burst into tears and she would fight against that with all her will. Because if Leah knew that Vieri had broken her heart she wouldn't put it past her to insist on confronting him, to rush to take a chunk out of him there and then.

'Well, if it was an act, it was a very good one.' Leah gave her sister a narrow-eyed look. 'It certainly had me fooled.'

'But that's not exactly difficult, is it, Leah?' Harper snapped back. 'I seem to remember you getting fooled by a certain Max Rodriguez and losing all that money being the reason we are in this mess right now. Or should I say *I* am in this mess.'

'And you know how sorry I am about that, sis.' Leah reached for Harper's hand, her eyes imploring.

'I know. I'm sorry, Lea, I don't mean to keep punishing you.' Harper dragged in a breath, fighting to keep the emotion at bay, acutely aware that Leah was watching her intently. 'It's just…it's all been a bit much. What with the wedding and everything and now Alfonso dying.'

'Of course.' Leah pulled an apologetic face. 'I'm sorry about Alfonso, really I am. He seemed like a lovely man and I know how fond you were of him. But…' her face brightened '…it does mean that your ordeal is over now.' She paused, searching Harper's face. 'Doesn't it?'

If only. If pretending to be Vieri's fiancée, and then his wife, had been the ordeal, then what she felt now, the thought of being separated from him for ever, was more akin to torture. She swallowed down her misery and focussed on the practicalities.

'It would be if we didn't happen to be legally married.'

'Well, presumably that can be annulled or something,

can't it?' Leah persisted, her eyes not leaving her sister's face. But when Harper didn't immediately reply she leaned in closer. 'Harper?'

'I don't know…yes… I suppose so.' Even amongst all the trauma of the day that particular worm of worry had managed to niggle at the back of her brain. She and Vieri had consummated the marriage, more than once. Did that mean it could no longer be annulled? But right now that problem would have to wait. Right now, all she could think about was getting away.

She had assumed that she and Leah would travel back to Glenruie together, but Leah, being Leah, had had other ideas.

'So are you planning on staying at Glenruie, when we get back?' She asked the question casually as she moved around the room collecting her belongings.

'Yes, of course. What else would I do?'

'Only I was just wondering, if you are there to keep an eye on Dad, could I maybe be excused, just for a week or so? It's not like he needs both of us on his case.'

'And what would you be doing for this *week or so*?' Harper helped her close her suitcase.

'Well, the thing is—' Leah affected a nonchalant air '—Jaco, he's invited me to go to Licata to see his vineyard.'

'Has he now?'

'And obviously I said no, because I thought I had to get back to Glenruie.'

'Obviously.'

'But now…'

Harper shook her head, even managing a small smile. She had never been able to deny her sister anything. And there was no reason why one of them shouldn't be happy. Jaco had seemed like a nice guy, and as Vieri's oldest friend he had to be trustworthy, didn't he?

'I mean, I will come back with you now if you want me to, that goes without saying.'

'No, it's fine!' She took Leah's hand. She had to admit that a part of her was glad that Leah wouldn't be accompanying her back home. She wasn't sure her fragile armour would be able to withstand several hours of Leah's questioning. At least this way she would be able to nurse her misery in peace. 'But promise me you won't do anything stupid.'

'Who, me?' Leah had feigned an innocent look, before pulling her sister into a hug.

So Harper had travelled alone. Now, as she paid the taxi, picked up her bag and trudged across the crunchy grass to let herself into Gamekeeper's Cottage, wondering what havoc would greet her inside, she felt more desperately miserable than at any time in her life.

Vieri hastily gathered together his belongings, the urge to get away from the *castello*, from Sicily, suddenly overwhelming. He would fly back to New York right away, concentrate on getting his life back on track. A life that had recently become dangerously derailed.

Today he had buried his godfather. In the same chapel that he had married Harper only forty-eight hours before, he had had to endure the ceremony, then watch as Alfonso's body was lowered into the ground. And as the priest had given his final blessing and Vieri had scattered a handful of soil against the polished wood, he had never felt more alone.

But he only had himself to blame. Because there was only one person who could have made this day more bearable. *Harper.* And he had driven her away, banished her. Today he had missed her presence like a physical pain but the suffering was no more than he deserved. Much as he had longed for the feel of her hand in his, for the comfort and support she could have given him, he had had no right to it. Far from it.

And the brutal fact was, even with the funeral over, he still missed her. With Harper gone it felt as if a huge void had opened up. As if a part of him had died.

And this was he, Vieri Romano, a man who prided himself on needing no one. Who had learned from a very young age to stand on his own two feet, to fight his own battles. To look to no one for emotional support, or any other support come to that. Even his beloved *padrino* had had to use his cunning and intelligence to circumnavigate Vieri's fierce pride before he could offer any guidance or advice.

Moving over to the wardrobe, he started to roughly pull his shirts off the hangers. He had ordered Harper to leave the *castello* and she had done just that, even though missing Alfonso's funeral must have hurt her terribly. He had behaved like a heartless bastard—he knew that. But he also knew that he was doing this for her own good, to save her from himself. Because the longer she was around him, the more deeply they became involved, the worse it would be for her in the long run. He would end up destroying her. And he couldn't bear for that to happen.

Plucking his wedding suit from the hanger, Vieri started to shove it into his suitcase when he felt the rustle of something in the jacket pocket. Sliding his hand in, he pulled out an envelope. Alfonso's wedding gift. Caught up in the events of his wedding night he had completely forgotten about it. Now he sat down on the edge of the bed and withdrew the handwritten piece of paper. He read it quickly, his godfather's reassuring voice speaking the words in his head.

To my dearest Vieri and Harper,
It is my final wish that you accept Castello di Trev-
ente as my wedding gift to you. I know it was agreed,

Vieri, that my entire estate would be distributed amongst my charities, but I hope you will allow me this small change of heart.

The thought of the two of you living here, raising a family, gives me the greatest of pleasure. I know you would never deny me that.
Your loving godfather,
Alfonso.

Vieri put his head in his hands, screwing up his eyes against the shame and guilt. Alfonso's gift, so generously given, so optimistically stated, felt like a ton of salt poured onto an open wound. Because he and Harper would never be living together at Castello di Trevente, let alone raising a family here. The whole thing had been a big fat lie. And Alfonso's kindness had only exposed the nasty little fraud for what it really was.

Getting to his feet, he raked a hand through his hair, then turned and stuffed Alfonso's letter into his suitcase, slamming down the lid. He would tell Harper about the 'wedding present' at a later date, when he had calmed down. She could have the whole *castello* as far as he was concerned, to live in or to sell, or to give to her wretched sister if that was what she wanted. It didn't matter to him. All that mattered was getting away from here.

Picking up his suitcase, he cast one last look around him and then headed out of the door. He couldn't get back to New York fast enough—back to the ordered, controlled life he had had before this whole wretched debacle had kicked off. Before Harper had happened. Only then would he be able to think straight again.

CHAPTER THIRTEEN

HARPER STARED AT the tester stick held in her shaky hand. *No*. She screwed up her eyes, refusing to believe it. It wasn't possible; it couldn't be true. But when she opened them again, they were still there, the two bright pink lines. There was no doubt about it—she was pregnant.

She let a couple of seconds pass, waiting for the reality to sink in. *Pregnant*. The room did a giddy spin. Whatever was she going to do? However was she going to cope?

Grasping hold of the washbasin beside her, she pulled herself to standing and faced herself in the mirror. She was pregnant with Vieri Romano's baby. And she had absolutely no idea what to do about it.

'Harps, hurry up, I need the loo. Whatever are you doing in there?' The bathroom door rattled and the old bolt that had never been very secure obligingly slid open. Spinning round, Harper saw Leah standing in the doorway. 'Oh, God, sis, you look dreadful. Are you ill?'

'No, no, I'm fine.'

'Well, you don't look fine. Whatever's the matter?'

'Nothing, I told you. Can't I even get five minutes' peace in this house?'

Leah advanced into the room. 'What are you hiding behind your back?'

'Nothing.'

'Oh, Harper!'

'What?' In her befuddled state Harper had failed to re-alise that the tester stick, still clasped in her hand behind her back, was reflected in the mirror.

'You're not!'

Letting out a long, juddering breath, Harper nodded miserably.

'Oh, my God!'

Flinging her arms around her sister, Leah hugged her tightly, then pulled away so she could see her face. 'It's Vieri's?'

Harper nodded again. She didn't have the strength to ask who the hell else's it was likely to be.

'But you said…'

'I know, Lea. It was just that one night, the night of the wedding.'

'Golly.'

'Yes, golly.' Somehow the use of the old-fashioned and ridiculously understated word broke the tension and suddenly the two sisters started to laugh, clinging to each other for all they were worth.

'So, what are you going to do?' Finally breaking away, Leah studied Harper's semi-hysterical and now tear-stained face.

'I… I don't know.' She accepted the bunch of tissue that Leah had plucked from the toilet roll and blew her nose. 'I mean, obviously I'm going to keep it. And I'll have to tell Vieri at some point. But not yet. Not until I've got used to the idea.'

'Don't leave it too long.' Leah dabbed at her sister's eyes. 'It will only make it harder in the long run.'

'I guess so.' A sudden panicky thought occurred to her. 'But whatever you do, don't you go telling him, Leah! You must promise me that.'

'Yes, of course, I promise. I wouldn't do that. What do you take me for?'

Harper shot her a look, which Leah studiously ignored.

'Oh, sis, this is so exciting! I'm going to be an auntie.' She clasped Harper's hands in hers, which only set Harper's lip trembling more violently.

Exciting was one word for it—petrifying another one. However was she going to get through this? Not just with the pregnancy or the birth or the prospect of raising a child on her own. But the fact that this was Vieri's child.

She had worked so hard to try and forget about him, done everything she could to block him from her thoughts, erase him from her mind. But of course it had been impossible. Six weeks had passed since she'd left Sicily, six torturous, lonely weeks when there had been no contact between them at all. And far from finding any relief, each week had felt more bleak, more desolate than the one before. Despite Harper keeping herself frantically busy, watching her father like a hawk, overseeing his job as well as working shifts at Craigmore Lodge, Vieri still managed to consume her every waking moment. More than that, he had tortured her dreams, images of the night they had spent together filling her head, crowding her sleep until she woke to the gnawing agony of being alone again.

And now this. A baby. A living, breathing child that would tie them together for ever. Somehow she was going to have to protect her shattered heart from the onslaught of having Vieri in her life. Because he would insist on being there for his son or daughter; instinctively Harper knew that. Supposing he tried to take the baby away from her? Supposing he decided to fight her for custody?

'Don't look so worried!' At the sight of her troubled face, Leah pulled her into a hug again. 'Everything will be all right. We'll do this together. I'll be there every step of the way.'

Harper gave a weak smile, surrendering to her sister's embrace. Somehow that statement did absolutely nothing to reassure her.

Getting out of the car he'd hired at the airport, Vieri slammed the door and looked around him. This place was picturesque, he'd give them that, but right now picturesque didn't cut it. Right now he just wanted to reach his destination. It felt as if this journey to Glenruie had gone on for ever—first the flight from New York to Glasgow and then following the seemingly endless road along the side of a glittering loch. And now the sat nav had brought him to some ancient-looking contraption that called itself a car ferry, and, even though he had been ready to leave as soon as he'd bumped the car up onto it, it seemed that the two men in the tugboat that pulled the thing across the inlet were going nowhere. He marched over towards them.

'Can we get a move on, please?' He tapped his watch for emphasis. They looked back at him with mild lack of interest. 'I'm in a hurry.'

'We're a waitin' more vehicles.' The older one spoke through the window of the tug in a language that Vieri only barely recognised as English.

More vehicles? They could be here all night. Apart from the odd battered old Land Rover he hadn't seen a car for twenty minutes. Vieri scowled.

'Where ya headed, any road?'

'Glenruie.'

'Craigmore Lodge?'

'Yes, well, the Craigmore estate.' Vieri hesitated, having no desire to discuss the reason for his visit with these two. But if it meant getting there more quickly… 'I'm looking for the gamekeeper's cottage. I have business with Harper McDonald.'

'Do you now?'

Irritation spiked inside him. Hadn't he just said that?

'Yes. So, could we get going?' Vieri attempted to keep his impatience in check.

'Aye, why not?' With an incomprehensible but immensely welcome change of heart, the old man started the engine of the tugboat. 'Close the gates, Jim. We cannae keep this man away from Miss McDonald any longer. He looks like he's fair set to bust.'

Turning on his heel, Vieri went back to sit in his car, drumming his fingers on the steering wheel as the ferry chugged its way across the inlet of blue water that was supposedly quicker than driving around this peninsula. He wasn't entirely sure what *set fair to bust* meant, but he could hazard a guess. Clearly he wasn't managing to hide his feelings anything like as effectively as he'd thought.

His decision to come to Scotland had been made on the spur of the moment. He'd been in a board meeting at his New York office, staring out at the city skyline when he should have been concentrating on the latest capital investment accounts, when the idea had come into his head. Picking up the phone, he had instructed his jet to be put on standby, telling his driver to take him to the airport there and then, before logic and common sense had the chance to change his mind. As the board members had been hastily shepherded out of the room they had exchanged nervous glances. What was Romano playing at? What the hell had come over him these past few weeks?

The fact was, Vieri didn't know what had come over him. Only that he had been back in New York for two months now and that time had done absolutely nothing to erase Harper from his mind. Being halfway across the other side of the world had done nothing to free him from the power of her spell. Even throwing himself into work, where he normally felt his most comfortable, had failed spectacularly. Instead of finding any relief there he had ended up making questionable judgements, bad decisions.

Which meant only one thing—he had to see Harper. As soon as possible. Right away. He was done trying to forget about her; he was sick of hearing his own damned voice telling him that he had to get over her. This was the only way.

As the ferry finally docked on the other side Vieri started the car engine, gritting his teeth at the casual way Jim was sauntering over to open the gates. Now that he was so close he could almost sense Harper's presence, almost feel her in his arms.

Mio Dio, how he had missed her. From the toss of that auburn-coloured hair, to the pout of her pink lips, the way she wrinkled her nose when she was annoyed, bit down on her lip as she thought. Her bright intelligence, her sexy body, her slow smile, he missed them all. With a passion that was burning him up inside.

One thing was for sure, if he didn't get off this ferry and reach his destination very soon, there was a good chance that he might indeed be *fair set to bust*.

Harper eased herself up against the pillows, checking how she was feeling. The cramps had definitely stopped. It had to be, what, at least a couple of hours now since the last one? She allowed herself a sigh of relief, the hope in her chest starting to bloom. Maybe, just maybe, it was going to be all right.

The first muscle spasm had woken her early that morning. Low in her abdomen, it hadn't been painful, but enough to see her fumbling for the bedside light and lying very, very still. Then the second one had come, followed by a third until a cold rush of fear had swept over her that something was wrong. Levering herself gently out of bed, she had stood in the cold first light, hoping against hope that being upright might help, that each spasm might be the last, but still they had come.

Clutching her stomach, she had tried to swallow down the panic. It was only two weeks since she had done the pregnancy test but already the thought of losing this baby was too terrible to contemplate. Already she knew that the child inside her was more important, more precious than anything in the world. No matter what obstacles lay ahead, no matter that being tied to Vieri would break her heart a thousand times, she would fight with everything she had to keep it safe. Starting now.

Pulling on her clothes, she had crept downstairs, trying not to wake Leah, surprised to find her already in the kitchen, nursing a mug of tea. Apparently she had got up to make their father his breakfast and seen him off to work. And of course one look at Harper's face had been enough for her to know that something was wrong. Refusing to take no for an answer, she had leapt into action, bundling her into the Land Rover and delivering her to the local doctors' surgery just as they were opening their doors.

And the doctor had been reassuring. After taking down the details, her professionalism slipping only very slightly at the news that Harper McDonald, who she had known since she was a baby, was pregnant by some unknown man, she had given her a quick check over and made an appointment for her to have an ultrasound scan.

'And try not to worry.' She had patted Harper's hand, now devoid of both the engagement ring and the wedding band that Harper had tugged off her finger and hurled onto the dresser before fleeing from the *castello*. 'It's early days and we can't completely rule out that there may be a problem but sometimes these cramps are just the baby bedding in. I suggest you go home and have twenty-four hours of bed rest. Let your sister look after you.'

Bedding in. It had been such a cosy, comforting expression. Leah, who had insisted on coming in with her, had turned to give her a smile full of hope, reassuring the doctor that she would wait on Harper hand and foot for the whole nine months if necessary.

Which was why Harper now found herself in the unfamiliar position of lying in bed with absolutely nothing to do. And that meant too much thinking and all thoughts inevitably led to Vieri. She rearranged the pillows and sat back, staring out of the window at the dark shape of the mountains against the thundery grey sky. *She was in love with him.* It was as simple and as complicated as that. And there was absolutely nothing she could do about it. But he still didn't even know she was pregnant. Closing her eyes, she let herself drift off to sleep, promising that she would find the courage to tell him as soon as she knew for sure that everything was all right.

Vieri pulled the car up in front of the cottage. So this was where Harper lived. It was smaller than he'd imagined; a long, low, white building with dormer windows set into a slate roof. But he could see the logic in building low to the ground in this rugged landscape. It was beautiful but it was also tough and wild, the climate unpredictable. Attributes that might describe Harper herself.

Pulling up the collar of his cashmere coat against the fat drops of rain that were starting to fall, he rapped hard on the knocker of the weather-beaten door. His heart, he suddenly realised, was beating over-fast. From inside he heard a dog bark and a female voice telling him to shush. There was a rustle as she came closer, the skittering sound of the dog's claws against a hard floor. Vieri took in a breath, pulled back his shoulders.

But it wasn't Harper. As the door opened, Leah appeared, holding the straining dog by its collar. She stared at him in open-mouthed shock.

'What are you doing here?' Her question was straight to the point, but Vieri could hear the panic in her voice.

'I have come to see Harper.'

'Well, I'm sorry, it's not convenient.' She made an attempt to bar the door.

'Then I will wait until it is.' Firmly planting his feet and towering over her, Vieri made it quite clear that he was going nowhere.

'Look, the thing is…' Leah went for a different approach. 'Harper's in bed. She's not well.'

'What sort of not well?' A thrum of alarm moved through him and he took a step forward, leaving Leah no option but to move aside to let him in. Ignoring the growl of the dog, he ducked his head and stepped inside until the three of them were squashed in the small hallway. Leah squeezed past him, dragging the dog behind her. Vieri followed them into the kitchen, where the dog was finally persuaded to go and lie down in his basket next to the Aga. Leah turned to face him.

'Can I get you a drink of anything?' Vieri could see her struggling to hold her composure. 'Tea or coffee, I mean— we don't have alcohol in the house.'

'No, nothing.' The more he looked at Leah, the more convinced he was that there was something seriously wrong. 'Tell me now, Leah, what's the matter with Harper? Is she ill?'

'Umm, not…not really.' Leah turned to fill the kettle but Vieri was behind her in a couple of strides, his hand on her shoulder, turning her to face him.

'And what exactly does that mean?'

'It means that she's not ill in the conventional use of the word.'

'For God's sake, Leah.' Irritation and alarm thrummed through him. 'I refuse to stand here listening to your riddles. Either you tell me what is wrong with your sister right now, or I climb those stairs and find out for myself.'

'No!' Leah clutched at his elbow. 'Don't do that. She needs quiet. She mustn't have any stress.'

'Then tell me what's going on.'

'I can't!' Shrugging from under his grip, Leah moved into the room, backing towards the wall. 'Harper made me promise I wouldn't say anything to you.'

'About what?' The blood was beginning to roar in his ears. 'You have precisely three seconds, Leah.'

'About the baby!' She blurted out the words with a cry of anguish. 'Oh, God...' She looked at him with beseeching eyes. 'Harper is going to kill me.'

But Vieri wasn't listening any more. The roaring in his ears had intensified to the point where he couldn't hear anything anyway. A red mist had descended, clenching his fists, making his whole body tremble with a flood of thundering rage that had all but engulfed him.

The baby. Leah's words ricocheted inside his head. So Harper *was* pregnant? Or at least she *had been* pregnant. He screwed his eyes closed against the violent realisation that the deed must have already been done. Why else would Harper be in bed? Why else would Leah look so damned shifty? *Guilty.*

A thousand splintered thoughts shattered in his brain. When had it happened? If he had got here yesterday could he have stopped it? Or even earlier today, if the journey hadn't taken so long, if that infernal ferry hadn't been so slow? Why had he let his pride keep him away for so long? Why had he ever let Harper out of his sight?

But most of all was the hideous sense of history repeating itself. He had done it again. Let down his guard, let someone in. First Donatella and then Harper. And once again he had been betrayed.

Anger surged inside him, hot and febrile. He forced himself to drag in a breath, dimly aware that Leah was speaking. No doubt she was complicit in this; she had probably arranged the whole thing. Vieri couldn't bring himself to look at her. She was irrelevant. But Harper... *oh, Dio*... His beautiful, seductive, tormenting Harper. Was it possible that she could really have done this? He lifted his head, squaring his shoulders. There was only one way to find out.

He moved through the kitchen, Leah leaping ahead of him, trying to bar his way, holding her hands up against his chest.

'No, Vieri, you mustn't go up there.'

'Get out of my way, Leah.'

'No, really, the doctor said she needed rest.'

'I said get out of my way.'

The dog had joined in now, growling loudly. Stepping past them both, Vieri headed for the stairs, Leah following him before turning to shut the dog in the kitchen.

'Please, Vieri, I'm begging you.' She called up from the bottom of the stairs. 'Don't go upsetting her. I know I shouldn't have told you but now it's done...'

Now it's done. With his thumb on the iron latch of a bedroom door, Vieri turned to look down at Harper's twin. So there was his proof. Giving Leah one last glance of utter revulsion, he clicked the latch down.

CHAPTER FOURTEEN

THE LOUD RAP on the front door, followed by Timmy's barking, woke Harper from her doze. She heard Leah going to answer the door, but the next sound froze her with shock. A male voice, deep and impatient. *Vieri!* No, it couldn't be. Clutching at the bedclothes, she told herself she must have made a mistake. Her sleep-fuddled state, her anxiety over the pregnancy, had obviously conjured him up from the shadowy recesses of her mind, where she had tried so hard to banish him. But then she had heard it again, his voice raised now as they went into the kitchen. There was no mistake. Vieri was here, in this house, under this roof.

Oh, God. Harper tried to rationalise her thoughts over the frantic thudding of her heart. *What was he doing here? And why did it suddenly feel as if all the oxygen had been sucked from the room?* She forced herself to calm down, for the sake of the baby, if nothing else. But still her mind madly darted in all directions as she tried to figure out how she was going to face him, what she was going to say. She just hoped Leah would be able to distract him long enough for her to pull her defences in place.

I am pregnant, Vieri, she tried the words in her head. *But I intend to raise the child myself.* No, that sounded too contentious. *I feel that any decisions regarding the child's future should be left to me.* As if he would accept that. But before her poor frazzled brain could come up with anything remotely workable she heard the commotion going on downstairs. Timmy was growling, Leah pleading and Vieri... He sounded so angry. So filled with rage. A rage that was coming closer and closer with his every thunderous step. And then, with a click of metal and a creak of the hinges, the door flew open.

Vieri stared at her. Propped up in bed by pillows, she was clutching the duvet under her chin, as if it could somehow protect her. Well, there was no chance of that. There was nothing in the world that would be able to protect her from the storm that raged inside him now.

He advanced towards her, trying to ignore the way his heart flipped at the sight of her, the fact that, somewhere at the calm centre of that storm, the sight of her was still managing to affect him in a way that had nothing to do with rage or retribution. He exhaled sharply.

'Vieri!' She backed further into the pillows.

'I'm sorry, Harper, I couldn't stop him.' Leah was in the doorway behind him.

'That's okay, Leah. You can go.'

'I'm not going to leave you.'

'Please, Leah.'

'You heard what she said.' Speaking over his shoulder, Vieri's chilling tone could not be disobeyed. As Leah shut the door he jammed his hands into his coat pockets and for a long moment he and Harper stared at one another. Vieri could feel the muscle twitching along his jaw.

'So...' Finally Harper broke the silence. 'What are you doing here, Vieri?'

'You can cut the pretence.' Vieri advanced towards the bed. 'Leah has told me.'

'Ah.'

'*Si*, ah.'

'Look, Vieri, I know I should have said something before but…'

'But what, Harper?'

'But I needed to sort things out in my head first.'

'So that's what you call it, is it? Sorting things out?'

Harper stared back at him. She had expected shock, anger maybe, but not directed at her, and not like this. His whole body was taut with cold fury, as if his rage had solidified the very bones of him.

Pulling back the covers, she got out of bed and, in a futile attempt to stand up to him, placed herself squarely before him. So close now, she could feel the heat of his temper, almost smell it on his skin. Never had she seen him like this before.

'Look.' She reached out to touch his arm but he recoiled in horror. 'This has obviously come as a shock to you, but maybe if we could just sit down calmly and talk it through…?'

'It's a little late for that, Harper.' His voice leeched scorn. 'I'm sure you think you have fixed this problem, the way you fix everyone and everything else in your life. But believe me, Harper, there is no fixing me.'

'I'm sorry you feel like that, Vieri.' She pushed the hair away from her face, still trying to inject some calm, soothe his rabid temper. 'But if it makes you feel better, I am prepared to take full responsibility.'

'Better?' He cursed violently in Sicilian, reaching towards her with a hand that shook with emotion before changing his mind and shoving it back into his pocket, as if he couldn't bring himself to touch her. 'You think your taking *full responsibility* is going to make me feel better? Are you mad, woman?'

Harper stared at him aghast. If she was to question anyone's sanity, it would be his. His rage had turned him from the cool, controlled man that she thought she'd known into some sort of raving beast. She wouldn't have been surprised to see him foam at the mouth. Never had she seen this side of him before, never had she expected him to react like this, as if it were all her fault. And yet still she knew she loved him. Still her heart melted at the sight of him.

'Why are you behaving like this?' She wanted to reach out to touch him so badly, but instead she folded her arms across her chest.

'And tell me, Harper, how exactly am I supposed to behave? How should a man appear on learning that his…his wife has made a unilateral decision to end her pregnancy?'

'What?' She stared at him, shock and confusion knotting her brow, dulling her brain.

'You heard.'

'You…you think that I have had an abortion?'

'Don't insult my intelligence by trying to deny it. Leah has told me the truth.'

'No, Vieri, she hasn't.' Now she reached for his shoulders, her hands shaking with raw emotion. 'Or at least, whatever she has told you, you have misunderstood.'

Vieri felt Harper's slim hands on his coat, fluttering like a trapped bird. And this time he didn't try and shrug them off. Standing there in her sensible pyjamas, her tawny eyes wide, imploring, she looked so adorable, so vulnerable. He rapidly searched her face for clues. He saw confusion and hurt, but not guilt. Had he got this wrong? Instantly another terrible thought flashed through his mind. What if she had lost the baby, suffered a miscarriage?

'Harper?' He cupped her face in his hands, staring deep into her eyes. 'Tell me now. What have I misunderstood?'

'I haven't got rid of our baby, Vieri.' Her eyes held his. 'I would never do such a thing.'

Our baby. Vieri briefly closed his eyes against the painful wonder of that word.

'So, what, then? You have had a miscarriage?' The words felt like boulders in his throat.

'No.' Harper shook her head beneath his grasp, her hands leaving his shoulders to rest on her stomach. 'I thought that was what was happening when I woke up this morning with stomach pains but I went to see the doctor and she said—'

'You are still pregnant?' With a leap of hope, Vieri tilted her face so he would finally see the truth. And what he saw melted his heart.

'Yes.' Fat tears leaked from her eyes. 'Yes, I am.'

'Grazie Dio!' He pulled her against him, crushing her in his arms. Relief flooded through him, hot and heady, stirring up other emotions in its wake. Joy, hope, *love*.

Harper let him hold her, her body moulding against his, wonderfully soft and responsive to his embrace. But then the moment passed and she stiffened, moving against him. 'You are pleased?' She muffled the words against his coat, then pushed herself away to look up into his face.

'Si, certo, of course.' But at the sight of her anxious face Vieri's fears crept in again. 'What exactly did the doctor say?'

'She said that I should rest and if the spasms stop and I don't get any more then everything should be okay.' She sniffed, brushing away the tears with the back of her hand. 'She has booked me in for a scan in a couple of days.'

'And have they stopped, the pains?'

Harper nodded, but she had to bite down on her lip before she could meet his eyes. 'I haven't had any for several hours now.'

'So that it good, *si?*' Relief flooded his voice.

'Yes, it's good.' She gave him a watery smile. Of course

it was good; it was more than good. But having Vieri here, standing in her bedroom looking ridiculously out of place in his dark coat, seeming even taller than usual beneath the low ceiling, had brought another pain that was nothing to do with her pregnancy. She loved him so much. Seeing him again, after several weeks' absence, only made her realise it more.

'You should get back into bed.' Suddenly Vieri was swooping her up into his arms and carrying her over to the bed, where he pulled back the duvet and settled her underneath. 'There.' He tenderly brushed the hair back from her forehead. 'You must rest.'

Fat chance of that. As Harper gazed at him, every nerve ending in her body tingled with awareness, every cell longed for him, yearned for him. But she knew she had to be strong, be sensible.

Vieri's extreme reaction to the pregnancy had shocked her. His anger when he had thought she'd had a termination was perhaps understandable, although she suspected there were many men who would have greeted that news with relief. But Vieri wasn't like other men. He was proud and he was strong and just the sight of him filled her heart to overflowing. But he wasn't hers. And even though now he knew the truth his attitude had dramatically changed and he appeared to be so happy about the baby, thrilled even, that didn't mean that anything had changed. In terms of what they were going to do now, how they would raise the child, how she would cope with the agony of loving a man who didn't love her back, she had no idea.

One step at a time, she decided, arranging the duvet around her. Somehow they would make it work. They had to.

'So what are you actually doing here, Vieri?' She delved down into her shallow reserves of reason to try and sound normal. 'You didn't think to tell me you were coming?'

'It was a spur-of-the-moment thing.' Vieri shrugged off his coat and pulled up a chair, positioning it by the bed.

'Can I ask why?'

'I wanted to see you.' He made it sound like the most natural thing in the world, especially when he took hold of her hand that lay outside the covers and laced his fingers through hers. 'Though it was never my intention to come storming in like a wild beast. I'm so sorry.'

'That's okay. You were upset.'

'No, it's not okay. It was unforgivable. Especially when you are supposed to be getting peace and rest.'

'There's no harm done.' She gave him a reassuring smile.

'Thankfully not.' He gave her a solemn stare. 'But I owe you an explanation.'

'No, really, there's no need…'

Raising a finger, he pressed it against her lips to silence her.

'Yes, Harper, there is. There is something I need to tell you.' He hesitated and Harper could see the internal struggle playing across his face, as if he was waging war with himself. 'Many years ago I fathered another child.' He watched her intently, searching for her reaction. 'I was eighteen. I thought she was the love of my life, but it turned out I was wrong.'

'Oh, Vieri.' Harper gripped his hand more tightly.

'She had an abortion without even telling me she was pregnant. I only found out by chance afterwards.'

'I'm so sorry.' Suddenly realisation dawned. 'And you thought I'd done the same thing?'

Vieri shrugged his apology. 'Stupid, I know. I just jumped to the wrong conclusion. Forgive me, Harper.'

'There's nothing to forgive. This girl obviously hurt you very much.'

'That's just it—she wasn't a girl. She was a woman.'
He hesitated again, before dragging in a deep breath. 'It
was Donatella Sorrentino.'

Donatella Sorrentino. Harper felt the pain of her name
spear through her. She should have known. The woman
whose dark presence had always been swirling around in
the background. Who Harper had long suspected meant
more to Vieri than he had ever admitted. Now she knew
the truth.

She pulled her hand away from his clasp.

'And you still love her?' Her voice sounded very small.

'No!' Vieri's reply was immediate, vehement. Too vehement. 'Whatever makes you think that?'

Harper looked down at the bedclothes, unable to meet
his gaze, frightened of what she might see there.

'Because I saw the way you reacted when I told you she
had chosen my dress for the ball. And again at Castello
di Trevente after Alfonso died. Both times you behaved
like a man possessed...' she picked at the duvet cover '...
or a man in love.'

'No!' Vieri could only repeat the word in astonishment.
He gazed at Harper's bent head, at the soft auburn curls
falling to cover her face. How could she have got this so
wrong? How could she have misunderstood him so completely? But then it was hardly surprising when he thought
of the way he had treated her. All the harassment and bul-
lying, using her for his own gain, or, even worse, his own
satisfaction. Forcing her to marry him and then banish-
ing her from the *castello* before turning up here hollering
like a raving lunatic. It was no wonder Harper jumped to
wrong conclusions, thought so badly of him, had no real
measure of who he was. Who could blame her?

Shame coursed through him, hot and strong. He had
to try and put things right. It was time to come out of the

murky shadows and be honest with Harper, show her the man he really was. Except he was no longer sure who that man was.

A few months ago it would have been easy. Hugely successful billionaire businessman with a formidable reputation for working hard and for enjoying the fruits of his success. A man at the top of his game, always in control, a man who had taken on the world and won. Invincible, ruthless, *heartless*.

But now…now as Harper slowly raised her head to look at him again and he caught sight of her beautiful face, he realised that none of that material success mattered. None of it actually meant anything. His whole life had been a hollow shell…until now.

Getting to his feet, he moved over to the window, trying to order his thoughts, make some sense of this astonishing shift in his values. But first things first—he had to put Harper right about Donatella. Drawing in a breath, he turned to face her again. 'I promise you, Harper, any love I may have felt for Donatella died a very long time ago. Now all I feel is anger. That's what you have witnessed.'

'But so much anger?' She refused to let go. 'And after all these years? Surely time should have allowed you to put it behind you, move on.'

She was right, of course. He had carried this hatred for Donatella for far too long. So long that it had become part of who he was, almost as if letting go of it would be losing a chunk of himself. It had become his own personal vendetta. And deep down he knew why. Not just because Donatella had betrayed the Calleroni family, the callous way she had as good as signed her own father's death warrant and broken Alfonso's heart. Not the vile way she had groomed him on the orders of the Sorrentino family, used him and then dumped him. Not even the actual act of the abortion. His problem was more basic than that, more fundamental. He had never analysed the root cause before—he had never needed to. But suddenly he wanted Harper to understand.

Moving towards the end of the bed, he gripped the iron railing, the metal cold against his hot hands.

'I know how important family is to you, Harper. I have seen the way you care for your loved ones.' He started slowly, trying to keep his voice level, neutral, aiming for facts rather than emotion. 'And despite the impression I may have given you, I really admire you for that.'

Harper stared at him, waiting.

'But I grew up without a family. Apart from Alfonso, I had no one to show me any love, or to love in return.'

'That's so sad.' Her soft, gentle voice immediately pulled at the threads of his composure. Vieri shrugged.

'I never really knew any different. But when Donatello had that abortion, she terminated my only known blood relative. That was why my reaction was so extreme.' He swallowed hard. 'With that one, selfish act, she denied me the possibility of a family of my own. Someone to care for, for the first time.'

'Oh, Vieri.' Pulling back the covers, Harper scrambled to the end of the bed, kneeling before him and placing her hands over his clasped fists.

'And I believe that is the reason I have found it so hard to let it go.' He pushed on to the end, determined to be honest with himself—with her.

'Of course. I understand completely.' Reaching up, Harper touched his cheek with the back of her hand, a gesture so gentle, so simple, but so right. Vieri felt his heart melt. 'And all those emotions were stirred up again when you thought I had done the same thing.'

'No.' For the first time Vieri realised that wasn't true.

He reached for her hand. 'No, this is different. The reason I reacted so violently when I thought you had had an abortion is because…' he hesitated, discovering the truth as he spoke the words '…because I want this baby. So very much.'

'I see.' Harper withdrew her hand and sat back on her heels, a wariness creeping into her voice.

'No, you don't.' He moved to the side of the bed. 'This has nothing to do with my childhood or what Donatella did or the family I have never had. It is simply because this baby is ours, Harper, yours and mine. That's what makes it so special.'

'Well, thank you for sharing that with me.' She turned her head away, as if unwilling or unable to process his words.

'It is I who should be thanking you.' Suddenly Vieri realised how true that was. Catching hold of her chin, he turned her to face him again, searching deep into her eyes. Beneath the vulnerability he could see such tenderness, such compassion that something shifted inside him. Like a beam of light shining through the gloom of his past existence, he realised that the anger that had been with him so long had lifted, gone, miraculously evaporated. Donatella meant nothing to him any more. *And Harper everything.*

But still he hesitated, still he tried to hold back the surge of emotions that was straining to break free. He had to think about Harper now, what was best for her. The cruel way he had treated her in the past tormented him, but he had always been so sure it had been for her own good. To protect her from the man he was—from his blackened heart. A heart that had been so badly damaged all those years ago that it had petrified inside him, like a chunk of fossilised wood. But now as he looked into those remarkable autumn-coloured eyes he realised he had been wrong all along. His heart hadn't been irretrievably damaged after all. He had just never come across anyone to breathe life into it. Until now.

Outside the rain was coming down heavily, the wind lashing it against the small window, darkening the room. Taking hold of Harper's hands, Vieri solemnly held them before him.

'I have so much to thank you for, Harper.' He spoke quietly, feeling his way, his voice competing with the sound of the rain. 'You are the most remarkable, beautiful, caring woman I have ever met. But it is time for someone to take care of you. I am that person. From now on I am going to look after you, you and the baby. I promise you, you will want for nothing.'

Harper held herself very still. She could see the sincerity in his eyes, feel it in his voice, almost believe that, for once, she was all that mattered. *Almost.* She gave her head a small shake. 'You don't need to do that.'

'Oh, but I do, *cara.* More than you could possibly know.' He stroked the palms of her hands with his thumbs. 'From now on you and our unborn child are all that I care about. Your happiness is everything to me.'

'Vieri... I...' Harper pulled away her hands and, slipping off the bed, came and stood before him. Vieri could see her bottom lip staring to quiver, hear the threat of tears in her voice.

'Please, Harper,' he quickly tried to intercept. 'Let me do this. I know that you have every right to hate me after the way I have treated you but let me try and make it up to you.'

'That's just it, Vieri. I don't hate you.' Now the tears were starting to fall, silently rolling down her cheek. 'I could never hate you. I almost wish I did.'

'But why?' He frowned down at her anguished face, uncomprehending.

'Because to hate you would be much easier.' She took in a short, brave breath. 'Loving you is the hard thing.'

There, she had said it. Like stepping off a cliff, Harper felt herself go into freefall, the world spinning around her. By opening up to her, Vieri had released her to say the thing that had been haunting her for so long. And to her surprise she felt a profound sense of release. A calm sense of 'what will be, will be'. *Que sera sera.*

'What are you saying, *cara*?' Vieri leant in, searching her eyes for answers.

'I'm saying that I love you, Vieri. With all my heart.'

With tears still blocking her throat, she waited as Vieri took in this information, refusing to let herself try and analyse the fleeting expressions of shock and surprise that were flitting across the face that she loved so much. Finally, silently, he wrapped his arms around her, pulling her into a tight embrace.

'But why do you cry, *cara*?' He breathed into the tangle of her hair.

'Because I never meant for this to happen.' Buried against his shoulder, Harper felt the torrent of words begin to tumble from her mouth. 'And I know you don't feel the same way and that's fine because we will still be good parents and raise our child together and I don't expect anything from you, romantically I mean, because I know you couldn't give that and…'

'Harper!'

'…and I would certainly hate you to think that you had to stay with me out of some sort of pity. That would be awful and totally unacceptable, of course.'

'Harper, stop!' Pulling away, he gazed into her face. 'Let me speak. I need to tell you something. I need to make you see what is here, in my heart.' He spread his hand across his chest. 'You mean everything to me, Harper, *everything*.

With or without the baby, you are the centre of my world. My world would have no meaning without you in it.'

A delirious sensation flooded through her, weakening her bones, stealing all words. But Vieri hadn't finished yet.

Brushing a strand of hair away from her heated face, he held her gaze with an intensity that permeated her very soul. 'Because I love you, Harper. With my whole being. With everything I have to give.'

'You do?' Her eyes were bright with shock.

'I do. And I am only sorry that it has taken me this long to realise.' Clasping her hands, he poured out his confession, determined that she should see it, *feel it*. 'Now I know the truth I realise it has been there all along. I love you, Harper, and I want to spend the rest of my life with you. That's if you will have me, of course.'

'Oh, Vieri!' With a certainty that set her heart alight, she realised it was true. He really did love her. Every bit as much as she loved him.

His lips came down on hers, softly at first, but immediately deepening as the ecstasy took hold, the heat of their love spreading between them until they melded together as one. Until they were kissing, not just with their mouths but with their breath and their blood, their hearts and their souls. All that they were.

'Can I take that as a yes?' Pausing for a second for them to catch their breath, Vieri pulled back to gaze down at her.

'Yes, Vieri.' She tipped her chin, her eyes shining. 'You can.'

'*Mille grazie, mio amore.* I can't tell you what that means to me.' He brushed her lips again. 'I'm just wondering...' He looked over her shoulder. 'D'you think there is room in that bed for two?'

With a wide smile, Harper took his hand. 'Don't you mean three?'

'I do, don't I?' Vieri stared at her, shaking his head in amazement. 'You and the baby—I have to be the luckiest man alive.'

Outside the window the rain had stopped and a brilliant rainbow arced across the sky. Whether it was in agreement or celebration or merely a meteorological coincidence didn't really matter. Snuggled up in bed, lost in the wonder of their joy and very, very much in love, Vieri and Harper knew that, no matter what, their happiness would last for ever.

EPILOGUE

'WE ARE HERE, *mio figlio*.' Bringing the car gently to a halt outside the *castello*, Vieri turned to look at his precious cargo. His wife, Harper, and beside her, asleep in his car seat, his newborn son. 'Welcome to Castello di Trevente.' Harper smiled back at him and Vieri's heart swelled with tenderness and love.

Being there as his wife gave birth to their child had been the most exhilarating, terrifying, astonishing experience of his life. The labour had been long and seeing Harper in pain hard to endure and at times his concern for her had almost got the better of him. Only Harper's calm insistence that she was in control had stopped him from roaring down the corridors to demand somebody did something, or summonsing every medic in the land to come to her aid if necessary.

But in the end his beautiful, brave Harper had done it all on her own, with just the help of the midwife, who had made it clear she had no time for Vieri's histrionics. Seeing his son take his first lungful of air, then lovingly held against Harper's chest, had all but undone him, the whole miracle of life almost too much to take in. And when the baby had been wrapped in a towel and handed to him, when he had gazed into his son's deep blue eyes for the first time, the full swell of emotion had taken over. And Vieri had done nothing to try to hide it.

Now, only twenty-four hours later, here they were, back at Castello di Trevente. And their life together as a family could finally begin.

'Here, let me.' Opening the car door, he helped his wife out, then went round to unbuckle the baby's car seat. Coming beside him, Harper slipped her arm through his and together the three of them ascended the steps to the entrance.

'Wait a minute.' Putting down the car seat, Vieri lifted out the baby and, cradling him in the crook of one arm, clasped Harper's hand with the other. 'There, that's better. Alfie needs to have a better view of his new home. Look, Harper, he's opened his eyes.'

It was true, he had. And as Harper gazed at her baby son cradled in Vieri's arm she thought she might burst with happiness.

The housekeeper opened the door, duly fussing over the baby as if he was the most remarkable infant in the world, which clearly he was. Going into the salon, they settled themselves on the sofa as she bustled off to bring them some refreshments.

Harper looked around her, at her husband, her son, at the beautiful room they were now in, still having to pinch herself that it was real. Discovering that Alfonso had left them Castello di Trevente as a wedding present had been the most wonderful surprise. They had been living here for a couple of months now, and, although in some ways it still felt like a dream, it was also starting to feel like home. The whole place had been beautifully refurbished, a project that Harper had loved overseeing during her pregnancy, apart from when Vieri was fussing over her and insisting that she was doing too much. Now it was the most amazing for ever home that Alfonso had wanted for them. All the more so since baby Alfie had joined them.

'Are you comfortable? Can I get you anything?' Slipping one arm around her shoulder, the other still holding Alfie, Vieri pulled her close.

'No, I'm fine.' She reached for his hand, threading her fingers through his. 'In fact, everything is perfect.'

'It is, isn't it?' Leaning in, Vieri kissed her softly on the lips. Alfie, pressed between them, gave a small grunt of disapproval.

'Though we had better make the most of the peace and quiet.' Harper pulled a mirthful face. 'We've got Leah and my father descending on us tomorrow.'

'Don't remind me!' Vieri looked down tenderly at his son. 'Don't worry, *figlio*, I will protect you from your mad auntie Leah.'

Harper laughed. 'She's just excited, that's all.' It was true that Leah's constant calls as she had waited for news of the birth had been a bit over the top, eventually leading to Vieri insisting they turned off their mobile phones. But, of course, she had been the first one Harper had called when Alfie had finally arrived—Harper's eardrums were still recovering from her shrieks of joy. 'I'm so glad Dad has agreed to come with her.'

'Me too.' Running the palm of his hand over Alfie's soft, downy head, he addressed his son. 'From now on we guys have to stick together.' He looked back at Harper. 'I have to say I like your father. I think we are going to get on fine.'

'He is a good man. It was just that after Mum died he lost his way.'

'Grief can do strange things to a man.'

'Indeed.' They locked eyes, Vieri acknowledging Harper's knowing look with a wry smile. 'And the project you have involved him in has given him a new lease of life. He's a changed man. Thank you so much for that.'

'*Nessun problema.* Your father has such a wealth of knowledge and I intend to exploit that to the full while he's here. I have set up meetings with a couple of my land managers to see about starting to keep game birds on some of the estates. It could turn into a lucrative business. I'd happily employ Angus full time if he'd let me.'

'Dad's roots are in Scotland and the Craigmore estate is his life's work. You will never persuade him to leave. Leah, on the other hand…'

'No-o-o.' Covering Alfie's small ears with his strong hands, Vieri recoiled in mock horror. 'We didn't hear that, did we, Alfie?'

Laughing, Harper gave him a playful punch on the arm and Vieri pulled her in for another kiss. 'I don't mean it. Your family is my family now. And I have to say, that feels surprisingly good. Plus, of course…' he gave her a cheeky grin '… I am very much looking forward to increasing its numbers. I think it is our duty to provide lots of brothers and sisters for Alfie.'

'Our duty, eh?' She raised her eyebrows at him.

'There may be some pleasure involved along the way.'

Harper laughed again, knowing for certain that there would.

'And to think this is all down to Alfonso.' She offered her finger to Alfie, who took it in his tiny grasp. 'We have so much to thank him for.'

'We do indeed.'

'I hope he would approve of what we've done with the *castello*.' She glanced around her. 'It looks very different from when he lived here.'

'Believe me, Alfonso won't be worrying about the decorations. He'll be too busy gloating over the way his plan has come together. I bet he's looking down feeling thoroughly pleased with himself.'

'You think?'

'I know. And his spirit will always be here at Castello di Trevente. He is part of the fabric of the place.'

'That's true. And of course his name will live on in this little one.'

'So it will.'

Kissing the top of his son's head, Vieri turned to his wife. 'And together, my most beautiful Harper, I know we will make him proud. The future starts here, *amore mio*, with you, me and baby Alfie. And it is going to be the most wonderful future ever!'

* * * * *

HER
WEDDING NIGHT
SURRENDER

CLARE CONNELLY

For Kylie Adams,
who has supported and encouraged me from the start.

PROLOGUE

'SO, LET ME get this straight.' Pietro stared across his desk at the man he'd idolised for the better part of two decades. 'You're actually asking that I marry your daughter—a woman thirteen years my junior, a woman I barely know. And why, exactly, do you suppose I'll say yes?'

Across from him Col shifted in his chair, his own gaze direct. 'Emmeline is a beautiful and intelligent woman. Why are you so offended by my suggestion?'

Pietro's scepticism on that score wasn't something he wished to communicate to his friend. Nor the belief he held that Emmeline was either painfully shy or vapid.

'I have no intention of marrying anyone,' Pietro said, neatly sidestepping the question. 'Ever.'

'Even better. Marrying Emmeline isn't going to skittle any lingering love affair for you.'

Pietro's lips were a gash, scored across his face. He spoke emphatically and with the kind of iron-like command that had his corporate opponents running scared. 'There will be no marriage.'

Col smiled at the swift rebuke. Apparently the commanding tone that Pietro's business adversaries feared was inconsequential to Col.

'I love you, Pietro. Like a son. You and Emmeline are the most important people in my life. I *need* you to marry her.'

'Why? Where has this come from?' Pietro leaned forward, analysing every flicker of the older man's face.

'I've been thinking about it for a few weeks.'

'Why?' Pietro pushed, certain now that he wasn't seeing the full picture.

Col exhaled slowly and his eyes dropped away from Pietro's. 'Emmeline wants to go to university. She's found a place in Rome. I've told her she may come here to study, with my blessing. But only so long as she marries you.'

'And she has agreed?' Pietro snapped scathingly, his impression of Emmeline as a limpet who'd signed her life away on a dotted line increasing.

'It took some discussion,' Col admitted gruffly. 'But, yes, she agreed.' His eyes held a defiant glint in their depths. 'Emmeline would do anything I ask of her. She's always been a good girl.'

A good girl? Pietro had to concentrate hard to stop himself rolling his eyes. Good girls were boring. Predictable. Dull. The description served only to reinforce his dim opinion of the Senator's daughter.

'So?' Pietro laughed, the sound rich with disbelief. 'I can keep an eye on your daughter without marrying her!'

'Damn it!' Col shouted, the words an angry curse on his lips. 'That's not enough.'

'Why not?' Pietro narrowed his eyes. 'What am I missing?'

Col's glare was defiant, his expression rich with displeasure. But after a burning moment of silence he nodded. Just once, but it was enough to signal a surrender of sorts.

'What I'm about to tell you stays in this room.'

Perplexed, Pietro jerked his head in agreement.

'Swear it, Pietro. Swear you will keep my confidence.'

'Of course.'

Pietro had no concept of what he was agreeing to, at that point, so it was easy to go along with the Senator's insistence.

'There are only two people other than myself who know what I'm about to tell you. Not even Emmeline knows.'

A *frisson* of anticipation drummed along Pietro's spine. He stayed silent, waiting for the Senator to continue.

'There's no easy way to say this. I'm dying.'

Pietro froze. He felt his body go into a kind of shocked

stasis. 'What?' he heard himself query after a long moment, and the word was almost sucked out of him.

'Dying. My oncologist thinks I've probably got a few months in me yet.'

He leaned forward, and the determination in his gaze sent shivers running down Pietro's spine.

'They won't be *good* months, though. I want Emmeline as far away from me as possible. I want her happy. Safe. Protected. I want her blissfully unaware of what's happening to me.'

Pietro felt as though a slab of bricks had landed on his chest and was determinedly squeezing all the air out of him. He'd lost his own beloved father to cancer twenty years earlier. The idea of going through that again turned his blood to ice.

'That can't be right.' He ran a palm over his eyes and stared at the Senator with renewed interest. He looked so well. Just as always. 'Have you had a second opinion?'

'Don't need one.' Col shrugged. 'I saw the X-rays. Cancer everywhere.'

Pietro swore in his own tongue. It had been a long time since he'd felt so powerless. 'I'm sorry.'

'I don't want your apology. I want your help. Damn it, I'm *begging* you for it.'

Inwardly, Pietro groaned. He would do almost anything for the older man. But marrying his daughter...?

'Surely Emmeline would prefer to find her own partner...'

'Who?' Col scoffed. 'Some fortune-hunter? She's going to be worth billions of dollars when I die. *Billions*. Not to mention inheriting the estate and the oil rig off Texas. And she's got no experience with the world.' He grunted angrily. 'That's *my* fault. After her mother died I wanted to protect her. I wanted to keep her away from all that was ugly. I did a damned good job. But now I find myself with a twenty-two-year-old daughter who's about to be orphaned—and, hell, Pietro, I need to know that someone will look after her.'

'I will,' he assured Col, meaning it.

'The occasional email won't cut it. I need her living under your roof. Emmeline *needs* looking after.'

'You say she doesn't know about the cancer?'

'Absolutely not. And she's not going to.'

'What are you talking about?'

'I want to spare her this pain. I owe her that much.'

Pietro felt frustration gnawing through him. Of all the requests he'd expected, this was nowhere on the list he'd prepared.

'It's the only thing I've ever asked of you, Pietro. Promise me you'll do this. For *me*.'

CHAPTER ONE

'YOU DON'T LIKE ME, do you?'

She regarded the handsome Italian thoughtfully, taking in his expensive suit, thick dark hair, dark chestnut eyes and lips that looked as if they were made to curse and kiss. Lower, there was the cleft in his chin, then broad shoulders and a muscled chest. Yes, even though he was wearing that suit she knew it would be muscled. There wasn't an ounce of spare flesh on him—just toned, honed body.

A shiver ran down her spine as she wondered just how the hell she was going to go through with this.

Marriage to this man? Talk about a baptism of fire. No experience—and she had very little anyway—could have prepared her for this.

He didn't answer. Had he even heard? She'd asked the question quietly, in a sort of stage whisper.

She sucked in a breath and focussed on him anew. 'I said—'

'I know what you said.'

His voice was accented. Thick with spiced consonants and mystery. He drummed his fingers—long fingers, with neat nails and a sprinkling of hair over the knuckles—on the arm of his chair.

'It's late. Would you like a coffee? Something stronger?'

Emmeline shook her head and her hair, which was long and lay flat down her back, moved a little, like a shimmering curtain. 'I'm fine.'

He compressed his lips and stood, moving across the room with a stride that spoke of raw, feral power. She watched as he took the glass lid off a decanter and tilted it, filling a round highball tumbler with amber liquid. He threw at least half of it back in one go and then spun the glass in his hand, his fingers moving easily around its circumference as he rotated it purposefully.

'I know this all seems crazy…' Emmeline murmured, her eyes large as they found his.

The force of meeting his gaze startled her and she looked away again just as quickly.

His lips curled in an expression of derisive acknowledgement. '*Un po,*' he agreed. 'A little.'

'The thing is, I don't want to upset my father. I've never been able to bear the idea of hurting him.'

Her eyes flicked to his again, and this time she held his gaze, forcing herself to be brave. If she wanted this man to be part of her plan, her bid for freedom, then she needed him to know she wasn't afraid. Even though the charcoal depths of his eyes made her stomach flip and churn, she kept her courage.

'Since my mother died he's wrapped me up in cotton wool. And I've let him.'

She bit down into her lower lip. Contrary to his first impression, it was a full, pleasingly shaped lip, Pietro realised distractedly, before throwing back another measure of Scotch.

Emmeline's sigh was a soft exhalation. 'I've felt for years that I should assert myself more. That I should insist on the freedoms and privileges that any other person my age would have.'

'So? Why have you not?'

For Pietro's part, the very idea of Emmeline's rarefied existence was abhorrent. Virtually from infancy he had bucked against restraint of any kind. He had always wanted more of everything—particularly independence and maturity.

'It's hard to explain.' *Even to herself!*

She had struggled for years to come to terms with the life she was leading—*choosing* to lead, in many ways.

'After Mom's suicide he fell apart. Keeping me safe,

knowing I was protected—it became an obsession for him. I couldn't bear to see him hurt again like he was when she died.'

Pietro froze, his body stiff, his expression unknowingly wary. The expression in Emmeline's face touched something deep inside him, tilting him way off balance.

'Yes,' she said, answering his unspoken question, interpreting his silence only as surprise. 'I do know how she died.'

Her face drained of colour and she crossed her slender legs in the opposite direction, her hands neatly clasped in her lap.

'Your father went to great lengths to…to protect you from the truth.'

'Yes.' Her smile was twisted, lop-sided. 'I just told you—protecting me from *everything* has become somewhat of an obsession to him.'

When had Emmeline come to realise that her father's protection was hurting her? That his well-intentioned benevolence was making her miss out on so much in life?

'How did you find out?'

The gravelled question dragged her back to their conversation, and to a dark time in her life that she tried her hardest not to think about.

'I was fifteen—not five,' she said with a lift of her shoulders, her expression carefully neutral. 'He wrapped me up as best he could, but I still went to school and kids can be pretty brutal. She drove into a tree, sure—but it was no accident.'

Her eyes showed all the emotion that her face was concealing. Perhaps under normal circumstances he might have comforted her. But these weren't normal circumstances and she wasn't a normal woman. She was to be his bride, if he agreed to go along with this.

As if he had any choice! The loyalty and affection he felt for Col, combined with the older man's terminal diagnosis, presented him with a black and white scenario.

'I don't think he ever got over losing her, and he's terrified of something happening to me. As much as this all seems crazy, I can see why he feels as he does.' She cleared her throat. This next part was where she really had to be strong. 'So, yes. I think we *should* get married.'

The laugh that escaped his lips was a short, sharp sound of reproach. 'You don't think I'm the kind of man who'd like to ask that question myself?'

'Oh...'

Her eyes narrowed speculatively and there was a direct confidence in her gaze that unsettled him slightly.

'I think you're the kind of man who has no intention of asking that question *ever*. Of *anyone*.' She cleared her throat again. 'If the gossip pages are to be believed, you're more interested in installing a revolving door to your bedroom than settling down.'

His smile was laced with icy disdain. 'Is that so?'

'Your...*exploits* are hardly a tightly guarded secret.'

She bit down on her lip again, her eyes dropping to the floor. The lighting was dim, but he could see the flush of pink in her cheeks.

'No,' he agreed softly.

The word should have been a warning, but Emmeline had no experience with men at all. And definitely not with men like Pietro Morelli.

'I don't propose you stop...um...that...' She waved a hand in the air, the dainty bangles she wore jingling like windchimes on the eve of a storm.

'Don't you? My, my—what an accommodating wife you'll be.'

'I won't *really* be your wife,' she pointed out quickly. 'I mean, we'll be married, but it will be just a means to an end. I imagine we can live perfectly separate lives.'

She tilted her head to the side thoughtfully, recalling the details she'd seen of his sprawling mansion on the outskirts of Rome.

'Your house is enormous. We'll probably hardly see one another.'

He rubbed a hand over his stubbled chin, somewhat mollified by her realism in the face of such a ludicrous suggestion. At least she wasn't getting carried away with fairy tale fantasies, imagining herself as a Disney princess and he as her long-awaited Prince Charming.

'And that wouldn't bother you?' he drawled, his eyes raking over her from the top of her bent head to the curved body and crossed legs.

She was the picture of boring, high-society America. No fashion, no sense of style or personality—just a beige trouser suit with a cream blouse and a pearl choker wrapped around her slender, pale neck. Why would *any* twenty-two-year-old choose to style themselves in such a fashion?

'Of course not,' she said, the words showing her surprise. 'I just told you—it wouldn't be a real marriage. My father will be comforted by knowing that we're married—he's so old-fashioned—but I don't think he expects it to be some great big love-match. It's a dynastic marriage, pure and simple.'

'A dynastic marriage?' he heard himself repeat.

'Yes. It's hard for people like us to settle down. To meet a person who's interested in us rather than our fortunes.'

She shrugged her shoulders and Pietro had the impression that Col had been fundamentally wrong about Emmeline. She didn't strike Pietro as particularly vulnerable. If anything, she had an incisive grasp of the situation that he hadn't expected.

'I definitely don't want your money. In fact I don't want anything from you. Just the freedom our marriage offers me.'

Why did that bother him? Her calm insistence that she would take his name and nothing else?

'My mother would like grandchildren,' he was surprised

to hear himself say. Baiting her, perhaps? Or trying to un-
settle her?

She laughed—a sound that caught him off-guard completely. It was a musical laugh, full of the colour that was
otherwise lacking from her.

'She probably already has several, given your reputation.'

Dark colour slashed across his cheeks. 'Are you sug-
gesting I have unacknowledged children running about the
place?'

She shrugged. 'Well, I guess it's a possibility you should
consider.'

His eyes narrowed thoughtfully. She had more spark
than he'd appreciated. It was hidden deep beneath the veneer of cultured, polite society heiress, but her intelligence
and acerbic wit were obvious now that he was actually in
a conversation with her.

'There aren't,' he said with finality. 'The responsibility
of parenthood is not one I would abandon.'

Yes, she could tell that about this man. He had a sombre,
ultra-responsible air.

'Then your mother may have to live with disappointment. At least she'll have the satisfaction of not seeing her
son in the society pages for all the wrong reasons every
weekend.'

She stood up, pacing across the room thoughtfully, reminding him powerfully of his own back and forth with
Col earlier that same evening.

'You would need to be far more discreet, though. I'm not
marrying you just to be embarrassed or ashamed. The outside world would have to think it was a normal marriage. I
suppose we'd have to attend some events together, be seen
out in public from time to time—that kind of thing. But
within the walls of your home you can do what you want
and with whom.'

'So if you were to walk into this room and find me having sex with one of my lovers you would not be concerned?'

Her heart *kerthunked* but she kept her expression neutral. 'Only from a sanitation perspective.'

He bit back a smile at her prim response. 'I see.'

'Daddy seems to think a quick wedding is for the best, and if we were to get married within the month I'd have time to enrol in a couple of subjects for next semester…'

'Subjects?' he asked, a frown marring his handsome face for a moment. Then he remembered her plans to study in Rome. The revelation of Col's cancer had thrown everything else from his mind, particularly Emmeline's reasons for pursuing this marriage.

'Yes. University. I presumed Dad told you?'

'He did,' Pietro agreed.

'Well, then, you see? I'm not going to be in your hair. I'll be out doing my own thing much of the time.'

'And there we may have a problem,' he said thoughtfully. 'While I appreciate your generosity in agreeing that my social life shouldn't be disrupted, I would have no such tolerance for you in return.'

Emmeline tilted her head to one side, her eyes meeting his with obvious confusion. 'What do you mean?'

'I won't marry a woman who wants to go out with other men. Who wants to sleep with other men.'

Emmeline pulled a face full of surprise. The possibility hadn't even occurred to her, but his hard-line stance wrought instant confusion. 'Why not?'

His eyes narrowed dangerously. 'Because it might create the impression that I can't satisfy my wife.'

'Oh, heaven forbid anyone should cast aspersions on your big macho libido,' she said, with a roll of her caramel eyes.

'That is a deal-breaker for me, *cara*.'

She darted her tongue out and licked her lower lip. She hadn't planned to go out looking for a boyfriend. The thought had really never entered her head. But, as she spoke to him now, the injustice of his being allowed to continue sleeping his way around Rome but having no such opportunity herself seemed manifestly unreasonable.

'Then maybe you should abstain as well,' she murmured, tapping a finger on the side of her mouth.

'That's not a very clever suggestion, is it?'

'Why not? It seems only fair.'

He prowled towards her. Yes, *prowled*. She felt like a bird pinned under a rock, with an enormous growling lion circling her, waiting for his moment of attack.

'Because I like sex,' he said, when he was only a step away from her. 'I am a red-blooded male and it's a part of my life. So if you force me to give up sex with other women that leaves only you...'

He left the rest of the sentence unfinished, hanging in the air between them like a plank she would definitely never walk.

'Okay...okay.' She lifted her hands in surrender, but it was too late to stem the wave of sensations that were besieging her body. 'No sex.' Her voice was thready. 'I mean, sex is fine for *you*.' She closed her eyes softly. 'And I'll talk to you if I meet someone I like...deal?'

He compressed his lips, his eyes studying her face. Her cheeks were flushed, her eyes wide, her lips slightly tremulous. Fascinating. Was that because she was annoyed? Or were more pleasurable emotions fuelling her physical response?

'*Si.*'

She expelled a shaking breath, nodding slowly. 'So we'll get married?'

'There are a few other matters to consider,' he said quietly, the words thickened by emotion.

'Such as?'

'Your appearance.'

She froze, her eyes shocked into clashing with his. Arcs of electricity shimmied and sparked between them. 'You mean how I look?'

His lips twisted into a tight, displeased smile. 'That is generally what a person's appearance means, is it not?'

She nodded, moving further away from him. She needed breathing room if she was going to keep a level head about her—particularly given this subject matter.

'What about it?'

'No one is going to believe I chose to marry you.'

He said it simply. So simply that she believed he hadn't meant to wound her.

'Why not?' She narrowed her eyes, hoping her face wasn't showing the effects of the cruelty his words were lashing her with.

'Because you're nothing like the kind of women I date. And, as you so rightly pointed out, there's more than enough images of me with that kind of woman available to anyone who cares to search for my name on the internet.'

As Emmeline had. And she'd seen glamazon after glamazon in those online images: tall, thin, voluptuous, and all stunning. Pietro Morelli had a 'type', all right.

'I like how I look,' she said, but her mind cursed her for the lie it was. Concealing her body and playing down her looks was a habit that had formed many years earlier, and she wasn't sure she had any desire to revise it.

'It would not take much effort,' he said quietly, his eyes moving over her dispassionately, assessingly.

A distant memory flashed before him of the first time he'd seen her, and the quick, instinctive desire that had warmed his blood before he'd remembered how young she was. She was naturally beautiful; why did she hide her looks?

Fire and outrage burned in her blood. 'No.'

He compressed his lips, hiding the amusement that shifted through him at her determined recalcitrance. 'If I'm going to go through with this I expect you to start dressing as if you actually have a figure and some kind of budget for clothing. It is what people will expect of my wife.'

She stared at him, agog. 'You're joking?'

'No, *carissima*. It's no joke.' His eyes roamed her face analytically. 'This is Roma. Find a boutique and worship your body, then I'll consider it.'

His arrogance and his grim, scathing indictment infuriated her, but the realisation of her dream, the closeness of her escape were things so close she could smell freedom and liberation and she wasn't going to let her appearance stop her.

Not for the first time, though, she felt the sharp needling of injustice at the lengths she had to go to in order to earn what most people perceived as a God-given right. What if she refused? Refused not just his request that she start to pay attention to her looks but also her father's suggestion that they marry? What if she took a credit card and just ran away?

It wasn't as if she hadn't thought about it. But the thought of what it would do to her father had always brought her swiftly back into line. She couldn't hurt him. But here she had a way to be independent *and* make her father happy. She just had to tick a few boxes along the way.

'Fine.' Determination and resilience still glinted in her eyes.

'Good.' He nodded crisply.

He reached into his pocket and pulled something out. Something small and white. When he handed it to her she saw it was a business card with a woman's name on it: *Elizabetta Ronimi.*

'This is my secretary's number. She will organise the details with you. Any time in the next month is fine for me.'

'You want *me* to organise our wedding?'

He shrugged, as though it didn't matter one bit to him. 'I presumed you'd hire someone to do it, actually, but you'll need to speak to Elizabetta regarding my availability and to co-ordinate your move to my villa. *Si?*'

'*Si,*' she mumbled wearily. 'I suppose that makes sense.'

'Good.'

She stared at him for several seconds before the penny dropped that she was being dismissed. Colour warmed her cheeks as she moved towards the chair she'd occupied and scooped up her clutch purse.

'I'll have Remi take you home.'

'Remi?'

'My driver.'

'Oh, right.' She nodded, but then shook her head. 'I can grab a cab,' she murmured.

He stopped her on the threshold to the room, his hand curving around her elbow. Warmth spiralled through her body, making her blood pound. Her gut twisted with something like anticipation and her mouth was dry.

'He will soon be your driver too, *cara*. Go with him.'

She didn't want to argue. She wanted to get out of there by the quickest means possible.

'Thank you.'

'Non ce di che,' he said softly. 'See you soon, Mrs Morelli.'

Emmeline's eyes swept shut as she stepped out of his office, one single question pounding through her brain.

What the hell have I just agreed to do?

CHAPTER TWO

THE SUN WAS high in the sky and beating down over Rome, but Emmeline barely felt it. She was cold to the centre of her being, anxiety throbbing through her.

In the end it had taken five weeks to get all the paperwork in order, including a swift visa application for Italy, helped in no small part by the last name that had always opened doors for her.

But who was this woman looking back at her now? She had a growing sense of desperation as she studied her own reflection, doubt tangling in her gut.

'Aren't you glad we went with the Vera?' Sophie asked, wrapping an arm around her best friend's shoulders, her own expression not showing even a hint of doubt. 'You're a vision.'

Emmeline nodded slowly. Sophie was right. The dress was exquisite. A nod to nineteen-twenties glamour, with cap sleeves and a fitted silhouette, its beading was perfect, and the shoes she'd chosen gave her an extra lift of height— not that she needed it.

Her hair had been styled in a similarly vintage look, pulled to one side and curled lightly, then held in place with a diamond clip that had belonged to Grandma Bovington. At her throat she wore a small diamond necklace, and vintage earrings completed the look. Her make-up was the work of some kind of magician, because the woman staring back at Emmeline actually looked...*nice*.

Beautiful?

Yes, beautiful.

'I guess we should get going.'

'Well, yeah, we're a little late—but that's your preroga-
tive on your wedding day, isn't it?'

Emmeline grimaced, lifted her head in a brief nod.

'Honey, you're going to need to work on your happy
face,' Sophie said quietly. 'Your dad's never gonna believe
this isn't torture for you if you don't cheer up.'

'It's not torture,' she said hastily.

Though she'd kept the truth behind this hasty marriage
to herself, Sophie knew Emmeline well enough to put two
and two together and get a glaringly clear picture of four.

'It had better not be. I've seen your groom already and—
whoo!' She made an exaggerated fanning motion across her
face. 'He is hotter than a spit roast in hell.'

Emmeline could just imagine. Pietro Morelli on *any*
given day of the week was more attractive than a single
human being had any right to be, but on his wedding day…?
Well, if he'd gone to half the trouble and expense she had
then she knew she'd better start bracing herself.

'Suit?'

'Yes. But it's how he wears it!'

Sophie grinned, and it occurred to Emmeline that Sophie was far more the type of Pietro's usual love interest.
With silky blonde hair that had been styled into a volumi-
nous bun on the top of her head and in the emerald-green
sheath they'd chosen for her bridesmaid's dress, there was
no hiding her generous curves in all the right places and
legs that went on forever.

Sophie was also a political daughter—though of a congressman rather than a senator—and yet she had a completely different attitude to life and love than Emmeline.
She'd always dated freely, travelled wherever and whenever she wanted. For every measure of obsessive attention
Col had suffocated Emmeline with, Sophie had been given
a corresponding quantity of freedom and benign neglect.

Emmeline had read her emails from Sophie with rapt

envy, studying the photographs and closing her eyes, imagining herself alongside her friend. What had Paris on a spring evening smelled like? And how had Argentina been in the summer? And what about that time she'd travelled on a yacht around the Mediterranean, stopping in the French Riviera for a month just because it had taken her fancy?

But all that was ahead of Emmeline now. Soon it would be *her*!

This marriage was crazy in no small part, but it was also the smartest thing she'd ever done. Marriage to Pietro was freedom—freedom to live her own life without hurting her father. Freedom to explore, travel, to *live*—away from Annersty and yet not carrying the burden of having let her father down.

Was there any other way? A way that would give her *true* freedom? The kind of freedom that *wasn't* purchased by marriage? The freedom of knowing she could live her own life?

She bit down on her lower lip, her eyes unknowingly haunted. Of course there was. She could have packed a bag and announced that she was leaving home at any time.

So why hadn't she? Because she'd been with her father when her mother had died. She'd seen the way it had killed a part of his heart, withered it forever, and she didn't dare do the same to him. She couldn't hurt him.

She was making the right decision. She'd get what she wanted, albeit in a not particularly easy way, and her father would be placated. And then, eventually, she'd divorce Pietro and all would be well.

A renewed glint of determination shifted through her eyes. 'Let's go.'

Sophie nodded her approval. 'Attagirl. That's better.'

She sashayed to the door of the small room at the back of the ancient chapel, craning her head out and nodding.

Music began to play—loud and beautiful. A mix of

organ, strings and woodwind. It was Pachelbel's *Canon in D*, a piece that Emmeline had always loved.

She watched as Sophie disappeared ahead of her, counted the ten seconds Maria her wedding co-ordinator had advised and then stepped out of the anteroom into the back of the chapel.

It was packed. The pews were crammed full of well-dressed guests. Many of her father's political friends had come, a few of her schoolfriends, and apparently all of Italy's upper echelons of society had turned out to get a look at the woman who'd finally brought renowned bachelor and commitment-phobe Pietro Morelli to his knees.

She moved along the back of the church, behind the last row of guests, smiling as she caught the eye of someone she vaguely remembered having met once or twice on her visits to the Capitol.

The smile clung to her lips as she saw her father waiting for her. His eyes were moist with unshed tears, his body slim and lean in a fine suit. He wrapped her in a bear hug, almost squashing her, and then kissed her cheek.

His eyes, when he pulled back, searched hers. 'Ready?'

She nodded, smiling brightly at him. She wouldn't let him think she had doubts. Having agreed to this, she wouldn't let him live with any kind of guilt over the fact that he'd pressured her into marrying a man she didn't know—a man called Pietro Morelli, no less!

'Good.' He nodded. 'I'm glad.'

He turned his body slightly and she turned with him, towards the front of the church. She looked past the acres and acres of guests, standing and staring with undisguised curiosity, and there was her groom.

Oh, boy.

Sophie really hadn't been exaggerating. In fact she might have waxed a little more lyrical about just how freaking gorgeous her groom looked. *All other Italian pin-ups—eat your heart out.*

His skin was darker than it had been a few weeks ago, as though he'd been out in the sun a lot. Emmeline tried not to imagine him sunbaking on the Riviera, with a suitably gorgeous companion all too willing to rub oil over his body. Was it an all-over tan? Of course he'd have a private spot to go around in the altogether...

Her father was walking, and she had no choice but to walk with him. One foot in front of the other. But as she got closer her trepidation doubled. Up close to Pietro, she was reminded powerfully of that handsome face with its permanent scowl and the dark, intelligent eyes, his chiselled jaw and symmetrical features. The broad body that she somehow just *knew* would be hard and warm.

His eyes met hers and there was something in them—challenge? Admiration? No, not that. But his look was intent. He stared at her long and slow, uncaring of the hundreds of guests assembled, nor the priest who was waiting patiently.

Col extended a hand and Pietro shook it. This evidence of their firm, long-held friendship gave Emmeline a much-needed boost. A timely reminder that he wasn't a wolf—well, not *just* a wolf. He was someone who had every reason and every intention to be just what they'd agreed. A convenient husband. He was simply a very handsome means to a definitely necessary end.

'*Cara,*' he murmured, low and deep, in a husky greeting that set her pulse firing and spread goosebumps over her flesh. He leaned in close, whispering to her through the veil that covered her face. 'This is more like it.'

Her heart turned over at the compliment, but something like impatience groaned in her chest—impatience that he might think she'd gone to all this effort for *him*; impatience at the fact that he was right.

She arched a brow and met his eyes without showing a hint of her turmoil. 'I thought about wearing a suit, but, you know... This seemed more appropriate.'

'Definitely. I almost wish I was going to be the one to remove it.' He straightened, the hit having met its mark.

Her cheeks glowed with warm embarrassment at his comment, and the effect it had had on her body.

Traitorous flesh.

Her nipples peaked, straining against the soft fabric of her bodice, and an image of him doing just that spooked into her mind. His suit would be rumpled, his jacket discarded, the tie gone, the shirt half unbuttoned with its sleeves pushed up to expose his tanned forearms. There were seemingly a thousand buttons on her dress—probably actually only fifty—and it had taken Sophie the better part of a half-hour to pull the dress together. Would he move slowly or quickly?

She swallowed, staring straight ahead.

The service itself was surprisingly swift. A simple recitation of vows, just as she'd seen in dozens of movies and television shows, preceded by the question about whether or not anyone objected.

That part had had Emmeline holding her breath, waiting, wondering—and strangely hoping no one would say *Yes, this is a sham!* She'd waited, watching intently as the priest's eyes had skimmed over the congregation.

Finally he turned to the couple, smiling brightly.

'Then without further ado, I now pronounce you man and wife.'

Not *husband* and wife, she noted in the small part of her brain still capable of rational thought. 'Husband' and wife would suggest that he too had been altered in some significant way by what they'd just done. 'Man' and wife made all the changes hers.

'You may now kiss your bride.'

She winced unknowingly. *Your* bride. A possessive phrase that spoke of ownership and rankled. Well, what had she expected? She'd chosen this path to freedom because it was easy. Because it meant she wouldn't have to upset her father. She deserved to feel a little objectified.

Her small facial expression of displeasure was easy for Pietro to discern. Seeing it pass across her face like a storm cloud, he wrapped an arm around her waist, drawing her closer to his body quickly, easily, giving her no chance to question his actions. His eyes briefly met hers and there was sardonic amusement at the heart of his gaze.

She tilted her chin defiantly, inadvertently giving him the perfect angle of access. He dropped his lips to hers, pressing them against her mouth, separating her lips easily and sliding his tongue inside.

It was an invasion of every single one of her senses.

Did he know it was her first kiss? Yes, her first kiss—at the age of twenty-two and on her wedding day. Shame made her toes curl and yet desire heated her up, right to the base of her abdomen. His fingers on her back feathered across her nerve-endings, and she made a small whimper low in her throat that only her groom could possibly have heard.

He broke the kiss, his eyes meeting hers laughingly.

Was he laughing at her?

Her heart was racing, banging against her ribs so hard she thought it might crack them. Her breath was burning inside her body and she stared at him in a tangle of confusion. It took at least ten seconds for her to remember where she was and who she was with.

'I would slap you if all these people weren't watching us,' she muttered under her breath, pasting a tight smile to her face.

His lip lifted in sardonic mockery. 'Or would you rip my clothes off?' he pondered.

But before she could respond, he reached down and took her hand in his.

'They *are* watching, so keep pretending this is the happiest day of your life.'

By the time they'd reached the end of the aisle, having

paused several times to accept good wishes and hugs of congratulation, Emmeline's mouth was aching from the forced smile she'd adopted.

A crowd had formed beyond the church and there was a throng of paparazzi. Inwardly, Emmeline trembled at the idea of being photographed. Her husband apparently had no such qualms.

'Ready?' he asked, pausing just inside the door, sparing a quick glance at her face.

Then again, why *would* he hesitate? This was his life. If the number of photographs of him on the internet proved anything it was that he was followed and snapped often. He probably couldn't walk down the street without someone taking his picture.

But Emmeline's life hadn't been like that. A handful of society events had led to her picture sometimes being splashed in the papers, though not often. She was too drab. Boring. Ugly. Why print a picture of Emmeline Bovington unless it was to compare her unfavourably to the renowned beauty her mother had been?

She closed her eyes, sucking in a deep breath, and was unaware of the way Pietro's eyes had caught the deceptive action.

He studied her thoughtfully. He'd seen panic before, and he saw it now. Was this idea *so* unpalatable to her? Hell, she'd suggested it and her father had railroaded him. If anyone should be panicking it was Pietro.

Her hesitation annoyed him—probably more than it should. He stepped out through the door, holding her hand and bringing her with him into the brightness of the Italian afternoon. The steps towards the street were empty, but beneath them was a large crowd, and as they erupted from the church applause broke out. Rose petals were thrown high into the air. The noise was deafening.

He smiled, lifting a hand in acknowledgement, and turned towards his bride.

There it was again.

Panic.

Blinding, devastating panic.

Impatience crumpled his common sense and quickly ate up his judgement. He caught her around the waist and this time he tipped her back in a swoon worthy of an old black and white Hollywood movie.

His lips on hers were an assault; it was a kiss that gave voice to his annoyance when he wasn't otherwise able to. Her hands curled around his neck, her fingers tangling in the hair at his neck, and she made that noise again. That little whimper of confusion that made him hard all over.

That annoyed him even more, and he pressed his hands into her back, lifting her higher, pressing his arousal against her abdomen, leaving her in little doubt of just what kind of man she'd married.

It lasted only seconds, but when he eased her back to stand and pulled away from her the crowd broke out into thunderous applause.

Her eyes were thunderous too. Thunderously pissed off. He could practically hear the storm brewing.

Good. Let Little Miss Refined work on *that.*

'I swear to God, kiss me again and I'll wait until you're asleep and do some serious damage to you,' she said angrily, but her smile was plastered on again seconds later as Col came up behind them.

'I know I wanted this for you both, but seeing you together…' He shook his head wistfully, tears in his eyes. 'I could die a happy man right now.'

Emmeline laughed, not noticing the way her husband had stiffened at her side. 'God, Daddy, don't say that. You'll tempt the heavens.'

'Che sera, sera,' Col said with a shrug.

Emmeline dismissed that attitude. Her father was clearly thrilled that the wedding had taken place, and she wasn't going to take that away from him. Now there were several family photographs to pose for.

Emmeline had met Pietro's mother Ria a few times over the years, and it was easy enough to make conversation with her. His brother Rafe was similarly easy. At least five years younger, Emmeline wondered why *he* hadn't been suggested as a possible groom by her father. He boasted the same pedigree and was equally handsome. Less established in his career, it was true, but with their family fortune what did that matter?

'So, you're now my sister-in-law, eh?'

She returned Rafe's smile, and felt herself relaxing as they posed in the sunshine for the requisite shots.

Nonetheless, it was a relief when the photographer declared she had enough 'for now' and they were free to return to their guests. For Emmeline, that meant Sophie and a hint of normality.

'Ah, the woman of the hour.' Sophie grinned, passing her half-finished champagne flute to Emmeline.

'Don't remind me.' She took a sip, and then another, closing her eyes as the cold bubbles washed down her throat.

'So, Maria was just running through the details with me.'

'Ugh—there's still more, isn't there?'

Sophie laughed softly. 'The reception. But don't worry—that's just a cocktail party at a gorgeous restaurant overlooking the river.'

'Okay, I can cope with that.'

'Then you and Pietro will take your leave—insert catcalling and whistling—and the rest of us young, hip and happening people will have an open bar at some club that's just opened. Apparently your husband had something to do with the financing of it.' Sophie shrugged. 'Sounds kind of fun.'

Emmeline pulled a face. 'Not to me. I can't think of anything worse.'

'Yes, well… I'm sure you'll have your hands full anyway…'

Emmeline sent her friend a scathing look. 'Yeah, right.'

'Hmm, I saw the way you guys kissed. I know passion when I see it.'

Emmeline practically choked on her champagne. She coughed to cover it, lifting a hand to her mouth.

'Trust me—that's not what this is.'

'Then you need to get to a hospital, because if you can be in the same room as that guy and not need CPR then you are some kind of cold fish.'

'Or just a very sensible woman,' she said quietly.

The formalities seemed to last forever. Speeches. The cutting of the cake. Their first dance as a couple…

Emmeline stood in Pietro's arms, trying her hardest to pretend not to be affected by her husband's touch when a single look had the power to turn her blood to lava.

'So…' he drawled, the single word imbued with more cynicism than she'd known was possible. 'You are my wife.'

The sentence brought a smile to her face, but it wasn't a smile of pleasure.

'Don't sound so thrilled about it.'

He slowed the movement of their bodies, his eyes scanning the crowd. 'I can name three people who are beside themselves,' he said coldly.

She followed the direction of his gaze. Her father and his mother stood to one side, each of them beaming with obvious pleasure.

'Yeah, I guess this is a dream come true for Daddy,' she said with a small shake of her head.

There was a look of frustration in her eyes that Pietro thought about probing. But the last thing he wanted was to get to know his inconvenient bride any better.

'And for my mother,' he said simply. 'I'm sure she's imagining a lifetime of calm now that I've apparently hung up my bachelor shoes.'

'*Apparently.*' She repeated the word, rolling it around in

her mouth, wondering about the practicalities of what they'd agreed to. The idea that he'd be free to see other women so long as he was discreet.

It didn't bother her. At least that was what Emmeline told herself. And yet a pervasive sense of confusion filled her.

They would be living under the same roof, seeing each other in the hallways, the kitchen, the lounge, the pool. Despite her protestation that they'd be like flatmates, was it possible that she would be able to ignore her husband at such close quarters?

From the first moment she'd seen him she'd found him worryingly distracting, and the years hadn't stilled that awareness.

And now they were married...

'You are as stiff as a board,' he complained. 'Did you never learn to dance?'

Her cheeks flushed pink and the look she cast him was laced with hurt. 'I was lost in thought,' she mumbled, making an effort to pay attention to her husband.

'Dancing does not require your mind. It is something you feel in your body. It is a seduction.'

He rolled his hips and colour darkened her cheekbones. His body was every bit as fascinating as she'd imagined. All hard edges and planes, strong and dominating, tempting and forbidden in equal measure.

It would be playing with fire ever to touch him in earnest. This was different—a dance at their wedding was unavoidable. But Emmeline had to keep her distance or she'd risk treading a very dangerous path.

'Relax,' he murmured, dropping his head towards hers. 'Or I will kiss whatever it is you are thinking out of your mind.'

She started, losing her footing altogether. She might have fallen if he hadn't wrapped his arms more tightly around her waist, bringing her dangerously close to his body.

'Don't you dare,' she snapped.

His laugh was like gasoline to a naked flame.

'Then smile. Relax. At least pretend you are enjoying yourself.' He dropped his mouth to her ear and whispered, 'Everyone is watching us, you know.'

She swallowed, her eyes scanning the room over his shoulder. The room was indeed full of wedding guests dressed in beautiful clothes, all smiling and nodding as he spun her around the dance floor.

Emmeline's heart sank.

Pretending to be married to Pietro Morelli was going to require a hell of a lot more patience and performance than she'd envisaged.

It was late in the night and Emmeline stifled another yawn. Sophie had found a group of friends—as always—and was charming them with her wit and hilarity. Emmeline listened, laughing occasionally, though she knew all the stories so well they might as well have been her own. Still, sitting with Sophie and pretending to laugh at her hijinks was better than watching her husband.

Her eyes lifted in his direction unconsciously.

He was still talking to her. The redhead.

Emmeline's frown was instinctive—a response to the visual stimulus of seeing a stunning woman so close to the man she, Emmeline, had married only hours earlier.

The woman had auburn hair that tumbled down her back in wild disarray, and she was short and curvaceous, but not plump. Just the perfect kind of curvy—all enormous rounded boobs and butt, tiny waist and lean legs. Her skin was honey-coloured and her lips were painted bright red. Her nails, too. She wore a cream dress—wasn't it considered bad manners to wear white to someone else's wedding?—and gold shoes.

Who *was* she?

Pietro leaned closer, his lips moving as he whispered in the woman's ear, and the woman nodded, lifting a hand to his chest as she dragged her eyes higher, meeting his. From all the way across the room Emmeline could feel the sexual tension between them.

She stood without thinking, her eyes meeting Sophie's apologetically. *I'll be right back,* she mouthed.

Sophie barely missed a beat. She carried on with the story of the time she'd got caught flying from Thailand to London with very illegal monkey droppings in her handbag—she'd been sold them at a market and told they would bring good luck…whoops!—and Emmeline walked deliberately across the room towards her groom and the woman she could only presume to be a lover—past or future. She didn't know, and she told herself she definitely didn't care.

She was only a step away when Pietro shifted his attention from the redhead, his eyes meeting Emmeline's almost as though he didn't recognise her at first. And then his slow-dawning expression of comprehension was followed by a flash of irritation.

He took a small step away from the other woman, his face once more unreadable.

'Emmeline,' he murmured.

'Pietro.' Her eyes didn't so much as flicker towards the woman by his side. 'I need you a moment.'

His lips twitched—with amusement or annoyance, she couldn't have said. He walked towards her, putting a hand in the small of her back and guiding her to the dance floor.

Before she could guess his intentions he spun her around, dragging her into his arms and moving his hips. Dancing. Yes, he was dancing. *Again.*

She stayed perfectly still, her face showing confusion. 'I don't want to dance any more.'

'No, but you want to speak to me. It is easier to do that if we dance. So dance.'

'I…' Emmeline shook her head. 'No.'

He slowed his movements and stared at her for a long, hard second. 'Why not?'

'Because it's not my...thing,' she mumbled, looking away.

Mortification filled her. So many things she'd never really done. Experiences she'd blindly accepted that she would never enjoy. She'd made her peace with that. But now, surrounded by so many people who'd all lived with such freedoms as a matter of course, wasn't it natural that she was beginning to resent the strictures of her upbringing?

Her voice was a whisper when she added, 'As you so wisely pointed out.'

'Then let me show you,' he said.

And his hands around her waist were strong and insistent, so that her body moved of its own accord. No, not of its own accord; she was a puppet and he her master.

Just as she remembered—just as she'd felt hours earlier—every bit of him was firm. His chest felt as if it was cast from stone. He was warm too, and up close like this she could smell his masculine fragrance. It was doing odd flip-floppy things to her gut.

'You told me you'd be discreet,' Emmeline said, trying desperately to salvage her brain from the ruins of her mind. 'But you looked like you were about to start making out with that woman a moment ago.'

'Bianca?' he said, looking over his shoulder towards the redhead. Her eyes were on them. And her eyes were *not* happy. 'She's a...a friend.'

'Yeah, I can see that,' Emmeline responded, wishing she wasn't so distracted by the closeness of him, the smell. What was it? Pine? Citrus? *Him?*

'Are you jealous?'

'Yes, absolutely,' she said with a sarcastic heavenwards flick of her eyes. She leaned closer, lowering her voice to a whisper. 'We have a deal. I just don't want our wedding guests to see you with another woman. What you do in *pri-*

vate is up to you.' She let the words sink in and then stopped moving. 'I'd like to go home now.'

Pietro wasn't used to being ashamed. He was a grown man and he'd lived his own life for a very long time. But something about her calm delivery of the sermon he really did deserve made a kernel of doubt lodge in his chest.

He knew he should apologise. He'd been flirting with Bianca and Emmeline was right: doing that on their wedding day wasn't just stupid, it was downright disrespectful. To his bride, sure, and more importantly to their parents.

He stepped away from her, his expression a mask of cold disdain that covered far less palatable emotions. 'Do you need anything?'

'No.'

'To say goodbye to anyone?'

She looked towards Sophie, enthralling her newfound friends, and shook her head. 'I'd rather just go. *Now.*'

Silence sat between them and she waited, half worried he was going to insist on doing a tour of the room to issue formal farewells.

But after a moment, he nodded. 'Okay. Let's go, then.'

He put a hand on her back but she walked away, moving ahead of him, making it obvious she didn't need him to guide her from the venue. She'd walk on her own two feet.

She hadn't made this deal with the devil to finally find her freedom only to trade it back for this man.

Emmeline Morelli was her own woman, and seeing her husband fawning all over someone else had simply underscored how important it was for her to remember that.

CHAPTER THREE

SHE'D EXPECTED A LIMOUSINE, but instead Pietro directed her to a low, sexy black Jaguar, parked right at the front of the restaurant.

He reached for the front passenger door, unlocking it at the same time, and Emmeline sat down quickly, stupidly holding her breath for some unknown reason. What did she think would happen if she breathed him in again?

He closed the door with a bang and a moment later was in the driver's seat. The car throbbed to life with a low, stomach-churning purr, and he pulled out into the traffic with the consummate ease of a man who'd grown up in these streets and knew them well.

Silence stretched between them and it was far from comfortable. The car had a manual transmission and required frequent gear changes from the man with his hand curved around the leather gearstick, his strong legs spread wide as he revved the engine, his arm moving with the gears.

There was an athleticism in his movements even when simply driving a car.

Emmeline ground her teeth together and focussed on the passing view of starlit Rome. Her new home.

She hadn't thought about what it would mean to leave Georgia behind. At most she'd contemplated the sadness that would come from not seeing her father so often. But there was so much more than that. Annersty was the plantation she'd called home all her life, in the town where she'd grown up, with all the people she knew...

'Tell me what you see for yourself, in the future, pumpkin?' her father had asked her.

'I don't know, Daddy. *This*. I like it here...'

'But one day I won't *be* here.'

His voice had been soft, yet it had cut like glass through her flesh.

'*One* day,' he'd said to calm her, and the words had been reassuring, referring to a time that was distant-seeming. 'But I'd want to know you've got a family of your own to make you happy.'

'I hardly know Pietro—and what I do know I don't think I like.'

He'd given a laugh of genuine amusement. 'He's a good man. Do you think I'd be pushing for this if I didn't thoroughly believe that?'

Her eyes had met his and she'd seen the truth in them. She'd nodded then, sealing her fate with that single gesture.

A soft sigh escaped her lips. She had agreed to this and there was no sense in getting all remorseful now. She'd married Pietro Morelli and they both knew it was a marriage in name only. She held that reassurance close like a talisman.

Yet what was that vitriolic acidity in her gut? It frothed angrily when she remembered the way he'd been looking at that redhead—Bianca—as though he wanted to lick her all over.

An angrier sigh pressed from her lips and Pietro turned his head, studying her in the intermittent light cast by the streetlamps they drove beneath. She looked pretty damned good, despite his assertion weeks earlier that she was far from the kind of woman he was attracted to. It wasn't as though she'd made any major changes—only it was the first time he'd seen her in a dress, wearing make-up, heels, and with her hair done in a style other than a plain ponytail.

He fought the urge to ask her how she was feeling. It wasn't his business and he sure as hell didn't care.

He pressed his foot harder onto the accelerator, chewing up the miles to his home.

The gates swung open as they approached and he eased the car along the curving drive, pulling it up outside the garage. His fleet of vehicles was housed inside and his mechanic would be waiting to give the Jaguar a once-over. He cut the engine and turned to say something to his bride, though he wasn't sure what.

There was no point, in any event. Her hand was on the door and she was pushing it outwards before he could articulate a thing.

She stood tall and proud, her eyes running over the façade of the building, studying it as if for the first time.

'Nothing's changed,' he said, the words darker than the night that surrounded them.

She flashed him a tight smile. 'Yes, it has.' Her eyes looked bigger somehow, and the moon was drawing out flecks of amber and gold from amongst their caramel depths. 'I live here now.'

Pietro's expression was grim, and Emmeline flinched inwardly. Her own shock at the fact that they were now married was dwarfed only by his, and yet he made a decent show of pretending normality.

'I'll show you to your room. Come.'

She thought about making a joke—wasn't it a tradition to carry a bride over the threshold of her new home?—but the tightness of his back as he walked away, the firm angle of his head, showed how little he wanted to laugh about this situation.

Emmeline followed, her gaze wandering over the façade of his house as she went. It was an impressive building. If she had found her host…no, her *husband*…less intimidating she would have asked him a little about it. Still, a place like this had to be in the history books; she could do her own research. Especially once she was at uni and had access to a fantastic library.

She breathed in, imagining the scent of all those books. Renewed purpose reassured her. There was a reason she'd married him. She had to keep that firmly in mind and then all would be well.

'It's late. I won't give you the tour now. Tomorrow the housekeeper will show you where things are.' He stood with his hands in his pockets, his attention focussed squarely ahead.

'That's fine, only...'

'*Si?*' It was an impatient huff.

'Um...where am I supposed to sleep?'

His expression contorted with irritation but he moved forward, down a long corridor, then turned left and took her up a flight of stairs.

'These rooms are for your use.'

He pushed a door inwards, showing her a practical space that had been set up with a desk, a bookshelf and a tread-mill. The latter made her smile, though she covered it with a yawn.

'Very good.'

'There is a bathroom through there. And your bedroom is here.'

He nodded towards a third and final door and she turned the handle and pushed the door inwards, her eyes scanning the room with interest.

It was not dissimilar to a particularly lovely five-star hotel. A king-size bed made up with nondescript white bed linen and silvery grey throw cushions, a white armchair near the window and yet another book case, and double doors that presumably concealed a wardrobe.

With increasing interest she stepped into the room, the thick beige carpet soft underfoot.

'No books?' she murmured, eyeing the almost empty shelf. The sole book in its midst was a tourist guide to Rome and she refused to believe its placement had anything to do with her husband. He wasn't thoughtful like that.

'This has been used as guest accommodation in the past,' he said softly. 'The décor is neutral in order to accommodate the guests I've had staying here. You are free to add your own touches—furnish it with whatever books you wish.'

She fluttered her eyelids exaggeratedly. 'Even if I want to paint the walls lime-green?'

His smile was dismissive. 'Your choice. It is not as if I will ever be in here to see it.'

She laughed, but there was a thunderous rolling in her gut that she didn't want to analyse. Anxiety, she told herself. She had taken herself out of the comfiest little nest in the world and dropped herself like a stone into the deep end of a raging river.

'So, hot pink then?' she joked, walking towards the window.

She hadn't noticed at first, but as she got closer she saw that it was in fact French doors, and beyond the window was a small Juliet balcony.

Her heart fluttered as she turned the handle and opened the door, feeling a warm breeze breathe in off the city. They were far enough away that she could make out Rome's landmarks with ease, see their place within the cityscape.

'Your suitcases are in the wardrobe,' he said, definitely impatient now, calling her attention back to the important business of getting settled. 'I wasn't sure if you'd find it invasive for the housekeeper to unpack for you. Let me know if you'd like me to send her up…'

Emmeline waved a hand in the air dismissively. 'I can manage.'

'Fine.' A curt nod. 'My room is down at the other end of the hallway. Last door on the right-hand side. If you need me.'

As in, *Don't bother me unless you're on fire, your room is falling away from the building, and there is no one else you can think of to call.*

'Okay.' She smiled—out of habit rather than happiness.

He paused on the threshold for a moment, his eyes glittering like onyx in his handsome face. *'Buonanotte, cara.'*

'Goodnight.' The word came out as a husky farewell. She cleared her throat but he was gone.

Emmeline stretched her arms over her head and then moved towards the door to her room, pushing it shut all the way until it clicked in place.

This was her home now.

She shouldn't think of herself as a guest, nor of this arrangement as temporary. She'd married him—for better or for worse—and, while she wasn't stupid enough to imagine they'd stay married forever, this was certainly her place in life for the next little while.

The doors did open on to a wardrobe, as she'd suspected, and her two suitcases sat in the centre. She'd unpack in the morning, she thought, when she had more energy. She pushed one open and pulled out a pair of cotton pyjamas and the prospectus for her university course, putting them on the foot of the bed.

Her feet were aching, her body was weary, her mind was numb. What she needed was a hot shower and the pleasant oblivion of sleep.

She reached around to the back of her dress and groaned out loud. The buttons. The damned *buttons*.

The mirrors in the wardrobe showed exactly what her predicament was. There were what seemed like hundreds of the things; they'd taken Sophie an age to do up, and without help Emmeline would never get out of her dress.

Obviously she could sleep in it. Sure, it was heavy and fitted, and she wouldn't exactly be comfortable, but it would save her any embarrassment and she could simply ask one of the staff to help her the following morning.

Or... a little voice in the back of her mind prompted.

She grimaced. Yes, yes. *Or...*

She pulled the door inwards and peered down the corridor. It was longer than she'd appreciated at first, and somewhere at the end of it was the man she'd married.

Refusing to admit to herself that she was actually a little bit scared, she stepped into the hallway and walked down it, paying scant attention to the artwork that marked the walls at regular intervals. At the end of the corridor she waited outside the last door on the right, taking a moment to ball her courage together.

She lifted her hand and knocked—so timidly that she knew there was no way he would have heard the sound.

Shaking herself, she knocked harder:

Once.

Twice.

Her hand was poised to knock a third time, and then the door seemed to be sucked inwards. Pietro stood on the other side, his face unforgiving of the interruption.

'Yes?' It was short. Frustrated.

'I...' Emmeline swallowed. 'Am I interrupting?'

'Do you need something?'

Her eyes clashed with his—angry gold against unreadable black.

'This is in no way an invitation...'

His lips flickered for the briefest second into a genuine smile. It was so fast she thought she might have imagined it.

'Fine. What is it?'

She spun around, facing the wall of the corridor directly opposite. 'There's a billion buttons and I can't undo them. I guess wedding dresses are designed with the fact in mind that a bride won't be undressing alone...'

'Apparently,' he murmured, moving closer.

She knew that because she could feel him, even though he didn't touch her. His warmth seemed to be wrapping around her like an opportunistic vine up an abandoned wall.

'Would you mind?' she asked quietly, keeping her attention focussed on the bland whiteness of the hallway wall.

'And if I did?'

'I suppose I could find some scissors somewhere...' she pondered.

'No need.'

And then, even though she'd come to his room for this express purpose, the sensation of his fingertips brushing against her back made her shiver. Her nipples strained against the fabric of her gown in a new and unexpected sensation.

'Are you cold?'

The question caught her off-guard. She bit down on her lip, willing her body to behave, her pulse to quiet, her heart to settle. But her body had its own ideas, and it continued to squirm, delighting in his closeness and his touch.

'I'm fine.'

His laugh was soft, his breath warm. It ran across her back like a wildfire she should have paid better attention to.

He pushed at the first button, flicking it open expertly. *One down, nine hundred thousand to go*, she thought bleakly. He dragged his fingers down to the next button and her stomach rolled with awareness.

Emmeline sucked in a deep breath.

He wasn't *trying* to turn her on; this was just how he was. The man oozed sensuality from every pore of his gorgeous, perfectly tempting body.

Still, as he undid the second button and moved on to the third the dress parted an inch at the top, and she was sure it wasn't an accident that his fingertips moved across her skin as he lowered them to button number four.

He worked slowly, and for every second she stood in front of him she felt as if her nerves were being pulled tight, stretched and tormented. At button number twenty he wasn't even halfway down her back, and a fever-pitch of heat was slamming through her.

Had he undone enough for her to take the dress off? She wasn't sure, at this stage, that she much cared if the dress got torn, so long as she could get it off without subjecting herself to another moment of...*this*.

Oh, maybe one more moment, she conceded weakly, sucking in a deep breath as his fingers grazed the flesh near where her bra should be. She hadn't needed one in the dress; its boning was sufficient.

Lower still, and the next two buttons came apart slowly. His fingers were achingly close to her lower back, to the inches of flesh that dipped towards her rear.

No man had ever seen her there, let alone touched her. His fingers lingered on her flesh, not moving downwards, just stroking her skin. Her pulse hammered and her eyes drifted shut on a tidal wave of imagining and longing, on hormonal needs that had long ago been relegated to the back of her mind.

'I… I…' The word stammered out as a dubious whisper. 'I can cope from here,' she said quietly, even though her body screamed in silent rejection of her comment.

He ignored her. His hands moved lower, to the next button, pushing it through its beaded loop, separating the fabric, and then his fingers were back, lingering on the flesh exposed by the undone dress.

'That's enough,' she said again, with more strength to her words, and she backed them up by moving a step forward, away from him, and slowly turning around.

His eyes almost electrified her. They were full of something—some strange emotion she couldn't process. His jaw was clenched tight and there was displeasure lingering in the harsh curves of his lips.

'Thank you,' she said softly, unaware of how pink her cheeks were, how enormous her pupils, how full her lower lip from the way she'd been savaging it with her teeth.

His eyes dropped to her mouth, and unknowingly she darted her tongue out and licked its edges. His own lips flickered in a small sign that he'd seen the nervous gesture, before his gaze travelled lower, to the curve of her breasts no longer held firm by the dress.

'Did you want to join me, *cara*?' he drawled, those eyes lifting back to hers with something like *knowing* buried in their depths.

She shook her head quickly from side to side, but still

she didn't move. Her throat was dry, parched, and it stung as though razorblades had been dragged along it.

'I think you do.'

His smile flickered again, but it was a harsh smile, thoroughly without pleasure.

'I think your nipples are tight and aching for my touch. I think your skin is covered in goosebumps because you want me to kiss you all over. I think you came to me tonight because you're curious about whether sleeping with me would feel like that kiss outside the chapel.'

She stifled a groan. 'But...'

'But?' he prompted, reaching out a hand and capturing hers, lifting it to his lips.

She had expected a kiss, but instead he dug his teeth into the ball of her thumb and arrows of heat and need shot through her, making her knees shake and her back sway.

She couldn't speak. She could barely think. Sensation and feeling were all that was left in her.

'But you are a virgin?' he prompted, her inexperience not even a question.

Was it emblazoned on her skin somewhere? Like the opposite of a scarlet letter and something only he could see?

'And you are saving yourself for someone you love?' He dropped her hand and let out a harsh sound of laughter. 'Rather a shame, given you've just married *me*.'

His eyes returned to hers with renewed speculation.

'How do women like you even *exist* in this day and age?'

There was anger in the question—an anger she didn't understand.

'Women like me?' She was surprised that her voice came out smooth and calm—cold, even.

'A virgin at twenty-two! Did your father lock you up in some kind of a chastity belt? Build a moat around Annersty?'

Emmeline shook her head. 'Neither.'

'So you just aren't interested in boys? In sex?'

Emmeline grimaced, her cheeks flushing darker. 'I guess not.'

'Your body's reaction to me would dispute that.'

'You're imagining it.'

His laugh was soft. 'Careful, Mrs Morelli. One touch and you melt like butter in my hands. Imagine if I pinned you back against that wall and kissed you as though I wanted so much more from you...'

The image filled her with a sense of strange confusion. She *wanted* him to do that. At least a part of her did. A crazy part. The part that had no pride and no rational ability to think.

'I'm sure I'd be very disappointing after the women you're used to,' she said stiffly, sounding so prim that she cringed inwardly.

He didn't say anything. His hand lifted and reached for the cap sleeve of her wedding dress, and slowly he guided it lower. So slowly that she had plenty of opportunities to say something. To object. But she didn't. She watched him with hooded eyes as he drifted it downwards, the fabric a torment as it pulled over the skin at her décolletage and then lower, exposing one of her breasts to the night air—and to his eyes.

They were neat breasts—not huge. But nor were they tiny—and they were firm. His eyes studied her, but she couldn't tell what he was thinking.

'Has a man ever touched you here?' he asked, the question gravelled.

She shook her head, biting down on her lip.

'Do you want *me* to touch you?'

A slick of moist heat formed between her legs and her eyes were anguished as they met his. She nodded. Just a tiny, almost involuntary movement of her head, accompanied by a mask of abject fear on her face.

He laughed softly, dropping his hands to her waist and yanking her closer. His body was hard all over, and she could feel the hint of his arousal through the fabric of her dress. A moan was thick in her throat.

'And I thought this wasn't an invitation,' he said with sardonic mockery, dropping his head so quickly she couldn't anticipate his intention, moving his mouth over the swell of her nipple and rolling his tongue over its unsuspecting tip.

She cried out at the stark feeling of pleasure. It came out of nowhere and it practically cut her off at the knees. His face was stubbled, and the contrast of his rough chin across her soft breast, and the warm wetness of his mouth, the lashing of his tongue...

She was melting—just as he'd said she would.

Swirling need pounded inside her, creating a vortex of responses she'd never imagined possible. Her body was experiencing its first awakening, and any thought of words or sense had fallen from her mind. There was only this.

She could hear herself mumbling incoherently, needing more than he was giving. A wave was building and she had no idea when and how it would crash. Only knew that it was imperative she stay on it, surf it right to its conclusion.

He dragged his lips higher and she cried out at this abandonment of her nipple. But his hand lifted up and cupped her breast, his thumb and forefinger taking the place of his mouth, twisting and plucking at its sensitised nerve-endings until she was crying out over and over, a fever-pitch of sensation rioting inside her.

His other hand pushed her forward, holding her tight against him as his lips sought hers, kissing her as his hands moved over her, and she cried into his mouth as the feelings became too much, her awareness of him too great.

'Oh, God, please...' she groaned into his mouth, with no idea of what she was asking for, only knowing that she needed *something*. Something he alone could give her.

He pulled away, lifting his head at the same moment as he dropped his hand and stepped backwards. His look was one she couldn't fathom. His chest was moving rapidly, his jaw clenched, but she couldn't understand why he'd stopped. Arousal was a raging river in her bloodstream.

'Go to your room, Emmeline.'

The way he said her name was like warm butter on hot toast. It dripped over her body.

Did he mean *with him*? Was he going to come with her? Her confusion was muddied by the way her body was crying out for him.

'I'm not interested in breaking in virgins.'

He turned away from her, stalking into his own room and picking up the glass of Scotch that was resting on the bedside table.

Her jaw dropped. She stared at him, confused and bereft. 'I'm sorry?'

'No need to apologise,' he said, with a shrug of those broad shoulders.

His hair was tousled. Had *she* done that? Had she run her fingers through it so that it now stood at odd angles, all messy and gorgeous?

'I'm not... I wasn't apologising,' she said, her voice thick with emotion. 'I don't understand why you stopped. I don't—'

His accent was coarse when he was angry. 'I'm not interested in sleeping with you. It would complicate things and undoubtedly be unsatisfying, for me.'

She drew in a harsh breath, her eyes flashing with pain.

'Don't be offended,' he murmured. 'I'm just used to more experienced lovers.'

Mortification curled her toes, flushing away any lingering desire. She spun on her heel, walking quickly down the corridor. It was only when she reached her room that she realised she'd come the whole way with her breast still uncovered.

Pietro stared into his whisky, his expression grim.

That had been a mistake. He could still taste her on his

lips, smell her on his clothes, hear her sweet little moans of fierce, hot need as though she were still with him. Worse, he could *feel* her—like a phantom of the night he *could* be having if only he hadn't pulled things to a stop.

He was hungry for her…hard for her.

Col's daughter.

A groan permeated the silence of the room and bounced off the walls, condemning him as it echoed back. He'd married her to save her. He'd married her because he'd felt obliged to help his friend out.

Desiring his wife had never been part of the equation.

And he had to damned well do a better job of remembering that.

CHAPTER FOUR

IT WASN'T AS though she'd lived a particularly active and busy life. Confined to Annersty, her company had been made up predominantly of the staff, her father and the schoolfriends she'd caught up with from time to time for lunch.

But life in the villa was utterly silent.

A week after their wedding, and she'd barely seen her groom.

Thank God! The less she saw him, the less she'd need to remember what a fool she'd been in his arms. What a weak, willing, stupid *idiot*. Shame over that night still had the ability to make her blush.

She wandered further along the citrus grove, reaching up and plucking an orange blossom from a tree as she passed, bringing it to her nose and smelling its sweet fragrance.

Oh, they'd seen each other a few times. Once the next day, when she'd been walking around the villa like a lost lamb having escaped slaughter.

He'd come out of a room which she'd subsequently learned was his home office, full of enough technology to power a spaceship. Their eyes had met and he'd arched a brow—a simple gesture that had conveyed derision and scepticism. She'd dipped her head forward and moved past him, her heart pounding, her cheeks burning, her whole body confounded by mortification.

Two days had passed before she'd seen him again, that time in the evening. He'd walked in through the front door just as she was passing. And he'd looked tired. World-weary. He'd loosened his tie so he could undo his top button, and his jacket had been removed. She'd managed a tight smile and a nod of acknowledgement before she'd scurried away, and even kept her head up as she'd gone.

There were oranges growing in this part of the citrus grove, and further down the gently sloping lawn were lemons and limes. Beyond them were quinces and then olives.

It was a perfect Mediterranean garden—just as she'd always fantasised such a spot would be. She paused at the end of the row, turning around and looking down the hill towards Rome. The sky was streaked with orange and peach: a hint of the sunset that was to follow.

The warmth was quite delicious. She felt it on her skin and smiled. Her first genuine smile since before the wedding.

University would help. She needed activity. Something to do to keep her mind busy. Distracted from *him*. Her husband. And the treacherous way her body had responded to him.

She needed to remember her reasons for embarking on this charade! For the first time in her life she had a semblance of independent freedom, and she didn't want to waste it by pining for a man who didn't even like her. Hell, he barely seemed to notice she existed.

This marriage wasn't about lust and need. It wasn't about him.

It was about *her*. It was her vehicle to going out into the world at last.

A whisper of discontent breezed through her but, as always, Emmeline ignored it. She had stayed at Annersty, stayed under the same roof as her father, because it had been the *right* thing to do. Just as marrying Pietro to assuage her father's obvious concerns was the *right* thing to do.

And the fact that it spoke of a lack of faith in her own abilities? That it spoke of her being infantilised to an unbearable degree? She wouldn't think about that. She *couldn't*. For she knew where that path would take her, and criticising her father, whom she adored, was not something she would countenance.

All that mattered was that she had left home—*finally*. She was in Rome. A smile tickled at her lips and once more she felt the sunshine warm her skin.

At twenty-two, she'd finally done it!

Her phone buzzed, startling her out of her reverie. She lifted it from the back pocket of her jeans and Pietro's face stared back at her from the screen.

Her heart pounded as she swiped the screen across. 'Hello?'

'Emmeline.'

There it was again. The warm butter oozing over her skin. She closed her eyes and sank to the ground so that she could give him the full force of her concentration.

'Are you there?'

'Oh.' She blinked her eyes open and nodded. 'Yes. What is it?'

'Your father is coming for dinner tonight. Seven o'clock.'

Silence prickled between them. Then, 'Daddy's coming...*here*?'

'*Certamente.* Naturally I presumed you'd want to see him again before he leaves for the States.'

Emmeline nodded, but consternation ran through her. She *had* intended to see her father again—only for coffee the following morning, when it could be just the two of them.

'Right.' She bit down on her lip.

'My assistant will let Signora Verdi know,' he said, referring to the housekeeper Emmeline had met once or twice. A matronly woman who filled her with a sense of awe.

'Fine,' she said, a little too sharply.

'Though he knows our marriage was arranged to serve a purpose, I think it would be good for him to see that we are...getting along.'

Emmeline's stomach churned. *But we're not.*

'Do you?' she asked.

'*Si*. He loves you very much,' Pietro said, but his tone was weary. Impatient. 'Seeing you happy will make *him* happy.'

'So you want me to fake it?' she snapped, before she could catch back the sarcastic rejoinder.

'I want you to think of your *father*,' he said softly. 'As you've proved yourself so very good at in the past.'

'What's that supposed to mean?'

'You married me to make him happy.'

A woman's voice filtered through into the call and acid spiked Emmeline's blood. She couldn't make out what the woman said, but the tone was low. *Personal*.

Jealousy—unmistakable—pricked at her flesh.

'I'll be home by six. And, Emmeline? Perhaps wear a dress.'

Outrage simmered in her blood as she disconnected the call. Wear a damned *dress*? He actually thought he could boss her into wearing whatever the hell *he* wanted? What *he* thought would be appropriate? True, since their wedding she'd gone back to the clothes she felt most comfortable in, and they were hardly the kind of clothes that would set the world on fire. But of all the rude, misogynistic, barbaric things to say!

She stood up, her hands shaking as she jammed the phone back in her pocket and stared out at Rome.

She'd show him, wouldn't she?

At ten minutes past six Emmeline walked into the formal dining room, intending to pour herself a stiff drink to steel her nerves. What she hadn't expected was to see her husband already at the bar, shaking a cocktail mixer.

She froze on the threshold, taking a deep breath. She had only a second to compose her face into a mask of calm before he looked up. And when their eyes met she was thrilled to bits that she'd put her plan into action.

It had involved hours of shopping—her least favourite activity by a mile—but the effect was worth it.

The dress was exquisite. It had the advantage of looking as though it had been made for her—in a silk fabric that clung to her breasts and hips and stopped several inches shy of her knee—and it had batwing sleeves that fell to halfway down her hands, giving her a sense of comfort. The front had a deep vee—far deeper than she'd worn in her life before. She'd teamed it with a pair of espadrilles, which made the look a little more casual for an at-home dinner.

'I'll have what you're having,' she murmured, with a veneer of confidence she was far from feeling.

He began to shake the drink once more with a tight nod. 'Nice dress.'

The compliment made heat flood through her body. 'Thanks.'

'It makes it almost impossible to remember that you're a sweet and innocent little virgin bride.'

Emmeline fought her natural reaction of embarrassment, which he must have been trying to goad her towards. She saw beyond it. Her eyes narrowed and she moved closer, watching as he poured the martini into a glass and curling her fingers around its stem before he could even offer it to her.

'That bothers you?'

'It confuses me,' he corrected, reaching for more bottles of alcohol and sloshing it into the mixer. 'Particularly when you are dressed like this.'

'So one's choice of attire is an indicator of sexual inclination?'

'No. But dressed like this you are…irresistible.'

She sipped her drink to hide her reaction, and then spluttered as the alcohol burned its way down her throat. 'Ugh—that's strong.'

'It's a martini,' he pointed out seriously. 'It's meant to be strong.'

She nodded, taking another sip, and this time it went down more easily.

'Why do you dress like you do?' He returned to their previous conversation.

'Why is it any of your business?' she fired back, her eyes holding his even when she wanted to look away.

'It interests me. You are an attractive woman who goes out of her way to hide her assets. It makes no sense.'

Emmeline turned away from him, surprised by how easily he'd surmised the truth of her situation. 'Not everyone thinks their worth is derived from their appeal to the opposite sex.'

He made a sound of disagreement. 'But to take pride in one's appearance isn't just about meeting someone, or attracting a lover. It's a sign of self-love to want to look your best.'

'I don't agree,' she murmured, even though she'd never really thought beyond the opinions she'd formed in her teenage years.

'But don't you feel *better* in this dress?'

He walked towards her, a glass in his hand, his eyes holding hers. She stared at him, refusing to cower even as nerves fluttered inside her.

'Don't you *like* the way you look tonight?'

'I don't like the way you're looking at me as though you want to rip it off,' she said thickly, sipping her drink.

His laugh was a slow, sensual cord, wrapping around her. And was she imagining there was something like tension in the harmless sound? The air in her lungs was burning, exploding...

'We've already discussed that. I'm not interested in being the man who teaches you to feel.'

He lifted a finger and ran it across her lower lip, then dragged it lower, and lower still, to the fabric that joined at the centre of her chest. Then lower to her navel. She gasped as he ran it over her womanhood and paused, lingering there, padding his thumb across a part of her body that no man had ever touched.

'Though I'd be lying if I said that right now it doesn't hold at least *some* appeal.' His words appeared to be almost dragged from him, as though against his will.

Confusion and doubt were back. Uncertainty. Her insides were swirling and without her knowledge her body swayed forward.

'I wonder if you would orgasm quickly...' he murmured distractedly, and a sharp swell of need made her groan.

She nodded—but what was she even nodding at?

His lips twisted into a hard-fought smile and he pulled his hand away. She made a small whimper of anger, and before she knew what she was doing her free hand had curled around his wrist, catching it and dragging him back.

'Careful, *cara*. I don't think you want to play with a man like me.'

'Why are you tormenting me, then?' she asked thickly, holding his hand still and pushing herself against him, her eyes wide, her body screaming with need. 'Why stir me up and then walk away? Is that *fun* for you? Do you *like* seeing me like this?'

'Fun? No. As for why I like doing this... I can't say. I suppose I'm a little like a cat with a ball of wool. The idea of a twenty-two-year-old virgin is not something I can understand. You fascinate me and I just don't seem able to help myself.'

'Then don't,' she whispered, sipping the last of her drink. 'Please.' She lifted her arms around his neck, and her lips sought his. *'Please.'*

'You're Col's daughter.' The words were gravelled. Dark and husky.

'And yet you married me.' She ground her hips against him, her eyes showing her every need and desire.

He swore into her mouth in his own language, and then his hand was running down her thigh, finding the hem of her dress and lifting it, pushing aside the fabric of her silky underwear. He brushed his fingers over her throbbing heat and she gasped, the sensation unlike anything she could have imagined.

'I'm not the right man for you to want,' he said.

And he was so right. But sensual need had overtaken any vestige of common sense.

'Shut up,' she said hungrily, and he laughed against her lips.

'Shut up and do this?' he asked, pushing aside the fabric of her underwear.

Her heart skidded to a stop. All she could do was wait. Wait for what came next.

If Emmeline had been capable of rational thought she might have cared a little more that they were in a room anyone could have walked into at any point. But she didn't. Fortunately her husband had his wits about him, and Pietro used his body to guide her back, so that she collided with a wall near enough to a corner to provide some cover.

His finger invaded her heat gently at first, nudging inside, preparing her slowly for the unfamiliar sensation. She whimpered as he pushed deeper, a cry catching in her throat as she throbbed around him, her muscles tensing and squeezing.

'God,' she groaned, grinding her hips, and he laughed softly, moving his finger in a swirling motion while his thumb found the cluster of nerves at her entrance and teased it.

Her blood was boiling beneath her skin like liquid iron. She breathed out hungrily, the rasping sounds punctuating the silence of the room, and then she bit down on her lip as the sensations began to overflow, making her face blotchy with heat and sweat bead on her brow. She curled her fingers into his hair, holding him tight, and scrunched up her eyes.

The overload of feeling was something she hadn't prepared for. Waves of arousal and satisfaction ebbed through her, rocking her to the core. She stayed perfectly still, letting them pound against her nerve-endings, and then she tilted her head back, resting it against the wall as her breathing slowed to normal.

He eased his finger out of her wet, pulsing core, and she made a small sound of surprise at the unwelcome abandonment. When she opened her eyes he was staring down at her, his cheeks slashed with dark colour, his eyes silently assessing.

The world stopped spinning.

Everything stopped except her breathing and her awakening.

She lifted a hand, curled her fingers into his shirt, needing him for support. She held him while she caught her breath—in and out, in and out—and he watched her the whole time.

Finally, after long moments of silent, stretching heat, he spoke.

'You are far too sensual to have been uninterested in sex. Were you forbidden from dating?'

Her mind was still reeling from what had just happened. 'I need a minute…'

She bit down on her lip but couldn't stop the smile that spread across her face. She was beautiful at any time, really, but like this she was angelic.

'What the hell was *that*?'

His frown showed confusion. 'What?'

'I… I just… *Wow.*'

His groan was somehow scathing. 'Tell me you have at least *touched* yourself?'

Should she have? God, she supposed she *should* have had at least a passing curiosity in her own sexual development. Shame that she hadn't ever explored this side of herself made her flush to the roots of her hair.

'I…'

'What the hell happened to you?' he muttered. 'How can you have ignored these feelings? This desire?'

She swallowed, but the insulting tone of his voice was making her defensive. 'Not everyone sees sex as the be-all and end-all…'

'Yes, they do,' he disputed, a rough smile in his voice. 'At least anyone who's had really great sex does.' He shook his head. 'I wish I'd known this about you before agreeing to this damned marriage,' he said angrily. 'You *need* to have sex. And fast. But not with me.'

Her heart turned over in her chest. 'Why not with you?' she prompted.

His eyes flashed with rich frustration. 'I told you. Educating virgins isn't my thing. I'm not looking for the complications of that.'

'Even with your *wife*?' she responded archly.

'Not a *real* wife, remember?'

She bit down on her lip and nodded. 'So? What am I meant to do?'

'Well, you've waited twenty-two years. I guess a few more won't kill you.'

But it might kill *him*, Pietro thought as he turned his back on her. Walking away as though he was completely unaffected was damned near impossible with the raging hard-on between his legs.

A virgin. And yet so gorgeous and wanton and sensual. God, he wanted to take her to his bed. Despite what he'd said, the idea of teaching Emmeline Morelli *just* what her body was capable of stirred all kinds of animalistic masculine fantasies in his mind.

Being the first man to move inside her… Hell, the need to possess her was so savage it was beneath him.

He couldn't do it.

He'd married her because he loved Col Bovington like a father, and he would resist the urge to sleep with Emmeline for that exact reason.

No matter how damned much he was tempted.

He was the adult. The *experienced* adult. He had to control this beast of desire that was burning between them or he'd never forgive himself.

'I've always liked Rome.'

Col's voice had a wistful note. Or maybe Pietro was imagining things, because, in the back of his mind—much as it must be in Col's—was one single question: was this the last time Col would come to Italy? Was this the last time he'd look down on this ancient city?

'It's a city like no other.' Pride pierced Pietro's statement.

'*Si,*' Col agreed, a smile on his face. His eyes scanned the skyline, taking in the glistening lights of the city in the distance set against the inky black sky. 'How is she?'

Guilt slashed through Col. A feeling that was as unwelcome as it was foreign.

'Is she settling in? Happy? Adjusting?'

Pietro could close his eyes and remember the way her body had felt. The way her body had closed around his finger. The sounds she'd made as she'd come—hard.

He clamped his teeth together and focussed on the cupola of *il Vaticano*, willing his libido to remember where he was and with whom.

'It's still very early,' he said noncommittally.

'But you *are* getting along?' Col pushed.

Pietro expelled a breath. 'Sure.'

If you could count barely seeing each other and then him making her come for no reason other than he'd wanted to the second he'd seen her.

'Good.' If Col had doubts he didn't express them.

Pietro propped an elbow on the bannister and turned to face his friend slowly, weighing his words with caution. 'I think you need to tell her the truth.'

'About what?' Col joked.

It fell flat.

'She's stronger than you think.' God, Pietro hoped that was true. 'She'll cope with it. What she *won't* cope with is discovering you've lied to her.'

'I know her better than anyone.'

Col's words held a warning and Pietro heeded it. Not because he was afraid, but because the older man was probably right. Col had drawn a line in the sand and Pietro had no intention of walking over it.

He sighed gruffly. 'Then *consider* talking to her.'

'I can't. I need her to have more in her life than me.' His eyes shifted to Pietro and his skin looked pale all over. 'If she knows she'll come home.'

'So? Let her.'

'No. *Damn it!* The whole point of this is… I don't want her to nurse me. She deserves better than that.'

Pietro was very still, watchful. Waiting. 'You don't want her to nurse you? She's your daughter. When my father was sick—'

'It's not the same.' Col seemed to wince at the abruptness of his answer. 'I'm sorry, Pietro. I don't mean to belittle what you went through. But it's not the same.'

'Why not?'

'Because she is my only child. She will be orphaned when I die. Because she adores me and idolises me and I will not have her seeing me weakened and bedridden.' His jaw clenched firmly. 'I love her too much for that.'

An aeroplane passed overhead, leaving a trail of white cloud shimmering against the night sky. Pietro stared at it for a moment, wondering about the plane's destination and the people that occupied its belly. He wondered too at Col's 'love'. *Was* it love that could so easily lie? *Could* you love someone and deny them an opportunity to say goodbye?

'Did you think he looked tired?' Emmeline asked when Pietro returned to the lounge room, having said farewell to the American Senator.

The question caught him off-guard in its directness and perception. Then again, she was the much-adored daughter of the man—of course she'd notice small changes.

'Perhaps.' He sidestepped the question with surprising difficulty, his gaze resting on Emmeline's face.

She was distracted, toying with the hem of her dress, her fingers running over its silky edge as she nodded slowly. He knew what that dress felt like because he'd held it in his hands. He'd touched it and run his fingers over it and then he'd found her heart and driven her crazy against the wall.

'He did. I suppose it's jetlag… Or something.' She shook her head. 'I don't know.'

He sucked himself back into the conversation with difficulty, his arousal straining against the fabric of his pants. It was unwanted. So was the guilt that was sledging through him. Guilt at deceiving her despite the fact he owed his loyalty to Col and not to Emmeline.

'I'm going out,' he murmured, speaking the words before he'd even realised what he'd intended.

'Out?' She frowned, flicking a glance to the slim wristwatch she wore. 'It's after ten.'

His laugh was softly mocking. 'In Roma that is still early, *cara*.'

Her cheeks darkened, and her eyes were huge in her face as she looked at him. Her pretty face twisted into an expression he didn't recognise, but then it was gone. She was herself again. Unfazed, uninterested.

'Fine,' she said. 'Thank you for tonight.'

'You're *thanking* me?' he said with disbelief. 'I invited your father here for my own purposes as much as yours.'

Her smile was a twist of pale pink lips and then she stood, moving towards him.

'I didn't mean for that.'

As she passed him he caught a hint of her vanilla and rosebud fragrance and his gut clenched with barely controlled need. The desire to snake his hand out and catch her around the waist, to pull her to him and make her come again, filled him like an explosion. His head turned as she left the room, following her by instinct. The way that dress pulled against the curves of her arse as she walked...the way her long legs glided as if she was in a damned ballet...

He needed to get out of the house before he did something really rash. Like give in to temptation and invite his wife to his bed...

CHAPTER FIVE

His bedroom was far enough away from hers that she wouldn't necessarily hear when he came home each night. But somehow in the month they'd been married her ears had trained themselves to hear the slightest noise.

Like the opening of his bedroom door and the shutting of it a second later.

She heard the tell-tale click and her eyes drifted to the bedside table. She reached for her phone, checking the time. It was just after two.

How did he do that so often and still look so damned fresh the next day?

She tried not to think about who he'd been with and where. Though she didn't need to be a genius to work it out.

He'd made no effort to hide his virility, and they'd agreed before marrying that he'd continue his life as before. And he was doing that. It was Emmeline's fault that it no longer sat well with her.

She turned over in the bed, flipping on to her other side so she could stare out of the window. It was still warm, with the breeze that drifted in offering a hint of relief—but not much. The day had been sticky.

Was there only one woman in his life? Was it the beautiful redhead from the wedding?

She closed her eyes and the woman's face came to mind. She'd been stunning—but so clearly cosmetically enhanced she should have borne her surgeon's signature somewhere on her body. Was that the kind of woman he went for?

Emmeline would never be like that.

She blinked her eyes open but it was too late. An image

of her mother had seared into her brain and she made a small sound in the dark room.

Patrice Bovington had been beautiful too. Stunning without cosmetic enhancement. But that hadn't stopped her from seeing her doctor regularly, having a little Botox dabbed into her forehead, a tad of filler in her lips. Over the years she'd changed, but so subtly that it was only in looking back at photos that Emmeline could recognise the fact that beautifying herself had become an unhealthy obsession for her mother.

And a foolish one too. For there would always someone more beautiful, more svelte, younger. Why make one's appearance the hallmark of one's self-esteem?

'You could almost be pretty if you put some effort in.'

She sat upright in the bed, the fever in her blood burning out of control. Did he *know* that looking pretty had led to all the problems she'd had with her mother? Guilt made her stomach flop as she remembered their last argument. The day before Patrice had driven her Mercedes convertible into an enormous elm around the corner from the house.

Emmeline rolled back to her other side, staring at the wall now. But it was no good. Her mind was wide awake, her legs restless, her body warm.

She sat up, then pushed her feet out of the bed.

She'd only swum a handful of times since arriving at the villa. Both times when she'd known Pietro was out of the house.

And now he was fast asleep—probably exhausted from seducing some beautiful woman all evening.

Emmeline changed into her swimsuit quietly. If she could hear the sound of *his* door clicking open and shut then he could certainly hear hers. She tiptoed out into the corridor, pausing for a second, her breath offensively loud in the silent evening.

The stairs were around ten steps away. She moved quietly but quickly, like some kind of night-time ninja.

She'd just wrapped her fingers around the top of the bannister when his door was flung open.

He stood there in a pair of shorts, otherwise naked, his scowl landing on her as though she'd driven a herd of elephants through the house.

'Did I wake you?' she whispered, not sure why she was keeping her voice down given the fact they were the only two in the house.

'No. I was up.' His eyes dropped to the swimsuit that was clearly on display, his frown deepening. 'It appears we've had the same idea.'

'Oh.' She didn't dare look at his shorts but, yes, she supposed they *could* be swimming trunks. 'It's a hot night...' she finished lamely.

His grunt was an agreement of sorts.

She prevaricated on the steps for a moment, contemplating going back to her room and then deciding against it. When he began to move towards her, though, her pulse kicked up a notch. Her breath was held in her throat.

'What are you doing?'

He looked at her as though she'd gone mad. 'Going for a swim. We just discussed this.'

'Oh. I thought...' She closed her eyes and breathed in deeply; it was a mistake. The smell of him filled her, reminding her of how it had felt when he'd touched her so intimately.

'The pool is more than big enough for the both of us.'

He was right, of course, and now she felt like an even bigger idiot. It was bad enough that he thought her some kind of inexperienced prim virgin. Worse when she confirmed those thoughts by acting just like one.

'I know that,' she snapped, resuming her journey down the stairs, moving quickly to stay ahead of him.

At the bottom she moved ahead—not waiting for him, not wanting him to think that she saw this as a joint venture.

He wanted to swim and she wanted to swim. That didn't mean they would be swimming *together*.

The air on the deck was noticeably cooler, but it was still a sultry, muggy night. It felt as though a huge bandage was pressing down on Rome, holding in its heat, making breathing difficult.

Emmeline dropped her towel onto a lounger and turned towards the pool—just as Pietro dived into the water, his body strong and flexed as he hit the surface and went underneath.

He was like a god, tanned and muscular, as if he'd been carved from stone. She watched the water separate as if to welcome him and then conceal him again, almost by magic. Her breath was held again inside her lungs—waiting, apparently, for the moment he reappeared at the other end of the pool when she let out a slow sigh.

'Well?' He turned to face her. 'Are you joining me, Mrs Morelli?'

Her eyes met his, and if she'd known about the look of anguished surrender in them she would have tried harder to conceal her feelings. But she didn't.

The moonlight sliced through her as she moved to the water's edge and dipped her toe in. As she'd hoped, it was deliciously cool.

She sat on the edge and then eased herself into the water. It reached up to her waist and enveloped her in its thick, luxuriant relief.

She didn't swim. Rather she walked across the pool, her face deliberately averted from his. He might have found it entertaining if he hadn't already been frustrated beyond belief. The idea of a cold swim had been essentially to serve the same purpose a cold shower might have. Instead his wife was swimming with him, her pert breasts outlined by the light cast from the moon, her enigmatic, aristocratic face tilted angrily away from him.

Was she angry with him? And, if so, why did he like the

idea so much? Why did he want to inspire that hot, fierce temper in her?

He dived underwater and swam the length of the pool, pretending not to notice as he passed her by and splashed water in her general direction.

When he surfaced she'd moved to the other end of the pool.

Was she hiding from him? The idea of her being the mouse to his cat was like a red rag to a bull. He dived underwater again and swam beneath the surface, stealthy and silent, and had the pleasure of seeing surprise on her face when he lifted himself up right beside her.

'Nice evening?' she murmured, her eyes scanning his face, her anger flashing more visibly now.

'Not really,' he said noncommittally.

Without developing some kind of mystical psychic ability she had no idea what he meant by that. She turned her head away, her eyes soaking in the view of Rome in the distance without really seeing it. Even at this early hour of the morning the city was alive, its buildings outlined with light, all its ancient stories winding around themselves, whispering through the walls to those who wanted to listen.

'Do you do this often?' He turned to face her, his body achingly close.

'No.'

'Nor do I. Strange that we both had the same idea tonight.'

'Not really. It's been muggy as hell today,' she pointed out logically. 'I couldn't sleep.'

He nodded, but his eyes were speculative. 'And in general?' he prompted.

God, she looked young like this—bathed in moonlight and the salt water of his pool.

Her eyes were blank. 'What do you mean?'

He compressed his lips. 'Are you settling in well to Rome?'

'Oh.' She was grateful for the night, grateful that it hid her blush. 'Yes. I've sent off my enrolment forms. I'll start university next term.'

'What will you study?'

'Psychology.' She looked away from his intense gaze, feeling that he saw way too much. 'It's always interested me.'

'I see.' He frowned thoughtfully. 'I would have imagined you doing history, or perhaps English literature.'

She lifted a hand and ran it over the water's surface, feeling its thick undulations beneath her fingertips.

'Why? Because I'm bookish? Because I look as though I'd be perfectly at home under bags of dust in an ancient library?'

His smile was perfunctory. 'No.'

He moved closer towards her, and again she had the sense that he was chasing her. Ridiculous when they were simply floating at the same end of the pool. Besides, why would a man like Pietro Morelli chase her?

'Because the last time I saw you, you spent the entire night staring at very old paintings as though they were the beginning and end of your existence.'

Emmeline's smile was genuine. 'I'd never seen works of art like that before. The Dutch Masters have always fascinated me.'

'So you can see, then, why I thought of history—perhaps art history—as your university subject of choice?'

'Oh, I *love* art.' She nodded. 'And old things in general.' She tilted her head back into the water, wetting her hair. It draped down her back like a silken curtain. 'But I've wanted to do psychology for almost as long as I can remember.'

Not quite true. She could recall the exact moment when it had dawned on her that a lot of people's minds needed fixing.

Apparently Pietro was drawing the same conclusion. 'When did you learn the truth about your mother's death?'

'I thought I told you?' she murmured quietly, feeling the night wrapping around them like a blanket. 'I knew at the time.'

'I'm sorry you had to experience that loss. And so young.'

Emmeline rarely spoke about her mother. Her father never wanted to talk about her, and Emmeline didn't really have anyone else to confide in about something of that nature. But, perhaps because Pietro had known Patrice, Emmeline felt her strongly held borders dropping.

'She'd been unhappy for a long time. I didn't expect her to die, but it wasn't a complete surprise, somehow.'

'Unhappy how?' Pietro pushed, moving closer.

His recollections of Patrice were vague. She'd been drop-dead gorgeous, and kind enough. Perhaps there'd been a coldness to her, a sense of disconnection. He'd been a young man when he'd last seen her and his thoughts weren't easy to recall.

'Oh, you know…' Emmeline's smile was uneven, her eyes not quite meeting his.

'No, I don't. That's why I asked you.'

How could Emmeline answer? There'd been that morning when she'd come downstairs to find her mother passed out, two empty bottles of gin at her feet, her make-up ruined by her tears. And there'd been all the little nips and tucks, of course. But the biggest clue had been the control she'd begun to exert over Emmeline.

Even as a teenager Emmeline had known it wasn't right—that there was something unhealthy about her mother's desire to infantilise Emmeline, to keep her from experimenting with clothes and fashion. Discouraging Emmeline's attempts on improving her image had been one thing, but knowingly pushing her towards unflattering hairstyles and prohibiting her from anything except the wardrobe she, Patrice, had selected…

It had taken years for Emmeline to understand her mother's motivations and they'd left her reeling.

'Lots of things,' she said vaguely, shaking her head.

Perhaps it was the raw pain in his wife's voice that stalled Pietro from pushing further. For whatever reason, he let the matter go for a moment.

'Psychology will no doubt be very interesting,' he said quietly. 'When do you begin?'

'A month.'

He nodded. 'There's still time for you to adapt to life here, then.'

'I think I'm just about adapted,' she said quietly.

He was so close now that when he moved the water rippled in response and it almost felt as though he was touching her. She knew she should put some distance between them, but she'd hardly seen him for a month. This nearness was like a highly addictive form of crack cocaine.

'You have been bunkered here in the villa,' he said softly. 'It's time for you to start coming out with me. You are my wife. There are events. Functions. Things to attend.'

'Oh.' She bit down on her lip and uncertainty glimmered in her eyes. She had been the one who'd suggested they needed to keep up a certain public persona. But now the idea filled her with doubts. 'I don't know if that's really necessary...'

'Not all the time, no. But there are certain things you can no longer avoid.'

'I haven't been *avoiding* anything.'

As soon as she said it she knew it was a lie. She *had* been holed up in his house as much as possible—reading, emailing, reading some more. Keeping her ears permanently trained on noises that might herald Pietro's arrival so that she could scamper away.

'My bank organises a banquet every summer. It is a Midsummer's Eve theme—very beautiful and enjoyable. You'll come with me.'

She arched a brow, instantly resenting his imperious tone. 'Oh, I will, will I?'

'*Si.*'

His fingers brushed against hers underwater. Surely it wasn't an accident? Her heart didn't think it was. It pounded hard against the fabric of her being with a thundering beat that he must be able to hear.

'I usually take a date. That would raise eyebrows this year.'

She smiled, but it was a distracted smile. He'd been late home almost every night in the month since they had been married. It was impossible to believe he hadn't been seen out with different women in that time.

The thought made her heart race, but for a less palatable reason now. *Jealousy.* Not because she cared for him or wanted him, she hastened to reassure herself. But because he was *hers*. Her husband. And she didn't particularly want people thinking that he was straying from the marital bed already.

Marital bed.

What a joke.

Longing surged inside her.

The need he had awoken was at fever-pitch.

She controlled it as best she could, but her mind continued to toss up images of just what it would be like to be made love to by a man like her husband.

The reality wouldn't live up to her fantasies, Emmeline was certain.

'It's Friday night,' he murmured.

Her eyes clashed with his and the longing was back, begging her to do something—anything—to indulge it.

'You want me to go?' she asked quietly.

'I think you should come, *si.*'

She bit down on her lip, and then spoke before she could question the wisdom of her proposition.

'Well,' she said thoughtfully, 'there's something I want too. I suggest we…trade.'

'Oh? And what is it that you want, Mrs Morelli?'

Say the words... Say the words... her courage pushed angrily.

'I want you to sleep with me.'

They blurted out of her on the warm breeze that rushed past.

Pietro barely reacted. Just a tightening around his lips showed that he'd heard her proposition and was digesting it.

'I told you—'

Emmeline waved a hand in the air. 'That you're not interested in being my first lover,' she said, with a shrug of her shoulders. 'But it's too late for that. You've shown me what my body can feel and I want to know more.'

'I'm not a damned *teacher.*'

'No. You're my husband.'

His eyes narrowed, and his breath was clearly tearing from his body.

'I'm not going to sleep with you,' he said with an angry shake of his head.

God, she was Col's *daughter*, and he'd married her to ease the mind of his dying friend.

But surely Col knew enough of Pietro's ways to know that this was a possibility.

Why was Pietro fighting it so hard?

The last month had been a living torture as he'd forced himself to keep his distance, never sure if the flame between them would burst out of control.

'I'll go to this…this banquet with you. And whatever else you want me to attend. But I need to know what it feels like.'

'Why now?' he asked, the question thick in his throat.

'I didn't *mean* to not sleep with anyone. I just never met a guy I was interested in. Honestly, I started to think I was kind of…sexually not all *there*. All my friends have been in relationships forever.' She bit down on her lip.

'You lost your mother at a vulnerable time in your life,' he said gently.

'Yes, that's true. It changed who I am.' Her clear amber gaze held his for a long moment. 'Life sort of got away from me. I feel like I've spent the last seven years in a sort of stasis and now I'm ready to start living again. I want to wake up.'

Be brave. Be brave.

She closed the distance between them, surprising him when she wrapped her arms around his neck. 'I want *you* to wake me up.'

His eyes were lightly mocking as they stared back down at her, but he didn't push her away. He didn't remove her touch.

'I'm not Prince Charming, Sleeping Beauty.' The words were cold. Determined.

'I know that.' She blinked her eyes. 'I don't need you to be.'

'I wouldn't have married you if I'd known,' he said with an angry shake of his head. 'You deserve to find someone yourself. Someone you care about.'

'She'll be vulnerable to fortune-hunters.'

Yes, Emmeline—the sweet, naïve virgin heiress—sure as hell would have been vulnerable. She might as well have had a target on her back for some guy to come along and sweep her off her feet.

All Col's reasons for pursuing this marriage were blindingly clear to Pietro. What had at one point seemed ridiculously absurd now made absolute sense. Even without the fortune she would inherit, her youthful innocence would mark her as the easiest target for no-good bastards on the lookout for an easy buck.

'This isn't about happily-ever-after,' Emmeline said with a grim determination. 'I'm twenty-two, and until our wedding day I'd never even kissed a guy.'

She dropped her eyes, the admission making her insides squirm with embarrassment.

'I feel like some dusty old antique no one's wanted to

pick up off the shelf.' Her throat moved as she swallowed. 'But when you look at me it's like… I *get* it. I get what everyone's talking about. I understand—finally—the appeal of sex. And I don't want to die a virgin.'

He couldn't help but laugh softly at her dramatic end note. 'You are not going to die a virgin. You are still young.'

'Yes, but…if not now, when? *Who?*'

An excellent question.

Suddenly the idea of someone else taking this precious gift was anathema to Pietro. The red-blooded man that was thick in his blood had begun to see his wife as *his*. Not just a bride of convenience, but a woman in *his* home, under *his* protection. Was he to let her go one day, knowing some other man would take what he, Pietro, had so nobly declined?

He groaned softly, knowing then that the devil was on his shoulder and he was listening to his urgings. He was listening when he should be speaking sense, reminding her of what they were.

'You are too young for me,' he said, with a finality that his hard-as-stone cock wasn't happy with. 'And too inexperienced.'

He reached up, wrapping his hands around her wrists, pulling them away from his neck. As he glided them through the water, resting them at her sides, her pert breasts pressed into him.

His arousal jerked and for the briefest moment his will-power left him. How easy it would be to do what she wanted! She was handing herself to him on a silver platter.

But he'd regret it.

One way or another he'd conquer this desire—because nothing and no one *ever* got the best of Pietro Morelli.

CHAPTER SIX

Dio. SINCE WHEN had she started wearing skirts like that?

Pietro stared out of the villa window, his concentration sapped by the image of his wife in a scrap of denim that barely covered her arse and a simple white strappy top.

Without a bra.

The pert outlines of her breasts were clearly visible, as were the hardened nubs of her nipples, straining at the fabric. She was tapping a pen against her mouth, her eyes intent on the book she had propped on her knees. But his eyes were lost on her lips. Lips that were slightly parted, full and pink, glistening as though she'd just licked them.

'I'm twenty-two and until our wedding day I'd never kissed a guy.'

A fierce burst of possession tore through him. Those lips had welcomed his claim on them, had sought his mouth and kissed him back. They'd parted for his invasion.

She'd tasted so sweet.

His eyes swept closed as he remembered the way she'd come to him on their wedding night, all pink-cheeked and nervous. The way she'd stood like a rabbit caught in bright headlights—which was exactly what she'd been! How could she have understood the onslaught of sensual heat that was flaring up between them?

Even for Pietro it was proving difficult to process. And impossible to ignore, apparently. Did she have any idea what her presence was doing to him? Here in his house… his virgin bride?

His for the taking.

The idea spread like wildfire through his body. It took

every ounce of his willpower not to give in to temptation and act on it.

But it would be so wrong. Other women were for meaningless sex. She was *different*. Not someone he could desire. She was someone he needed to protect. Yes, as a brother would protect his sister.

Ugh. Not as a brother!

She tossed her dark hair over one shoulder and her eyes lifted almost unconsciously. She was clearly lost in thought, her mind wandering as her eyes did the same.

Pietro jerked his own head down, returning his concentration to the marketing reports he'd been given that morning. Or at least pretending to.

But it was incredibly dull reading, and his wife was just metres away, her long legs calling to him...

With a noise of impatience he scraped his chair back and strode towards the glass doors, his expression grim.

'Are you wearing suntan lotion?' he asked, pushing the door open wider as he stepped through it.

Emmeline's frown showed that she'd been deep in thought—that his question had seemed to come from a long way away.

'Are you wearing suntan lotion?'

Her face showed bemusement. 'No. But it's after five. I'm sure I'll be—'

'The Roman sun still has bite.' He turned on his heel and disappeared, returning a moment later with a small yellow tube. 'Here.'

He tossed it down on the lounger and she picked it up, unscrewing the lid slowly. His eyes followed her progress and he crossed his arms over his chest, his manner imposing.

He had been imposing even *before* Emmeline had factored in her embarrassing confession and request in the pool last night. No. Not last night: in the early hours of that same morning.

The colour in her cheeks now had nothing to do with the fact that she'd been reading by the pool for hours. Though why she'd chosen to return to the scene of the crime was beyond Emmeline. In that moment, confronted by the ghost of what a fool she'd been, she wished she was anywhere else.

She flicked the cap off the bottle and squeezed some cream into her hands, then rubbed it over her exposed arms and the vee of her neck.

Pietro watched, but his temper wasn't improved by the display. Nor was it improved when she placed more cream into her palm and reached down to spread it over her legs. Legs that were long, tanned and smooth...

He looked away from her, his arms still crossed.

But he could see her in his mind. As she'd been in the pool early that morning—her hair like a shimmering black veil, her eyes enormous, her lips curved into a smile.

Her question hadn't been unreasonable. Hell, he'd backed her up against a wall and slid a finger into her wet heat until she'd come in his arms. Of *course* she was curious.

He'd stirred something inside her and now he was preventing her from experimenting. From exploring that side of her.

It wasn't fair.

Was she annoyed that he'd turned her down?

'The thing is,' he said, as though their conversation from the night before was still going, had simply been paused for a few hours while they slept and he worked. 'You're my wife, and if we were to sleep together it would be too complicated...'

Her eyes flew to his face, the statement knocking her off balance completely. She hadn't expected this, but she managed to pick up the threads of their negotiation as though it were just that—a simple business deal.

'Complicated how?'

'I have nothing to offer.' He spoke stiffly, his shoulders

squared. 'I'm not interested in a relationship, and I suspect you'll blur those lines if I do what you ask of me.'

She nodded slowly and then shrugged her shoulders. 'Sure.'

Her easy acceptance was insulting. 'If you came to want more from me I can promise you I wouldn't offer it.'

She bit down on her lip and shrugged once more. 'Whatever. It's not important. Forget I mentioned it.'

He looked away once more. *Why* did she have such beautiful legs? Out of nowhere he pictured them wrapped around his waist as he pulled her closer, pressing into her.

His arousal throbbed painfully.

'I know I can't hold a candle to your usual…um…lovers. It was stupid of me to even suggest it.'

'You are *very* different,' he agreed softly.

Her battered pride was almost debilitating in its intensity. He didn't need to *tell* her how different she was. She'd seen the photos. He'd all but told her that she wasn't attractive. God, she'd thrown herself at his feet! Of all the foolish, embarrassing, childish, stupid things to do!

Regret washed over her heart. But pride was beating its drum, forcing her to remember who she was and what she wanted in life. This marriage was a stepping stone for Emmeline—a brick path to freedom.

'I think I just got carried away last night. The moon… The water… The heat…' Her smile was dismissive. 'It won't happen again.'

She briefly met his eyes and then looked back to her book, pretending fascination with the page she was on even as the words swam before her eyes.

It won't happen again.

'That is for the best, *cara*.'

He spun on his heel and stalked back inside the villa before he gave in to temptation and pulled her to her feet, roughly against his chest, and plundered those sweet lips that had been tempting him all afternoon.

* * *

Rafe let out a low whistle, his eyes locked on some point across the room. Pietro followed his brother's gaze, though he knew what he'd see.

His wife, Emmeline Morelli, looking as if she'd walked out of a goddamned *Vogue* photo-shoot. Her dress was beautiful, but every woman at this event was draped in couture and dripping with diamonds. It was Emmeline he saw.

Her long dark hair had been set in loose curls that waved around her back, and the dress itself was a sort of Grecian style, in a cream fabric that gathered beneath her breasts then fell in floaty, gauzy swathes to her feet, which were clad in shimmering gold sandals. She wore a snake bracelet on her upper arm, and a circle of gold around her head.

She looked like a very beautiful, very sexy fairy. Something the two men she had been locked in conversation with for the past twenty minutes seemed eminently aware of. Her face was animated as they spoke, her eyes illuminated and her laugh frequent.

Hot, white need snaked through him.

'Married life seems to agree with Mrs Morelli,' Rafe said, and grinned, grabbing a glass of wine from a tray being walked past by a waiter.

'*Si,*' Pietro agreed, willing himself to look away but finding it almost impossible.

'And you?' Rafe turned to study his brother, a smile twitching at the corners of his lips. 'I would ask how *you're* finding the leap into married life, but I can see for myself that it is no hardship.'

Pietro's expression was shuttered.

'No comment, eh?' Rafe laughed good-naturedly.

A muscle jerked in Pietro's jaw. 'There are too many of these twinkling lights,' he snapped, changing the subject. 'I feel like they are everywhere I look.'

Rafe's laugh was annoying Pietro. *Everything* was annoying him. Who the hell *were* those men? Had she met them before? It was possible that they had dealings in America…that they knew Col. Perhaps she'd hosted them at the plantation. Maybe they were old friends.

A groan of resentment died in his throat. He nodded dismissively at his brother. 'I'll speak to you later.'

Pietro moved quickly, cutting through the crowd, ignoring any attempt to draw him into conversation. But there were so many people between him and his wife and he was the man of the hour, in huge demand.

He spent a few minutes in curt exchange with a board member, and then smiled briefly at his cousin Lorena before getting within striking range of his wife.

He paused, watching her up close for a few seconds, seeing the way her face moved while in conversation.

Guilt was not something he was used to and yet he felt it now. Her father was one of his most valued friends, and yet he'd hardly taken the time to speak to Emmeline. What was making her laugh like that? What did she find funny?

He compressed his lips and moved closer, but at the moment of his approach the two men stepped away—not before one of them pressed a kiss against Emmeline's cheek and almost earned an angry rebuke from Pietro.

'Oh, Pietro.' She blinked up at him, her expression shifting swiftly from enthusiasm to confusion.

His chest felt as if it had been rolled over by a car. He manoeuvred his body, placing himself between Emmeline and the crowd, her back almost touching the wall, so that both of them would be reminded of the night he'd made her come.

Her breath snagged in her throat. She stared up at him, a pulse beating wildly in her throat.

'Who were those men?'

A frown tugged at her lips, but only for a second. Then the enthusiasm was back in her eyes, apparently irrepressible.

'Oh, they're professors at the university! One of them is

a lecturer in the psychology department. It's going to be so helpful to have people there I know already.'

Great. She'd continue to see people who looked at her as though she was an ice cream they wanted to lick regularly.

Anger made common sense impossible. 'You should be with me,' he grunted angrily. 'Not talking to strange men.'

'They weren't *strange* men—they were perfectly nice. And staying with you at something like this is impossible,' she responded curtly. 'Everyone wants to talk to *you*, not me.'

'I don't care; you're my wife.'

'Yes, your *wife*. Not an accessory,' she pointed out softly, keeping her voice low purely out of recognition of the fact that there were people everywhere.

'We agreed that we wouldn't draw attention to our relationship or lack thereof. I will *not* have people gossip that my wife's interest is straying.'

She blinked up at him, her face pale. 'You must be kidding me! Your ego is wounded because I was talking to two probably married professors from the university I'm going to attend?'

'You weren't just *talking*. You were…'

'What? You think I was *flirting*?' she said with disbelief. 'You're unbelievable.'

'Forse,' he acknowledged. 'Nevertheless, I want you to stay with me tonight.'

Emmeline glared up at him angrily. She might have moved hell and high water to please her father, but that was where her submissive tendencies ended.

'No way.' To her chagrin, tears sparkled on her eyelashes. She blinked them away angrily. 'Right now you're the last person I want to see.'

And then, with her back up against the wall—literally—he placed a hand on her hip and stroked her flesh gently, teasing her, making her pulse throb.

'Why do I find that so hard to believe?' he asked throatily, the words a hoarse demand.

'Don't.'

She bit down on her lower lip, and there was such a look of need in her eyes and confusion in her face that he almost dropped his hand.

Almost…but not quite. 'Don't what?'

Don't use this against me, she thought, her heart hurting. This desire she wasn't used to was tormenting her enough already.

He moved a little closer, dropping his head by degrees, so that when he spoke his words were whispered into her ear. 'Go and wait for me in the car. It's time for us to leave.'

'We've only been here an hour,' she pointed out huskily, her body attuned to every shift in his.

'Fifty-nine minutes too long,' he responded.

'Why are we leaving?'

Because I don't want to watch you being drooled over by any other man.

Because I want to make love to you.

Because you're mine.

He shook his head. 'It's time. I'll be out as soon as possible.'

But it was not so easy for Pietro to depart. By the time he'd said goodbye to the more influential of the guests Emmeline had been cooling her heels in the car for almost a half-hour, and it was clear that she was in a foul mood.

'Am I being punished for enjoying a conversation?' she demanded, the second he was in the driver's seat.

'No.' He revved the car to life and floored the accelerator.

He shifted a sidelong look her way. Her jaw was clenched, her hands gripped tightly in her lap, her body vibrating with barely suppressed anger.

'I went to a lot of effort to come to this damned thing tonight because you told me you wanted me to! No, you told me I *had* to! I don't appreciate being frog-marched out like some errant schoolgirl.'

Oh, God. The last thing he needed was to picture his wife as a schoolgirl. *Hell.* She *had* been a schoolgirl the first time he'd seen her, around the time of Patrice's funeral. She'd appeared in the hallway in a navy blue dress, with a blazer that fell to her hips, and even then Pietro had known she had the potential to be trouble for him.

He had unconsciously stayed away from the plantation after that, avoiding her as much as he could. It hadn't always been possible—there'd been a few dinners and parties, in the intervening years—but for the most part he'd kept a very wise distance.

Something about Col Bovington's daughter had sent all his warning sensors haywire, and now he knew how right his instincts had been.

'I was having a good time,' she continued angrily, her gaze focussed on the streets of Rome as they drove.

She didn't know it well enough yet to recognise that they were heading out of the city—away from his villa.

'I'm glad,' he said quietly. 'But those men were all over you and you were encouraging them.'

'How can you *say* that? We were just talking.'

'Believe me, *cara*, with you in that dress no man will be "just talking" to you.'

Her jaw dropped and she whipped around to face him, her face lashed by pain. 'It's a *nice* dress. A *respectable* dress.'

'You look good enough to eat—and I'm sure as hell not the only man who thought so.'

Emmeline's face drained of all colour, and all the fight seemed to leave her in one second.

Pietro didn't notice.

'You're my *wife*! It doesn't matter that our marriage is unconventional. I will not have you dragging my name through the mud…'

'Your name…' She rolled her eyes, but her words were just a whisper. 'For such a powerful, successful guy, you've got major insecurity about your reputation.'

He slammed his palm into the steering wheel, anger coursing through him. It wasn't about that! Didn't she understand? He had *no* insecurities; his virility left him little room for doubt on that score. It was just a stupid excuse. Something he could say that would achieve the desired result—which was what? Her total isolation? *Dio.* What kind of barbaric son-of-a-bitch was he turning into?

'*You* said I should change how I look.'

She was shivering now—a reaction Pietro finally recognised, though he couldn't understand it. Unconsciously he drove faster, turning the car onto the highway and picking up speed.

'You said that I had to be what people would expect of your wife. Haven't I done that?'

He gripped the steering wheel tighter, his eyes focussed on the night sky ahead. She'd done it—only far too well for his liking.

'You would have complained if I'd come to that thing tonight wearing something I was comfortable in—something I usually wear. Now you're complaining because I'm dressed like any of those other women who were there.' She shook her head from side to side. 'That's not fair.'

It wasn't—she was right. But nothing about this was fair! He'd been *happy* before marrying Emmeline. Happy in his life…happy with the endless parade of women he'd taken to his bed.

And now?

He had no damned idea.

'Where are we going?' she asked, as if waking from a dream and suddenly realising that they were well outside the city.

'Not much further,' he promised, his eyes flicking to the

clock in the centre of the dashboard, willing the distance to shorten. 'Close your eyes, *cara.*'

'I'm too angry to sleep,' she snapped, but she did sit back in her seat, and a moment later her eyes fluttered closed.

Her steady, rhythmic breathing informed him that she'd drifted off despite her protestations. He drove the rest of the way in a silent car, but his thoughts were still screaming at him.

What he was planning was stupid, crazy, and he'd decided firmly against it. But after seeing her with those men… He no longer had a choice.

He pulled the car through the electric gates to the farmhouse and then crept up the gravelled driveway.

Though no one lived there, he had a team who kept it permanently tidy and stocked.

His headlights illuminated the pots of geraniums and lavender that stood on either side of the green-painted door.

He went inside, checking from room to room, leaving the bedroom until last. It was an enormous space, with an old iron bed in the middle. The floor was tiled and the shutters were closed over the windows, making it pitch-black. In the morning light would filter through the cracks, and when the shutters were open a stunning view of the countryside would open up, with the ocean glistening beyond the rolling hills.

It didn't take him long to make the room ready, and then he went back to the car.

Emmeline was still asleep, and he knew the kindest thing to do would be to carry her inside and leave her to sleep.

But fire was raging through his body, tormenting him as much as it was her, and there was only one answer to that.

He opened her door and crouched down, hesitating for a second before pressing his lips to hers.

In her drowsy state, she opened her mouth to receive his and moaned, lifting her hands to curl them around his neck, her fingers twisting in the dark hair at his nape.

'Pietro…' she moaned, and he undid her seatbelt then lifted her out of the car in one easy movement. He cradled her against his chest, carrying her with grim determination into the house. He moved up the stairs at the front, through the corridor and then up the flight of internal stairs.

'Where are we?' she asked, looking around and then, as if remembering that she was annoyed with him, pushing at his chest. 'I can walk.'

'I'm aware of that.'

He shouldered the door of the bedroom open and Emmeline looked around, a soft gasp escaping her lips. Dozens of candles had been lit, casting a golden glow in the room.

The *bedroom*.

Music was coming from somewhere, a lilting song in his native language that did something strange to her heartbeat.

He placed her down on her feet with care and then straightened, catching her face between his hands. 'You have two choices, Emmeline.'

'And what are those?'

'You may use this room to sleep,' he said softly, stroking her cheek. 'Or we will be together here tonight. Your first time. *Our* first time.'

He dropped his lips to hers softly, studying her, waiting. He felt as if he'd been waiting an eternity already…

CHAPTER SEVEN

THE AIR STRETCHED between them, thin and tense. Emmeline's heart was rabbiting about in her chest. She'd wanted this for a *really* long time. Since their wedding? Or since her father had first suggested this hare-brained idea?

The thought of marriage to the charismatic tycoon she'd adored from afar for as long as she could remember had scared the heck out of her—mainly because she'd known she'd find it impossible not to fall head over heels in lust with the confirmed bachelor.

And love? Would sleeping with him blur the lines of what they were, just as he'd said? And was she brave enough to reject him when he was offering something she wanted so badly?

She blinked up at him, doubt making her voice quiet. 'I'm not tired.'

He expelled a breath he hadn't realised he'd been holding.

'Thank God for that.'

And now his patience deserted him.

He balled a hand into her hair, tilting her head back to allow him access, and kissed her as she'd never been kissed before. His tongue duelled with hers, lashing her with his need, and his body was hard and erect as he pushed her backwards onto the bed. She fell and he went with her, lying on top of her as his kiss pressed her head into the mattress and her body writhed beneath him.

A fever of need was spinning from her womanhood through her whole body, making her pant with desperate hunger. And he understood it. It burned in him, too.

'This is so beautiful,' she gasped, watching the candlelight flickering against the wall, casting shadows that did something to her insides.

'*Si.*'

His hands pushed at the fabric of her dress, lifting it higher, moving it up her body, exposing her long legs to him so that he groaned into her mouth as he felt the expanse of her thigh.

'*You* are beautiful,' he added, dragging his mouth lower, teasing the flesh at the base of her neck.

After a lifetime of not wanting to be beautiful it was strange for her to find those words so seductive, so pleasing. She swallowed.

He flicked the pulse point in her neck that was pounding hard and fast, his tongue a call to arms she couldn't ignore. Her hands pushed at his jacket and he groaned low in his throat as she arched her back at the same time, needing more, so much more, wanting her to touch him, to feel him.

Despite her complete inexperience she was driven by an ancient feminine dance, the power of which had been implanted into her soul at birth.

She rolled her hips, cursing the fabric between them. But his length was hard and it pressed against the sensitive flesh of her need. He thrust it towards her as though they were naked. He ground it against her and heat rose inside her. Her eyes had stars dancing in front of them and her breasts were tight, her nipples straining against the fabric of her dress, desperate for attention.

He ran his palms over her flesh and she cried out at the unexpected touch. As he ground his arousal tighter, harder, faster, his hands moved over her breasts and an orgasm split through her, its intensity almost ripping her apart.

She arched her back, moaning, crying out, her hands pushing at his shirt as the strength of the feelings he'd stirred made breathing, speaking, *anything* almost impossible.

But Pietro wasn't close to finishing. He was going to

make this a night Emmeline Morelli would never forget. A night worthy of her first time.

As her breath softened and her cheeks glowed pink he crawled down her body, his hands worshipping her through the dress, his mouth running over the soft folds of fabric until they connected with her underpants. They were simple white cotton, and that brought a smile to his face. He liked to imagine her in them. That alone would fuel his fantasies for years to come. But for now they served no purpose.

He slid them down her body, over the shoes she still wore, discarding them at the foot of the bed. She was writhing, her body still on fire. He traced circles along her legs with his fingers, moving towards her thighs.

She gasped, and the sound made him smile.

'You want me to touch you here?' he said softly, padding a thumb over the sensitive cluster of nerve-endings.

'I want everything,' she moaned.

His erection jerked hard in his pants. As hard as it could, anyway, when it was already taking up more room than was left inside the fabric.

'You are going to get it,' he promised darkly.

His hands were gently insistent as they separated her legs, pushing them wide apart to reveal her whole self to him. Before she could guess what he intended to do he ran his tongue across her seam.

She cried out into the room as new pleasures began to swirl around her, but he held her legs still, keeping her open to him. Keeping her right where he wanted her.

It was both an invasion and a sensual adventure. The intimacy of the act should have embarrassed her, or shamed her, but it did neither. She tilted her head back and stared at the ceiling as his tongue lashed her sensitive nerve-endings and euphoric delight careened over her body. She was at the top of a rollercoaster and the ride was only just getting started.

Emmeline didn't try to control herself as cry after hoarse

cry came from her mouth. She couldn't. She was completely subjected to the pleasure he was creating. He was her master.

'I want you to come,' he said against her body, and the words were a command that started a fever inside her.

She reached up and grabbed the duvet in her fingers, wrapping her hands around it and arching her back as his tongue moved faster, deeper, harder. Finally the muscles deep inside her squeezed hard, wet and desperate, and then, overjoyed, she felt pleasure fill her. It rioted through her, ricocheting off her body.

'God…' she whimpered at the candles in the room, shivering and yet covered in perspiration at the same time. 'I can't believe you just did that.'

His laugh was slightly unsteady as he dragged his mouth higher, over her flat stomach to her gently rounded breasts. He flicked one nipple with his tongue and then moved his mouth to the other, clamping his teeth over it just hard enough to make her cry out with renewed awareness.

'Why can you not believe it?' he prompted, his smile lazily indolent, his eyes hooded as his head came level with hers.

'I just… You kissed me…down there.'

'Down *here*, you mean?'

He curved a hand possessively over her womanhood and she sucked her lip between her teeth, nodding slowly.

'I want to do that again and again,' he promised, the heel of his hand pressing on her flesh just hard enough to keep the tremors of sensation going.

'Okay.' She smiled up at him, her body strangely lethargic in the midst of the passion he'd stirred up.

His laugh was a rumble…a coarse sound. He stood up, and for a moment she was assailed by loneliness and concern. *Was he stopping?*

But his fingers flicked at his buttons, loosening his shirt, pushing it off his body to reveal the full expanse of his tanned naked chest. She'd seen him like this before—in the pool—and the memory of that had burned itself into her fantasies.

But this was different.

He was undressing for *her* now. Undressing with his eyes hooked to her body, his fingers moving with determined speed as he slid the clothes from his body until he was in just a pair of black briefs. His arousal was evident through the fabric, straining against it, pushing outwards so her eyes couldn't help but be drawn to it.

'Am I right in thinking you have not *seen* a man before, Emmeline?'

The question was asked impassively, with no judgement, but Emmeline's face flushed with blood. Embarrassment made her look away and swallow.

'Of course I've seen a man,' she said quietly.

'Naked?' he prompted.

She shook her head, still unable to meet his eyes.

'Come here.'

Her heart thundered inside her body but she stood, closing the small distance between the bed and him. Even her own nakedness didn't shame her, though she'd never been this way before.

As if instinctively understanding her thoughts, he caught her around the waist. There was something in his expression—a confusion, a newness—that made her breath hitch in her throat. He drew her against the hard planes of his body and she made a soft sound of anticipation as his arousal pressed against her.

'I didn't want to marry you,' he said thickly. 'But now I can't think of anything I want more than what we are about to do. You are…uniquely beautiful.'

The words made her heart flutter; it felt weightless, without gravity, and she felt it might lift out of her body altogether.

'I'm not.' She shook her head.

'You try to disguise your beauty,' he corrected. 'And I cannot understand why, when most women do everything they can to enhance what they have.'

For a moment pain lanced her. A pain so deep, so embedded, that it had always been a part of her.

'It's who I am,' she said quietly.

'I want to get to know who you are,' he murmured. 'I didn't want to marry you, but you're my wife. And I'm glad.'

Her stomach churned and emotions ransacked her body, filling her heart with something new.

A sense of belonging.

He caught her hands and lifted them to his underpants. 'Undress me.'

Her eyes flew to his; doubt and uncertainty warring with temptation. 'I've never done this…' she babbled.

He laughed softly. 'I'm aware of that.'

She drew her brows together, her face a mask of doubt. 'I thought educating virgins wasn't your thing?'

'Not just any virgin,' he said in a gravelled tone. '*You*, Mrs Morelli.'

'What if I'm not…? What if this isn't…?' She closed her eyes, forcing herself to think clearly and speak what was on her mind. 'You told me you're used to experienced lovers. What if I'm terrible in bed?'

That unfamiliar stroke of guilt slashed through him anew. *He'd* said that. In fact he'd said words to that effect several times. Why had he been such a bastard to her?

'Tonight I want to show you what your body is capable of,' he said thickly, pulling her closer and making her gasp when his arousal throbbed hard against her body.

He felt her knees tremble. Her eyes were huge in her face, all honey and caramel, awash with far too many thoughts and doubts. Doubts *he'd* put there. Doubts he wanted to remove one by one, kiss by kiss.

'I'm scared,' she said, with such simple honesty it broke his heart.

'I know.' He kissed the tip of her nose.

His tenderness made her heart swell. Her fingers moved of their own accord, pushing at his underwear, lowering it over the hard line of his erection and then down, over his thighs. He stepped back, moving out of his underwear as he guided her to the bed.

She fell backwards, but he didn't immediately join her. Instead he reached into the drawer beside the bed and pulled out a foiled square.

'Protection,' he said with a half-smile.

'Ah. No grandkids.'

She nodded, her wink reminding him of the first day they'd discussed this marriage. When she'd been so sure of herself. Sure that she was getting a convenient husband, a ticket to her university studies and to…freedom. The word lodged in his mind as incongruous, as it had done back then.

'Not tonight.' He grinned.

Their eyes met and the air sparked with something neither had ever felt before. Though Pietro had slept with more women than he could easily remember, he'd never taken a woman's virginity. Even as a young man he had gravitated towards experienced lovers. This was new ground for them both.

How could he reassure her? Drive that doubt from her mind properly?

A strange sense of uncertainty ached in his gut. But she pushed up on her elbows and stared at him.

'I want this,' she said with soft confidence. 'I don't care what happens next. I want to *feel* this.'

He nodded and lowered himself onto the bed, kissing her slowly, sensually, marvelling at the feeling of flesh on flesh. Her naked breasts were flattened by his hair-roughened torso. His arousal was close to her—so close he could take her. The way she was trembling beneath him was a reaction to the newness of this, even as her eyes looked at him as though he was the air she needed to sustain life.

He dragged his mouth lower, rolling one of her nipples with his tongue while his hand slid down and splayed her legs wide, giving him more room, more access.

'You tell me if you need time,' he said thickly, not even sure the command made sense.

But she understood. She understood as though he'd spoken in a language made just for them.

She nodded and he lifted his head, one hand cupping her cheek as he kissed her hard. His tongue was passion and flame and she writhed beneath him, lifting her hips, searching for him, welcoming his invasion.

And God knew he wanted that too.

He pushed into her gently, gliding only his tip into her warm, tight core, giving her time to adjust to each incremental sensation as he filled her anew.

She moaned into his mouth as he moved, and all his control was required to stop himself taking her as he wanted to—hard and fast. He pulled out slowly, then pushed in deeper, before removing himself again. As he did so each time he took more and more of her and her muscles relaxed, welcoming him deeper, without restraint, without reserve, until he was pressing against the barrier of her innocence.

He kissed her, holding her tight as he thrust past it, removing it forever, imprinting himself on her as the first lover of her life. The first man who'd touched her like this.

Finally his whole length was sheathed by her, wrapped up in her, squeezed by her, and he paused, giving them both a moment to adjust to how it felt. He pushed his face higher so he could see her properly, could read her face. He saw wetness in her eyes and something turned in his gut.

'You're in pain.'

He moved to pull out of her but she shook her head and wrapped her legs around his waist.

'No, no, it's…' She shook her head and her smile was tight. Self-conscious. 'It's fine.'

Perfect, she amended inwardly. Everything about the

moment was more perfect than she could ever have fantasised or hoped. It was sublime.

'"Fine" is a good starting point,' he said darkly. 'But it
requires improvement.'

And then he moved quickly, his body thrusting into her
and pulling out, each movement sparking an electrical current beneath her skin until she was almost out of breath. The
assault on her senses was unlike anything she'd expected.
Even when he'd touched her and brought her to orgasm it
had been different from this. Now every nerve-ending in
her body was twitching, as though he was stirring her from
the inside out.

And he was, she realised, arching her back as the feelings began to overtake everything.

The galaxy was bright and hot and she was intimately
aware of her part in it: like flotsam, bright and floating,
powerless and yet powerful. A contradiction in her heart.

She dug her nails into his shoulders as wave after wave
of pleasure swallowed her, devoured her, making her eyes
leak hot tears she didn't even feel. Only when he caught one
with his tongue and traced it up her cheek did she realise
she was crying—but she couldn't stop.

She was incandescent, the explosion of her pleasure like
a fire in her blood. He held her as she came, held her tight,
reassured her, whispered to her in Italian, his words stirring
her up more, hotter, faster. She clung to him as the tornado
swirled around her, held him as though he alone could save
her, and then she cried out, sweat beading on her brow as
the storm broke.

Pleasure saturated the room, thickened her breath. She
clung to him until the craziness slowed and she was once
more herself.

But she was not herself. She'd never be herself again.
She had shaved off pieces of her being and handed them to
him, bound them into his soul and his flesh, uniting herself
with him even if he didn't want that.

She fell back onto the bed. The beauty of what they'd shared was incredible. Yet it was almost immediately eclipsed by a sense of guilt. Of self-doubt.

She'd just experienced the most unimaginable delight and he...he'd simply had a good workout.

'I'm sorry,' she muttered, turning her face away and staring at one of the flickering candles. 'I told you I wouldn't be any good at this.'

'Hey.'

He caught her face in his hand and turned her back to look at him, even though she couldn't bear to see the pity and disappointment in his eyes.

'What are you talking about?'

'Nothing,' she muttered.

It was impossible to give voice to the embarrassment that was quickly usurping her delight. Uncertainty and inexperience were horrible accomplices, and they dogged her every thought.

'Cara...' He spoke quietly, bringing his mouth to her earlobe and pulling it between his teeth, wobbling the flesh and breathing warm air over her delicate pulse-points so that she shivered anew. 'Do you feel this?'

He thrust into her again, deeper, harder, his body like a rock.

'Yes, but you didn't—' She bit down on her lip.

His laugh was soft recrimination. 'I did not finish because I didn't want this to be over. Believe me, it is taking every ounce of my willpower not to.'

Her eyes clashed with his, trying to read truth in his statement.

'You answer my needs perfectly,' he promised.

She wasn't sure she believed him, but then he began to move once more and she was lost to thought. She arched her back, her body held by his, and this time as he rocked her to new heights of awareness and fulfilment his mouth tormented her breasts, so there were fires raging in every part of her body.

She ran her fingers over him, wanting to touch and feel every inch of him, to enjoy his body as he was hers. And as she began to fall apart at the seams, a tumbling mess of sensation and feeling, a tangle of emotions, he kissed her, his mouth holding hers as he made her world shift once more.

Only this time he came with her.

Feeling him throb inside her, feeling his body racked by a pleasure he couldn't control and knowing it was being with *her* that was doing that to him made an ancient feminine power rock her. She held him tight and kissed him back, her mouth moving over his as he lost control of himself, as though she felt he needed some kind of reassurance.

Later she would find that instinct absurd, but in that moment it filled her, made her desperate to comfort him somehow.

He swore in his own language, the harsh epithet filling her mouth and her soul.

'You were worried I wouldn't enjoy myself?'

He rolled away from her, pulling out of her and sitting up in one motion. His face was angled down towards her, his smile bemused.

'How do you feel?'

Emmeline blinked up at him and stretched her body. She was covered in a fine sheen of perspiration and her nipples were taut; there was a red rash on the parts of her body his stubble had grazed, including her thighs, and at the top of her legs. She arched her back, tossing her arms over her head and stretching like a cat in the sunshine.

'I feel…*whole*.' She smiled and closed her eyes, her breathing soon deep and soporific.

He studied her for a moment, hearing the reality of what they'd done banging on a door in his mind—one he was going to ignore for as long as possible.

'Tell me,' he said thickly, running a finger over her abdomen up to the swell of her breast.

'What?' She flicked her gaze to him.

'Explain to me why you haven't done that before.'

'Maybe I was waiting for you,' she murmured, the words incongruous in their sweetness. She broke the spell by smiling teasingly. 'Or maybe I just didn't meet anyone who tempted me.' She pushed up on one elbow, her eyes not shying away from his. 'Is that so strange?'

'Yes.' He shook his head. 'Yet it also makes sense.'

Her eyes dropped to the sheet between them. 'I'm glad you made an exception to your "no virgins" rule for me.'

His laugh was a soft caress. 'That was rude of me.'

'It was *honest* of you,' she corrected, stretching again, her body lean and long and begging for his touch.

He cupped her breast possessively, his eyes simmering with tension as they locked to hers. 'Do you need anything? Food? Water? Wine? Tea?'

She shook her head slowly. How could she need anything when he'd just made her feel like that?

She smothered a yawn with the back of her hand and he smiled.

'Sleep, then.'

'Mmm...but then I might think this was all a dream.'

He covered her with the duvet that was folded across the bottom of the bed. 'Which will give me the perfect opportunity to remind you otherwise,' he said, with a deep husk to his words.

Her eyes were closed, her breathing even, but she was still awake. He watched as she breathed in and out, her face calm, her cheeks still pink from the heat of their lovemaking. He watched as the smile dropped and her wakefulness gave way to slumber...as her breathing grew deeper and steadier and her eyes began to dance behind their lids. Her lashes were two sweeping fans across her cheeks.

And still he watched. Without realising it he was being

pulled into a spell; it wrapped around him, holding him immobile.

There were mysteries surrounding his bride. Mysteries of her choice. Her being. The contradiction that lived deep inside her. She was stunningly beautiful and yet she did everything she could to hide that fact. She had lived like a prisoner for years—a prisoner of her father's love and concern, but a prisoner nonetheless—and yet she was brave and spirited, strong and independent. Why had she sacrificed her independence for so long?

She was sensual and desirable and yet she'd never even been kissed. How had she subjugated that side of her nature for so many years? She was twenty-two years old but she lived like a Victorian. Most women her age had their heads buried in their smartphones, sending glamorous selfies to their social media followers. She read books by the pool and covered herself from head to toe. *Why?*

These were questions to which he badly wanted answers, but there were other overriding questions that poisoned the perfection of the moment.

How would she react when she learned the truth about her father's health? Would she be able to forgive him for keeping it from her?

And, most importantly of all, why did the idea of lying to her, disappointing her, inadvertently hurting her with his dishonesty, make his skin crawl all over?

CHAPTER EIGHT

HER BODY THROBBED in an unusual new way. She stretched in bed, and wondered at the strangeness of everything. Not just her body, but the smells that enveloped her. Sort of citrus and lavender, clean and fresh. And the sounds—or lack of sounds. No busy motorways or bustle of a nearby city.

Her eyes blinked open, big pools of gold in the darkened room—dark save for the flickering of a couple of candles and the glow of a laptop screen beside her.

'*Ciao.*'

His voice was a warm breath across her body. She looked up at Pietro—her husband...her lover—and a lazy smile curved her lips.

'I had the strangest dream,' she murmured, pushing up onto one elbow so that the duvet fell from her body, uncovering her breasts for his proprietorial inspection.

He dropped his eyes to the display, unashamed of enjoying her nakedness. 'Are you sure it was a dream?' he prompted, folding his laptop closed and placing it carelessly on the bedside table nearest to him.

'It must have been,' she said softly. 'It was too perfect to be anything else.'

She was so beautifully unsophisticated. He couldn't remember the last time he'd been with a woman who didn't dissemble in some way. Her honesty was as refreshing as her body was tempting.

He brought his frame over hers, so large against her slender fragility that Emmeline couldn't help but feel safe in his presence. As though nothing and no one could hurt her if he was by her side.

The thought evaporated when his lips touched hers, his kiss perfection in the midst of her body's awakening.

'I want you again,' he said.

Her smile was broad. 'Good.'

He dropped his eyes for a moment. Something was clearly bothering him.

'I want you too,' she reassured him.

His laugh was a kernel of sound—a husk in the night. 'I hated seeing you with those men.'

She blinked, having no idea at first who he was talking about. Then, 'I was just talking.'

'I know that.' His smile was self-deprecating. 'It is possible that I overreacted.'

She burst out laughing. 'Is that some kind of extremely hesitant apology?'

He ran a hand over her hair, stroking its dark glossy length thoughtfully. 'Yes.'

'Apology accepted. But, Pietro? You can't really expect me never to speak to another man...'

'*Lo so.* I know.'

'Good. Because I came to Rome to find my feet—to be myself. I can't do that with you getting all shouty every time I have an innocent conversation with someone...'

'I know.'

He lifted himself up and straddled her, the strength of his want for her evidenced by the rock-hard arousal that was already pressed against her abdomen.

'But I will bring you to my bed each night and make it impossible for you to even *think* of another man.'

He dropped his head, placing a kiss on her temple.

'I will be all you think of and your body will crave mine.'

He thrust into her without warning and she cried out at the sweetness of his invasion, the possession that she was already hooked on.

'Starting now.'

'Starting a couple of hours ago,' she corrected breathily.

He grinned. 'Yes.'

He made love to her as though she was his only lover—as though he'd been dreaming of her for years. As though he needed her and only her. He made love to her with an intensity that blew her mind and filled her with the kind of sensual heat she hadn't believed could possibly exist.

She refused to acknowledge the truth: that she was one of many lovers for him and he was her only.

Afterwards, as she lay with her head resting on his chest, listening to the strong, fast beating of his heart and feeling the steady rise and fall of his chest, all was silent in the bedroom.

Except for the rather loud and insistent rumble of her stomach.

She burst out laughing, self-conscious but mostly amused. 'Apparently I'm starving.' She sat up straight, turning her face towards his. 'I hardly ate today,' she said after a moment, thinking back to her shopping trip and then the time she'd spent styling her hair and applying make-up.

'Why not?'

He stroked a hand over her back as though it was the most natural thing in the world, and his touch stirred a deep sense of rightness right down in the bottom of her soul.

She chewed on her lower lip. 'Just busy, I guess. I don't suppose there's anything here though…?'

'If so then someone's going to find themselves out of a job tomorrow.'

'Why?' she asked, looking around the darkened room. Only a few candles remained alight, flickering lazily against the white walls.

'Because I retain a full-time housekeeper to maintain this estate.'

'Estate? What *is* this place?'

His hand stilled on her back and then resumed its contact, as though he couldn't bear not to touch her. 'It is what you would call a bolthole,' he said after a small pause. 'My own little slice of the world.'

'Why would you need a bolthole, Mr Morelli? Is it for when your hordes of admirers and past lovers get too much?'

It was meant to tease him, but his face flashed with true annoyance. 'There is significant media intrusion in my life—something you might have noted if you'd been with me more.' He winced at the way that had sounded and shook his head. 'Sorry. I'm sure you're no stranger to that sort of invasion.'

'No,' she agreed, and she wasn't offended or upset—only interested. 'Though staying on the plantation as often as I did meant I wasn't really a figure of much interest,' she said quietly, conveniently glossing over the articles that had been so painful to her teenaged heart. The articles that had so callously compared her boring appearance to her mother's legendary beauty.

'You're lucky,' he said, taking her statement at face value. 'For years I was followed everywhere I went, with paparazzi eager to catch a photograph of the kind of mess I'd get into next.'

His wink hid genuine pain; she wasn't sure how she knew that, but she did.

'Including your escapade with that very much married Brazilian model?'

He grunted. 'Apparently.'

She expelled a soft breath—a sigh that meant nothing. It simply escaped her lips without her knowledge.

'I didn't know she was married,' he surprised her by saying gruffly. 'We didn't have that kind of relationship.'

She nodded thoughtfully. 'What kind of relationship *did* you have?'

He looked at her thoughtfully for a moment and then pushed out of the bed, striding across the room and grabbing a pair of shorts.

'You don't want to talk about it?' she asked as he pulled them up his body, leaving them low on his hips.

'I'm happy to talk about it if you would like. But let's get you something to eat as we speak, hmm? I don't want your energy fading.'

She hid her smile and stood, keeping a sheet wrapped around her as she moved.

His laugh was mocking. 'Why are you covering yourself?'

She sent him a droll look. 'Because I'm naked.'

'And you are worried I might see you?' He crossed the room, dislodging the sheet from beneath her arms, dropping his head to kiss her shoulder. 'Really? After what we've shared?'

Her cheeks flushed pink and something inside Pietro twisted painfully. So her innocence wasn't just a question of virginity. It was simply *her*. She had a sweetness, a naivety that was so unusual he doubted he'd ever seen anything like it.

'*You're* wearing something.'

'Yes, but I don't look like you.' He grinned, pulling her close. 'I want to *see* you.'

'Believe me, I feel the exact same way.'

His laugh was a little off-kilter, but he stepped backwards and slowly slid his briefs from his body so that he was completely naked.

'Better?'

Emmeline felt as though she'd eaten a cup of sawdust— her mouth was completely dry. 'Uh-huh.'

He laughed, kissing her cheek, and then reached for her hand. He laced his fingers through hers and she grinned.

'What?' he asked.

'First time I've held hands with a guy. Other than my father.'

He pulled a face that perfectly covered the way his heart

was rabbiting about like a wild thing in his chest. 'I don't want to think of your father right now.'

Or the fact that he had cancer. Was dying and lying to his only daughter. Nor the fact that he was using Pietro to cover that lie.

Emmeline's laugh covered the unpleasantness of his thoughts. 'Sorry. It's just this is all so strange.'

'Si. Quest'e verita.'

He pulled her after him, out through the door and down the stairs, and for the first time Emmeline spared a thought for the dwelling they were in. It was a very unassuming rustic farmhouse. Large terracotta tiles lined the hallway and the walls were cream. The furniture was nice, but certainly not designer.

'It came like this.' He answered her unspoken question.

'When did you buy it?'

He squeezed her hand. 'Here.'

He guided her into a kitchen and lifted her hand to his lips, kissing it before releasing her fingers from his grip. He opened the fridge and she watched, waiting.

'Five years ago.'

'Why?'

He thought about not answering, but what was the point in that?

'I'd broken up with a girlfriend. The press thought we would get married. So did she, I suppose. It was a messy split. Acrimonious. Bitter. Public.' He grimaced. 'I learned a lot from that experience. Most of all the importance of having somewhere to go when things get heated. I should have taken the time to calm down.'

'You didn't?'

He shook his head, pulling a box out of the fridge and opening it. 'I stayed in Rome.'

'That was bad?'

He laughed. 'I did a lot of drinking to forget her. A *lot*. It was not a good phase of my life.'

'I'm sorry,' she murmured, hating the lash of jealousy that whipped her spine.

'Don't be. We are still friends, and I realised that I needed somewhere all to myself. No one knows about this farmhouse. It's owned by my corporation, but I never bring anyone here.'

Pleasure soared at the fact that she'd made the cut, but there was envy too. 'How...*admirable* that you're still friends.'

His eyes met hers, his smile making her feel as though she'd been sledged in the gut. 'Jealous?'

'Not at all.' She looked away, hating how transparent she must be to him. Unfortunately she had no experience in pretending not to give a crap about her husband's past. Especially when his past must so radically outstrip her own experience.

'Why does that annoy me?' he mused, lifting a piece of meat out of the container and placing it on a dark timber chopping board. He reached for a knife; it glinted in the light.

'I don't know,' she said softly, distracted by the motion of the knife as it cut easily through the meat. 'Even with this place you're still in the press more than I can ever imagine.'

'And you are *never* in it,' he said thoughtfully, placing the pieces of sliced beef onto a plate and then turning back to the fridge.

'Well, there's nothing interesting about me,' she said softly.

'That isn't true.' A frown tugged at his lips. 'You are an anachronism.'

'I know.'

She couldn't help it. She reached over and lifted a piece of meat, placing it into her mouth just as he turned around.

Her eyes met his and she shrugged. 'I'm starving,' she said through a full mouth.

He grinned. 'I'm glad to see you eating. You need energy.'

Her pulse raced. 'Do I?'

'Oh, yes, *cara*.'

He paused, his eyes scanning her face so intently that she froze.

'What is it?'

'When you smile like that you look so much like your mother.'

Something flashed in her expression. Something that was definitely not pride or pleasure. It was doubt. Guilt. Pain.

Curiosity flared in his gut. 'That annoys you?'

'Of course not,' she said stiffly. 'My mother was very beautiful. I'm flattered.'

'No, you're not.'

'Why do you say that?'

'Because I know you,' he said simply.

And her stomach flopped because she didn't doubt he was being honest.

'So why do you not want to look like Patrice?'

'You'll never be like me! Take this off! Wipe it all off! It's too much rouge, too much mascara. You look like a porn star gone wrong.'

Emmeline shuddered, her smile as fake as the night was dark. 'You're wrong,' she insisted, even as the memory scratched its fingers over her spine.

'I'm never wrong.' His eyes sparked with hers. 'But I can be patient.'

He placed a handful of strawberries on the plate, then a wedge of cheese and some bread.

But I can be patient.

Did he have some mysterious super-ability to know just what she needed to hear?

'It's complicated,' she said, after a moment of silence had passed.

'Family stuff often is.'

His smile showed a depth of experience that she understood.

'Are your parents pleased you've "settled down"?' She made inverted commas with her fingers and he lifted his broad shoulders.

'I suppose so. Rafe thinks you're quite irresistible,' he added as an afterthought. 'I think he's more than a little jealous that your father chose *me* as your groom *du jour*.'

Emmeline made a sound of amusement and lifted a strawberry to her lips. Strangely, she was not remotely self-conscious in her nudity. Everything about that moment felt right.

'Have you ever been in love?'

Except that.

The question came from her lips completely unexpectedly, uninvited and unwanted. He stared at her for a moment, his expression unreadable.

'No.'

'Seriously?'

She reached for the plate but his hand caught hers, lifting it to his lips. He pressed a kiss against her palm and then took her finger into his mouth, sucking on it for a moment. Her stomach rolled.

'Seriously,' he murmured, coming around the kitchen bench to stand opposite her.

'But you've been with so many women.'

'Sex isn't love, *cara*.'

Just like that the floor between them seemed to open up; a huge hole formed and it was dark and wide…an expanse of confusion and heartache that she couldn't traverse.

Sex isn't love.

And it wasn't.

Sex was just a physical act. A biological function. A hormonal need.

Nothing more. Why had she asked that stupid question?

'What about that woman you broke up with? The one the press went into a frenzy over?'

'Which one?' he muttered, arching his dark brows.

'Five years ago—before you bought this place.'

'Bianca,' he said quietly. 'I cared for her. I still do.'

Jealousy was no longer just a flame in her blood; it was a torrent of lava bubbling through her, burning her whole.

'Bianca as in that beautiful redhead you were all over at our wedding?'

Contrition sparked inside him—and regret too. He'd forgotten that Emmeline knew her name. It was a stupid, foolish oversight that Pietro would never ordinarily have made.

'That was wrong of me.'

'You can say that again,' she snapped, reaching for a pistachio nut as a distraction. 'You're still seeing her?'

Her insides ached. Her body still throbbed with his possession, her nerve-endings were vibrating with the awakening he'd inspired, and she was jealous. So, *so* jealous.

'No.'

Emmeline stood up. She felt strange. Strange and achy.

'It's none of my business,' she said quietly, moving around to the other side of the kitchen bench—ostensibly to grab some more food, but in reality because she needed space.

'Of course it is. You're my wife.'

'But this isn't a *real* marriage, remember? We have a deal. You're free to…to do what you want.'

He stared at her long and hard. 'You don't think that's changed now, Emmeline?'

Doubts flickered inside her. 'What are you saying?'

'I don't want to see anyone else.'

He hadn't even realised that himself, but as he stared at his beautiful bride he knew it was the truth. And he knew she deserved to know it.

'I want to sleep with *you*. A lot. I want to be married to you. And I know we are doing this all the wrong way around, but I want to get to know you. There is so much of you that is a mystery to me, and for some reason I have become obsessed with uncovering all your secrets.'

He came around to her side of the bench and dug his hands into her hips.

'Every. Single. One.'

'This place is so beautiful.' She stared out at the rolling hills of the countryside, her eyes clinging to the fruit orchard in the foreground before moving on and landing on the glistening ocean. 'I don't know how you can ever leave.'

'Business,' he said simply. 'My office can't actually function for that long without me.' He thought of the emails his assistants had been forwarding and grimaced. 'I have to get back.'

Emmeline sighed. 'Today?'

'Now,' he agreed.

Or soon, he amended, sitting on the spot of grass beside her. After three days in the countryside he wasn't sure he could put off the reality of life for a moment longer. He wanted to, though.

'But it's so nice,' she said again, tilting her head to look at him.

She rested her cheek on her knees, which were bent against her chest, and he had to fight against reaching out and touching her. It was his 'go to' impulse now, and he suspected he might need some kind of 'Emmeline patch' to get through a day in the office without her.

How had he ever thought her ordinary and dull to look at? She was so breathtakingly beautiful that he derided himself for not having noticed. It didn't matter what she wore—these past three days she'd gone around in old shirts of his and she'd looked sexier than any woman he'd ever known.

No, she was simply Emmeline.

He saw every expression that crossed her face—including the slight flicker of regret that shifted her lips downwards now.

'You can stay here,' he said quietly. 'I can come back on the weekend. If you'd prefer it…'

'No.'

The response was instantaneous. How could she stay away from him? Her addiction was firmly entrenched. She couldn't remember a time when his body hadn't taken over hers.

'We'll come back some other time.'

She stood a little jerkily, wiping her hands across her knees.

He followed her and got to his feet, then caught her around her waist. 'I'm glad we came here.'

'Me too.'

Her smile was bright, but there was something in her expression that he didn't like. An uncertainty he wanted to erase.

Only he had no idea how.

He'd spent three days with her but he hadn't uncovered a single secret. Instead, he'd got to know her body intimately. He'd become acquainted with every single one of her noises, every single movement her body made that signalled pleasure, need, desire, an ache. He'd learned to read her body like a book, and yet her mind was still an enigmatic tangle of uncertainty…

'You seem nervous.'

She flicked her gaze to him, wondering at his perceptive abilities. 'I guess I am.'

Her smile was tight. Forced. Anxious.

Pietro slowed the car down, then pulled off to the side of the road. Emmeline's gaze followed a young child skipping down the street, his mother walking behind, her arms crossed, her eyes amused.

'What is it?'

Emmeline shifted her gaze from the child—his mother was next to him now, her smile contagious.

'Honestly?'

'*Si, certamente.*'

'It's stupid.'

'I doubt it,' he said reassuringly, his voice low and husky.

The statement was a balm to her doubts. Still, she hesitated before she spoke.

'What happened back there…' She bit down on her lip and cast a glance over her shoulder, towards the road they'd just travelled at speed. 'The closer we get to Rome, the more it feels like a fantasy. Like it never really happened. Like it won't happen again.'

'How can you say that?' he asked, a genuine smile of bemusement on his face. 'I was there. It happened. It happened a *lot*.'

Pink spread through her cheeks and she looked away, uncomfortable and disconcerted. 'But it doesn't feel real, somehow.'

He expelled a soft sigh. 'It *was* real.'

She nodded, but her uncertainty was palpable. 'I guess it's just…the last time we were in Rome everything was still so weird between us.'

His laugh caressed her skin.

He pulled back into the traffic, his attention focussed ahead. 'A lot's happened since then.'

And it had—but the fundamental truth hadn't changed, except in one crucial way. It was weighing on him more and more, heavy around his neck. Knowing that her father was dying and that she had no idea was an enormous deceit now. They'd crossed a line; they were lovers.

But Pietro wasn't overly concerned. Of the many things he excelled at, one of his strengths was managing people and situations. He just had to manage this situation tightly. Starting with his father-in-law.

CHAPTER NINE

'YOU DO NOT sound well,' he drawled down the phone, wondering at the sense of anger he felt towards this man he'd always admired and respected. A man he loved. A man who had helped him remember himself after the despair of losing his own father.

Col's cough was a loud crackle. 'I'm fine. The god-damned nurse is here, taking my temperature.'

'Rectally?' Pietro's response was filled with impatience. He softened it with a small laugh. 'Because you sound cranky as all hell.'

'I am. I'm a damned prisoner in this room.' Another cough. 'How's my girl, Pietro? Are you looking after her?'

Again, a surge of annoyance raged through Pietro's chest. 'She doesn't appear to need much looking after. Emmeline is stronger than I'd appreciated.'

Col's laugh was broken by a wheeze. 'Ah. I see you've come up against her stubborn side. Try not to judge her too harshly for it. She inherited that from me.'

'Mmm...' Pietro nodded, rubbing his palm over his stubble. He should have shaved. The pink marks of his possession had become regular fixtures on Emmeline's skin.

'Is there a problem?' Col's question was imbued with the strength that was part and parcel of the man.

'*Si.*'

'What is it? She's happy, isn't she? You told me you'd look after her...'

'She's happy,' Pietro agreed, thinking of her flushed face lying beneath him, her eyes fevered, her brow covered in perspiration. Then he thought of her uncertainty as they'd driven back to Rome the day before. The way she'd seemed pursued by ghosts unseen.

'So? What is it?'

'She deserves to know the truth about your health,' Pietro said heavily. 'She isn't going to understand why you haven't told her. You must give her a chance to see you. To say goodbye.'

A wheeze. Then another. Pietro waited, but his loyalty was shifting from the dying man to his daughter—the woman who loved her father and had no idea his life was ending.

'You can't tell her.'

It wasn't the response Pietro had expected. He shifted his weight to the other foot and braced an arm against the glass window that overlooked the city. In the distance he could make out the hill that screened his villa from sight. Was she there, looking out on the same blanket of stars he was? Was she staring up at the sky, wondering about him, missing him, wanting him?

His body throbbed with a need he fully intended to indulge. *Soon.*

'Someone has to,' he said, with a soft insistence that was no less firm for being quietly spoken. 'She deserves to know.'

'You aren't to say anything.'

Col's voice was raised, and in the background Pietro heard someone—a woman—telling him to calm down.

But Col was working himself up, his tone harsh. 'If I'd wanted her to know I'd have damned well told her. She's my daughter, Pietro. You've known her for a month—I've known her all her life. I know what she needs, damn it. You can't ruin this.'

'She deserves a chance to say goodbye.'

'No.' It was emphatic. 'I'm already gone. The man she thought I was…the man I used to be…that's not me now.'

There was a thick, throaty cough, then the scuffling sound of the phone dropping to the floor.

Pietro spoke quickly. 'Col? *Col?*'

A woman's voice came more clearly into the earpiece as the phone was lifted. 'Hello?'

Pietro expelled an angry breath. 'Yes?'

'I'm sorry, Senator Bovington needs to rest now. This conversation will have to wait.' The nurse lowered her voice. 'And next time please take more care not to upset the Senator.'

The call was disconnected before Pietro could ask to speak to Col for a moment longer. He shoved his cell phone back into his pocket and paced to the other side of his room.

And he swore, loudly, into the empty office, his temper ignited more than ever before.

The confidence he'd worn into the office earlier was morphing into doubt. Emmeline deserved to know the truth, but it wasn't Pietro's confidence to break. Perhaps with anyone else, he would, but Col was like a second father to him. He wouldn't share this secret until he had Col's permission. He couldn't.

But the knowledge that he was lying to Emmeline was a weight on his chest, and he found himself hesitant to go home to her that evening. The idea of looking at her, kissing her, making love to her, knowing that he was sitting on such a fundamental secret, made his situation unpalatable, to say the least.

He dialled Rafe's number on autopilot.

'*Ciao?*' Rafe answered, the single word slightly rushed and breathless.

'Are you free for dinner?'

'What time is it?'

Pietro gazed down at his gold wristwatch. 'After seven.'

'*Dio.* Already?'

'*Si.*'

'Okay. Dinner in an hour?' He named a restaurant near his own apartment. 'Is Emmeline joining us?'

Pietro's spine ached with rejection but he shook his head. 'Not tonight. She has…something on.'

Rafe was silent for a moment. 'You've always been a bad liar. I'll meet you soon.'

He disconnected the call before Pietro could refute the claim. Then he flicked his cell phone from one hand to the other and finally loaded up a blank message.

I have a meeting to attend. I'll be late. I'm sorry.

He grimaced as he sent it. Rafe was right; Pietro was a God-awful liar.

He saw the little dots appear that showed she was typing a message, but they went away again almost instantly, without any message appearing. He frowned, waited a few more moments and then put his phone back into his pocket.

Rafe was waiting at the restaurant when Pietro appeared.

'So?' he asked, nodding towards the martini that was sitting at the empty place on the table. 'What's going on?'

Pietro took the seat and threw back half the drink in one go. 'I need your complete discretion,' he said quietly, his tone showing the seriousness of his mood. 'This is a…a *private* matter.'

'Of course.' Rafe was clearly resisting the urge to joke about feeling like an extra from a bad World War Two resistance movie. He must sense it was not the time.

'Col's sick.'

'Col? Col Bovington?'

'Yes. Who else?' Pietro hissed.

'What do you mean, sick?'

'He has cancer; it's terminal.' He paused, in deference to the memories he knew would be besieging Rafe of the cancer that had taken their own father. 'He has months to live. Perhaps only weeks.'

'Poor Emmeline. She must be beside herself. I know how close they are.'

'Yes.' Pietro nodded angrily, his jaw clenched as he reached for his drink and twisted it in his hand. 'The thing is, she doesn't know.'

'She doesn't *know*?' Rafe repeated with disbelief, his dark eyes latching on to his brother's. 'What the hell do you mean?'

'Col wanted it that way,' Pietro responded with a defensive lift of his shoulders. 'And when I agreed to keep it from her I didn't… I hardly knew her,' he finished lamely. 'I didn't think it would be any hardship not to tell her the truth. I didn't care about her at all.'

'And now?' Rafe pushed.

The newness of what he was feeling was something Pietro wasn't willing to ruin by discussing it, though. He kept his answer vague.

'I know her well enough to know that she'd want the truth. She wouldn't want Col going through this alone. She'd want to be with him at the end.'

'Perhaps.' Rafe nodded. 'But Col is obviously seeking to protect her from the grief of watching a much-loved parent die…'

'We've been through that. But aren't you glad we got a chance to say goodbye to our father? To honour him? To ease his suffering?'

'We aren't Emmeline. If Col is right—and you must assume he knows his own daughter—then you'd be hurting her for no reason. And Col would never forgive you.'

'No. I gave him my word.' Pietro's response was stony. Cold. His heart was iced over by the thought of how that promise was betraying Emmeline. 'Until he frees me from that obligation I must keep it.'

'It sounds to me as though you've made your decision,' Rafe murmured gently. 'So what do we need to discuss?'

Pietro glowered. What he needed was for someone to absolve him of guilt, to tell him he was making the right decision. But no one could do that—and very possibly he wasn't.

'Niente.'

Emmeline turned the page of her book, having no idea what she'd just read. In truth, she'd covered several chapters, but she couldn't have recounted a single incident that had taken place.

Where was he?

And who was he with?

Her heart twisted in her chest as she thought of her husband with someone else. What assurance did she have that he wasn't still seeing Bianca, or any number of his past lovers?

Doubts filled her, making her feel nauseous and exhausted.

She should have gone to bed; it was late. But waiting for him to come home had become an obsession. She didn't want to fall asleep—to have him return at some point in the middle of the night and for her body to respond to his when he might well have been...

God. Was he sleeping with someone else?

A car's engine throbbed outside the door, low and rumbling, and her tummy flopped as her eyes looked to the clock. It was just after midnight.

Butterflies danced inside her, beating their wings against the walls of her chest, and her fingers were shaking as she flipped another page.

The door was pushed inwards and she waited, her eyes trained on the corridor beyond. Waiting, watching. He didn't see her at first. His head was bent, his manner weary. He stood dragging a hand through his hair, staring into space.

'Oh. You're home!' she said, in an admirable imitation of surprise.

He started. His eyes flew to Emmeline's and she knew

she wasn't imagining the darkening of his expression. The look of something in his face that might well be guilt.

'I didn't expect you to be awake, *cara*.'

'I've been reading. I guess the book engrossed me,' she lied. *What was it even called?* She folded it closed carefully, without attempting to stand. 'Did you have a good night?'

There it was again! That expression of uncertainty. Of wrongdoing. Her stomach churned and she looked away, unable to meet his eyes but knowing she had to speak honestly about how she felt. She needed to know where she stood.

'Have you been with another woman?' The question was a whisper. A soft, tremulous slice of doubt in the beautiful lounge of his villa.

'Oh, Emmeline...' He moved quickly to her and crouched down at her feet. 'No. Of course I haven't.' He put a hand on her knee, drawing her attention to his face. 'I had dinner with Rafe.'

'Yes.' She nodded jerkily. 'I know. He called hours ago, to say you'd left your jacket at the restaurant. He said he'd drop it by later in the week.'

Hours ago. Pietro understood then why his wife was so uncertain.

'I had to go back to the office to finish something,' he lied.

He'd needed to think. And he hadn't been sure he could face his wife with the knowledge he held—the lie he was keeping from her. What had seemed so simple was now burning through his body, making each breath painful.

'You can't seriously think I would be seeing anyone else?'

'I don't know,' she said softly, her eyes not able to meet his. 'I mean, I knew what I was getting when I married you...'

'No, you didn't. Neither of us did,' he said simply. 'I thought I was marrying the boring, spoiled daughter of a dear friend. I didn't expect my wife to be *you*. I thought I'd want to carry on with my life as before…'

'But you don't?' she pushed, her eyes huge as finally they met his.

'Not even a little bit,' he promised. He stood, holding a hand to her. 'You have to trust me, Emmeline.'

Guilt coursed through him. How could he ask that of her?

Emmeline bit down on her lip. She trusted Pietro with her life, sure, but her heart…? And it was her heart that was involved now. Her whole heart. It had tripped into a state of love without her knowledge, and definitely without her permission, and she couldn't say with any certainty that he wouldn't break it.

Not intentionally, but just by virtue of the man he was.

'Trust me,' he said again, cupping her face. 'I don't want anyone else.'

'It's crazy,' she said softly, doubt in her features. 'We only just met…'

He dropped his mouth to hers, kissing her with all the passion in his soul. She moaned into his mouth, wrapping her arms around his neck. So much for not responding, she thought with an inward snort of derision. She couldn't be in the same room as her husband and not feel as though a match had been struck.

'We've known each other for years.'

He kissed the words into her mouth and they filled up her soul.

'But not really.' She pulled away, resting her head on his chest, listening to his heart.

'I remember the first time I saw you,' he said quietly. 'I'd come for your mother's funeral. You were a teenager, and I think even then I knew that I was looking at you in all the wrong ways.' His smile was apologetic. 'You had just come home from school, do you remember?'

Remember? Of course she remembered. Her father's

handsome young friend had looked at her and a fire had lit in her blood.

'Yep.' She cleared her throat. 'You were the most gorgeous person I'd ever seen,' she said with mock seriousness. 'You fuelled *all* my teenage fantasies.'

His laugh was a soft rumble. 'No wonder you never met a boy you liked,' he teased. 'Who could live up to *me*?'

It was a joke, but Emmeline was falling back in time, her mind tripping over those painful years in her life.

She covered the direction of her thoughts with a flippant response. 'Who indeed?'

'I thought at the time that it was strange you were still at school. Your mother had just passed away, and yet you were carrying on with your life…'

'People handle grief in different ways,' she said softly. 'I needed to be around friends. The familiar. Sophie was a godsend.'

'How come you've never told your father what you know about Patrice's death?'

She looked up at him, her eyes awash with emotions. A part of him—the part of him that wanted his wife to be happy and at ease—felt he should back off. But the rest of him—the part that so desperately needed answers—pushed on with his line of enquiry.

'He thinks you believe she simply crashed.'

'She did crash.' Emmeline's smile was tight, her tone dismissive.

'But she drove into that tree on purpose.'

'Probably drunk,' Emmeline said, with the anger she tried so hard to keep a tight rein on taking over for a moment.

She stepped away from Pietro, pacing towards the window that overlooked the city. Her eyes studied its beautiful glow but she hardly saw it.

'Why do you say that?'

'Because she was always drunk at the end.' Emmeline

bit down on her lip but the words were bubbling out of her almost against her will.

Pietro frowned. 'Your father has never mentioned that. There was no hint of it in the media.'

'Of course there wasn't,' Emmeline said wearily. 'Daddy controls the local press, for the most part. *And* the coroner's office.'

Emmeline spun around to face Pietro, bracing her back against the glass window behind her.

'If she'd hit another car, hurt someone, then I don't think even Daddy would have been able to keep it hushed up. But as it was only Mom died, and no one could have gained anything from seeing our family name disgraced.' She swallowed, her throat a slender pale column that was somehow so vulnerable Pietro ached.

'How do you know about her drinking?' Pietro murmured.

Emmeline swallowed, looking away. Years of silence kept her lips glued shut even now.

'How do you *know*?' he insisted, staring at her lowered face, waiting for her to speak.

'Because she couldn't hide it towards the end. She was a drunk. A *mean* drunk,' she added quietly.

Pietro's eyes narrowed. 'Mean, how?'

Emmeline expelled a shaking sigh. 'Just mean.'

'To you?' he prompted.

'Of course. With Daddy away at the Capitol for much of the time, I was the only one around to *be* mean to. Well, other than the servants—but they were paid well and put up with it.' Emmeline swallowed back the sting of tears and pressed her palms to her eyes. 'I could never do anything right by her.'

She shook her head angrily.

'Everything about me offended her. Especially as I got older. I remember there was one dinner and Congressman Nantuckan made some throwaway comment about how beautiful I was, that I was going to be every bit as pretty as my mom when I grew up. I must have been all of twelve. He was probably just being kind,' she said, shaking her head. 'But Mom was furious. *Furious.* As though I'd planned some elaborate betrayal and laced her dinner with cyanide.'

A dark and displeasing image was forming for Pietro, but he took care not to react visibly. 'What did she do?'

'Nothing. Not straight away, anyhow. Mom would never show her hand publicly. But once everyone left she pulled all the clothes out of my wardrobe. She told me I was on the right track to becoming an A-grade whore if I didn't watch out. She—'

Emmeline gasped as a sob escaped her, and lifted a hand to her mouth to block it.

'I'm so sorry,' she said, shaking her head desperately. 'I never talk about this! But I've ripped off the Band-Aid and I don't seem able to stop…'

'I don't want you to stop,' he assured her, fighting the urge to close the distance between them. He wanted to comfort her, but he suspected that it would cause her to stop sharing, and he desperately wanted to understand more about her life.

She nodded, but her hands were shaking, and finally Pietro gave up on maintaining his distance. He walked to the bar and poured a stiff measure of Scotch, then carried it to his wife. She curled her fingers around it, sniffed it before taking a tiny sip. Her face contorted with disgust and she passed the glass straight back.

'Yuck.'

His smile was indulgent, but impatience burned inside him. 'You were twelve, and on the cusp of changing from a girl into a young woman…?' he prompted.

She nodded, pulling at the necklace she always wore.

'She couldn't stand that. When I was young she was such an attentive, affectionate mother. We were very close. But from around ten or eleven, as I shot up and started to develop a more mature body… Mom saw it as some kind of act of defiance. She started to see me as competition, hated the time I spent with Daddy. When people came to the house she'd send me to my room. I wasn't allowed to wear anything that drew attention to myself. Cosmetics were forbidden. So was dying my hair or having it cut into a style.'

'Yet you were still beautiful,' he said softly. 'And anyone would have been able to see that.'

Emmeline's eyes met his with mockery. '*You* didn't. You specifically told me that I didn't look good enough to be your wife.'

He groaned—a sound of deep regret. He *had* said that. 'Emmeline, I saw you as a teenager. I wasn't thinking straight the night you came to my office. And, if anything, I suppose I was…annoyed.'

'Annoyed?' she prompted.

'*Si.* Annoyed that you went to such effort to cover up your natural beauty.'

'Even after she died it was a habit. I don't know… I guess I got very mixed up. Any time I would even *think* about wearing something other than what she'd chosen for me I'd hear her voice, hear the things she'd called me, and I'd know I could never do it.' Emmeline blinked, her enormous eyes round and golden in her face. 'When you told me I needed to change how I looked…'

'I was a bastard to say that to you,' he said gruffly.

'Yes. An *arrogant* bastard,' she agreed, although the words were softened by her smile. 'But you freed me, in a weird way. It was almost as if I'd been waiting for someone to shake me out of that mind-set. To remind me that she was gone and the power she'd exerted over me had gone with her. There was an article in the papers not long after she died. It compared me to her and the headline was *Dull Heiress Can't Hold a Candle to Dead Mother.* Can you believe that?'

His snort was derisive. 'Ridiculous journalists.'

'Yes, and a ridiculous story. They'd taken a heap of long-lens shots of me leaving school, playing baseball—you know, generally the worst, most unflattering pictures. A normal girl would have been devastated by that.'

'You weren't?'

'No. I saw it as a tick of approval. I was doing just what I was supposed to. Mom would have been proud of me.' She shook her head again. 'It took me a long time to unwrap those thoughts and see them for the idiocy they were. For many years I couldn't gain that perspective...'

His eyes swept closed and he processed what she was telling him. He thought of the way he'd criticised her appearance—first telling her she was too conservative and then accusing her of looking too 'available' when she'd dressed as he'd suggested.

'You are beautiful to me no matter what you wear—and to any man. Your mother was playing a foolish and futile game, trying to hide you like that.'

'She wasn't exactly firing on all cylinders,' Emmeline pointed out with a grimace.

'I cannot believe your father wasn't aware...'

'He doted on her,' Emmeline said wistfully. 'There was a significant age gap between them, as you know. She was his precious, darling wife.' She shook her head bitterly from side to side. 'He had no idea.'

'I can't understand that.'

Emmeline shrugged. 'I think it's quite common. A lot of people who love someone with a dependency issue fool themselves into thinking nothing's wrong. They don't want to admit the truth, so they don't.'

'But—'

'I know.' She lifted a finger to his lips, her smile distracting. 'It doesn't make sense.' She dropped her finger lower, digging the tip into the cleft of his chin. 'The first thing that's gone right for me is actually...um...'

'Yes?' he prompted, the word a gravelled husk.

'This. Marrying you. It must seem crazy to an outsider but here…with you… I feel so alive. For the first time in a long time I'm myself again. Thank you.'

Guilt was heavy in his chest.

Tell her. Tell her now.

He wanted to so badly, and there was only one way to stop the words galloping from his mouth. He crushed his lips to hers, taking possession of her mouth with his, pressing her against the window, making her his once more. Here, like this, everything made sense.

Nothing and no one—no truth kept or lie uncovered—could hurt what they were.

CHAPTER TEN

THE NIGHTCLUB WAS full to overflowing and the music was low-key, electronic. It thumped around the walls. The lighting was dim. Even dancing with her husband, his arms wrapped around her waist, she couldn't make out his face properly.

'So this is where our wedding guests came?'

He nodded. 'I believe so.'

His hands dipped lower, curving over her rear, holding her against the hint of his arousal. Her eyes flared with temptation and desire.

'It's nice…' She wrinkled her nose as she looked around, studying the walls that were painted a dark charcoal and featured beautiful black and white prints of Italian scenes.

'I am going to take a stab in the dark and say it's not your usual scene,' he teased, kissing the top of her head.

'Not exactly!' She laughed. 'But that doesn't mean I can't learn to like it.'

'There is no need. I don't come here often.'

'But you have something to do with it?'

'I financed it,' he agreed.

'Uh-huh. That would be why they treated you like some kind of god when you walked in here.'

'Or it could have been because of the incredibly beautiful woman on my arm.'

She shook her head, her smile dismissive. 'I'm sure I'm not the first woman in a nice dress you've brought through those doors.'

He slowed for a moment, hating it that she was right—hating it that his past was as colourful as it was. Not once had he questioned the wisdom of the way he lived, but now, married to Emmeline, he wished more than anything that he *hadn't* slept with any pretty woman who'd caught his eye. He wanted to give her more than that, but he couldn't exactly wind back time.

'Have you spoken to your father lately?'

'Ah...' She expelled a soft sigh. 'A change of subject, I see. I take it that means I'm the hundredth woman you've come here with, or something?'

He compressed his lips, angry with himself and, perversely, with Emmeline for pushing this line of enquiry. 'Does it matter?'

She blinked up at him and shook her head. 'I guess not.'

She looked away, but the pleasant fog of sweet desire that had wrapped around them dissipated. A line had been drawn and she'd stepped back over it, warily.

'I was just thinking,' he said gently, 'that I wish I had come into this relationship with less baggage.'

'Fewer ex-lovers, you mean?' she murmured, moving in time to the music even as most of her mind was distracted by the idea of Pietro *ever* making love to someone else.

'*Si, certo.*'

'But why?' she asked softly, and stopped moving, staring up at him.

'You deserve better than someone like me.'

He was surprised to hear himself admit that. Until that moment Pietro would have classified himself as supremely confident and self-assured.

'But perhaps you wouldn't be such a sensational lover without all those women you've been with before,' she quipped, winking up at him.

His laugh was gruff. 'So practice makes perfect?'

'Yes. But now you get to practice with just me.'

'And you are perfect,' he said quietly.

He kissed her gently then, and the world stopped spinning, the music stopped playing. Everything was quiet and still—a moment out of time. A moment that resonated with all the love in Emmeline's heart.

And in his too?

She didn't dare hope that he loved her. She knew that what they were was changing, morphing, shifting every day. That he looked at her as though he'd never seen a woman before. That he held her after they'd made love until she fell asleep. That he was always holding her, still, in the soft light of morning.

She knew that he was choosing to work fewer hours in his office and instead spending time in the villa. Oftentimes he was propping up a laptop, but generally near her. By the pool, in the lounge, in their bedroom.

And that was the other thing. Since they'd come back from the farmhouse she hadn't slept in her own room once. His room was becoming 'their' room.

Still… Getting close to one another was one thing. Falling in love was quite another. Emmeline wasn't going to get her hopes up. Life had taught her that there was safety in low expectations and it was a hard lesson to shake.

The song came to an end, fading seamlessly into another.

'Are you hungry?' he murmured into her ear.

She looked up at him, her eyes meeting his with sensual heat. 'Not for food,' she said quietly.

His laugh set her pulse firing. 'Then let's get out of here.' He squeezed her hand. 'I just have to see Leon—the owner. Want to come?'

'Not particularly.' She smiled at him and he smiled back, and the world was quiet again, spinning softly around them as if Emmeline and Pietro existed in their own little space. 'I'll wait in the car.'

'Five minutes,' he promised, holding up his hand and flexing his fingers.

She nodded, watching as he cut through the crowd effortlessly. Or did it part for him? Either way, he moved unencumbered through the hundreds of dancing guests. Once he was out of sight she turned and made her way in the opposite direction, towards the doors of the nightclub.

'Emmeline.'

The sound of her name had her pausing, turning, a blank smile on her face as her eyes scanned the crowd. She didn't see anyone she knew at first, and was about to resume her progress towards the door when a beautiful redhead came into view.

And then she knew instantly who was looking back at her.

'Bianca.'

The woman's smile was bone-chilling. 'You know who I am? Good. That saves me the trouble of introductions.'

'I saw you pawing my husband at our wedding,' Emmeline heard herself say, and instantly wished she could pull the words back. They were rude and unnecessary, and the last thing she wanted was to make a scene.

'Being pawed *by* your husband is a more accurate description,' Bianca commented, with a purr in the words.

'Yes, well… That's ancient history,' Emmeline said, lifting her slender shoulders in what she hoped looked like an unaffected shrug.

'If that's what you want to believe,' Bianca said, her smile tight, her lips bright red. 'You know, I could *never* put up with a husband who was so easily tempted away. But then, yours is hardly a *conventional* marriage, is it?'

Emmeline's doubts, already so close to the surface, began to wrap around her anew. Her brain—logical, calm, cool—knew that Bianca had every reason to be unkind. That her gloating attitude was probably just a cruel manipulation aimed at hurting Emmeline. But the muddiness of what she actually was to Pietro, and the truth of what she *wanted* to be, made her heart ache.

'I almost wish *I* had married him,' Bianca said, tapping a fingertip along the side of her lips. 'But this way I get to have my cake and eat it too.' Her laugh was a soft cackle.

'I don't understand…'

'I get the best parts of Pietro—without the press intrusion and the expectations of being Mrs Pietro Morelli… You're good cover for him and me.'

Emmeline felt as if she was drowning.

She stared at Bianca and shook her head. 'I don't know if you're telling me the truth, or just trying to upset me, but either way it's time for me to go.' She blinked her enormous eyes, the hurt in them impossible to conceal. 'Please don't come near me again.'

'It's not *you* I want to be near,' Bianca purred as a parting shot.

Emmeline spun and made a beeline for the door, bursting through it and into the night air with an overwhelming sense of relief.

Pietro was only seconds behind her, his breath loud, as though he'd just run a marathon. 'Was that Bianca I saw talking to you?'

Emmeline didn't have time to hide the hurt in her eyes. She nodded bleakly, then looked around for their car.

A muscle jerked in Pietro's cheek just as a camera flash went off. He swore angrily and put a hand in the small of Emmeline's back, guiding her away from the nightclub towards his car. He opened her door without saying a word, then moved to the driver's side.

He revved the engine as soon as she was buckled in, and pulled out into the empty street. The silence prickled between them, angry and accusatory.

'What did she say to you?' he asked finally, as they cleared the more built-up streets of the city and went on their way to his villa.

'Nothing.' She frowned, then closed her eyes. 'I don't know if it matters.'

Pietro gripped the steering wheel until his knuckles glowed white. 'Tell me what she said.'

Emmeline swallowed, her mind reeling. She had gone

from the euphoria of being with Pietro to feeling as if everything was a sinister ruse.

'She told me our marriage was a convenient cover for your relationship with her. She implied that you and she are still very much a thing.' Emmeline shook her head. 'She knows that our marriage isn't conventional.'

The words were a sharp accusation and Pietro swore.

'That last part is true,' he said thickly. 'I shouldn't have said anything to her but I was…angry. I was wrong to expose you to that kind of gossip.'

'Yes, you were,' Emmeline muttered, her heart plummeting. 'I'm sure she's told anyone who cares to listen,' she added, mortified.

'I don't care. It's not true any more. You *know* how much everything has changed between us.'

He reached down and put a hand on her knee but she jerked away. Her eyes lifted to his and the pain and uncertainty in them had him swearing and veering the car off the road, pulling to a rapid halt in a space marked for buses.

'Please listen, *cara*. You know the truth about Bianca and me because I have told you. She has always wanted more from me than I have to give. She is very jealous of you.'

'I know that,' Emmeline said quietly. 'And I know she wanted to hurt me tonight and obviously cares very much for you. But it makes me wonder… What do I know about *you*?'

'You know *everything* about me.' He groaned. 'Please believe me, Emmeline. I have never had with any woman what I have with you. This is special, and different, and you and I are both finding our way with it. Don't let outsiders—someone like Bianca—cause problems for us.' He pressed a finger beneath her chin, lifting her face to his. 'I won't let you. I won't let *her*.'

'I wish you didn't have such a long list of ex-lovers,' she muttered.

'None of them matters to me. Not a bit.'

Her eyes clashed with his; she wanted to believe him so badly. 'Have you been with her since we married?'

He shook his head.

'In that first month?' she persisted, holding his gaze. 'When we weren't sleeping together? I hardly saw you, and you were home late almost every night.'

He shook his head. 'I had dinner with her once. But that's all. I think I *wanted* to sleep with her. To prove to myself that our wedding hadn't changed anything. But the truth is I'd kissed you by then and I no longer wanted any other woman.'

Her heart turned over in her chest. Was it true? Did she believe him? It took such a leap of faith for her to trust anyone—especially given the strange circumstances. But gradually she found herself relenting.

'Why were you always so late?'

'You need to ask?'

His smile was like sunshine on a rainy afternoon. She felt its warmth penetrating the storm and could have wept with relief.

'I didn't trust myself not to touch you,' he said thickly. 'It was bad enough on our wedding night, when I kissed you and touched you and tasted your sweetness for myself. But after the night you wore that dress...' He groaned. 'I knew I was in serious trouble.'

The truth in his words filled her. 'Why couldn't you touch me?'

His smile was lopsided. And sexy as hell.

'Because you were meant to be a bride of convenience. Ours was an arranged marriage. I wasn't supposed to be craving you. To be dreaming about you...obsessing over you.' His sigh was exaggerated. 'And yet I was. I *am*. I suppose initially I resented that. I wanted to prove to myself that I could resist you. Spoiler alert: I couldn't.'

She expelled a soft sigh, but the memory of Bianca was still too fresh for her to relax completely.

'I don't want to see her again,' Emmeline muttered.

His eyes glinted with a heated emotion she couldn't interpret.

'Believe me, you will *never* see that woman again.'

'Can we go home now?'

He nodded, and inside he felt as though he'd been spared from Death Row with a minute left on the clock.

He dropped his head and kissed her slowly, gently. 'Don't let anyone come between us, *cara*. I cannot change the man I was, but you are changing everything about the man I *am*. The man I want to be.'

Her stomach squeezed with happiness. Because she knew he was telling the truth.

She trusted him implicitly.

It wasn't long before they found their way back to each other's bodies, exploring every inch available and sating their appetites.

'You are crying,' he whispered, chasing a tear up her cheek, depositing it back in the corner of her eye.

She laughed through a sob, shaking her head, wrapping her hands around his waist. 'I'm sorry. It's just so perfect. I don't know what happened—what I did to deserve this—but it's just...'

He smiled—a smile that tipped her world off its axis—and then he thrust deeper, and she moaned into the cool night air, her body moving with his. They were completely in sync, completely together.

He kissed her as he ground into her and she wrapped her legs around his back, holding him close, needing him in her core. His tongue lashed hers and together they spiralled off the edge of the earth in a tangle of limbs, sheets, sweat and cries.

Afterwards he stroked her hair, his eyes smiling down into hers. He rolled onto his back, pulling her with him, holding her tight, and she listened to the beating of his heart for a long time. She thought for a moment that he'd fallen asleep, but after a long time he spoke.

His voice was a gravelled husk in the night. 'Have you spoken to your father lately?'

'No.'

She shook her head and her hair tickled his nose. He patted it down flat and then stroked her naked back, feeling every bone of her spine, knotting down to the curve of her rear.

Tell her. Tell her.

But the moment was so perfect. Some time he might find a way to be honest with his wife. But on this night, with the sound of their lovemaking still heavy in the air, he couldn't bring himself to do it. To ruin what they'd just shared.

'You don't speak often? That's interesting. I would have thought you'd find being apart from him more of an adjustment.'

Emmeline shrugged. 'I lived on the plantation but my father was often away. I did try to call him a few days ago and he emailed back. Something about house guests.' She shrugged. 'That will mean he's out showing off the horses, the cattle, his shooting prowess.' She wiggled her brows—he felt the movement against his chest. 'Knowing Daddy, he's never been happier.'

Pietro groaned inwardly. The lie was tightening around his chest.

'My father speaks of you often, you know,' she murmured, apparently having no clue that her husband was in a self-induced hell of sorts. 'He adores you.'

Pietro's smile was tight. 'It's mutual.'

'Why?' She pushed up on her elbows to study him. 'Why are you so close?'

That bleak time from his past sat like a weight on his chest. 'I've always admired him.'

'That's not the same thing.'

'No,' he agreed. 'Years ago, I was in negotiations with

your father. I was buying some commercial real estate of his—just off the Champs Elysées. I was devastated by my father's death—I got the call about it while we were in a meeting—and your father… Col…supported me. Not just that day, but afterwards too. I'd always admired him as a businessman, a politician, but as a friend he was irreplaceable.' He shrugged. 'He was a rock when I badly needed one.'

As Pietro spoke the words they reverberated around his soul. Col had been his rock when there'd been no imperative on him to be any such thing. He had been strength and resilience, and he had imparted those qualities to Pietro.

How could he be anything but loyal to the statesman now, in his own time of need? Pietro owed Col his allegiance, even though lying to Emmeline was beginning to poison him.

'That's just like him.' Emmeline smiled. 'He's so selfless…'

CHAPTER ELEVEN

'GOOD MORNING, MRS MORELLI.'

He dragged a finger down her body, finding her womanhood and brushing against it possessively. She writhed beneath him, remembering the way they'd made love the night before. Her body still throbbed from the strength of that pleasure.

'*Buongiorno.*' She blinked up at him.

'Do you know what today is?'

Her smile was irrepressible. 'My first day at university.' She grinned. '*Yay!*'

He laughed. '"Yay"?'

'Uh-huh. Yay. Just…*yay.*'

He dropped his head and kissed her gently. 'Which means we have been married two months.'

'And it feels like two weeks.' She stretched her arms over her head. 'Time really does fly when you're having fun.'

His wife—his beautiful wife—stared up at him with all the goodness in her soul and he felt as though the sun was beaming right through his chest.

'Are you nervous?'

'Nervous? God, no. I'm excited. I have been wanting to study for so long, Pietro. I can't believe I've put this off. I feel like there's a whole world out there—a world of learning and knowing—and finally it's going to be mine.'

She sat up excitedly, pushing the covers off her naked body and stepping out of the bed. He watched as she strolled across the room, uncaring of her nakedness. She pulled a pair of jeans off a hanger, and then a cream blouse, and took his favourite pair of briefs from her underwear drawer.

He groaned across the room. 'Not those.'

The smile she threw over her shoulder was pure impish cheek. 'Oh, yes. You can imagine me in them all day.'

'I'll imagine stripping them *off* you all day,' he corrected.

'That too.' She winked, sashaying into the adjoining bathroom and switching the fan on with the light.

The noise droned in the background and Pietro fell back against the mattress, staring up at the ceiling fan that was spinning lazily overhead.

The sense that he was betraying her had lessened. So, too, the feeling that he was living on borrowed time. After several more attempts at getting Col to tell the truth to his daughter Pietro had been forced to accept that the secret was there and that it existed beyond Pietro's control. They would deal with the fallout when it happened.

It never once occurred to him that there might be a fallout bigger than they could handle, because he and Emmeline had become a single, unified force. The idea of anything happening to them that they couldn't handle was impossible to contemplate.

He listened to the running of the shower and the soft singing that she did without even realising. Smiled wider when he caught the tone-deaf notes she seemed always to miss.

He stepped out of bed, strode across the room and pushed the door inwards. Steam swirled around him. She had her eyes closed, her face lifted towards the showerhead, and water was raining over her face and down her back. She hummed now, quietly, and he grinned as he pulled the shower door open and brought his mouth down on hers without warning.

Her eyes flew open and then she surrendered to the kiss, moaning as he pushed her back against the cold tiles, groaning as his body pinned hers and water ran over them both, down their faces and into their mouths.

'Remember what I said the night you were talking to those two professors?'

He asked the question as he brought his mouth down to take a nipple between his teeth and roll it gently, as he moved his hand lower, brushing over her feminine core, before he transferred his mouth to her other breast.

'No…' she moaned, rolling her hips, inviting him in. Needing him again.

How was it always like this for them? Would it ever not be? She felt as if an explosion had caught her in its midst, powerful and fierce.

'I will bring you to my bed every night, so that no other man ever, *ever* interests you.'

The passion in his words was wrapping around her, squeezing her, filling her with all the love in the world. 'You already do that,' she said huskily.

'It never hurts to take precautions, though, does it?'

She laughed, but any hint of amusement died inside her as he dragged his lips lower, falling to his knees so that he could kiss her in her most sensitive, private place. His tongue ran along her seam and her knees quivered as sensations began to drown her, to make thought impossible.

'I can't believe there was a time when you were not mine,' he said against her flesh, and she moaned, running her fingers through his hair as pleasure spiralled in her belly, driving through her, making her blood heat and her heart pound.

'I need you!' she cried out as an orgasm began to unfurl, spreading through her limbs, making them weak and aching.

'I'm glad.'

He didn't stop, though. His fingers dug into her hips and he held her where he needed her, his tongue dictating the speed of her release, and the intensity too. She cried out into the shower as the orgasm unfolded, her mind exploding, every conscious thought obliterated by the havoc he wreaked on her body.

He kissed her quivering flesh as he stood, but didn't

give her even a moment to recover. His hands spun her easily—she was weakened by the total meltdown of her bodily awareness—and he bent her at the hips. Holding her steady, he drove into her from behind and felt her tremble as his possession was complete—the ultimate coming together.

He throbbed inside her, his fingers massaging her wet, soapy breasts, his arousal rubbing against her sensitive nerve-endings, squeezed by her tight, wet muscles. He spoke in Italian—words that meant nothing and everything. He bent forward, kissing her back as he moved, stroking her, touching her, and finally, when her muscles squeezed him with all their need, he emptied himself into her, the feeling of ownership more complete than ever before. She owned him, and she was his.

Emmeline pressed her flushed face against the shower tiles, her mind reeling.

'I am going to find it very hard to concentrate today,' she said thickly, rolling her hips as he continued to pulse inside her, his length experiencing the aftershocks of the earthquake of their coming together.

'That makes two of us.'

He ran a finger down her back before easing himself out of her, away from her, releasing them from the agony and ecstasy of what they had been. She stood and turned to face him, and her eyes were so vibrant and her smile so broad that a dull ache spread through his chest.

He'd been fooling himself in pretending the lie didn't matter.

It did. Of course it did.

He ran a hand over her hair, wet and dark. 'Emmeline...?' he said softly, studying her cautiously.

'Mmm?' She wrapped her hands around his waist, holding him close to her body.

How could he tell her now? On her first day at university? It would derail her completely, and he'd already done his best to do that. No, he couldn't do it today.

But Col Bovington was going downhill, and enough was enough.

Pietro had an obligation to his wife. Soon, when the time was right, he would tell her.

Having made the resolution, he felt a thousand times better. As if simply by deciding to do something he had in some way enacted a small step of the deed.

Absolution was close at hand.

Emmeline hummed as she moved about the kitchen. There was a pile of textbooks in the corner, opened to the page she had most recently been reading. She cast a gaze over the *papas di pomodoro,* smelling the piquant sweetness of the tomatoes and the undertones of basil and garlic, then shifted her focus to the quails that were roasting in the oven.

It was the first time she'd cooked dinner for Pietro's family and she wanted everything to be perfect.

He'd laughed when she'd said as much. 'I have a house-keeper, a chef and a valet. Why do you not leave the food to them? You have too much on your mind already,' he had said, nodding towards the books that were littered around the house.

'I've only been at uni a week; it's still early days.' She'd smiled back. 'Besides, I want to. I like to cook and I think… I don't know… It just feels like something nice to do.'

Of course now she was regretting that impulse, as time marched on and food simmered and she worried that she would have nothing ready by the time they arrived.

There was nothing she could do but wait. The quail in *confit* needed an extra hour before they would be ready to remove. The soup was the entrée. There were olives, breads and cheeses ready to serve as antipasti.

She rubbed her hands together, checking the table for the tenth time. She'd set it with a simple white cloth and put several vases of old-fashioned roses in the centre. Sprigs of orange blossom lent them a beautiful fragrance. Plus, they reminded Emmeline of his farmhouse—the place where their relationship had come alive.

She smiled as she leaned down and breathed in deeply—then her back pocket vibrated. She reached down and fished her cell phone out, relieved and surprised in equal measure to see a text from her dad. She'd left several messages for him in the last week, and apart from a brief email she'd heard nothing.

Hi, Pumpkin. Sorry I've been hard to catch lately. I've got the flu and it's kept me in bed all week. Are you doing good? Love, Daddy.

A smile tickled her lips. It was something he had often asked her when she was younger.

I'm doing real good, Daddy. Uni is amazing.

She ran her finger over the phone, wondering what she should say about her husband and settling for, Married life suits me. Come over and visit soon?

She thrust her phone into her pocket and continued with her preparations. But as she showered and changed she couldn't help but let a kernel of worry infiltrate her happiness.

Her dad wasn't a young man. For the flu to have kept him in bed all week sounded serious. That and the fact that she hadn't spoken to him in rather a long time had her mind unpleasantly distracted.

She chose a black silk slip dress, teamed it with a long string of pearls and a pair of black ballet flats, then quickly applied basic make-up.

Pietro appeared just as she was bent forward, slashing mascara over her brows, and his eyes locked to her rear before she straightened and spun around.

'If it isn't my favourite husband,' she murmured, her eyes clashing with his in the mirror.

'Your *only* husband?' he prompted.

'For now.'

She winked and turned her attention back to the mirror, ignoring the serious tremble that assaulted her heart. Initially she'd felt their marriage would be of short duration. That she'd wean herself off life at Annersty, let her father adjust to her departure and then move on. For good. But now…?

'I have something for you,' he said softly.

Curious, she spun around, scanning his outfit, his hands, and seeing nothing.

'It's downstairs.'

'What is it?'

'Come and see,' he murmured, holding a hand out to her.

Emmeline walked to him, wanting to peel her dress off as she went, to expose her nakedness to him. She followed behind him, her curiosity increasing with each step, until they reached the front door.

He lifted his hand to cover her eyes. 'Wait a moment.'

She bit down on her lip, held her breath and listened as the heavy timber door was pulled inwards. Then his hand dropped from her eyes and she blinked, focussing beyond him.

A sleek black car sat before her. A Bentley with a soft roof that looked as if it would turn the car into a convertible.

'It's…it's beautiful,' she murmured. 'I don't understand…'

'Well, *cara*, you are a Roman now. You go to university here. You live here.'

He moved to the car and opened the driver's door; she followed, a frown etched in her face.

'Do you know what I have been thinking about lately?'

'What?'

'When we first discussed marrying, I remember you

saying something about wanting only the freedom it offered.' He cleared his throat. 'I didn't understand it at the
time. I still don't. But I know I want to give you everything in this world, and a car seems like an important step
to true freedom.'

Unexpected tears sparkled on Emmeline's lashes. 'Stop
doing this to me!' She groaned, a laugh breaking the seriousness of her mood. 'You're *too* perfect.'

'*Cara*, I'm not...'

Something flickered in his face—something that briefly
made her heart skid to a stop before she pushed the doubts
away.

He *was* perfect. She had no reason to worry that he'd
ever disappoint her or let her down. He was her match in
all ways.

'Thank you,' she said softly.

'Hop in,' he replied, and grinned.

She smiled brightly as she slid behind the wheel. 'You
know, I'm not actually a great driver...'

His laugh was husky. 'Then I shall have to teach you.'

As he'd already taught her so much. 'The thing is, I get
bored,' she said honestly. 'I find it all a bit dreary.'

'Not here, you won't. Roman roads are fun. They are
designed to test you.'

'I love my car. Even if I just sit in it to study.' She grinned
at him.

A plume of dust from further down the driveway her-
alded the arrival of another car, and Emmeline stepped out
with true regret. As she did so she saw a university parking
permit on the dashboard, and that single gesture of thought-
fulness meant more to her than the extravagant gift of such
an expensive car.

'I love it,' she said again, walking around the bonnet and
pressing a kiss to his cheek.

His eyes latched to hers and she had the strangest feeling that he wanted to say something else. That something was bothering him.

'Is everything okay?' she asked searchingly, her eyes scanning his face.

'Ciao, ragazzi!'

Pietro's mother stepped from the car, a vision in green, her hair styled in a topknot, a large gold necklace at her throat and a pair of gold espadrilles snaking up her legs. She sashayed towards them as though the driveway were actually a chic fashion show catwalk.

'Mother,' Pietro drawled, kissing Ria on both cheeks before she transferred her attention to Emmeline.

'Ah! My lovely daughter-in-law,' she said in her heavily accented English. 'Still too skinny, I see,' she said, with a disapproval that Emmeline guessed was only half joking.

'Mother,' Pietro scolded warningly. 'That is enough.'

'What? I want grandchildren. Can you blame me?'

Emmeline's heart squeezed painfully. The truth was, the image of a baby had begun to fill her dreams. How sweet it would be to grow their own little person in her body—to hold it and feed it and cuddle it and love it.

Maybe one day that would happen. But for now Emmeline was having her first taste of life as a normal adult woman and she wasn't ready to sacrifice her independence yet. Her life with Pietro was perfect and new, and she didn't want to add a baby into the mix.

Yet.

Her eyes met Pietro's over Ria's head and she smiled; she knew he understood. He wanted her to be happy. To be free.

Her eyes drifted to the car, and as they walked into his home, she saw the number plate: *Mrs M.*

Her smile stretched broader, making her cheeks hurt.

Rafe arrived only a few minutes after his mother. They were sitting at the table sipping rosé wine, when he strode in, relaxed in pale trousers and a T-shirt.

'Ah, Rafe. Off the yacht, I see,' Ria said critically, but her smile showed nothing but maternal pride.

'*Ciao*, Mamma.' He grinned, doing the rounds and saying hello to his family. 'This smells wonderful. So you cook, too?' he demanded of Emmeline.

'A few dishes,' she said with false modesty.

Emmeline had always loved cooking. She'd spent as much time in the kitchen as possible—especially when Patrice had been on the war path. It had been the perfect bolthole. A spot where she could make dishes and enjoy the therapy that cooking and baking offered. She'd mastered croissants from scratch at the age of fifteen—just before her mother had died.

'Tell me again why *I* did not get to marry you,' Rafe grumbled good-naturedly, taking the empty seat beside Emmeline.

'Hush,' Ria said, reaching across and batting at Rafe's hand. 'She is your brother's wife.'

'Still… A man can dream.' Rafe winked at Emmeline, then reached for a handful of *grissini*.

'Leave some for the rest of us,' Pietro drawled, taking the seat on the other side of Emmeline and passing a glass of wine to his brother.

Beneath the table, Pietro's hand found Emmeline's knee and he squeezed it. She turned to face him. Their eyes met and sparks flew that Emmeline was sure everyone must surely see.

She smiled softly and then focussed on the story Ria was telling. Or tried to. But beneath the table Pietro's fingers moved steadily higher, until they were brushing her thigh, teasing her, comforting her, simply *being* with her.

'I'll get the soup,' she said after a moment, scraping her chair back and moving towards the kitchen.

'Would you like a hand, darling?' Ria called after her.

Emmeline shook her head. 'I'm in control.'

In truth, a moment to herself was essential. A single

touch from her husband was enough to set her pulse skittering and stay that way. Was it possible that if she stayed married to him she was going to end up having a stroke?

The thought made her smile, but it also made something strange shift inside her.

If she stayed married to him?

Where had that come from?

She lifted four bowls out of the cupboard and ladled delicious soup into them, thinking about the arrangement they'd come to. Discomfort was like ice inside her. They'd never really talked about how long they'd stay married for. But everything had changed. The deal they'd made was surely redundant now. She was in love, and she was pretty damned sure he was too.

Which meant *what*, exactly? That they'd live happily ever after? Was that even what he wanted?

Uncertainty brought her happiness down a notch. Perhaps they needed to have a talk about that? A *Where are we going?* conversation…

She grated some fresh parmesan over the top of the soup, adding a glug of oil and few leaves of basil.

The thing was, they'd done everything in reverse. From her extensive experience with books and movies Emmeline had gathered that generally two people met, discovered they were attracted to one another, dated, fell in love and slept together, then moved in together or got married. But at some point before that crucial last step they discussed what they wanted. Where their future was going.

Could they discuss that now? Or would it be weird? Everything was so good she didn't want to ruin it.

With a small noise of frustration she lifted two bowls and moved through the kitchen and back into the dining room.

'Let me give you a hand,' Pietro said, as though he'd only just realised his wife would be ferrying four bowls on her own.

'Thanks,' she murmured, depositing the first in front of Ria before following her husband back to the kitchen. As she walked through the door he caught her around the waist and pulled her to him.

'I want to take you upstairs *now*...' He groaned. 'Why is my family here?'

She laughed, but her heart was thundering, her pulse racing. 'I don't know. It was a terrible idea. Let's send them away.'

'Definitely.' He kissed her hard and fast. 'A down payment,' he said with a wink.

'Good. I'll expect payment in full later.'

'How much later?' He groaned again, his expression impatient.

She kissed his cheek. 'Not long, I hope.'

The soup was a hit. She had been anxious about cooking such a quintessentially Italian dish for her husband's family, but they seemed genuinely to love it, and Emmeline had to admit it was one of her best. The quail was perfect, too. Served with some crispy potatoes and garlic-roasted green beans, it was an excellent mix of flavours and textures.

Pietro took over hosting after dinner, making espresso martinis in the lounge area that they progressed to.

Pietro had given her a car. That *meant* something. Not to mention his sweet sentiments about her wanting freedom. This marriage was so much more than either of them had anticipated. It was real.

'You're quiet,' Rafe remarked, taking the seat beside hers. *Whoops.*

'And you look concerned. Is everything okay?'

Emmeline hardly wanted to have a deep and meaningful conversation about her marriage with her brother-in-law, so she scrambled for the easiest explanation she could offer.

'Oh, you know...' She smiled at him, her mind turning over quickly. 'It's my dad. He's not well, and it's hard to be over here and so worried about him,' she said with a shake of her head.

Rafe's surprise was obvious, but Emmeline didn't understand it, of course. 'He *told* you?'

'Of course he told me,' Emmeline said with a small frown of her own. 'It's hardly a secret.'

'Oh, thank God. I know Pietro's been tearing himself up about all this. It must be a weight off his mind that you know.'

Emmeline's look was quizzical. It was just the flu, and she'd only recently found out about it herself. 'How does Pietro know?' she asked quietly.

Rafe froze, apparently sensing that they were speaking at cross purposes. He sipped his martini, his eyes scanning the room. 'Um…'

'How does Pietro know what?'

Pietro appeared at that moment, devastatingly handsome in the suit that she loved so much. But Emmeline hardly noticed.

'How do you know my father is sick?'

CHAPTER TWELVE

SILENCE STRETCHED LIKE a piece of elastic. Then it stretched some more.

Emmeline tried to make two and two add up to four but it wasn't possible.

'Rafe just said you've known for a while. That it's been tearing you up,' she murmured. None of this was making sense.

Rafe swore, standing up and setting his martini glass down in one movement. He tossed Pietro a look of deep apology. 'I thought she knew.'

Emmeline stood up too, the movement unknowingly fluid. 'Knew *what*?' Her voice was louder. More demanding. The fear in it was obvious.

'Emmeline?'

Ria appeared at her side, and only with every single ounce of self-control in her body did Emmeline manage to calm herself. To offer her a tight, terse smile. But her eyes were haunted, her skin pale.

'Thank you for a lovely dinner. I think I should leave you to it now,' Ria said.

'Me too,' Rafe added quickly. 'Don't see us out.'

Pietro glared at his brother before dragging his attention back to his wife. It was quite possibly the worst manner in which this news could have been dropped.

'What the *hell* is going on?'

Pietro expelled a long, slow sigh. 'Sit down, *cara*.'

'I don't want a damned seat,' she responded caustically, her eyes flying around the room as if answers might suddenly appear. 'Well?' She tapped her foot, her arms folded across her slender chest.

'Rafe seemed to think you knew—'

'Daddy has the flu,' she answered sharply. 'But that's not what you're talking about, is it? Pietro? What's wrong with him?'

Fear was written across her beautiful face; her eyes were haunted by it.

'Your father *is* sick,' he confirmed.

Emmeline made a grunting noise of impatient displeasure. 'I've gathered that. What's wrong with him?'

A muscle jerked in Pietro's cheek.

'Is it serious?'

'*Si, cara.*'

'Oh, God.' She reached behind her for the sofa, collapsing into it wearily. 'What is it?'

Pietro crouched before her, his hands taking hers. 'He has cancer. Advanced and incurable.' He rubbed a thumb over her hand, across the soft flesh of her palm. His heart hurt with the pain in hers. 'I'm sorry.'

Tears fell down her cheeks, but shock was numbing her to their balm. 'I don't understand. When...? How...? Why didn't he tell me?'

'He wanted you to be happy. He wanted to *know* you were happy, to die knowing that you weren't going to be left stranded by the loss of your father. He wanted to know that you have other things in your life. Other people.'

'You,' she said quietly, pulling her hands free and rubbing them along her thighs. 'When did you find out?'

Pietro reached up and touched her cheek but she jerked away from him.

'When?'

It was a primal grunt. She was skinning the situation alive, trying to boil it down to just bones and fact.

'The day he came to see me.'

Surprise resonated through the room as though an atom bomb had been dropped. 'Before we were married?' she responded angrily, her voice high pitched and stringy. '*Be-*

fore we were married? You've known this whole time. Oh, my God.'

She stood up jerkily, looking around the room as though she didn't recognise it. As though it were simply a set and she an actress—a character in a play with no real meaning, no real plot. Nothing was real.

She blinked, clearing the confusion from her mind and trying her hardest to hone in on what mattered. There would be time to come to terms with Pietro's betrayal. But in that moment more was at stake.

'How bad is it?'

'He's dying,' Pietro said, the words thick and guttural. He stood slowly, but didn't attempt to move towards her. 'He told me it was a matter of months. If that.'

'No. I don't believe you.'

She stared at him, all her grief and confusion and the bereft state of her soul silently communicating themselves to Pietro.

'My father is… He's never sick.'

Pietro's expression was bleak. 'The cancer is throughout his body.'

The words were like strange sharp objects. She could barely comprehend them. Her daddy was ill? Why had he sent her away? Was he in pain? Was he lonely? The thought of him going through something like cancer without anyone to hold his hand brought a lump to her throat.

'And you let me stay here with you, knowing I had no idea? Knowing that my whole world—' She stabbed her hand into her chest, her eyes wild in her face. '—my father, my only family, was dying on the other side of the world? How *dare* you make that decision for me? How *dare* you lie to me like that?'

'He wanted it this way.'

'It doesn't matter! You should have *told* me!' she roared, turning her back and stalking out of the lounge.

She took the stairs two at a time, pacing down the corridor and into his room, which they'd been sharing for weeks. She pulled clothes out of the closet at random. Jeans, a few skirts, shirts… She had more clothes at home—she didn't need to pack much.

Home. Annersty. The words whispered through her with sombre realism.

'I couldn't tell you,' he said with muted anger in his words. 'What are you doing?'

'*Why* couldn't you?' She spun around to face him, her eyes accusing.

'He made me promise and I owed it to him to keep that promise.'

'Even knowing how it would hurt me?'

'I didn't want to do that,' he said thickly. 'You must believe this is true. I was in an impossible situation…'

'Damn it, Pietro.' The words reverberated around their room. 'Don't you *dare* talk to me about impossible situations! This wasn't impossible. It should have been easy.'

'Your father—'

'Yes, yes…' She waved a hand in the air, cutting him off. 'You've told me. He didn't want me to know. But what did *you* think?'

He froze, the question so direct that he hadn't expected it.

'You must have thought about it. Did you think I wouldn't care? Did you think I'd be able to forgive you this?' She zipped her suitcase with such ferocity that her nail snagged in its closure and she swore under her breath. 'You've been sitting on a time bomb.' She dashed a hand over her eyes, wiping away her tears.

He made a visible effort to pull himself together, straightening his shoulders and wiping his expression clean. 'You want to go to him?'

Her eyes bore into his. 'Of *course* I do. I would have gone to him weeks ago if anyone had told me what the hell was going on.'

'Good…fine,' he murmured. 'I'll organise my plane…'

'No.' She reached for her phone with fingers that shook. 'I'll book myself on the next available flight.'

Her meaning was clear. She didn't want his help.

'I have a jet at the airport. It will take hardly any time to fuel…'

'I don't want your stupid jet,' she snapped. 'I just want to get to him.'

'This is the fastest way,' he promised. 'I know you're angry, but let me do this.'

Emmeline looked away, panic and worry making her uncertain.

Pietro's voice came to her as if from a long way away. He spoke into his phone in his own language, ordering the flight preparations to begin. In some part of her mind she was glad. She was furious with him—furious in a way she doubted she'd ever forgive—but she wasn't sure she could face this completely alone.

He disconnected the call and she spoke without meeting his eyes. 'When?'

'Now. Come. I'll drive.'

She kept her eyes averted as he lifted her suitcase easily, carrying it down the stairs and past the car he'd given her only hours earlier. She ignored the anguish that churned her gut.

Mrs M. What a joke. She'd been nothing to him. Was this why he'd married her? To keep this lie? To deceive her?

All her ideas that their marriage had begun to mean something real were obviously just stupid, childish fantasies. There was no way that he loved her as she loved him. If he'd cared for her at all he would have found a way to break the truth to her sooner.

She stared out of the window as he took the car to Fiumuncino, the countryside passing in a blur that eventually gave way to the built-up cityscape and then more industrial outlying buildings. Finally, it pulled up at a small air terminal.

'Here.' He nodded towards a hangar that was guarded by a single soldier.

It wasn't Emmeline's first time flying in a private jet—her father's was permanently stationed in the States—so it was no surprise for her to be ushered through a private building and customs area before being whisked across the deserted Tarmac to a jet bearing a golden 'M' on its tail.

He handed her suitcase to an attendant, but it wasn't until he climbed the stairs with her that it occurred to Emmeline he might be coming along for the trip. That she might have given herself a rather long flight with a man she never wanted to speak to again.

'What are you doing?' she asked, her words as cold as ice as she paused at the top of the plane's steps.

'What do you think?' He walked deeper into the plane, pausing at an armchair and waiting for her to follow.

She shot him a pointed look, but moved towards him. Fine. If he wanted to join her—to sit with her—then she'd make him sing for his supper. He could damned well give her some answers to the questions that were crashing around inside her.

'So he told you before you and I had even agreed to the marriage?' she said, sitting down in the armchair and buckling her seatbelt in place.

Her fingers were trembling so she clasped them firmly in her lap. Shock was a wave that was spreading around her, swallowing her in its depths.

'He bullied you into marrying me,' she murmured, her eyes locking on the view beyond the window. She had to focus on this conversation or she'd fall apart.

A muscle jerked in Pietro's cheek at her characterisation of their marriage. 'He asked me to help him.'

She pulled a face. 'To help him *manage* me? God! This was meant to be *my* decision. My first step to freedom.'

There was a throb of anxious silence, and if Emmeline had lifted her eyes to Pietro's face she would have seen the aching sympathy there. But she couldn't look at him. His face was now inextricably linked with betrayal.

'He was worried about how you'd cope. He didn't want you to see him unwell.'

Emmeline stared out of the window, the lump in her throat growing bigger by the minute. Was he in pain? Was the housekeeper Miss Mavis looking after him? Was he scared? Tears filled her eyes and she didn't bother to blink them away.

'I didn't agree with his decision, but I had to honour it.'

She whipped her head around, barely able to see him through the fog of her grief. 'Don't *say* that. You can't have it both ways! If you didn't agree with his decision then you should have *told* me.'

'I wanted to tell you.' A frown was etched across his face. 'I'd decided I would tell you one day, when the time was right.'

Her laugh was a harsh sound of fury. 'You just said he has months, maybe weeks, to live. What were you waiting for?'

'Excuse me, *signor*? *Signora*?' An attendant practically tiptoed down the centre of the plane, her expression professional. 'We're ready for take-off. Can I get you anything to eat? Drink?'

'No,' he snapped curtly.

'Yes. Scotch. Neat,' Emmeline demanded. 'And some aspirin.'

'Yes, *signora*.'

Pietro leaned forward and put a hand on her knee once privacy had been restored. 'This changes *niente*—nothing about what we are.'

'Like hell it does!' Her disbelief was a force-field of shock. 'You have been lying to me this whole time. *This whole time*.' She sat back in her seat, all the fight in her evaporating as quickly as it had appeared.

When the attendant appeared with her drink she threw it back, then lifted the aspirin.

'Don't take those,' he murmured. 'You've just had a ton of alcohol…'

She glared at him angrily and tossed the pills into her mouth. 'Go to hell.'

She woke somewhere off the coast of the States. Her head was pounding, her eyes were scratchy and there was a heaviness in her heart that didn't initially make sense. She was disorientated and confused.

She blinked her eyes open and looked forward.

Straight into the brooding stare of her husband.

The smile that was always so quick to come to her lips when she saw him did not come.

Sadness and grief sludged through her instead, and then it all came rushing back. The lie. The secrecy. The betrayal. Her father's cancer.

The fact that he was going to die.

And she hadn't been with him.

Instead she'd been living in Italy, believing everything was amazing, pretending she was normal, truly thinking herself to be happy.

'You told me I could trust you,' she said, so quietly he had to strain to hear the words. 'Do you remember?'

'Sì.'

'You were talking about Bianca and the other women. But I took it to mean you were generally trustworthy.'

'Your father trusted me,' he said softly, darkly, the words slicing through her resolve.

The betrayal—by both the men she loved—cut her to the quick.

'I can't believe he told you and not me. How dare he? How dare *you*?'

'He was concerned that you would be very vulnerable when he is no longer with us. You will inherit an enormous fortune, and he felt you hadn't had the experience necessary to remain safe from less desirable elements. He wanted to know you were protected. Is that so awful?'

'Yes!' she spat angrily. 'He was afraid of wild dogs and so he sent me to live with a wolf.'

Pietro's eyes flashed with suppressed frustration.

'Don't you *get* it? I will never believe anything you say again. You begged me to trust you and I did. Apparently I was just as naïve and stupid as Daddy thought.'

She glared out of the window, her heart thumping hard when land appeared below. She was back in her country—or the airspace above it, at least—and she never planned to leave it again.

She was home. At least, that was what she told herself.

'Oh, sugar.' Miss Mavis pulled the door inwards, her face lined with tears. Her middle was comfortingly round and she pulled Emmeline against her, holding her tight. 'I'm so sorry.'

Emmeline was aware of everything in that instance. Miss Mavis's sweet scent—like lemon and sugar and butter all rolled into one—the sound of an aeroplane droning overhead, the way Pietro stiffened at her side, and the way her own heart lurched and rolled with the certainty that it was too late.

'I came as soon as I heard. How is he?'

'Oh, Miss Emmeline…'

Miss Mavis's face crumpled and Emmeline knew. She just *knew*. Even the light was different as it glistened across the front of Annersty. The sun was bleak, mourning his loss.

'When?'

The quiet question came from behind her—a voice as much stained by grief as her heart was. And she didn't doubt the truth of his sadness. Pietro had loved Col like a father. Had loved him enough to marry her just to give Col some semblance of reassurance at the end of his life.

'An hour ago,' Miss Mavis sobbed. 'We tried to call you, but your phone...'

Miss Mavis, whom Emmeline had known from five years of age, was like family. She ran a hand over Emmeline's back, holding her tight, comforting her.

'Can I see him?' Emmeline whispered, sounding like the little girl she'd been the year Mavis was hired.

'Of course you can.'

Miss Mavis stepped inwards and Emmeline followed, but then she spun around, her eyes fiercely accusing as they locked to Pietro's.

'Don't.'

She lifted a hand to emphasise her point, then fixed her gaze somewhere over his shoulder. She didn't want to look at the pallor of his face, the haunted eyes. She didn't want to think about the fact that he'd lost someone he loved as well. That he was possibly as wrenched apart by sadness as she was.

'Don't you dare come into my house.'

He flinched as though she'd hit him. *'Cara...'*

'No. Don't you dare.'

Miss Mavis's hand on her back offered strength and comfort. She was feeling more and more like herself again.

'If I'd never married you I would have been with him. *I would have been with him.*'

Pietro braced a hand on the side of the door but otherwise made no effort to move inside. 'It's not what he wanted.'

'He was wrong. *You* were wrong.' She shook her head angrily. 'You should have told me. I should have been here. I'll never forgive you for this.'

She stepped backwards and slammed the door shut, sobbing as it latched into place.

CHAPTER THIRTEEN

ON THE THIRD day after her father died—the morning of the funeral—she found a note stuffed in a book. It had fallen beneath his bed, and she'd pulled it out, was unfolding it slowly, when a knock at his door startled her. She spun guiltily, jamming the piece of paper into her vintage Dior clutch.

Pietro stood in the opening, dressed in a black suit, his dark hair styled back from his face, and he looked so strong and handsome, so supportive and sexy, that she wanted to throw herself across the room and take every bit of strength he was willing to give her.

But she didn't. Because he'd destroyed what they were. Or maybe what they'd never been. The illusion of their marriage seemed like a dream now—one she would never have again. He'd kept his distance since they'd arrived at Annersty, and yet he'd always been there. Dealing with the lawyers, the servants, the mourners who arrived unannounced.

'It's time to go,' he said quietly, his face lined with sympathy and sorrow.

The childish urge to tell him to stay the hell away from the funeral evaporated in the midst of what she knew her father would have wanted and expected. Col had loved Pietro, and she knew her husband well enough to know that it was mutual.

'I'm not going with you.' She settled for that instead.

'Yes, you are.'

He pushed the door shut, leaving him on the bedroom side of it, and walked towards her. She froze like a deer in the headlights—as she had on their wedding night.

She tilted her chin defiantly, remembering all that had happened since that night. Changes had been wrought on her personality and her confidence—changes that couldn't be undone now.

'We *will* go together because if we arrive separately it will cause gossip and scandal.'

'Oh, heaven forbid anyone should cast aspersions on the great Pietro Morelli's marriage—'

'I don't give a damn what the papers say about *me*,' he interrupted firmly, his expression showing grim sympathy, 'but your father, on this day, deserves the focus to be on him. I will not provide the media with any distraction from the greatness he achieved in his long career of public service.'

'Oh, God.' She gripped his shirt for support as her body weakened, a wave of nausea rolling over her at the recognition of what this day was. 'I can't do this.'

'Yes, you can.'

'I can't!' she sobbed, shaking her head from side to side. 'I can't bury him. I can't. *I can't.*'

'Hush…hush.'

He stroked her back, her hair, held her tight, whispered words in his own language—words she didn't try to translate. She didn't need to understand what he was saying to feel comforted.

'I'm here with you.'

And he was. He stayed by Emmeline's side throughout the awful, necessary ordeal. As she said goodbye to the hundreds of lawmakers, donors and friends who'd come to pay their final respects. Pietro's mother and brother were there too, and it was strange to see them here in the church at Annersty. Her new family merging with her old.

Only they weren't her family.

And Pietro wasn't really her husband.

The funeral was a time to say goodbye to more than just Col. It was an ending of all things.

Late that night, when everyone had left and it was just Emmeline and her grief, Pietro found her on her knees in a room that he quickly surmised had been hers as a girl.

'What are you doing here?' she asked without looking, the tone of weary defeat thick in her words.

He crouched down beside her and handed her a mug. 'Coffee?'

She took it, her eyes red-rimmed. 'Thank you.' She curled her fingers around it and sat down on her bottom, staring around the room. 'I was just wishing I could lift a corner of the blanket of time and slip beneath it.' Her smile was vague. 'I want to be a little girl again.'

'The room is very...pink.'

She nodded. 'My favourite colour.'

'I'm surprised,' he said quietly. 'I would have thought perhaps green or red.'

Emmeline wrinkled her nose. 'Nope. Pink. Rainbow. Sparkles.'

She sipped her drink and then pushed herself up to stand, pacing over to the window.

'It was a nice funeral.'

'It was. A fitting service for a man like your father.'

Silence filled the room. A sad, throbbing ache of quiet that spread darkness through Emmeline's soul. She wanted to lift the blanket of time and go back days, not just years. She wanted to be back in Rome, lying in Pietro's arms, hot and slumberous from having made love to him all night, smiling as though the world were a simple place.

But she couldn't go back. Time was a one-way train and it had scooped her up, deposited her on tracks she didn't want to be on. Yet here she was, bound by grief and betrayal, and her destination was fixed.

'There's no point you being here,' she said softly. 'You should go back to Rome.'

'No.' A quiet word of determination. 'I'm not leaving you.'

She turned to face him, her expression blank. 'I don't want you here. Daddy was wrong to think I couldn't cope with this. And he was wrong to think you and he should keep it from me. It's all wrong. Everything we are has been a mistake.'

'It's not the time to make this decision,' he said stonily. 'You have buried your father today.'

'I know what the hell I've done today!' she snapped. 'Tomorrow, the next day—it doesn't matter. Nothing's going to change how I feel.' She sucked in a breath, her lungs burning with hurt. 'If you care about me at all, you'll go. Please.'

His eyes were impossible to read as they locked to hers. He stared at her for a long moment and then nodded softly, turning on his heel and leaving. He pulled the door shut with a soft click but Emmeline was as startled as though he'd slammed it.

Well? She'd been emphatic. What had she expected? That he'd sweep her off her feet and carry her to bed? Lie her down and stroke her back until she fell asleep?

That spoke of an intimacy that had been a lie. How could anything make sense when trust was broken between them? And, no matter what he said or did, he'd broken their trust in the most vital of ways. Robbing her of the chance to be with her father in his last months. To love him and care for him.

She had another sip of coffee, her eyes following the moonlight that danced over the rolling hills of the estate. The trees she'd always loved…the hills she'd rolled down as a young girl.

Strange that she no longer felt the same ties to Annersty she had at one time believed unbreakable. It was no longer the home she saw when she closed her eyes. Instead, her mind was filled with visions of fruit orchards and a tumbling down farmhouse.

She blinked her eyes open, determined not to let her traitorous thoughts go there.

Emmeline slept fitfully, her dreams punctuated by loneliness and grief, her mind heavy with sadness and need. When she woke she was pale, and there were bags under her eyes. She didn't bother to hide them. It was only the housekeeping staff here, and Miss Mavis had seen her in all modes over the years.

Emmeline pulled on a pair of jeans and a sweater. It wasn't a particularly cold day, but she was cold inside.

When Emmeline had finished senior school, and decided not to attend college so she could keep an eye on her father, she'd moved out of her old bedroom and into a larger suite of rooms. It had been more appropriate, given the fact she'd been of an age when most people were moving out of their parental homes for good. She had a large bedroom, a walk-in wardrobe, a beautiful bathroom that had always made her feel as though she was in an old-fashioned book like *Gone with the Wind*, and beyond that a sitting room and office that had a beautiful view over the lake in the East Lawn.

Her eyes were focussed on that window as she crossed the sitting room, seeking out the view that had always provided such a balm to her soul, so it wasn't until she heard a movement that she realised she wasn't alone.

Pietro was on the sofa, scruffy as hell and even more physically beautiful for his air of dishevelment. He wore the trousers from the suit he'd had on at the funeral, and the shirt too. The jacket had been discarded somewhere. He'd pushed his shirtsleeves up and his hair was thick and tousled, as though she'd been dragging her fingers through it all night even though she knew she'd never do so again.

She froze, her eyes unable to do anything but drink him in. To stare at him as though he was the answer to every question that had made her toss and turn all night.

'*Buongiorno.*'

His voice was gravelled perfection. She sucked in a breath, steadying herself, blinking her eyes to clear the image of him as the man she loved. How could she forgive him? He was her father's friend. And a liar.

'What are you doing here?'

He stood, and if she had ever seen him in the boardroom

she would have recognised the look of unshakable determination that set his face.

'I'm staying with you.'

'I told you to go.' It was a bleak rejoinder.

The wind ran around the house, wuthering against the walls and shaking the glass behind her. She jumped as it banged loudly in its ancient timber frame.

He stood, crossing the room so that he stood before her. He didn't touch her, but he looked at her so intently that he might as well have.

'I love you,' he said simply. 'If you are here then I am here.'

She made a noise of exasperation. 'You don't need to pretend any more! Daddy's dead. It's over. You did what you were supposed to do. We can let this charade go.'

She wrapped her arms around her chest, hugging herself tight.

If anything, his expression simply assumed an air of even greater determination. 'You need to eat something.'

'I'm not hungry.'

'You look terrible.'

Her eyes flashed with pent-up emotion. 'Just as I did when we first became engaged? This is who I *am*, Pietro. You might have tried the Cinderella treatment on me but I'm just this person. Here.'

It took all his strength not to respond angrily. He *was* angry! Bitterly so. But he smiled gently instead.

'I mean you look like you *feel* terrible. You look as though you haven't slept. You look as though you have lost weight even in the few days we have been in America. Please, come and eat something.'

'This is *my* house,' she said coldly. 'I'll do what I damned well please.'

She stalked out of her suite, her shoulders square, her gaze focussed on the stairs ahead. But her heart was breaking and her eyes were leaking hot, salty tears of misery…

* * *

Days passed in a strange fog. Pietro was always there. Sleeping on the definitely too short sofa just outside her bedroom, keeping his distance but also watching her constantly. After a week she stopped wanting him to go. She stopped wishing he would go. Or rather she began to accept that she was glad he'd stayed.

Her world had been rocked off its axis with Col's death, and having Pietro with her offered comfort that she knew she couldn't get from anyone else. Even Sophie, with her cheery visits and bottles of wine, couldn't erase the throbbing ache deep in her heart.

Emmeline didn't speak to Pietro. Not beyond the obligatory morning greeting and an occasional comment about the weather. But his constant presence was doing something strange inside her. Something she needed and resented in equal measure. She was starting to feel like herself again, and she hated it that it was because of Pietro.

A month after Col's death Emmeline came home to find her father's lawyer in the lounge, locked in conversation with Pietro.

'We've discussed this,' Pietro was saying firmly. 'The estate passes in its entirety to Emmeline.'

Emmeline paused on the threshold, a frown on her face, before sweeping into the room. Pietro's expression was wary, his concern obvious. Emmeline knew why. She had continued to lose weight and she didn't have any to spare.

She ignored his concern and smiled politely at Mr Svenson. 'Can I help you with something, Clarke?'

'Oh…um…er…'

'It's handled,' Pietro said firmly, standing.

Clarke Svenson followed his lead, smiling kindly at Emmeline as he moved as quickly as possible towards the door.

As soon as they were alone, Emmeline whipped around to face her husband. 'What was that all about?'

Pietro expelled a sigh and reached down for his coffee

cup. He took a sip and she realised, with a sudden flash of guilt, that he hardly looked his best either. He looked tired, and she hated the way her heart twisted in acknowledgement of the fact.

'There are the usual scum looking to get in on your father's will. Long-lost second cousins twice removed—that sort of thing.' He rolled his eyes. 'It's being handled.'

Her eyes were round in her face. 'By you?'

'*Si.* Someone has to evaluate the claims on their merits.' He moved towards her, slowly, cautiously, as though she were a skittish horse he needed to calm.

She nodded, but without understanding. 'And you've been doing that?'

'*Si.*'

'Why?'

'Because I'm your husband,' he said softly. 'Because you needed me to.'

His eyes ran across her face and he took a step closer, but she shook her head.

'And because my father expected you to,' she added softly.

So much of what they were came back to that, and Emmeline couldn't shake the feeling that she'd been traded. That she was not so much an asset as a bad debt that her father had needed to hand off before he'd died.

Her grief was never-ending.

'We must talk,' he murmured gently.

'I know. But I'm not... I can't... I can't. Not... I'm not... ready.'

'Okay—that's okay. I understand.'

'God, *stop* being so understanding. Stop being so kind. I don't want you here, picking up all these pieces. No matter how kind you are now, nothing can change what happened.'

He ground his teeth together, his eyes clashing with hers. 'I hated lying to you.'

'That's *bull*. You aren't the kind of man who would do anything he hated.'

'It was the perfect rock and a hard place,' he said with understated determination. 'Your father made me swear I wouldn't tell you...'

'How did you think I'd forgive this?' she asked. 'How did you think we'd move past it?'

'I don't know,' he said honestly. 'But I knew we would. I know we *will*.'

'How? How *can* we?'

'Because I am me, and you are you, and together we have found something so special, so unique, that it is irreplaceable.' His eyes forced hers to meet his, and the challenge was impossible to ignore. 'I worried about you not knowing. I worried about you finding out and about you losing your father. I worried about your anger and your hurt. But I never once thought it would be the end for us.'

He stared at her still, his eyes begging her to see, to understand.

'Can you look at me now and think there is a life which we don't share?'

'It was all a lie.' She was numb.

'Nothing about what we are was a lie.'

'Yes, it was! You were my... You woke me up, remember? With you I became a proper, full person. I felt whole and mature, and the most like myself I've ever felt. And really you were just an extension of Daddy. Managing me and infantilising me out of a mistaken belief that I can't look after myself. I thought you saw me as an equal, but instead I was your obligation.'

'At first,' he said, the words a thick concession. 'But you dressed me down at our wedding and I knew that Col was wrong about you. You were naïve, yes, but not weak. Not incapable of handling yourself.'

He reached out and took her hand in his, and his relief at her letting him hold it was immense.

'I'm not here to protect you. I'm here because I need you—and right now you need me. That's marriage.' He stroked the soft flesh of her inner wrist. 'I want more than anything to be married to you. Not because your father sought it, but because of who you are and what we have come to mean to one another.'

The words were like little blades, scraping against the walls she'd been building brick by brick around her heart.

And yet she wasn't ready.

She couldn't forgive him.

'It's too soon. Too much.' She blinked away tears and pulled her hand back to herself. 'If you'd slept with another woman I would find it easier to forgive.'

His laugh was a harsh sound of disbelief. 'You are grieving, and I am trying to give you the space you need. I do not want to crowd you. And I certainly don't want to fight with you. But ask yourself this question: What could I have done differently? I spoke to your father weekly, urging him to tell you about his illness. He was adamant that you should not know.'

'You spoke to him *weekly*?' If anything her sense of betrayal yawned wider.

'He wanted to be reassured you were happy.'

'Oh, *what* a good friend you were!' she snapped, but the indignation of her words was somewhat marred by the sob that strangled them. 'You went above and beyond to make me happy.'

A frown was etched over his handsome face.

'You made it so obvious that you weren't attracted to me, and still you seduced me. You made me think I was *very* happy.'

'None of that had anything to do with your father.'

She rolled her eyes. 'It was *all* because of him. He pulled the strings—just like he did with me my whole life.' She stamped her foot. 'You were supposed to be *mine*. Rome was meant to be *mine*.'

'I didn't marry you with any expectations that it would become a real marriage. That was all *us*. I fell in love with you, Emmeline. Not because of Col but because of you and me.'

The words were sucking her in—so sweet, so exactly what she needed to hear that she rejected them instantly.

'No.'

She held a hand up in the air. To silence him? Or slap him?

'Lying to me about Dad, keeping his secret—that's completely incompatible with love. Love is honesty and truth. It's trust.'

'In a perfectly black and white world, perhaps. But nothing about this was simple. My loyalties were split from the moment I met you. I made him a promise before I even properly knew you. I felt obligated to stick to it. That's the man you love.'

She blinked, felt her heart bricking itself up, its walls forming more easily now they had well-worn foundations.

'I don't love you,' she mumbled tightly. 'I never did. I see that now. I loved Rome. I loved sex. But you? No. I don't even *like* you.'

She spun on her heel and walked quickly from the lounge, waiting until she was in her own room before she let out the sob that was burning inside her.

That night, her dreams were terrifying.

Her mother stood behind Emmeline, her face pinched, dressed all in black.

'See? This is what you deserve, Emmeline. You are alone. All alone. Nobody will be there for you. And that's as it should be.'

It was the crying that woke him. Emmeline had been tossing and turning and crying out in her sleep almost nightly for the whole month they'd been at Annersty. But this was different.

Her sobbing was loud, and when she began to say, 'Go away! Go away! Go away!' again and again in her sleep he felt a cold ache throb through him.

He'd stayed because he'd believed it to be what she needed. But was it possible he was hurting her more with his presence?

I don't even like you.

That was possibly more damning than her insistence that she was angry. It was such a cold denial of all that they were.

Torn between going to her and letting her settle herself, he was just standing to move into her bedroom when she went quiet. All returned to normal.

Pietro took up his cramped space on the sofa, his mind an agony of indecision. Torn between what she needed and what he wanted, he knew there was only one option open to him.

If she needed him to go so she could have the space to realise what they were, then he had to give it to her.

CHAPTER FOURTEEN

EMMELINE STARED AT herself in the mirror with a frown. The dress was beautiful. Her hair was neat. Her make-up flawless.

But she looked wrong. Different. Something was missing. The tan she'd acquired in Rome? The smile that had permanently framed her face? The glint she'd become used to seeing in her eyes—one of utter happiness?

No matter.

She wasn't that girl any more.

She blinked and stepped away from the disappointing image in the mirror. She had no time for maudlin self-reflections. She was late.

Thankfully Sophie was permanently at least fifteen minutes behind schedule, but Emmeline still felt stressed as she lifted her vintage clutch and tucked it under her arm. She pulled her bedroom door inwards, and the lurch of emptiness as she crossed the threshold and stepped into the small area that Pietro had used as a makeshift bedroom was like falling into a pit of quicksand.

There was nothing left of him. Not even the faint hint of citrus and pine that had lingered a day or two after he'd told her he would go if that was what she'd really wanted.

The horrible truth was she *hadn't* wanted that—not really. She'd nodded as he'd said the words, seeing that his mind was apparently made up, but her heart had been screaming. Begging him to stay, willing him to ignore everything she'd said and just be with her.

He'd driven away only an hour after they'd spoken, and the sense of grief and loss had almost eclipsed anything she'd felt since her father had died.

He'd messaged her every second day over the fortnight since he'd left but she hadn't replied. Not because she'd wanted to be childish or to punish him, but because she had no idea what to say. How to express feelings that she couldn't even comprehend herself. The grief, the betrayal, the disbelief. The worry that he'd been pushed into a marriage he'd never wanted. That she'd been falling in love while he'd been making do. The worry that she'd never be able to trust that there had been truth in *any* of their interactions.

She slipped behind the wheel of her car, her expression bleak as she started the engine and began to make her way into town.

The Bowerbird Lounge was doing a roaring trade, despite the fact it was a grey November day. The tables outside featured patrons wrapped in brightly coloured blankets, and the heaters beneath the awnings were on and glowing warm.

As she'd expected, Sophie was nowhere to be seen, but their reserved table was available so Emmeline took a seat and ordered a Diet Coke. She enjoyed people-watching. With her dark sunglasses firmly in place, she gave herself the freedom of scanning the room, watching the guests and catching snippets of conversation.

Ten minutes later her phone began to buzz and she reached into her clutch, pulling it out and answering it when she saw Sophie's face beaming back at her from the screen.

'Hey, hon, I'm just looking for a space. I'll be a few minutes, okay?'

'That's fine,' Emmeline murmured.

'Seriously… What the hell? There's no spaces on this whole damn block.' Sophie made a grunting noise of complaint and Emmeline smiled, tinkering with the clip on her purse.

A piece of the lining, old and fine, ran across her fingertip. She tried to pull it straight, then realised it wasn't the lining at all. It was a piece of paper, folded several times, with her name on the front.

Her heart was pounding so hard and fast that she could no longer hear the din of the restaurant. She disconnected the call and dropped her phone to the table, her fingers shaking as she unfolded the letter. The letter she'd thrust into her bag on the morning of the funeral and forgotten about.

How had she forgotten? Disbelief raged inside her as she sat, ready to read whatever the note contained.

Her dad's handwriting was barely recognisable to Emmeline. It was spidery and fine, weak and pale.

Pumpkin...

Emmeline felt tears sting her eyes. She could hear Col's voice so clearly. She sucked in a deep breath and kept reading.

At the end of one's life I suppose it's natural to reflect. On choices, decisions, roads not taken. Having you as a daughter is the best thing I've ever done, but I wonder now if I've done it all wrong. Have I failed you? More than likely. That's hard for me to admit, because I have always tried to do everything in my power to make your life a good and rich one.

I didn't want to lose you so I kept you close, and I got in the way of you living your own life. I've been selfish.

These last few months...knowing you to be in Rome, on the brink of so much excitement in your life, so happy with Pietro... I have finally seen you as you should have been all along. Your happiness and independence is the most precious gift I have ever received. I wish I could have helped you find them sooner.

I know my death will have come as a surprise. But while I know you are shocked, you must know that I wanted it this way. Please don't be angry with me for keeping my diagnosis from you. I wanted to spare you as much pain as possible, and I know you would have deferred your own pleasure and adventures to stay close to me. You've done far too much of that already.

Pietro disagreed with my decision, but he was faithful to the last. I am grateful to him for upholding my confidence even when he felt strongly that you would prefer to know the truth. Sparing you the pain of seeing me as I've become is my last gift to you— and it is a gift, Pumpkin. I am not this man.

I hope you can both forgive me for making him stay the course. Or perhaps I have been selfish to the last.

Be happy together. He is a good man and he loves you very much.

As do I.
Forever,
Daddy

Emeline didn't realise she was sobbing until the young girl at the table beside her reached across with a tissue.

'Oh, I'm sorry…'

Emmeline stood up, the table jerking loudly as she moved. She wove through the restaurant and caught Sophie just as she was bursting through the door.

'I have to go,' Emmeline said quickly. 'I'm sorry.'

'Is everything okay?'

Emmeline shook her head, then nodded, her face showing all the confusion that was rich in her heart. 'I… I don't know.'

She handed the letter to Sophie and wrapped her arms around herself as her best friend scanned its contents.

Afterwards, she lifted her eyes to Emmeline's face, trying very hard not to react. 'Where did you get this?'

Emmeline's voice was a sob. 'It was...it was in his book. I found it on the day of the funeral but I... I put it in my clutch and I just found it now. I didn't even think about it again. I suppose I presumed it was just... I don't know. Why didn't I read it sooner?'

Sophie tsked sympathetically. 'Would it have changed anything?'

Emmeline's expression bore anguish. Sophie knew the truth of the situation now—including her real reasons for marrying Pietro.

'How can he have thought it was the right decision?'

Sophie expelled a soft breath. 'Your father was a very proud man.'

'God, I know that. I *know* that! But he was also selfish.' Her voice cracked as she spoke the condemnation. Hot guilt at betraying him spread like wildfire through her body. 'He had *no right* to decide to cut me out.'

'He wanted you to be happy.'

'So he sent me away?'

Sophie sighed. 'Imagine if you'd stayed. You'd have nursed your father and you'd have been by his side when he died, sure. You'd have seen a great, strong man become weak and no longer in control of his body. And when he died you'd have been alone. Bereft. Miserable. Instead you have a new life. A life you love.'

'A life my father *chose* for me,' Emmeline scoffed. 'Don't you *see*, Sophie? I should have been free to find my own way!'

'If you had every choice in the world before you, would you want anything other than what you had with Pietro? Would you have chosen any differently for yourself?'

Emmeline's heart skidded at the mere mention of her husband's name. It spurred an ache deep inside her gut, for it was not just a random collection of letters. It was a call that her body instinctively wanted to answer. It was a promise and a denial. It was everything.

'You can choose now, Emmeline. It's not too late. You have the world at your feet. What do you want to do?'

Pietro was on fire, and then he was ice-cold. His brow beaded with perspiration as once again he read the letters at the top of the document. Did he miraculously expect them to alter in some way? To rearrange themselves and say something else.

PETITION FOR DIVORCE
Emmeline Morelli v Pietro Morelli

He swore, using every curse he knew, and then repeated them for good measure, scraping his chair back and moving to the door of his office even as he wrenched his phone from his pocket. For the second time in two months he ordered his jet to be made ready at a moment's notice, the urgency in his voice instantly communicating itself to his unflappable assistant.

He stared at the document for the entire drive to the airport, and then again as the plane lifted off. It was a straight-up divorce petition. No dispute over assets or ongoing entitlements, despite his considerable wealth—then again, her own fortune was formidable. She had no need to make a claim on his.

But it bothered him because everything about the document spoke of a woman who wanted to wrap their marriage up swiftly—to bring it to an official conclusion in the fastest possible way.

Did she really think he'd sign the damned thing? Without so much as a conversation?

His plane touched down in the early evening and Elizabetta, with her usual efficiency, had organised a driver to collect him. He stared broodingly out of the window as the car cut through the miles between the airport and Annersty.

But when it pulled up at the front of the grand estate the

adrenalin that had brought him the whole way to Georgia seemed to disappear. He swore under his breath and pushed himself out of the car, the divorce papers clutched in his hand.

Miss Mavis answered the door and her smile was warm. Precisely the opposite of what he expected from Emmeline.

He was unable to dredge up more than a grimace of acknowledgement. 'Is she home?'

'Yes, sir.' Miss Mavis stepped back, holding the door wide open. 'She's swimming, I believe.'

'Swimming?' He arched a brow. Well, he hadn't expected *that*.

He stormed through the house, anger taking the place of adrenalin. How dared she end their marriage like this? Without the courtesy of so much as a phone call? Hell, she hadn't even answered his text messages!

As he got closer to the indoor swimming pool the sound of her splashing made him slow. He tried—and failed—to get a grip on his temper. The doors were made of glass. He saw her even before he'd shouldered into the marble-floored room. She was moving slowly through the water, her stroke elegant, her legs languid as they kicked along the length of the pool.

Desire kicked hard in his gut; he forced himself to ignore it.

He ground his teeth together and began to stride on at the side of the water, all the way to the end of the pool. He reached it before she did, and crouched down so that when her fingertips grazed the tiled edge he was able to reach down and touch them. He'd meant simply to alert her to his presence, but the moment he felt her soft flesh beneath his a visceral ache overtook his body—a need to touch more than her fingers, more than her hand.

He straightened in physical rejection of the idea.

She emerged from the water and all he could do was stare at her. Her face was wiped clean of make-up, her hair was slicked back, and her expression showed nothing but shock. He felt something like a stabbing pain in his gut. She was so young, so innocent and so beautiful.

If she wanted a divorce, what kind of bastard was he to fight it? Didn't she deserve her freedom? True freedom? Not the kind that was bargained for and arranged by her father, but the freedom that came of being a young woman who had her own place in the world.

All the fight and the anger he'd brought with him, the disbelief that she wanted to end their marriage, evaporated.

He had to let her go.

He had to do what Col hadn't been able to.

He had to acknowledge that she was a mature woman with every damned right to make her own choices in life.

'Pietro.'

It was a groan and it broke through his resolve. Her eyes dropped to the document in his hands and at the moment of recognition she blanched. Her eyes held desperate anguish as they met his.

'You got the papers.'

'*Si, cara.*'

Why did she look as though he was killing kittens in front of her? This was *her* choice. *Her* decision.

He looked away, the sight of her making him want more than anything to argue with her. To use any tool at his disposal—yes, even sex—to get her to agree to give their marriage another chance.

But she'd been railroaded enough for a lifetime.

'You didn't have to hand-deliver them.'

Her words were so quiet. So pained. God, how he wanted to swoop down and take that pain away.

'That wasn't my intention.' He stepped back from the water's edge, feeling utter disbelief at what he was about to do.

'Wasn't it?'

The water made a rippling sound as she lifted her arms

out of it and braced her forearms against the coping, then pressed her chin into the back of one hand.

'So why *did* you come?'

He shook his head, forcing himself to look at her. But the pain was back—an ache that seemed to rip through him when he met her eyes. The change in her was marked. The happiness that had seemed to shimmer out of her pores in Rome was utterly absent now.

'I was surprised to receive these,' he said, without answering her question.

'Why should you be?'

Visibly, she seemed to tighten her resolve, to assume a mask of unconcern. How did he know it to be a mask? Because he *knew*. He knew everything about her.

'Our reasons for marrying are gone now. He's dead.' Her voice cracked. 'You're free.'

Pietro's head whipped back to hers. He crouched down. Urgency perforated his tone and he spoke before thinking. 'What do you mean, I'm *free*?'

'You did everything he wanted. You were a very good friend to my father. But it seems only fair to absolve you of this responsibility.'

Now it was Emmeline whose eyes were jerking away, refusing to hold his.

Pietro's mind moved quickly, rapidly sifting through her statement, trying to comprehend her words.

'You're divorcing me because you want to free me from our marriage?' He held the papers up. 'This is for *me*?'

She opened her mouth, surprise obvious in her face. She shook her head, and her eyes showed panic. 'I... It's the right thing to do.'

'*Why* is it, *cara*? Do you think I no longer love you?'

Tears sparkled on her lashes, mixing with the water of the pool. 'Please...don't. Don't say those things. It's not fair.'

His gut whooshed to the floor. She was right. Hadn't he just been telling himself that? And yet...

'I'll sign the papers, Emmeline. If that's what you really want. But I want to hear you say it.'

'Say what?' The words were a whisper and yet they echoed around the pool room.

'Tell me you don't love me.' He crouched down once more. 'Look in my eyes, see all the love I feel for you there, and tell me you don't feel the same.' The words were so deep, so gravelled. 'Tell me you don't want to live in Rome with me, as my wife, that you don't want to be in my bed, that you don't want to continue your studies. Tell me that you want to end our marriage. That *you* want that.'

Her sob was heartbreaking but he didn't withdraw.

'I don't want to be married to you. Not like this.'

Her addendum at the end was a lifeline in the midst of a turbulent, terrifying ocean.

'Not like what?'

'Not because of him. Not because you felt forced to protect me. Don't you see? I'm not the girl he thought I was. The girl *you* thought I was.'

'I know that,' he agreed urgently. 'You never were. I married you because Col asked me to, yes. But I want to stay married to you because of how I feel. How *you* feel. Because of what we *are*.'

Tears ran down her cheeks. She bit down on her lip and looked away from him, trying—and failing—to rally her emotions into order.

'I don't think I believe you.'

The words were agonising to both of them.

'I need us to divorce. It's the only way.'

None of it made any sense. He expelled a soft sigh as he tried to comprehend his wife's viewpoint.

'Then say it.' His eyes held a silent challenge. 'Tell me you don't love me and I'll sign these papers and drop them off at your lawyer's on my way out of town.'

Her sharp intake of breath told him everything he needed to know.

'But if you love me—as I think you do—say that. Tell me that. Be honest with me.'

'Our marriage has no future,' she murmured, ignoring his question. 'I'll never trust you. I'll never believe you're not with me because of a sense of obligation…'

'My God, Emmeline! If this was about obligation do you think I would have slept with you? I tried so hard to fight that, to not want you as I did, and yet you became my obsession. Think about it, *cara*. You had given me *carte blanche* with other women. But I didn't want them. I wanted *you*. I have wanted you from the moment we married. Hell, probably from that moment in my office when you were laying down the ground rules for our marriage.'

She rejected his assertion with a skyward flicker of her eyes. 'Sure. You thought I was so sexy you told me I had to change how I looked.'

He nodded angrily. 'Yes! Because you were so obviously trying to make yourself as uninteresting as possible. And I was right about that. Because even then I knew you. I don't care what you look like, for heaven's sake. I care about how you *feel*. I want you to be happy. I want you to be happy with *me*. But if you want to be here at Annersty alone, or—*God*—with another man eventually, just tell me. Say it and I'll sign these.'

'I can't… I told you. I can't… This marriage…'

He made a sound of frustration, and before she knew what he was doing—perhaps before even Pietro knew himself—he was sliding into the pool beside her, fully dressed. He kicked his shoes off as he wrapped his arms around her waist and drew her to him. And then he kissed her, the surprised 'O' of her mouth giving him the perfect opportunity. He kissed her and she kissed him back.

At least she did for a moment, before her hands lifted to his chest and she sobbed. 'I'll never trust you.'

'Yes, you will.' He stared down at her earnestly. 'I think you already do. I think you hate what happened, and I think you're mad as hell, but I think you love me and you want to find a way to make this work. Do you think that divorcing me will make you happy?'

She stared at him, her expression one of abject fear. And then she shook her head slowly. 'But I need to know you're not trapped. That you're not with me because of him.'

'I'm not.' He arched a brow and pulled her closer, dropping his mouth so that his lips were just a millimetre from hers. 'You gave me a perfect escape clause. You sent me the divorce papers. If I didn't want to be with you do you think I would have flown halfway around the world the second I got them? No. I would have signed them, posted them and heaved a sigh of relief.'

He watched her face, watched it carefully, so that he saw the play of emotions in her features and particularly the moment comprehension seemed to overcome doubt.

'I am *yours*, Emmeline Morelli, for the rest of your life. Married or not, I will never not love you. I will never be with another woman. I will never marry again or have a family. Nothing. Because all that I am…all that I will ever be…is tied up in you.'

Her breath was held in her throat. But still he wasn't sure she understood. So he kissed her again. He kissed her and he whispered into her mouth, over and over and over, like a spell being cast just for her. *'Ti amo, mi amore. Ti amo.'*

In response Emmeline reached up, out of the pool, sliding her fingers across the tiles until they reached the divorce papers. She pulled at them and then, without breaking their kiss, dropped them into the water.

'I love you too.'

'Per sempre?' he groaned.

She nodded. 'Yes. Forever.'

EPILOGUE

Three years later

EMMELINE STOOD IN her graduation robe, clutching her degree, a beaming smile on her face. In the front row sat Pietro, so handsome, so beautiful, and beside him Rafe, Ria and Sophie. Emmeline smiled down at them, waving her fingers as Pietro snapped a photograph, then moved off-stage.

Three blissful years, a university degree, and now she was on the cusp of a life that was about to change forever.

There was a swirling sense of celebration and she took part in all of it—smiling through the after-party, making polite conversation with the university professors who had been so helpful to her.

Finally, though, she was alone with her husband.

'I have something for you,' he said, with obvious pride.

'I have something for *you*,' Emmeline repeated. 'Let me go first?'

'*Certo.*' He grinned. 'Though it hardly seems fair. You are the one who graduated with distinction today. Surely the gifts should all be for you?'

'My gift is a present to me, too.'

She reached into her bag and pulled out an envelope, handing it to him. She watched as he lifted the flap and then looked at the front of the card. It was just a generic *I love you* gift card she'd picked up at the pharmacist. Nothing special.

But when he opened it to read the contents inside, and lifted his eyes to her face, she saw his shock and surprise and she laughed.

'This says we are going to be parents.'

'I know. I wrote it.'

His jaw dropped and he read the card again, his eyes scanning it over and over just to be sure.

'Are you serious?'

'Uh-huh.'

'But…when?'

Emmeline laughed. 'I think we've given ourselves plenty of opportunities, don't you?'

'We're going to be *parents*.'

He closed his eyes, and when he opened them they were swimming with emotion. He dragged her against his chest and kissed her, and she kissed him back, her heart soaring with love and optimism.

What they were—who they'd become—had taken a leap of faith, a mountain of trust and all the courage Emmeline possessed. And it had been worth it.

She stood in the arms of the man she adored, knowing without doubt that they would live happily. *Per sempre.*

* * * * *

MILLS & BOON

Coming next month

CLAIMING HIS HIDDEN HEIR
Carol Marinelli

'We were so hot, Cecelia, and we could have been good, but you chose to walk away. You left. And then you denied me the knowledge of my child and I hate you for that.' And then, when she'd already got the dark message, he gave it a second coat and painted it black. 'I absolutely hate you.'

'No mixed messages, then?' She somehow managed a quip but there was nothing that could lighten this moment.

'Not one. Let me make things very clear. I am not taking you to Greece to get to know you better, or to see if there is any chance for us, because there isn't. I want no further part of you. The fact is, you are my daughter's mother and she is too young to be apart from you. That won't be the case in the near future.'

'How near?'

Fear licked the sides of her heart.

'I don't know.' He shrugged. 'I know nothing about babies, save what I have found out today. But I learn fast,' he said, 'and I will employ only the best so very soon, during my access times, Pandora and I will do just fine without you.'

'Luka, please...' She could not stand the thought of being away from Pandora and she was spinning at the thought of taking her daughter to Greece, but Luka was done.

'I'm going, Cecelia,' Luka said. 'I have nothing left to say to you.'

That wasn't quite true, for he had one question.

'Did you know you were pregnant when you left?' Luka asked.

'I had an idea…'

'The truth, Cecelia.'

And she ached now for the days when he had been less on guard and had called her Cece, even though it had grated so much at the time.

And now it was time to be honest and admit she had known she was pregnant when she had left. 'Yes.'

Continue reading
CLAIMING HIS HIDDEN HEIR
Carol Marinelli

Available next month
www.millsandboon.co.uk

LET'S TALK

Romance

For exclusive extracts, competitions
and special offers, find us online:

📘 facebook.com/millsandboon

📷 @millsandboonuk

🐦 @millsandboon

Or get in touch on 0844 844 1351*

For all the latest titles coming soon, visit
millsandboon.co.uk/nextmonth